THE BOY FROM REACTOR 4

THE BOY FROM REACTOR 4

ORSET STELMACH

THOMAS & MERCER

The characters and events portrayed in this book are fictitious. Any similarity to real persons, living or dead, is coincidental and not intended by the author.

Published by Thomas & Mercer
P.O. Box 400818
Las Vegas, NV 89140

ISBN-13: 9781612186085
ISBN-10: 1612186084

For Robin

PROLOGUE

HE CAME FROM NOWHERE. NO ONE HAD EVER HEARD OF HIM or seen him before. No one knew who he was.

On the first day of tryouts for the hockey team at Fordham Prep School in the Bronx, he dazzled the coaches with speed, agility, and puck-handling wizardry that belied his age. They whispered giddily to each other and scurried for their cell phones to call friends and wives. They knew they had just witnessed the arrival of a future pro, and possibly a once-in-a-generation talent. They needed to share the news with someone. They needed to share the news with everyone.

He had the uncommon name of Aagayuk Kungenook, and he was an orphan from the Arctic Circle along the northwest coast of Alaska, an Inupiat from Kotzebue, population three thousand. In addition to their Inupiaq names, Inupiat take on a given English name later in life. This name is often based on someone the person admires. In Aagayuk Kungenook's case, his given English name was Bobby. Hence, his full name was Aagayuk Bobby Kungenook.

Bobby made the varsity team as a sixteen-year-old walk-on. During his first four games, he scored seven goals and assisted on three others. This would have been a staggering achievement for any center or wing, let alone a freshman, but he was neither. Bobby was a defenseman. He wasn't expected to score any goals.

Prior to this offensive outburst, his teammates kept their distance from him. At school, kids called him "Shark Bite." Half ears jutted out from the side of Bobby's head, with jagged, square tops that ended just above the canal. Some said a shark had attacked him while he was swimming in the Kotzebue Sound, while others insisted his father had cut them as punishment for not listening to him and then committed suicide.

Once the team opened the season undefeated, however, Bobby's teammates stopped calling him Shark Bite. The upperclassmen began confronting anyone at school who dared speak disrespectfully to their young star. Assuming he'd taken his English name from the greatest defenseman ever to play hockey, his teammates modified it further to fit his talents. They combined a living legend's first and last names, rolled them into one, and created a new moniker for their prodigy. They began to call him simply "Bobbyorr."

Every December, the New York Rangers hosted their annual Ice Hockey Night in Harlem, featuring current and former players. During that event, at Lasker Rink in northern Central Park, sixteen-year-old Bobby Kungenook took on Ranger superstar Martin Gaborik in an impromptu one-lap race around the rink.

Gaborik, previously the NHL's Fastest Skater award winner with a lap time of 13.713 seconds at the all-star game, finished with a time of 13.736 seconds outdoors. Bobby Kungenook, previously unknown, unseen, and unheard of, finished the same lap with a time of 13.573 seconds.

The conclusion was obvious yet unfathomable to everyone in attendance: the sixteen-year-old orphan from the Arctic Circle was arguably the fastest hockey player in the world.

Within a week, three videos of the race surfaced on YouTube and collected 230,000 hits around the world. The sports network aired the video on its news shows. It also dispatched Lauren Ross to the next Fordham game to interview Bobby. Lauren was determined to someday become a prime-time news anchor. She'd spent ten years in the business and had won three Emmys, but was still looking for a story to catapult her out of sports and into the upper echelons of mainstream broadcast journalism.

A standing-room-only crowd jammed The Ice Hutch in Mount Vernon for Fordham's game against archrival Iona Prep, the first since the Gaborik race. The game began sloppily, as though both teams were distracted by the publicity. A collective murmur of expectation rose from the crowd whenever Bobby took the ice. He was about six feet tall on skates, with a body that looked as though it had been spliced together from two separate molds. Above the waist, his jersey hung loosely on sinew and bone. Below the waist, quadriceps and calf muscles bulged against the fabric of his pants, as though he'd been building up his legs since he'd left the womb.

With Fordham trailing 1–0 in the second period, a bruising Iona forward crushed Bobby against the boards. Bobby lost his balance and tumbled. Rather than get up and resume playing, however, Bobby stayed on his knees and began searching frantically for something on the ice. A necklace had fallen from his neck and spilled to the ground. During the ensuing five-on-four, Iona scored another goal to go up 2–0.

Boobirds rang from the stands. Bobby found his necklace and limped to the sidelines. The coach chewed him out and benched him for the rest of the period.

During the second-period intermission, Lauren asked her cameraman to replay the incident. Fortunately, he'd kept his lens on Bobby the entire time, even while Iona scored its goal. Lauren thought she'd seen something interesting that could distinguish her interview from others. The video confirmed her suspicion.

The necklace had broken into two pieces. The first was a long gold strand. The second was a locket that must have been attached to the necklace. It landed between Bobby's skates. Lauren asked the cameraman to zoom in, and saw Bobby scoop up the locket. He fired a quick glance in each direction afterward, as though he feared someone were going to steal it from him.

There it was. Her edge. The other reporters wouldn't even notice it. They'd give the necklace short study, thinking the orphan couldn't stomach losing one of his only material possessions, perhaps a family heirloom. But that wasn't the case. What Bobby feared losing was the locket. That meant there was something precious inside it.

With five minutes left in the intermission, Lauren went down to the visiting coach's office. Coach Terry Hilliard looked as though he'd allowed too many sirloin hockey pucks past the crease of his lips since his days as a Rangers goaltender.

"Is Bobby okay after that fall?"

"Oh, sure. Kid's tough as nails. Or ice picks. Or whatever the heck they use up there in Alaska."

"So we're still good for that interview after the game?"

"You bet. As long as I'm present and the cameras are off and you take it easy on him. He's just a kid, Lauren. He's been through a lot. You brought an interpreter, right?"

"What?"

"Your people told you, right?"

"Told me what? Bobby doesn't speak English?"

"I wouldn't say he doesn't speak English. He's picking it up quickly. But he's not fluent enough to make it through an interview without some help."

"You're kidding me. What does he speak, then? Some Eskimo language?"

"Nope. His first language is Ukrainian. Second is Russian. English is third."

"Ukrainian and Russian? You're kidding me. Why?"

Hilliard shook his head. "Not entirely sure. It's a Jesuit school. The priests only told us so much. And you don't push around a Jesuit priest. He's such a good kid. We don't want to pry.

The priests said the Russians discovered part of Alaska. I guess there's some history there."

"Huh. Interesting. But how am I supposed to conduct an interview if we can't communicate?"

Hilliard scratched one of his chins. "Bobby's guardian is here tonight. Her name is Nadia Tesla. She's a young woman. From the city. Like yourself. I could ask her. She might be willing to translate."

"Would you, Terry? That would be really kind of you, thanks."

As the third period began, Lauren wondered how an orphan from a small town in Alaska had learned to play hockey so well. She wondered why he spoke Slavic languages better than English. She wondered who his guardian was and how he had ended up in a prep school in New York City.

But most of all, Lauren wondered what was in that locket.

CHAPTER 1

EIGHT MONTHS EARLIER

Anything can happen in New York City. Any dream can be fulfilled.

After a punishing winter, April revitalizes the dreamers. Scarves loosen, steam evaporates. Subways and sidewalks buzz with renewed hope.

Nadia Tesla bounded through the East Village, soaking in the scene. Tourists mixed with Ukrainian immigrants and rambunctious NYU students in Japanese noodle shacks and bodacious tattoo parlors. Soon she would have reason to party, too. A man had called. A man had called with the answers she needed.

Seventh Street was deserted compared with St. Mark's Place. A pair of black torches illuminated the sign for The Bourgeois Pig with burgundy-colored light. Nadia peeked inside the wine bar. Still early, a sparse crowd. The oldest guy looked Nadia's age, mid-thirties. She glanced across the street.

A sliver of a man stood on a corner beside a charcoal garage door, a plume of smoke twisting from his hand. He looked more like a shadow than a person, the offspring of Marlene Dietrich and Checkpoint Charlie, born with a genetic predisposition to survive in the catacombs.

He took a final drag on his cigarette. The tip flamed orange-red. He tossed it to the ground and stomped on it. Inched out of his nook and glanced in each direction, as though confirming he wasn't being followed. Nadia wondered if something was wrong or if he was just a paranoid old soldier. As he limped quickly toward her, Nadia scolded herself. The man was just crossing the street carefully. She was the paranoid one. After the last six months, who could blame her?

"Mr. Milan?" Nadia said in Ukrainian.

He nodded. His peppercorn eyes were kind but steeped in worry. "Nadia Tesla?"

"Yes."

"The mathematician?"

"Well, I majored in math."

He peered over his shoulder again. "The odds are not in my favor."

"I beg your pardon?"

"We have to keep moving. This way."

He pointed toward Avenue A. They walked side by side.

Nadia hugged herself. "Is something wrong?"

"Let's speak in English." He spoke with only a slight accent, suggesting he'd immigrated a long time ago. "You work on Wall Street?"

"No. I used to work for a private investment firm, but my job was eliminated. I'm starting a business on my own as a forensic security analyst." Nadia didn't add that she was starting her own business because she couldn't find another job. There were always too many applicants.

He turned to her and frowned, as though that were the wrong answer. Shrugged and kept moving.

"You knew my father?" Nadia said.

"What?"

"How did you know my father? When you called and offered to meet me, you said you knew my father back in Ukraine. That you could tell me stories about him. Were you in the Partisan Army with him?"

"Oh. That. No. I'm afraid I wasn't being honest."

Nadia stopped in her tracks. "What? What do you mean, you weren't being honest?"

"I know of him. But I didn't know him. It was just an excuse to meet you."

Nadia stepped backward. Now she was the one glancing over her shoulder. There was no one behind her. "Meet *me*? Why?"

"To discuss a matter of the utmost importance."

"Uh, I don't think so." She forced a smile. "I don't know what you want from me, but you've made a mistake."

"No. You must listen for a moment." Milan's eyes shone with intensity. "The fate of the free world depends on it."

Nadia croaked with laughter. The man was nuts.

Her giggling must have sounded rude. Her hand shot up to cover her mouth. "I'm so sorry." She took another step back. "Really, I am—"

Nadia bumped into a display window. A sign said MUSEUM JEWELRY REPRODUCTIONS. The name of the store was stenciled in tiny white print: THE SHAPE OF LIES.

When Nadia turned back, Milan was a foot away from her, the creases in his face looking like a grid of tunnels. "I beg of you, please—"

A car backfired. Milan collapsed to the pavement.

"Oh my God." Nadia dropped to his side. "What happened? Are you all right?"

Eyes wild, mouth agape, he clutched the left side of his chest.

Heart attack. Had to be a heart attack. Nadia leaned over. Her shoulder bag slid to the ground. She opened his gray sports jacket.

His crisp white dress shirt was drenched in blood.

Nadia screamed. Not a heart attack. He'd been shot. By whom?

A symphony of horsepower rose to a crescendo.

Her head swiveled to the street.

Ten feet away. Big old American sedan. Driver's window open. Barrel of a gun aimed at her.

A finger squeezed the trigger.

CHAPTER 2

A SECOND CAR CRASHED INTO THE REAR OF THE SEDAN. A clap of metallic thunder erupted. The big old American sedan lurched, sputtered, and quaked.

The barrel of the gun disappeared, as did the hand that held it. Tinted windows prevented Nadia from seeing more.

The second car was a muscular coupe. Its nose was smushed, but the engine was still burbling, ready to go again. The door opened—

Nadia's head snapped downward. Milan's hand grasped her collar. He pulled until his lips almost kissed her ear.

"Find Damian," he said, his spittle warm and disgusting as it rained against her flesh. "Find Andrew Steen...They all... Millions of dollars...Fate of the free world—"

His hand fell limp to his abdomen. His chest stopped heaving and his eyes went dead.

"Mr. Milan!"

Nadia grabbed her shoulder bag and tore it open. *Get cell phone. Dial 911. Check pulse, check airway, begin rescue breathing—*

A man in her peripheral vision. Coming at her from the sports car.

Nadia looked up. Blue jeans. Long legs. Cobalt button-down shirt stained with white chalk. Short dark hair, touch of gray on the side. Face practiced in composure. Moving fast.

"He's been shot," she said. "I don't know if he's—"

"I called for help," the man said, his tone even but incredulous. "They were going to shoot you next. I'm a doctor, let me—"

A second gunshot exploded.

Nadia ducked. The doctor did the same. A man in the American sedan pointed a weapon through his window at her. Nadia caught a glimpse of a round face and a shock of red hair.

A third gunshot.

Nadia fell flat to the ground.

"My car," the doctor shouted. He grabbed Nadia by the arm and urged her toward his car, shielding her from the gunman. "Let's go."

A fourth gunshot.

Nadia grabbed her bag, kept her head low, and raced around the car. The doctor flung her door open. She jumped in.

The interior smelled of talcum powder and gas. A partially deflated airbag hung from the center of the steering wheel. Nadia tossed her bag between her legs and strapped on her seat belt.

The doctor jammed the gear into reverse, put his right hand behind Nadia's seat, and sent the car hurtling backward. He swerved onto Avenue A, powered into second gear, and took off uptown.

Nadia grasped a door handle and kept her eyes glued to the side-view mirror.

"You see them anywhere?" the doctor said.

"No. I don't see anything."

"Me neither. I think we lost them."

A car spun out of Tenth Street behind them, tires squealing. As it straightened, Nadia caught its profile.

It was a big old American sedan.

CHAPTER 3

VICTOR BODNAR SAT BEHIND THE SIMPLE WOODEN DESK IN his mock courtroom on Avenue A, listening to the sweet child. Back and hip aching, hemorrhoids burning like the time in the forced-labor camp—the *gulag*—when the guards chained him to a toilet bowl filled with kerosene-drenched rats and lit them on fire. None of the above killing him as much as the sight before him now.

"Once I gave Misha all my money," Tara said in broken Ukrainian, "he never called again. When I told him I was pregnant, he said I had to get an abortion or he'd have me and my baby killed. That if I told anyone about it, he'd have me killed. I don't want an abortion." She started sobbing. "Victor, I don't want to die."

Victor pushed himself upright and gave her his handkerchief. "There, there, *Tarochka*," he said. "How much money did you give Misha? And why did you give it to him?"

"When my uncle died, I got a hundred thousand dollars in life insurance. Misha said he could double my money in one year with no risk. Something about gasoline arbitrage."

"And when you called to tell him you were in a family way, did you ask for your money back?"

"Yes, but he told me the thing with the gasoline had gone bad and he'd lost it all."

Victor smiled like a cat that had just been told the wolf was dangerous. "Of course he did. Of course he did."

Four years ago, she was the doe-faced belle of the debutante ball. Now she looked like a malnourished slab of Slavic cheeks dipped in mascara-colored tears.

"You have a job?" Victor said.

She shook her head. "I was working at Macy's, but Misha told me to quit. He didn't want his woman working. Now they're not hiring."

"Where are you staying?"

"With my aunt. In her apartment. On Avenue B."

"Good. Go there. I'll speak with Misha. I don't think I'll be able to get your money back, though. Misha is young, rich, and powerful. As you know."

"But you're a powerful man, too, Victor."

"Thank you for saying that, *Tarockha*. But I'm afraid I'm a relic. The time for me and my kind has passed. Still, I promise that you and your baby won't be harmed. That I guarantee."

"Thank you. Oh, thank you so much, Victor."

"Keep me informed. Now, wait outside for a few minutes. Stefan will make arrangements to send you some money to tide you over."

Tara protested, but Victor insisted. She hugged him. The experience left him dizzy. He longed for her to return as soon as she left. Worried that New York was unsafe for a young woman, especially one carrying a child. Dreamed of putting a bullet in Misha's brain.

Stefan, Victor's most trusted adviser, came in. He'd been the open-weight alternate on the Soviet Judo Olympic Team of 1972, though no one in America knew that. In fact, there was no record of his existing in America. He'd snuck into the country on a freighter thirty-three years ago.

"Wire ten thousand dollars into her bank account," Victor said.

"But the bank account is empty."

"Empty? The hell you say."

"We're bleeding cash since they shut down our antiques business."

"How much do I have in my personal savings account?"

"What?"

"How much?"

"About twelve thousand."

"Send it all to her."

"All of it?"

Eyes shut, Victor remembered Tara's mother when he first saw her, fresh off the boat, groceries spilling from the bottom of her paper bag on Avenue A. "Her mother used to bake *pampushki* for me."

"That will leave us with no money."

"Don't worry about it. When I was fifteen, I was the best pickpocket in Kyiv. Maybe I'll go to Grand Central and rob bankers on their way home from work. Do you think they'd even arrest me if I got caught?"

"Hard to tell the thieves from the citizens these days."

"Just like home. Who's next?"

"The courier from Kyiv."

"Ah. Right. The courier. Give me a minute to use the bathroom. And pat her down. Twice. Then send her in."

CHAPTER 4

THE DOCTOR YANKED THE WHEEL TO THE RIGHT AND THRUST the car onto Eleventh Street, toward the heart of Alphabet City. The later the letter, the tougher the neighborhood.

An SUV barreled down the street toward them.

"Wrong way," Nadia said. "It's a one-way street the other way."

"I know."

The doctor mashed the pedal. The car surged forward, and Nadia braced herself.

The SUV blared its horn and veered left beside a column of parked cars along the sidewalk. The doctor blew past it. He took a sharp right onto Avenue C and negotiated a maze of sequential turns. Nadia suppressed a wave of nausea.

They hit a red light at the corner of Houston. An ambulance sped by them toward Seventh Street, lights flashing and siren blaring.

No sign of the American sedan. There was no way that old heap could keep up. Nadia released her grip on the passenger door.

"Where are we going?" she said.

"Police station?" the doctor said, his hands loose around the wheel.

"Right. Fifth Street. Between Second and Third."

"Got it."

"My name is Nadia,"' she said. "Nadia Tesla. Thank you. Thank you for saving my life."

"You're welcome. I'm Brad. Brad Specter."

He offered his hand, and Nadia shook it. While hers was limp and covered with a light sheen of sweat, his was strong and dry. He touched her shoulder and peered into her eyes with his cornflower blues.

"Are you okay, Nadia? Are you hurt in any way?"

Nadia shook her head. "No, no. I'm fine." Her face flushed, and she turned away. She couldn't remember the last time a man had looked at her with genuine concern.

Specter turned right on Houston to double back toward Fifth Street. "What happened back there? Did you know that man? The one who got shot."

"Who? Oh, him. Uh, no, not really."

"Do you know his name?"

"I never saw him before tonight."

"Huh. That's bizarre. What did he say to you?"

"Pardon?"

"I saw him grab you and whisper something into your ear. What was that all about?"

She'd forgotten all about that. *Find Damian. Find Andrew Steen. They all—millions of dollars. Fate of the free world.*

"Just some random gibberish," Nadia said. "He was in shock. I couldn't understand a word of it." Nadia gathered her resolve and looked at him. "What kind of doctor are you?"

"ER," he said.

"Ah. That explains it."

"What?"

"Cool under pressure."

He took a turn on Third Avenue, two blocks from Fifth and the police station.

"Sorry for the beating your baby took back there," Nadia said.

"Excuse me?"

"Your car."

He laughed. "The computers are so sophisticated it drives itself. Even an idiot like me can look like a hero. It's my first new car ever. No worries, really. It's just a material thing."

Interesting perspective, she thought. Her ex-husband used to go bonkers when she dropped a crumb on the floor of his Volkswagen.

Traffic slowed to a crawl. Specter took another turn.

"Were you visiting someone in the East Village?" Nadia said.

"Yep. My mother. I try to come down and spend Sunday with her a couple of times a month. We go to church in the morning, have brunch. Maybe go shopping before she cooks dinner. I'm working tomorrow, so I came down today."

"You're a good son."

"Hey, she's my mom."

Nadia imagined what a first date might be like. The circumstances were all wrong for her to even go there. Milan was either dead or dying. But she couldn't help herself. Something casual, maybe lunch at a French bistro and a matinee.

He said, "Let me ask you. Just out of curiosity. You said the man who got shot spoke gibberish in your ear. What exactly did he say? The things people say in circumstances like that fascinate me."

A car ahead of them hit the brakes hard. Specter did the same. The lurch jolted Nadia. What had he just asked her? She looked beyond the car. Fifth Street was two blocks away. Funny, they kept moving but never got any closer to the police station.

"You remember, don't you?" he said, eyes on the road. "His exact words?"

He was pushing that question too hard. Nadia reached between her legs and put her hand inside her bag. "Sure, sure," she said. "But first, let me ask you a question."

"Okay. Shoot."

"What is an arteriography?"

He laughed. "What?"

"You heard me. What is an arteriography, and how is it done? They did it to my ex-husband. In the ER. Before he died. After his car crash."

"Are you kidding me?" Still laughing.

"No, I'm not kidding you. Tell me what it is."

His laugh dissolved into a look of thorough confusion. "I don't understand. What's the problem?"

"The problem, Dr. Specter, is that you don't know how to check for artery damage, do you?"

No answer. One beat. Still confused. Two beats. Confusion fading. Three beats. Neutral expression. Air in the cabin like nitro.

Specter lunged across Nadia's body and hammered the glove box with his palm. The lid fell open.

A shiny silver gun in a black leather holster.

Nadia whipped a canister out of her bag and blasted him with pepper spray.

He screamed and slammed the brakes. The car stopped on command. His hands went to his face.

Nadia jumped out the door. Raced toward First Avenue. She told herself not to glance over her shoulder. It would only slow her down.

A yellow cab with a vacant light.

Nadia shouted, "Taxi."

The driver slowed but didn't stop. He'd heard her voice but didn't see her coming down the street. He was rolling away.

At the end of the sidewalk, Nadia didn't bother looking both ways. She ran onto First Avenue.

A car swerved to miss her. A truck hit the brakes to avoid the car. Horns blared.

The taxi stopped.

Nadia ignored the insults being hurled at her. She ran to the cab, jumped inside, and told the driver to take her to the police station on Fifth Street.

She gave the driver a twenty-dollar bill for a six-dollar fare and didn't bother waiting for change. Instead, she sprinted into the station.

She told the desk sergeant she'd witnessed a shooting and wanted to report a crime. He took down some basic information and asked her to wait for a detective.

Only when she sat down did she realize her hands were shaking.

CHAPTER 5

AFTER WAITING THIRTY-THREE MINUTES, NADIA WAS escorted to the squad room by a detective named Hyland. He was a sturdy veteran with suspicious eyes and love handles above the shirt collar around his neck.

Nadia took a seat in a chair beside his workstation. Stacks of papers, folders, and nine empty Diet Coke cans covered his desk. A flyer promoted the NYPD Museum Car Show.

She told him everything that had transpired that evening, omitting nothing. The problem was, the words coming out of her lips sounded preposterous, especially to a cop who worked Alphabet City. By the time she was done, Nadia could smell his disbelief.

"Did you happen to get a license plate?" he said, twirling a pen that looked like a Montblanc except the black lacquer paint was peeling.

"No."

"No as in nothing? Not even a partial? On either car?"

"No, I'm sorry. When I was on the sidewalk, both cars were parked parallel to me. When I was in the sports car, we were moving fast. And when I got out of the sports car, I didn't look back. I was running for my life."

"Right," Hyland said, dunking the word in a vat of sarcasm as he looked down at his notes. "From the doctor who turned out to not be a doctor. Which you figured out when he kept asking you what the dying man whispered in your ear. Which was that Damian and Andrew—was it Stein or Steen?"

"Steen."

"Right. Steen. Damian someone or other and Andrew *Steen* control the fate of the free world."

"No. That's not what he said. He didn't say they controlled the fate of the free world. He just said, 'Fate of the free…'" Nadia's voice trailed off. It didn't matter what he had said.

Hyland placed his pen on his notes with both hands as though laying it to rest in a casket.

She sighed. "I know. I know how it sounds. Look, I'm not a good liar. I don't even pretend to be. You must be a good judge of character after all your years as a policeman. Do I look like I'm lying to you?"

Hyland tilted his head at Nadia and leaned back in his chair. "Have you been drinking tonight, Miz Tesla?"

"No, I have not been drinking."

"Not one drink?"

"No means no."

"Have you ever been arrested?"

"Excuse me?"

"Have you ever been arrested and charged with a crime?"

Nadia looked around to see if anyone else was listening. The other detectives in the room were on the phone or conducting their own interviews.

"Yes," she said.

His eyebrows shot up. "What was the charge?"

"Weapons possession."

"In New York?"

Nadia shook her head. "New Jersey." She told him how she'd inadvertently taken a bag with an old family gun to the airport.

"What was the disposition of the case?"

"I pleaded guilty to a misdemeanor disorderly-persons charge."

"When did this happen?"

"March."

Hyland sat up straight. "Of this year?"

"Yes."

"You're on probation now?"

"Yes."

"Do you have any weapons in your possession now?"

"No, I don't have any weapons—"

"What about that pepper spray you used? Did you buy it in New York?"

"No, I bought it at a sporting goods store in Connecticut. I gave my mother one canister and kept the other. Pepper spray is legal in New York."

"Not if it was bought outside the state. It has to be bought in New York State. If it was bought in Connecticut, you're actually carrying an illegal weapon that is a violation of your probation."

"What? This is ridiculous. I came here to report a crime, and I told you the complete truth. A man got shot, for God's sake. He got shot. And you're worrying about where I bought my pepper spray?"

"Oh. About the man you say got shot. Officers responded to a nine-one-one call earlier tonight. It was a muffled voice from an untraceable cell phone. Said a man had been shot on Seventh Street."

"That's it," Nadia said. "That must have been Specter calling in the shooting of Mr. Milan."

"Oh, I'm sure it was," Hyland said with disgust, the kind honed by a lifetime of listening to lies. "In your mind."

"Pardon?"

"There was no victim when our officers arrived. There was no man. There was no shooting. Some residents said they heard a car backfire a few times, and there was a crash. But both cars moved on. No one was shot, Miz Tesla. There was no body at the scene."

Nadia lost her breath. "What?"

"The only crimes that have been committed here are yours. False reporting of a crime. Possession of an illegal weapon. Both are violations of your probation and could result in your immediate incarceration. Do you want to go to prison, Miz Tesla?"

Nadia opened her mouth to fight, to argue with the fat bastard, but what was she going to say? Her head started to fall, but she caught it. Raised her chin, looked Hyland in the eye, and stood up.

"Thank you so much for your time, Detective," Nadia said.

She started to leave. What if Brad Specter was waiting for her outside? She'd told him to take her here. He could be planning to kidnap her right now. She turned back. She didn't mind pushing her luck.

"Excuse me, Detective Hyland? Would it be possible for an officer to drive me home?"

He looked at her like the principal who'd just shelled out detention instead of expulsion to the school sociopath.

"How about the subway station at Astor Place?" Nadia said. "It's a five-minute drive, at most. Please."

He waddled up to her and stuck his chins in her face. "I think you've wasted enough taxpayer money tonight, don't you, Miz Tesla? And if you pull a stunt like this again, you're going in. Do we understand each other? Have a nice evening."

When Nadia stepped outside, rain was pouring from the sky. Pedestrians scattered for cover. Head on a swivel, she sloshed her way to Third Avenue. All the taxis were occupied. The subway was the only way home.

She hugged the curb to stay out of the shadows in case someone was waiting to kidnap her. Cars plowed through puddles. Water thrashed her shoes, clothes, and face. She soldiered on, wishing it were all a practical joke, uncertain if she would make it home alive.

CHAPTER 6

THE COURIER WORE AN ELEGANT BLACK BUSINESS SUIT A SIZE too big for her wiry body. Her platinum-blonde crew cut shone in the dimly lit room. She could have been a former lingerie model or a ravenous zombie from a postapocalyptic world. For a Slavic woman trying to keep her figure past her thirties, it depended on the lighting. It didn't matter. At his age, Victor wouldn't turn either one away.

A sealed bottle of vodka, two empty shot glasses, and a manila folder rested on Victor's desk. The courier stood before him, a slim, rectangular object in her hand. It looked like a book or picture frame wrapped in simple brown paper. String hung loosely around it, and the paper had been dislodged when Stefan searched her for weapons.

She placed the package on the table and pulled an index card from an inside jacket pocket. She read from the card in Russian, not Ukrainian:

The mind withers in the wind.
A thief grows old.
Time to retire and reflect,
And rob and steal.

"*S Dniom Rozdenija*," she said, wishing him happy birthday. "From Ilya Milanovich and the *Bratsky Krug*."

The Circle of Brothers. The twenty most senior former Soviet bloc criminals in the world. Most of them were Russian, while he was Ukrainian, so they would always be extra wary of each other. Still, it was a classy move on their part. Victor closed his eyes and let her words hang in the air for a few seconds, nodding with appreciation.

"Thank you. It is good to be remembered by old friends, especially when they are oceans away." He pointed toward the vodka. "Let's have a drink. But first, tell me a little bit about yourself."

The courier put her left hand on her hip and thrust it to one side. Victor felt a slight stirring in his groin he hadn't experienced for months. Victor knew she wasn't part of his birthday gift, but he was certainly willing to play along. She circled around and sat on the desk facing him, legs spread wide. Victor caught a whiff of orange blossoms, violet, and tobacco.

She nudged her right shoe off with her left one. It thumped to the floor. Her toes were snuggled in panty hose. She slid them onto his crotch and extended her right hand toward him, palm down. Tattoos. The kind earned in a Russian or Ukrainian prison. And in the outside world as a reward for criminal achievements and loyalty. They told a person's life story in pictures.

Victor put on his reading glasses and studied the tattoos in the center of her hand in a clockwise fashion.

A circle with a bull's-eye in the middle. "You grew up an orphan. You spent time in the Round Stone, an educational labor colony." Her toes massaged him. "They taught you well."

A sickle with a stake driven through it. "You began stealing out of hunger during your Soviet life."

Five bold dots: four watchtowers and a convict. Prison. "You've been through the Crosses."

A little girl clinging to a goose flying through the air. "You are a single mother." She pressed harder with her toes. "You know when to put your foot down."

The word *OMYT* in bold letters. Russian for "whirlpool." "It's hard for a man to get away from you once he's in your clutches." Victor closed his eyes for a moment and savored the pleasure. "Why would he want to?"

He shifted his attention to her knuckles. If she was known in the criminal world by a certain name, this is where it would be spelled out. He read the letters on four fingers just above the nail.

"Puma," he said.

She pulled her foot back and dropped it to the floor.

"No. Don't stop—"

Puma hissed and flashed two more tattoos on the back of her *other* hand.

A leopard grinned with its mouth open, gun in its left paw and knife in its right. "Death to bitches and traitors," Victor said, breathless.

Puma snarled. "When you're a woman, men search your breasts real careful…"

An X beside three skulls and crossbones: An executioner. A hit man.

"But no one ever pats down the forearms," she said.

She snapped her arms out and made a cross with her body. Small black revolvers sprang into her palms from under her jacket.

"Your cousin, Kirilo, sends you birthday greetings from Kyiv. He says to tell you your father was a bitch." Puma turned her guns on Victor. "Death to bitches and their sons."

"Anya," Victor said, barely managing to get the name out in time.

She froze.

Victor tapped the manila folder. "I have pictures of Anya."

Puma's lips parted with astonishment, flashing the promise of yellow-and-black teeth.

"Would you like to see some pictures of your beautiful daughter? Playing an hour ago in Shevchenko Park?"

CHAPTER 7

WHEN NADIA GOT HOME TO HER APARTMENT ON EAST Eighty-Second Street at 11:55 p.m., she bolted the door and called the doorman to make sure he remembered: "No visitors under any circumstances."

Water dripped from her clothes and pooled at her feet. She went straight to the refrigerator and opened a bottle of Mount Eden chardonnay. Crystal trembling in her hand, she downed a glass of the buttery anesthetic in two takes. She poured another one and took it with her into a hot, steaming bath.

After a forty-five-minute soak, Nadia showered, washed her hair, and wrapped it in a towel. She lay down in bed to rest her eyes for fifteen minutes and woke up two hours later. She dried her hair, slipped into her favorite pajamas (the ones with the pink gorillas), and ordered a succotash of green beans and corn from Gracie's Diner.

While waiting for her dinner to arrive, Nadia studied Internet search results for Andrew Steen. Google had 2.4 million hits for such a spelling. Another 815,000 if she spelled it "Stene." That was over 3.2 million matches for the two most likely spellings alone.

Find Damian…Find Andrew Steen.

As Nadia's mind drifted, her eyes scanned the amethyst sticky notes taped to the border of her iMac: *call Marko, mail COBRA payment, call Mama* (that one was so old the color had faded to lavender), *schedule lunch with Johnny Tanner, Milan's phone number—*

Nadia grabbed her cell phone and tapped the digits into the keypad.

"The number you have dialed is out of service."

She sank back in her chair. It was probably a prepaid phone.

When her godfather was murdered a year ago, Nadia returned home to Connecticut for his funeral. She grew up in an insular Ukrainian community. Her parents were immigrants. Although she was born in Hartford, Nadia went to kindergarten speaking only Ukrainian. She went to Uke school twice a week for seventeen years and even served as an altar girl at the Ukrainian Catholic Church. In fact, that was her nickname in the community. The "Altar Girl." Her parents put enormous pressure on her to be a good Ukrainian American and a superior student in both schools. Once she left for college at Colgate, she never came back until the funeral.

The deeper she dug into her godfather's killing, the more she realized she never really knew the Ukrainian American people she had grown up with. Among them was her father, the scowling and screaming family man who seemed to hate every minute of his life. He died when Nadia was thirteen, before she ever had a chance to ask him about the source of his perpetual discontent.

Her investigation put her life in jeopardy. Nadia uncovered a multimillion-dollar smuggling ring for priceless icons and relics from Ukraine and solved her godfather's murder. The FBI shut down the ring and arrested the killer, a childhood friend of Nadia's. The event was reported in local papers. People in the Uke community knew who she was now. Milan must have heard about her exploits. He must have assumed she was a proven troubleshooter of some kind, and now he was probably dead.

Millions of dollars. Those were Milan's words. His shooting and abduction off the street implied they might be true. Nadia's savings were running out. It didn't matter if Milan was referring to a pot of cash or an object of value.

She had to find out more, and she knew who had the answers.

CHAPTER 8

PUMA SAT SOBBING QUIETLY IN A CHAIR. HER TWIN REVOLVers lay unloaded beside the pictures of her daughter on the desk. Victor rubbed her shoulder as he circled around her like a nurse comforting a terminal patient.

"There, there," he said. "It's not your fault. I had my suspicions when an old friend from the *Bratsky Krug* called to tell me they were sending you with a special package. I thought you might be working for my cousin. But I wasn't sure until the guns appeared in your hands." Victor pointed to the package she'd brought. "Is that for me?"

She nodded.

"May I?"

He didn't wait for her to answer before removing the paper. In the framed photograph, Victor stood posing beside two members of the *Krug* in front of a three-story cinder block building. The grim looks on their emaciated faces told their story.

"*Brygidki*," Victor said, holding the picture for her to see. "It used to be a nunnery in Lviv until the NKVD—the secret police under Stalin—took over. I did seven years for stealing a shipment of grain. One day, the NKVD took a local priest and crucified him for giving a sermon in the underground church before

Christmas. They nailed him to a wall. Cut a hole in his stomach while he was still alive and put a dead fetus in it."

Puma looked away, fresh tears flowing.

Victor scowled. "Why are you crying?"

"Anya. My daughter. She is sick. That's why I took this job."

"What's wrong with her?"

"She has trouble swallowing and breathing. She needs thyroid surgery, or she will die."

"I see."

"Her father was a liquidator in Chernobyl. He bulldozed cars, trucks, and ambulances under the ground so the nuclear particles on top of them wouldn't blow to Kyiv. They told us not to have children…but…these pictures of Anya…How did you get them?"

Victor glanced at the snapshots of a sad, malnourished girl playing on a swing with a babushka. "They were taken by the sons of an old friend of mine—twins, to be exact—and sent by computer. Young people. They know all about these things."

"Where is she now?"

"She is wherever her grandmother has taken her. No one has touched her. And no one will."

"She won't be hurt?"

"Not only won't she be hurt, I'll arrange for her to have her surgery at the best facility in Kyiv, where they are experts on this disease. You have my word as a thief."

Puma regarded Victor with disbelief. "You would do that? You would pay for my Anya's surgery?"

"Yes."

Puma's eyes sparkled. She raised Victor's hand to her lips, but he pulled it away before she could kiss it.

Victor squeezed her shoulder. "It's time."

She blanched. "Is there anything I can do?"

"I'm afraid not."

Victor opened the door. Stefan and two of his men came in. Stefan saw the guns on the table. He looked at Victor, the guns,

Puma, and back to Victor again. They stared at each other without saying a word.

Stefan ordered his men to take Puma away. Victor nodded his head with approval as she left with the stoic expression of a true thief.

Stefan closed the door behind them. He walked over to Victor's prized possession, the only painting in the room. A dove fluttered in the palm of a maiden dressed in a colorful peasant shirt as she danced in a field of wheat. The deceased artist, Edward Kozak, had arrived in New York on the same boat as Victor.

"The maiden and the dove, the dove and the maiden," Stefan said. "I love them so."

"Me too. Especially since that appraiser said it's worth a hundred thousand." Victor told him about the surgery for Puma's daughter. "Find out how much it will cost. Then call Milanovich in Moscow and ask him for a loan."

Stefan nodded at the painting. "You could sell…"

"Never. I'd rather die. Make the call."

"We have no money, and now you're going into debt with Moscow for sentimental reasons. You're scaring me. I think you're going senile and maybe I should leave you."

"The day I stop scaring you is the day you should leave me."

"We both have to truly believe the money situation is hopeless. Only then will we get a windfall."

"Hopeless? By God, you *are* going senile. Why?"

"Because the greatest opportunities present themselves when all hope is lost. Now, I have to go," Victor said, reaching for the beret and coat on the corner hanger. "I'm late for my chess match in the park."

CHAPTER 9

NADIA JUMPED IN A TAXI ON SUNDAY MORNING AND arrived at St. George's Ukrainian Catholic Church on Seventh Street at 10:00 a.m. When she got her job on Wall Street, she stopped practicing her religion, which is to say she changed her affiliation to the greenback. Sundays were for sleeping in after six consecutive twelve-hour days. Once she lost her job, however, Nadia started attending Mass regularly again, just like all the other pathetic people who worshipped only in times of need. The self-loathing this inspired was exceeded by the tranquility provided by her childhood sanctuary. She was learning to forgive herself. For losing her job, being childless, and living alone.

After the liturgy, Nadia stayed alert to her surroundings. An ethnically diverse crowd mixed beneath the warm sun on Second Avenue. Some headed to church in jeans, others to brunch in their Sunday best. The street teemed with pedestrians. No one could harm her without drawing attention to himself.

At Veselka on Second and Ninth Street, Nadia sat with her back to a wall, facing the entry to the Ukrainian soul food restaurant. She ate a plate of cheese-and-potato dumplings called *vareniky* and nursed a second cup of coffee until 1:00 p.m., when the Duma bookstore opened.

Paul Obon beamed when he saw Nadia and shook her hand with both of his. He was the living incarnation of the Monopoly Man, with a single strand of gray hair atop his bald head. He smelled of old books and rolled around the nooks and crannies of his cramped store with unfettered zeal.

"How did your meeting with Milan go?" he said.

Nadia had called Obon before meeting Milan, to confirm he was a legitimate member of the community.

"Fine," Nadia said. "Have you seen him today?"

"Who, Milan?"

"Yes."

"No. Why? Didn't you get along?"

"Oh, yes. No, everything was fine. Just fine. I was wondering...Do you have a minute to talk?"

"Of course. I have some books that need protection. Would you mind helping?"

"My pleasure."

They moved to a small table in the center of the room. A neat stack of old books sat beside a box of plastic book covers. Obon folded a sheet of plastic to fit the binding of the first book.

Nadia said, "Does the name Damian mean anything to you?"

"Damian. A fine name. Parents don't choose it enough. Greek origin. Divine power. Fate."

"No. I mean, is there a Damian in the community here?"

He slipped the front book cover into the plastic sleeve he'd created and paused. "Damian...Damian...No, I don't think so."

"Hmm. What about people you deal with outside New York? Anyone well-known in the broader Ukrainian American community by that name?"

He gave it some more thought and shook his head. "No. It's an unusual given name, and I'm sure I'd remember anyone who answered to it. Why do you ask?"

He finished covering the first book and asked Nadia to put it in a glass-enclosed bookcase. *The Minstrel,* by Taras Shevchenko. Poet laureate who dreamed of a free Ukraine in the 19th century.

"I overheard the name in a conversation between two people on the street," Nadia said.

Obon studied the binding of the next book. "That sounds mysterious, Nadia. Of course, there was the infamous Damian, well-known in less savory circles, but I'm sure you're not referring to him."

Nadia's ears perked up. "Really. Tell me anyways. Why less savory circles?"

"Because he was a *vor.*"

"A *vor*?"

"A member of *Vorskoi Mir,*" he said in Russian. He switched back to Ukrainian. "'The Thieves' World.'"

"Ukrainian and Russian *mafiya*?" Nadia said.

"If you are thinking of the crime groups that are popular in the press and films—Range Rovers, mansions, villas, and big-haired blondes—no. That is the *avtoritet.* 'The authority.' They are a younger generation defined by the pursuit of material wealth and consumption."

He handed Nadia the second book. *Boa Constrictor,* by Ivan Franko. Poet, journalist, social critic. Author of the first Ukrainian detective novel.

"The *vor* is something entirely different," Obon said as he began work on a third. "The literal translation of *Vory v Zakony* is 'thieves with a common law.' A loose organization of criminals that have their own set of social norms. *Vory v Zakony* was formed in prisons in 1682 under Peter the Great. Their members swear allegiance to an austere code of ethics. They cannot marry, have families, hold jobs, or assist the government in any way. Their stature is depicted by tattoos on their bodies. Earned in and outside of prison. They were traditionally known for their *anti-materialistic* behavior. Sometimes they gave back to the poor in their communities. Like Robin Hood. Most *vory* were vicious, but some less so. Some were held in such high regard they resolved community disputes in private courtrooms."

"*Vory v Zakony* still exist today?"

"Yes, but their numbers are dwindling. It's old-school. Once the Soviet Union fell apart and capitalism came to Russia, allegiances among criminals went out the window. Young people just don't care about the old traditions. It's the same in prison as it is on the streets. Also, many *vory* died in the Bitches War in the 1950s."

"The what?"

"The Bitches War. Stalin drafted criminals during World War II. Some *vory* left prison and fought for their homeland. When they returned to jail after the war, their former cellmates dubbed them 'bitches' for helping the government. The Bitches War broke out. Stalin encouraged it, hoping they'd all kill each other. But they didn't. The bitches perished, the true *vory* survived."

"And they're in this country? In the United States?"

"They're scattered everywhere. Estimates I've read, maybe five hundred to a thousand true *vory* left. Power is based on money, weapons, and willpower. The young *avtoritet* with global reach and connections have no interest in the old ways. A few *vory* did well during *perestroika*, abandoned their oath, and became *avtoritet* themselves. But for the most part, the only place where *vory* remain powerful is in prison."

"And this Damian, the *vor* you mentioned," Nadia said, "is he in this country? Is he in New York?"

Obon handed her the third book.

"No," he said. "He died outside Kyiv some thirty years ago."

Nadia cursed under her breath. She glanced at the book. *The Noblewoman,* by Lesya Ukrainka. Preeminent female writer. Nadia remembered reading it in Uke school, which she had attended two nights a week, from kindergarten through high school.

"I'd like to buy this," Nadia said.

"Good choice. You know, former Prime Minister Tymoshenko wears her hair in a braid as a tribute to Lesya." Obon took the book and whirled to the register. "I do know someone nearby who can tell you more about Damian and the *vor*, if you care."

"Really? Who?"

"A wise old man. Made his money in the food business. People come to see him for advice on Sunday afternoons. I'm sure he'd love to meet you. Let me go in back, call him, and see if he's available."

A buzzer sounded. An old man with thick sunglasses sat in a wheelchair in front of the door.

"Ah. Be so kind as to let our friend in," Obon said as he disappeared behind a corner curtain.

"*Our* friend?" Nadia said.

"Why, of course. Our friend. Max Milan."

Nadia stood dumbfounded. "Who?"

The man in the wheelchair sounded the buzzer again.

Laughter emanated from behind the curtain. "For goodness' sake, Nadia," Obon said. "Look closely. It's Milan. You met him yesterday, didn't you? Let him in, please."

Nadia unlocked the door. The man took his glasses off. He had smooth skin, black shoe polish in his hair, and a birthmark on his right cheek.

He bore no resemblance to the man she knew as Max Milan.

CHAPTER 10

THE CAT WAS A LIVING, BREATHING FELINE TUXEDO. ITS LUSTROUS coat shined like black satin under the exposed kitchen lightbulb. A splash of white adorned its chest. It studied Nadia with gypsy eyes from its perch on the windowsill, unsure if it wanted to tango or tussle.

An enormous man escorted Nadia to the tiny kitchen of the two-story apartment when she arrived at 2:00 p.m. The kitchen was ancient but immaculate. He might have been a strong man in a circus, or a Ukrainian solar system unto himself. He offered her vodka or tea. Nadia sat at a bare wooden table and declined politely.

She couldn't stop thinking about her discovery at the bookstore. The real Max Milan was a retired insurance adjuster who'd emigrated from Ukraine twenty years ago. He'd never heard of Nadia or her father. Nadia had paid for the book and left without offering Obon further explanation. He appeared confused and concerned. Nadia didn't want to discuss the shooting, her subsequent rescue and betrayal, and the missing body. She'd tried that with the cops. She didn't need another exercise in humiliation.

Stairs creaked. The cat dove to the floor and skipped to the doorway, its tail vertical.

An old man sauntered into the kitchen and petted the cat. He was dressed in earth tones, with hair the color of ash. When he glanced at Nadia for the first time, a light flickered behind his eyes. It gave him the overall appearance of a cigar that had been lit a hundred years ago and could never be extinguished.

"Hello. My name is Bodnar," he said, in a coarse Ukrainian tongue.

"Mr. Bodnar," Nadia said, rising to her feet. "Nadia Tesla." Why had she stood up? Something about his carriage reminded her of her father.

He didn't offer his hand, and Nadia didn't offer hers. It would have been presumptuous. He was her elder.

"Call me Victor," he said, motioning for her to sit down. "Please. Did Stefan offer you something to drink? Vodka. Would you join me?"

Nadia didn't want to dull her reasoning, but it would have been rude to say no.

"Thank you," she said.

He brought a bottle that was two-thirds full, sat down beside her, and poured two shots. They raised their glasses.

"*Na zdorovye*," he said. He drank and swallowed in one motion, keeping his eyes on Nadia.

Nadia drank only wine but couldn't afford to look like a weakling. She knocked back the shot and managed not to cough during the ensuing burn. She returned her glass to the table with a celebratory bang.

Victor smiled, revealing a mixture of decaying and gold teeth. "Don't drink vodka much, do you?"

Nadia frowned. "I thought I fooled you. How could you tell?"

He chuckled. "I know things about people. So, Obon says nice things about you." His eyes lit up. "I love young people. Indulge an old man. Tell me a little bit about yourself first." Strangely, he glanced at her hands as he said this, as though he could have read her palms if she'd offered them.

"What would you like to know?"

"Where were you born?"

"Connecticut."

"What was your father's given name?"

"Maxim."

"Maxim Tesla. Where was he born?"

"A city outside Kyiv. Bila Tserkva. Do you know it?"

"Yes. I know it. Do you have any brothers or sisters?"

"Yes. One brother."

Victor leaned back and folded his arms. "When you were a child, did you play with dolls or other girls?"

"Neither. Toy guns."

His eyes narrowed to slits. "Whose voice from childhood do you miss the most?"

"My brother's."

He nodded and murmured his approval. "And if I offered you a clear conscience or ten dollars, which would you choose?"

Nadia considered the question. "That would depend."

"On what?"

"On whether my brother and I were hungry."

His lip curled upward.

The buzzer to the front door sounded three times in rapid succession.

Nadia said, "What can you tell me about the man named Damian?"

The cat popped its head out of its bed in the corner.

"Damian?" Victor said. The cat skipped over and jumped into his lap. "Yes. Obon mentioned you were interested." Victor stared into the cat's fur and stroked its back for a moment. "Damian was a thief. A notorious con man. He once stole the entire milk supply for Kyiv. He struck a deal with a mortician to buy the uniforms of dead militiamen in exchange for future payment. Then he and his friends dressed up like the local police and emptied the warehouse. Sold it on the black market for a fortune."

A commotion broke out in the background near the front door.

"How did he die?" Nadia said.

"Poorly. He stole ten million dollars' hard currency from an *apparatchik* who'd embezzled it from the government. When the little bureaucrat found out, he had Damian and his crew buried alive in hot asphalt. Never did learn what happened to the money."

The huge man who'd let Nadia in appeared in the doorway. "Misha," he said.

Victor frowned. The huge man walked away.

Victor asked more pointedly, "Why are you asking about Damian? Obon said you heard the name on the street in conversation. Whose conversation? On what street?"

"Oh. Um..."

Victor handed her the cat. "Excuse me for a moment. I have another visitor. It won't take long."

"Of course," Nadia said. She placed the cat on her lap and petted it gingerly.

"Because I thought you might be asking for a different reason," Victor said, poking his head back in. "I thought you might be asking because you found out his last name was Tesla. Because you found out Damian was your uncle."

CHAPTER 11

MISHA MARKOV BURST INTO A GRIN AS VICTOR APPROACHED. It was the arrogant grin of the carefree and immortal that Victor would like to pound on sight. A gold necklace large enough to double as a tire chain for his silly British truck jangled around his neck. A thin black jacket of the finest Italian leather hung off naturally muscular shoulders that had never seen an honest day's work. Victor heard that women swooned in his presence almost as much as he did in front of the mirror.

"Thank you for coming, Misha," Victor said in Russian. "But you're early."

"Of course I'm early. I'm early because I wanted some wisdom from my mentor." He spread his arms out. "I love you so much. Come here, man. Give me a hug."

Misha buried him in a hug. Victor suppressed a wave of nausea. His head didn't even touch the kid's chin.

"You all right?" Misha said after pulling away.

"Yes. I'm all right," Victor said. Misha was still smiling, but more like a lunatic now. "The question is, are you all right?"

Victor looked around for Stefan but couldn't find him. He had to be around the corner, in the living room.

"I am fucking awesome, Victor. Awesome." Misha moved to Victor's side and wrapped his arm around his shoulder. "Actually,

I'm early because I wanted to show you something. Come into your living room with me for a minute."

Misha guided him into the living room. Stefan sat in Victor's reading chair, surrounded by three of Misha's men, sportsmen who took chemicals to make their bodies bigger. Their right hands were buried beneath their black leather jackets.

Tara, the sweet child in a family way, sat on the couch to their left. An eggplant-colored bruise surrounded her left eye, which was barely open.

A vice clamped down on Victor's lungs.

"You see?" Misha said to Victor, pointing at Tara's eye with his free hand. "That is what happens to an ungrateful whore who talks about me behind my back. And now," Misha said, looking at Tara, "I want to show you something, too, bitch."

Something flashed before Victor's eyes. The back of Misha's hand?

Victor toppled toward the floor. His cheek stung. Had that bastard just hit him? Was he going to fall all the way to the ground? Couldn't he stop himself? Stefan was watching. Tara was watching. Oh, no. Not in front of her. He would look like…such a fool. He had to catch himself. He had to do something. Do something—

Victor crashed to the carpet. His vision blurred. His hip groaned. He tried to right himself and fight. Get up and fight. A spasm shot through his back. He winced and fell back to the carpet.

Tara screamed.

"Shut up," Misha said.

Stefan shouted. One of Misha's men pulled his gun out and pointed it at him.

Misha straddled Victor. "You gave her your personal guarantee she wouldn't get hurt? Who the fuck are you to give my woman a personal guarantee?"

Misha reached down and slapped Victor in the face. Open palm. Once, twice, three times.

Victor's nose burned. His eyes teared. Stefan swore in the background.

Victor searched his memory for a more embarrassing experience. Something his father had done to him? No. Something in the *gulag*? No.

"Old man, you make me so crazy," Misha said. "I let you keep a piece of your old businesses. I want to show respect for the old ways. I want to keep up the traditions. But you? Look what you make me do."

Misha sighed and threw a handkerchief onto Victor's lap. Victor tossed it aside. Misha offered his right hand, but Victor stood up under his own power.

Victor kept his eyes to the ground, unable to make eye contact with Tara or Stefan. After taking a few seconds to regain his composure, he pulled his own handkerchief out of his pocket, wiped his eyes, and smoothed his hair.

He looked around for the other man he'd invited. He, too, would be party to the dispute Victor would try to resolve. "Where is Amazov?" Victor said.

"In his car," Misha said. "With his men."

"Invite him in. The three of us—to the courtroom. Everyone else—out."

"You old-timers," Misha said, shaking his head with admiration. "You are tough as fuck."

"A man should never let personal animosities stand in the way of business."

"And fucking brilliant."

"Because eventually business gets out of the way of personal animosities," Victor said under his breath.

"Sorry. What was that?"

"Nothing."

Misha, grinning again, slapped Victor on the back. "Okay, Old School. Let's do this thing."

CHAPTER 12

NADIA STOOD IN THE KITCHEN CRADLING THE CAT, HEAD swirling from the vodka and Victor's revelation. Her father had told her he had a brother who died as a child, but they had never even discussed his name. If this Damian was, in fact, her deceased uncle, it might explain why the man posing as Milan had called her. She felt a strange tug, as though she had lost something she never even knew she had.

"Is everything okay?" she said when Victor returned. "I heard a sound. As though someone fell." His eyes looked puffy, his face flushed. "Are you okay?"

"Yes, I'm fine. Sometimes people in the community call me to help resolve disputes. This was a family matter, and things got a bit emotional. For all of us."

Nadia handed him the cat. "Perhaps I should go."

"No, no. That matter is completely resolved."

"Are you sure Damian's last name was Tesla?"

Victor placed the cat on the floor. "Your parents didn't tell you about him?"

"My parents didn't talk much about their past. They put all their energy into molding my brother and me into their vision for the next Ukrainian American generation. My father did tell me he had a brother who died at a young age. He never talked about him. But then, he never talked about anything."

"That's no surprise. Damian was a thief."

"I'd like to know more about my uncle. But...if this isn't a good time..."

The cat darted around Victor's legs in a perpetual figure-eight motion.

Victor said, "I have two guests with a business dispute they've asked me to help resolve. It'll only take ten or fifteen minutes. Would you like to have a seat and wait?"

"If you're sure you don't mind."

"Not at all." Victor rubbed the stubble on his chin and studied Nadia for a moment. "Actually, you know what? Why don't you come in with me as an observer? You might find it interesting."

"Oh. Really? I don't know...I don't want to intrude."

"Nonsense. You'll be my guest. A business went bad. Restitution is demanded. It's a simple matter. It won't take long. Verdicts are quick in my courtroom." He winked.

Victor led her upstairs to a stark room with a small wooden table and five chairs, three on one side and two on the other. Two men sat on one side with an empty chair and plenty of space between them. Neutral ground. A manila folder lay on the table in front of the empty chair.

Victor motioned at the two empty chairs facing the men. Their eyes undressed Nadia as she sat down beside Victor.

Both looked her age. One was well built, with lush lips and a chin carved from granite. Worth a kiss, but ultimately too pretty. A show dog. The other was stout, with curly hair, pugnacious cheeks, and a day's beard just past noon. A wolverine. Too menacing.

Diamond-crusted watches glimmered around their wrists. Black leather spilled into their laps. *Avtoritet*. Young, rich, powerful, and irreverent crime lords. The Show Dog looked Ukrainian or Russian—he had to be Misha. The Wolverine looked Georgian or Chechen. Ethnic distrust probably had exacerbated fallout from their business venture.

"We're here to resolve a dispute," Victor said in Russian. His choice of language meant one or both men didn't speak Ukrainian. "One party has been wronged, another stands accused. The wronged party is demanding restitution from the accused for lost income. This is a courtroom. Verdicts are final and cannot be appealed. Punishment for noncompliance will be immediate and severe. Does each of you agree to abide by this proceeding? Its verdicts and its remedies?"

Both men grunted in the affirmative.

Victor nodded. "Very well." He stood up, moved to the other side of the desk, and sat down in the empty chair between the two men, facing Nadia.

Nadia squirmed. What the hell?

"The three wronged parties sit behind this desk. Income was lost because our business of importing antiques and religious art from Ukraine was shut down in December by the FBI. The accused party is the one responsible for its being shut down.

"The accused party sits before us. The accused party's name is Nadia Tesla."

CHAPTER 13

NADIA GLANCED AT THE DOOR. A NARROW STRIP OF LIGHT shone along the floor.

The door wasn't locked. It wasn't even closed. She could run for it, but they were probably armed.

"You must forgive Obon," Victor said. "He didn't know what he was doing. He had no way of knowing we had business outstanding."

Nadia barely heard what he said. Pepper spray. She put her hand in her bag. Rummaged for a canister.

"Last year, you made inquiries into your father's past," Victor said, "and stumbled on our business. You got the FBI involved. Now we're out hundreds of thousands of dollars."

"And you're gonna pay," Misha said. "One way or another, you're gonna pay."

Nadia forgot. No pepper spray.

"We did a net present-value analysis," the Wolverine said. "The number we came up with is five hundred thousand dollars."

She'd left the pepper spray at home once the cop told her it violated her probation.

"That business was worth five hundred grand," Misha said. "You owe us five hundred grand."

The thin strip of light in the doorway beckoned to Nadia.

"Excuse me," Nadia said. She stood up. Took aim for the light. "I have to go now."

One step. Two steps.

"You are free to go," Victor said, reaching for the manila folder in front of him. "The doors are open, and no one will stop you."

Three steps. Four—

He wasn't kidding. None of them budged to stop her.

Five steps. Six—

"Marko," Victor said.

Nadia froze.

Victor tapped the manila folder. "I have pictures of Marko Tesla."

Nadia turned toward Victor.

"Would you like to see pictures of your brother at his nightclub yesterday?"

Marko. Whose voice from childhood she missed the most. He'd been the ultimate big brother growing up. They played Wiffle ball in the park. Consoled each other when one of them got the strap for getting a B in school. As adults, they'd grown apart. Now, on the rare occasions they saw each other, he was often drunk, and she was always unforgiving. Was it really him?

Nadia edged up to the desk and glanced at the photos. A worn and weathered rider straddling a purple Harley, filling up the entire frame. An unlit neon sign read BRASILIA in the background.

It really was Marko.

Victor extended an open arm toward her chair. "Have a seat, Nadia. Please. Let's discuss this like rational people."

Nadia stumbled back to her chair.

"You wandered out of your kitchen and accidentally stepped into our bread and butter," Victor said. "It happens. You're guilty of nothing intentional, or we wouldn't be having this conversation. But you're accountable for our losses."

"Go to hell," Nadia said. "I owe you nothing. And even if I did, I'm broke."

"You lost your job," Misha said.

"You're four months late on your rent," the Wolverine said.

Victor smiled. "A friend of ours owns your apartment building. We know you're broke."

Misha said, "We thought you might have some valuable information."

"Inside information?" Nadia said. "I don't know anything about any deals."

"That's not what we had in mind," Victor said.

"What did you have in mind?" Nadia said.

Misha leaned forward. "What did the dying man whisper in your ear?"

"What?"

"What did he whisper in your ear?" Victor said.

Light burst from the doorway. Brad Specter slipped into the room.

Nadia tried to remove her eyes from Specter but couldn't. He regarded her without expression of any kind, like a man doing his job.

"We've been following you for the last two weeks," Misha said.

"Why?" Nadia said.

"We weren't sure you'd accept an invitation to meet us," Victor said, "so we wanted to know your routine."

Specter said, "What did the man say?"

Resistance was futile, Nadia knew. Her only hope was deception. The best deception was rooted in truth. "Find Damian. Find Andrew Steen."

The Wolverine didn't react. The names meant nothing to him.

Misha looked up with a blank stare. "Steen. Steen. I know that name."

Victor nodded at Nadia. Now he understood why she was asking about Damian.

"That's all?" Victor said. "He didn't say anything else?"

"Well," Nadia said, "he did say something else. But I'm not sure I heard him correctly. I could barely make out his words."

"What?" Specter said. "What was it?"

"Millions of dollars," Nadia said.

No one said a word.

"Damian's millions," Victor said.

Misha snapped his fingers. "Steen. Steen. I got it. Money manager in Kyiv. He's connected to the top. To the top, I tell you."

"Who was this old man, and why were you meeting him?" Victor said.

"He called out of the blue," Nadia said. "He heard I was asking about my father and said he had answers. He told me his name was Max Milan. He checked out, and I agreed to meet him. When I saw the real Max Milan in Obon's shop an hour ago, I knew I'd been duped."

"Obon has nothing to do with this, or I'd know," Victor said.

Specter said, "Then who killed the old man, and why?"

"Someone else who wants the money," Victor said. "Whoever it was came back and removed the body to make sure there was no trace of it. To make sure no questions were asked."

Misha said, "So there's ten million dollars in play and two players. Us and someone else."

"We'll find out, won't we?" Victor said. "Here's what I propose. The three of us will find out what we can about this Andrew Steen in Kyiv. Meanwhile, you go home and ask your mother about Damian. And the money."

"My mother?" Nadia said.

"Yes, your mother," Victor said. "I knew her when I was growing up."

"You knew my mother?"

Victor shrugged. "It's a small community of immigrants. It was innocent, I promise you. As a child, she was like a squirrel always burying treasure. She probably has more secrets than the Kremlin. We meet again at Veselka in twenty-four hours. Three p.m. sharp."

Victor looked at Misha and the Wolverine. They nodded. He picked up the pictures of Nadia's brother, glanced at them, and looked at Nadia as though reminding her of his leverage.

As she squeezed out the door past Specter, Nadia's shoulders brushed his arm. When she glared at him, she thought she spied compassion in his eyes.

Outside, Nadia wobbled down the steps. At ground level, a sign hung in the display window for a clothing boutique beneath the apartment: CRY WOLF, NEW YORK CITY.

"Ah, fresh air," a voice said from the stairs above her.

Nadia turned.

Victor leaned against the rail.

Nadia studied him for a second. "May I ask you a question?"

"Of course."

"If I offered you ten million dollars or a clear conscience, which would you take?"

He considered the question. "Both," Victor said. "I am a thief."

The light flickered behind his eyes, but faded before he could finish his sentence.

CHAPTER 14

THE SUN CAST PURPLE STREAKS AS IT DISAPPEARED OVER THE horizon. Shadows gathered along the perimeter of Tompkins Park.

After their usual Sunday dinner at the East Village Restaurant, Victor and Stefan strolled through the park, watching the dogs play.

"You believe her?" Stefan said.

"We know there was an old man," Victor said. "We know there was a shooting, and we know the man whispered something in her ear. We know all this because we have a witness. Specter. As for what he said to her, it doesn't matter."

"Doesn't matter? How can you say that?"

"Because one man shot another man in the street in broad daylight, and it had nothing to do with a woman. Since *perestroika* happened and capitalism came to our homeland, why do men shoot each other in the street?"

"Money," Stefan said.

Victor grunted. "Exactly. Money. So whether the dying man told her about Damian's ten million dollars—which he very well may have—or something a bit different..."

"It doesn't matter. It's money."

"Yes. It has to be money."

A petite woman in black tights with a perfectly formed ass walked a pug on a leash ahead of them.

"Two cloves of garlic," Stefan said. "All they need is a loaf of bread and some salt."

Victor let Stefan enjoy the view for a moment. "Bread costs money," he said. "Have you wired that money out of my personal account to Tara yet?"

"How could I? Banks don't open until tomorrow."

"Change in plan. Wire her seven thousand. Get the other five thousand in cash. And I want to get it to her tomorrow so she can leave town before Misha does some damage she can't walk away from."

"I'll take care of that and the girl's surgery in Kyiv first thing in the morning. Speaking of Misha…"

"Yes?"

Stefan looked away. "He offered me a job."

"Of course he did. And you accepted."

Stefan regarded him with a look of surprise. "You don't seem surprised. Or upset."

Victor veered off the trail toward the wrought-iron fence, where darkness would hide the embarrassment on his face.

"The other day," Victor said, "when you joked I was scaring you because I was senile and you said you might leave me, what did I tell you?"

Stefan kicked a pebble out of his way. "That the day you stopped scaring me is the day I should leave you."

Victor stopped walking and faced his *sovetnik* of twenty-three years. "So tell me, Stefan. Do I still scare you?"

"No, Victor. You don't scare me anymore."

"Then it's time for you to go," Victor said.

They left in opposite directions.

When Victor got home, he sank to the floor in the corner of his dark kitchen. The cat meowed and jumped in his lap. He wrapped his arms around it and kissed its head.

"It's just you and me," he said. "It's just you and me, Damian."

CHAPTER 15

On Sunday evening, long after most churches conducted their services, another form of worship began at 7:00 p.m. at Brasilia in Willimantic, twenty miles outside Hartford.

Giant speakers suspended above a runway stage thumped with a Joan Jett rock-and-roll anthem. Two women gyrated on the floor, arching their backsides within inches of the faces of their worshipping clientele. Nadia counted thirty-three customers scattered around her brother's club. None of them wore fine black leather coats, and none of them looked familiar.

Marko came around from behind a bar the length of a destroyer and gave her a lukewarm hug. With his shiny head and gray goatee, he looked like a prematurely old Cossack. A blast of mint gave way to the inevitable stench of alcohol.

"Oh, man," she said in Ukrainian. "You're drinking again."

He blinked. "I can control it."

"Last month, you told me you were sober for twenty-three days straight. What happened?"

"I think I can handle one cocktail."

"Oh my God, you've got to be kidding me, Marko."

"Just stop. You call me from your car all frantic and shit, telling me to be careful like my life is in jeopardy. Then you show up here with your holier-than-thou attitude. I don't need this, Nancy Drew. I really don't."

Nadia looked around to make sure someone hadn't crept close enough to listen. She pulled her checkbook out of her purse.

"I'm giving you an early birthday present," she said. "It's going to be a big one to make up for all the years we were incommunicado." She wrote her brother's name on the check. "I want you—no, I *need* you—to leave the country for two weeks. Immediately."

He laughed in disbelief. "Whoa, whoa, whoa. Ain't no one leaving the country"—he stopped laughing—"unless it's you. What the hell's going on?"

Nadia started filling in the amount. "I don't have much money left, or I'd make it more. Three thousand dollars. The Bahamas. Or maybe Aruba—"

Marko grabbed her wrist and lifted the pen off the check. "Stop. Stop writing."

Nadia tried to force the pen down, but Marko wouldn't let her hand budge.

"Talk to me, little sister," he said. "What's going on? What's this all about?"

She pulled her hand away and rubbed her wrist. "I can't."

"Why not?"

She looked around again. No one suspicious. "It's not safe for me to do so."

"What?"

"I can't tell you anything except that your life is already in danger. If I tell you more, someone could try to get it out of you, and I won't put you in that position. You have to trust me on this."

"Trust you? Listen to yourself. I'm your brother, and you won't trust me by telling me what's going on."

Nadia remembered when Marko had secretly tracked her during her three-night survival test on the Appalachian Trail to make sure she didn't get hurt. She was twelve years old at the time. Her father had insisted she become the youngest girl in the history of the Ukrainian scout organization PLAST to earn the survival merit badge. Marko had saved her from a pair of criminals who'd escaped from prison. Now his life was in jeopardy because of her.

"I'm so sorry this is happening," she said. "I'm so sorry we're having this conversation."

Nadia resumed writing the check.

Marko said, "Does this have something to do with that antiques ring you busted up last year?"

Nadia didn't answer.

"Does it? Were the people you put away just a front for someone else?"

Nadia signed the check.

"Oh no," Marko said. "They were, weren't they? Oh, shit. Uke or Russian?"

Nadia tore the check out of her book and slid it across the bar toward him. "Will you please leave the country? For your own protection."

Marko glared at her, slipped off his stool unsteadily, and raised both pant legs. A gun was strapped to the left, a twelve-inch Bowie knife to the right. "Got all the protection I need right here."

"No. No, you don't," Nadia said. "Not from these people."

Marko's face darkened, as though he understood her message.

"I'm begging you," Nadia said, pushing the check closer to him. "Please go on a vacation. For me?"

Marko tore the check into eight pieces.

"Asshole," Nadia said under her breath. "I knew this would be impossible."

"Then why did you bother coming?"

She added a dollop of sarcasm to her voice. "Because I hate you and I want you to get hurt."

Nadia gathered her purse and started to leave.

"Yo, Nancy Drew," Marko said.

She turned. As a child, Nadia had escaped from her parents' demands that she be the perfect student, Ukrainian, and daughter by reading mysteries. She always had a Nancy Drew in her hands, and it was Marko who supplied them. He delivered newspapers before school and bought her books with the proceeds.

"I'm leaving for Bangkok on Monday. Bunch of us are hiking to Burma. Two weeks. You need me to cancel and stay, just say the word."

"Why didn't you just tell me that from the beginning?"

"That would have been the normal thing to do. Not our family way, though, is it?"

Nadia managed a smile. "Watch out for the snakes."

"You too, Nancy Drew. You too."

CHAPTER 16

NADIA ZIPPED DOWN THE HIGHWAY TO ROCKY HILL, A BEDroom community between Hartford and New Haven. Her mother's condo conveniently abutted Dinosaur State Park. Yellow paint peeled from the clapboard exterior. The glass on the bottom half of the storm door was missing, as though her father were still alive and had kicked it during one of his tirades. She remembered how his temper had frayed when she resisted taking the three-day survival test. She didn't need to be the youngest Ukrainian Girl Scout ever to win the most coveted merit badge, she told him. He screamed at her that she would never make it in America. That she had to be stronger, tougher, and more fearless than the other children because she was an immigrant's daughter.

Her mother's role in her upbringing had been one of tacit participation. When her father berated her for a less-than-stellar teacher assessment at an American school or a rival's victory in a Ukrainian spelling bee, her mother fixed Ukrainian comfort food and gave Nadia compliments. But Nadia's rewards were always conditional on her scholastic and community achievements. Both mother and father acted the same in that regard. Any and all affection she received was always conditional.

When Nadia entered the kitchen, her mother was arranging photographs at the circular wooden table. She didn't get up. She didn't even glance Nadia's way.

Nadia wrapped her arms around herself. "What happened to the bottom of your door?" she said in Ukrainian.

"A T. rex got lost and kicked it when he saw his reflection. What do you think happened? The juvenile delinquents next door were playing soccer. When I told their mother she should fix it, she told me to go F myself. Can you believe that?"

"That's terrible, Mama."

"They're Puerto Rican. What do you expect? This country will let anyone in now. This country is going to hell. You want some tea?"

"Tea would be nice."

Nadia's mother glided to the stove, her elongated, birdlike jaw leading the way. The belt from her black satin robe dangled behind her like the tail of a pterodactyl that had escaped with the T. rex. After preparing two cups, she joined Nadia at the kitchen table.

Nadia looked at the photographs scattered all around. In one, her father stood beside Marko on Mount Carleton, the Canadian peak of the Appalachian Trail. Her father, windswept hair like an angry lion. Marko, a pipsqueak, about eight.

"Do you have any pictures of Father when he was young? When he lived in Ukraine?"

"I have some pictures when we met in Lviv. After he was bit by the nationalist bug and moved from Kyiv. And I have some wedding pictures, but of course, we got married here in '71. Why are you asking? Are you still obsessing over what your father did and didn't do for the Partisans? What's wrong with you?"

"What's wrong with me? When I lost my job, I took a look at my life."

"Oh, really. And what did you see?"

"Nothing, Mama. I saw nothing, because other than my career, I have nothing. I have no one."

"You have nothing," she said under her breath. "You have a college education, you have your health, and you're an American citizen. You have everything."

"That's not what I mean."

"I know what you mean. And what does this have to do with your father? Wait. Let me guess. Your father didn't dote on you, and after he died, there was no man around the house, so you have trust issues, right? You can't hold a relationship with any man, and he's to blame."

"No, he's not to blame—"

"No, he's not. You are. Because your entire life has been about money. You're just another in a long line of Tesla quick-buck artists. Working with those criminals on Wall Street. You could have stayed in Hartford and been a mortgage banker. Helped people buy homes."

"Yeah. That would have been much better."

"You want a man? Be a woman. Go get a man. Stop blaming your father."

"I'm not blaming him. I'm just trying to find out who he was. You never want to talk about him. You never answer any of my questions. So I have to do it on my own, don't I?"

Nadia studied a photo of Marko and her in Ukrainian scout outfits, army-green shorts and matching knee-high socks.

"This is a nice one of Marko and me," Nadia said. "I was hoping you might have one of Father and *his* brother."

The teacup froze at the edge of her mother's lips. "Well…I don't know…I don't think…You know, it was a tragedy. He died so young." She blew on the tea and took a sip. "Why the sudden interest in your father's brother? You never asked about him before."

Nadia squeezed lemon into her cup. "Because I met someone who knew him. My uncle didn't die as a child, like you and

Father said. His name was Damian, and he was a *vor.* A thief, as in Thieves-in-Law, right?"

Her mother's face dropped. "Who told you this?"

"An old friend of his."

"What old friend?"

"Victor Bodnar."

Nadia's mother lowered her teacup nervously. It rattled to its place on her plate. "Dear God. Victor Bodnar. I would have thought he was in hell by now. I can't believe his name is coming out of my daughter's mouth."

"I didn't know who he really was."

"He's a thief. A con artist. He makes a living stealing from honest people. How and why did you meet him?"

"It's complicated. One thing led to another..." Nadia motioned at the photos. "What's with all the pictures? Why the trip down memory lane all of a sudden?"

Nadia's mother waited a beat. "I'm looking for the same thing you are."

"What do you mean?"

"Your father's brother. Damian. I'm looking for pictures of Damian."

"Why?"

"Because I've been getting letters from Ukraine from a man claiming to be him."

Nadia's mother slid two sheets of faded white paper across the table.

Dear Vera,

How do you start a letter to your sister-in-law when fifty years have passed since you last saw her? When she thinks you're dead?

You don't.

But I have to.

So let me try again.

Dear Vera,

I'm not dead. I'm alive. I know you won't believe this until I offer you some proof. And even then, you may not care. But it's not for my sake that I write. Let me explain.

I was found guilty of theft of state funds and sentenced to hard labor at Sevvostlag in 1960, when I was twenty. I was not buried in asphalt, the way everyone was told. Three members of my crew were. Three weren't. The man who I robbed wanted me to suffer daily for the rest of my life. He spared my life so the gulag could kill me every day.

Five years later I killed a man in the gulag in self-defense, but they gave me a life sentence anyways. I was in the gulag until they closed it down in 1972. After that, I was allowed to settle in Kolyma, where I remained a prisoner. I worked on the Kolyma Highway—the Road of Bones—until 1983, and then on the Trans-Siberian Railway until 1998.

In August of 1998, a man came looking for volunteers. We were told the work was dangerous but that the pay was high. He told us we would be pardoned and allowed to leave Kolyma and resettle in Ukraine. I have lived outside Kyiv since then.

In 1994, I had a son with a woman who was doing the same work. She has died since then. My boy's name is Adam, and it is for his sake that I write this letter.

My health is not good. I am dying. Adam is sixteen. I want a better life for him. Would you be willing to sponsor him? Let him come to America, the best place on Earth. He is a good boy. He has done nothing wrong. He does not deserve this fate.

I do not have an address because I do not want anyone to find me. I do not have a phone because I cannot afford one.

There is a woman in Kyiv. She knew the woman who bore my child. She agreed to give me her phone number and address for the sake of the boy.

Clementine Seelick
Yaroslaviv Val 8

Kyiv 01021
Ukraine
Phone: 244-3683

It was I who first kissed you beneath the apple cart when you were twelve, not my brother. You kissed me back, and then slapped my face and ran off. You stepped on my ankle as you ran. I limped for the next two weeks.

I am not dead, Vera. I am alive. Please help my boy.

I eagerly await news of your response.

With respect,
Damian

Nadia slid the letter back to her mother. The prospect that her uncle was still alive, that she had family in Ukraine, struck a chord inside her. She wondered if he looked like her father and what he could tell her about him. The thought of a younger cousin was even more exciting. What was his daily life like? What were his dreams and aspirations?

"That was the first one," Nadia's mother said. "I got two more after that."

The second letter was the same as the first one, except the tone was more urgent. The envelope contained a grainy picture of a boy in gray sweats and skates on a pond. His face was a contrast with his thin upper body: full cheeks, hearty eyes, and an unusually dark complexion. A red-and-white chimney encased in scaffolding and the top of a cement tomb loomed above the trees on the horizon.

Nadia's mother grabbed the picture and bristled. "Look at this boy. He doesn't even look Ukrainian. He looks more like one of those Mongolian reindeer people. Pathetic. You'd think whoever's trying to pull this scam on me would have put a nice-looking Ukrainian boy on ice skates. Like Wayne Gretzky."

The third letter was dated April 2. That was two weeks before the man posing as Milan had called Nadia to set up a meeting. The handwriting was so weak it was almost illegible.

Dear Vera,

A friend of mine has some very important information that he must share with someone who can be trusted. We are surrounded by scavengers, killers, and thieves. I am told by an old friend in America that your daughter is a person of integrity. That she can be trusted. Please ask her to call Clementine immediately. I beg you.

The fate of the free world depends on it.

Damian

He had scribbled Clementine Seelick's address and cell phone number again at the bottom of the note.

"There's no mention of his son this time," Nadia said, hearing the disappointment in her voice. "As though that was just a pretense to start a dialogue with you. And there was no more time for games."

Her mother scoffed. "There is no Adam. There is no Damian. *Fate of the free world*? Spare me. I can see it now. Once you get there, they'll tell you they need fifty thousand dollars in fees to release the money or something Nigerian like that. It's a scam, Nadia. Don't get sucked into it."

Nadia wasn't so sure. "What about the kissing under the apple cart? Did that really happen?"

"Well..." Nadia's mother swallowed, blushed, and looked away. "It just can't be him."

"Who else would know a detail like that? Who would remember it?"

"Someone Damian confided in as a boy. Some other con artist."

"Who surfaces now? Fifty years later?"

Nadia's mother stared into space for a second. "Maybe it's him, then." She turned back to Nadia with a fierce expression. "And *he's* the one that's going to rip you off."

Nadia knew there was only one way to be certain. "Do you have a pen and some paper? I need to copy this woman's name and phone number."

"Don't bother."

"Why?"

"I already called it. Three times."

"And?"

"It's a beauty salon. They've never heard of any Clementine Seelick. I spoke with a hairdresser, the bookkeeper, and the owner. Nothing."

Nadia shook her head. "That makes no sense."

Her mother wasn't so cynical now, though. "You came here asking about Damian. It's too much of a coincidence. Why? What's this business with Victor Bodnar?"

"Do you know anything about the ten million dollars Damian stole?"

Nadia's mother's eyes shot up. "Ten million..." Her breath expired before she could finish the sentence. "He stole *ten million dollars*?"

Nadia pulled out her checkbook. "I'm writing you a check for fifteen hundred dollars."

"Finally."

"Get out of town. Take one of your many male suitors and go on a vacation. Preferably out of the country. I don't want to scare you, but it may be dangerous for you to stay here. I did the same for Marko, but he tore it into pieces."

She took the check, folded it in half, and stuffed it deep in her bosom.

Her mother was always practical. "Your brother's an idiot," she said. "My daughter's wish is my command."

CHAPTER 17

A RESTLESS CROWD WATCHED THE AMTRAK DEPARTURE board overhead at Penn Station. Some carried briefcases, others dragged suitcases. None looked happy.

The bars on the board spun forward and rotated. The revolving numbers sounded like a giant roulette wheel. One of the bars landed on the 8:45 a.m. Empire State to Albany. It was now boarding at Gate 13A.

Victor handed Tara a fanny pack. "Wrap this around your waist under your coat. There's two thousand dollars in it. Another seven thousand was wired into your bank account this morning."

"Victor—"

"A woman will meet you at the train station. She will take you to her home in a town called Voorheesville. When it is safe for you to come home, your aunt will call you from New York. Until then, you must not speak to anyone. Otherwise, Misha will find you, and you will never be free from him."

"Okay, I understand. But what about you? Here," she said, pushing the fanny pack into his chest. "This is too much."

"No, it's not. You see…I need you to do me a favor."

Tara hesitated. "What kind of favor?"

Victor reached down and picked up what looked like a small duffel bag. One end was vented. He unzipped the other. A black-and-white cat poked its head out and chirped like a parakeet at Tara.

"I need you to take care of him for me," Victor said. "I have no one else."

Tara froze, mouth open, as though she weren't a cat person but didn't want to admit it. "Why can't you take care of him?"

"I'm pretty sure I'm going to be traveling soon. He answers to Damian, but you can call him whatever you want. He's a good boy."

Tara swallowed and forced a smile. "Okay. I'll take care of him. Damian and my baby will be friends."

"That would be…so nice. Thank you. Thank you so much."

He took a final look at Damian and zipped up the carrier. Tara reached out and grasped it by its strap.

"You have it?" Victor said.

"Yes, I have it."

"Because he doesn't like to be dropped."

Tara laughed and tightened her grip. "Yes, Victor. I have it."

Victor let go of the strap. His hand fell to his side, still clutching an imaginary strap. He handed her a second bag that contained some food, the cat's favorite toys, and its vaccination history.

He cleared his throat. "I'll be right back. I'm going to get a porter to help you with your suitcases."

Victor walked away. He resisted the urge to turn back. To tell her how much joy she'd brought him the three times he'd seen her. Instead, he found a man in a red cap pushing a trolley. He gave him twenty dollars and asked him to help Tara board the train early. Afterward, Victor did not return to say good-bye to Tara.

Instead, he circled the waiting area until he found an intense young woman in a business suit typing away like a nutcase into one of those small phone-like contraptions everyone is obsessed with these days. She was sitting in a corner against a wall. Perfect. Victor slipped behind a support beam, removed his right arm from its jacket sleeve, and replaced the coat around his shoulder.

He sat down beside the woman. She paid no attention to him. With the sleeve of his jacket hanging by her side as it normally would, Victor slipped his right arm around her waist. He dipped into her purse, rummaged around, and lifted her wallet. The entire exercise took ten seconds.

Victor tucked the wallet inside his jacket and sauntered out of the waiting area. He looked around. The police weren't rushing from their booth toward him. No one sounded an alarm.

He wiped a trace of sweat off his brow. Just like the old days in Kyiv Central Station.

"Excuse me, miss," he said, after returning to the waiting area. "I think you dropped this."

The startled young woman took her wallet and thanked him profusely. Victor bowed slightly and walked away.

He still had it. After all these years, he still had the edge. Good.

He was going to need it.

CHAPTER 18

NADIA CLIMBED THE HILLTOP TO THE CAROUSEL IN CENTRAL Park at 10:00 on a crisp morning. A smattering of children gathered with their nannies and parents at the ticket window. A vendor sold popcorn and cheap T-shirts featuring a prancing horse. People crisscrossed the path below toward the skating rink or the zoo.

Nadia's optimal course of action was obvious. Still, she was having trouble picturing herself on a plane, landing in Ukraine, and walking the streets of Kyiv. She spoke the language well enough, but she'd be a stranger in a foreign land. She needed the money to solve her troubles, though, and now that its mystery was wrapped in her family history, she couldn't resist the temptation to see it through to her ancestral homeland.

She found her attorney, Johnny Tanner, waiting on a bench. She'd met him a year ago when she accidentally walked into an airport with a gun in her bag. Johnny had gotten the charges reduced to a misdemeanor. A fine and probation. He wore a ponytail, a black pinstripe suit, and a look of unequivocal dread.

He started reading from a file as soon as Nadia sat down.

"Misha's full name is Mikhail Markov," Johnny said. "Thirty-eight. Born in Moscow. Immigrated at age seven. Grew up in Brighton Beach. He's been investigated for gasoline sales-tax evasion, prostitution, extortion, murder, and selling a Russian submarine to the Colombians. Two priors for assault. Did six months at Mohawk Correctional."

"Extortion and murder," Nadia said, swallowing hard. "What about Victor Bodnar?"

"Nothing."

"Nothing?"

"Nothing."

"Brad Specter?"

"Master's degree in art history from Rutgers. Convicted of fraud for selling art forgeries. Did two years in Mohawk at the same time as Misha."

At the carousel, a homely girl and her young father climbed atop a pair of emerald-and-silver horses with cherry tongues hanging out of their mouths.

"I have to find the money to pay these people," Nadia said. "There's no running away from them."

"You're kidding yourself, Nadia. Once they start squeezing, they'll never stop."

"No, you're wrong. The old man, Victor Bodnar, he's different. I don't know why, but I trust him. They just want to be compensated for their antiques business in their own sick and twisted way."

"You really believe that?"

"Yes. But I hear you. I may be wrong. So I'm going to try it my way. If I find the money to pay them and they keep squeezing, then I'm going to the cops. In the meantime, I have to follow this trail on my own. If they're with me when I find the money, there's too big a risk they'll kill me and take everything. Whatever it is, cash or commodity, I have to bring it to America, make it my own, and then pay them. Otherwise, I'm as good as dead."

An organ-based version of "Raindrops Keep Fallin' on My Head" started up. The carousel began to turn.

Johnny said, "So you really want to go through with this?"

Nadia watched the carousel. "I have no choice." It was a snap decision, the kind that had made her career on Wall Street, based on a decisiveness she'd inherited from her father.

"As your attorney, I have to advise against this. You should go to the police and the FBI and tell them what happened. That business with the stolen-art ring was dangerous last year. But this thing…with these people…"

"I appreciate it, Johnny, but my mind is made up. I'm going to get that money before anyone else does."

"Your next meeting with your probation officer in Jersey is in twenty-five days. Be sure you're back by then."

"Twenty-five days? Please. In twenty-five days, I'm treating you to a hamburger and fries at the fast-food restaurant of your choice."

Johnny managed a smile. "You big spender, you."

The carousel spun round and round. The little girl stayed two lengths behind her father, unable to catch up to him no matter how much she willed her horse to run faster.

CHAPTER 19

VICTOR SAT AT HIS USUAL TABLE, WATCHING EXHAUST BILlow from a black SUV through a window beside the entrance to Veselka. Two of Misha's men sat in the front seats, pounding raspberry blintzes. Inside the restaurant, two other bodyguards sat at the counter across from the dining room, downing pints of pilsner. They blended in with a cross section of New York City: students, artists, lawyers, bureaucrats, and businesspeople.

"Amazov can't make it," Misha said, reading from his infuriating little electronic device. "He wants me to fill him in later."

Misha put the device aside. A sizzling kielbasa appetizer cooled on his plate. He reached for a pickle and studied its texture and color as though judging a contest. He bit off the end and chewed quickly.

"Not bad," Misha said. "Good garlic. Good crunch. They must have aged it in cold water, not hot. Good spices."

Victor grimaced. "You eat pickles with kielbasa?"

"I eat pickles with everything, man. Major flavor with zero calories. You can't beat it with your rhythm stick."

Victor shook his head and sipped his coffee. They were seated at a table for four in the far corner, Victor with his back against the wall. Misha's plate smelled of spicy pork and garlic. Victor hadn't eaten for twenty-four hours and still wasn't hungry.

Misha said, "I have an appointment with the money manager, Steen, in Kyiv tomorrow afternoon. I leave on the seven o'clock tonight."

A pang struck Victor. "Are you sure it's wise for you to go? I know the city better. I can go in your place, if you'd like."

Misha grinned. "So you can accidentally disappear with ten million dollars? A sudden attack of Alzheimer's? I don't think so, Old School. If Damian has ten million on account that is due his niece—his rightful heir—I'm going to tell him she's ready to accept delivery of the money. In no uncertain terms."

A man entered the restaurant and looked around. He wore his hair pulled back in an elastic band like a schoolgirl but had the build of a man who once really worked for a living. The women in the diner looked up from their soups and salads to check out his black suit, which seemed like something an Italian fashion designer or a mortician would wear.

The man dismissed the hostess with a glance and wound his way through the tables toward them.

"Victor Bodnar? Mikhail Misha Markov?" he said, glancing at each of them.

Misha's men approached quickly from the counter, hands under their coats.

Victor and Misha remained mute.

"There's been a change in plan. Nadia won't be joining you for coffee today. My name is Johnny Tanner. She sent me in her place. May I?" He motioned to the chair beside Misha, unbuttoned his jacket, and sat down without an invitation. "So, what's good here?"

Misha motioned for his men to return to their beer.

Victor called in Ukrainian for the waitress to come over. He eyed Johnny Tanner's ponytail uncertainly. Was a man who referred to himself as Johnny trustworthy in any way?

"Coffee?" the waitress said.

"No, thanks. I won't be here long enough to enjoy it." Johnny Tanner waited until the waitress couldn't hear them. "So what have you guys learned about Andrew Steen?"

Victor looked at Misha, who returned his blank stare.

"Do I know you?" Misha said. "Because you're talking to me like I know you. And I don't. Just like I don't have any idea what you're talking about. Who are you again?"

"Johnny Tanner. I'm Nadia Tesla's attorney. And friend. Her very good friend."

"I know a Nadia Tesla," Victor said. "The book man, Obon, introduced me to her yesterday. Nice girl. Very intelligent. I like her very much. She was looking for information about her uncle. A man named Damian. You heard of him?"

"Sure," Johnny Tanner said. "He's alive."

Victor didn't say anything. He couldn't have if he'd tried. Misha paused to digest what the man said and licked his lips.

"Say again?" Misha said.

"Damian Tesla is alive."

"Who told you this?" Victor said. "What proof do you have?"

"Nadia made some inquiries. That's all she knows for now, but she's working on it."

"What do you mean, she's working on it?" Misha said. "Why isn't she here?"

Misha's electronic machine sprang to life. It vibrated and danced in place. Victor bit his tongue. Misha picked it up and began to play with it.

"Where is Nadia now?" Victor said.

"On the way to Kyiv," Johnny Tanner said.

Victor and Misha glanced at each other sharply. Misha resumed reading. The table remained silent for several seconds.

"You looked surprised to hear that, Victor," Misha said, face down in his device. He turned toward Johnny. "KLM. Flight 8579. Newark to Amsterdam to Kyiv." Misha glanced back at the screen. "She's in 14E in the emergency exit aisle. And she's drinking red wine." Misha started typing furiously with both hands.

Victor would have tipped his cap at Misha if he were wearing one.

"See, Old School?" Misha said. "The guy with the most money isn't always the stupidest one at the table."

Johnny Tanner showed no emotion, no tangible fear that his friend was in deeper trouble than she could have possibly imagined, until his Adam's apple moved just a bit.

"Kyiv is no place for a woman on her own," Victor observed.

"I'm sure you're right," Johnny Tanner said. "But Nadia is her own woman."

"You guys got nothing to worry about," Misha said. "She's not on her own. She just thinks she is." He leaned over to Johnny Tanner and lowered his voice. "Tell her I'm disappointed she wasn't here like she said she would be. And tell her I'm on the seven o'clock from JFK tonight."

Misha left the diner with his men. Johnny Tanner followed shortly afterward.

Victor's stomach growled. All of a sudden, he couldn't remember ever having been so famished. He called the waitress over and ordered a bowl of hunter's stew and a bottle of Obalon beer.

Misha was on his way to Kyiv. It was the best possible news. Although Tara was safe for the moment, she and her unborn child would always be at risk until Misha was killed.

Victor considered that prospect. Getting away from New York would be good. His old stomping grounds would provide Victor plenty of opportunity to make sure Misha never returned home.

CHAPTER 20

NADIA COULD SLEEP ON PLANES AT WILL, BUT NOT THIS TIME. She bolted upright every ten minutes, convinced someone was watching her. Yet when she walked the length of the coach cabin, no one paid attention to her. She even stumbled into business class, pretending to need to use the restroom, before getting kicked out by a flight attendant. She didn't recognize anyone. Still, she couldn't sleep.

She landed at Boryspil Airport after a twelve-hour flight with a stop in Amsterdam. As the plane taxied down the runway, Nadia adjusted her watch. It was 1:30 p.m. on Tuesday, April 20, seven hours ahead of New York City. She checked for e-mails from Johnny on the GSM cell phone she'd rented.

Meeting as planned, Johnny wrote. *Wolverine a no-show. Victor quiet. Misha headed your way. You have 7–8 hour head start. Phone is on 24/7. Call if you need me. J.T.*

Misha was en route to Kyiv?

Nadia grabbed her suitcase from the stowaway bin and raced to Customs and Passport Control. The scene at Terminal B was reminiscent of any American airport, except the people spoke Ukrainian instead of English. Although Nadia had studied and spoken the language her entire life, she'd never been among so many native speakers. It was exhilarating.

The local process for queueing, however, was not as pleasant. People didn't wait in orderly lines. They jumped and jostled for position. Nadia channeled her innermost New Yorker to conform. It took her twenty minutes to get to the head of the line. A suspicious young man interrogated her, searched her bags, and motioned for her to pass.

When she burst into the arrival area, a gang of gypsy-taxi drivers tried to rope her into their cars. Nadia ignored them and continued to the taxi stand. The sun shone on a mild day, but the air smelled of diesel. Peugeots, Fords, and Mercedeses purred in line. While twenty people waited for a ride, five men argued loudly in the yellow hut.

A thirtysomething driver with dirty-blond hair and cynical blue eyes stood beside his cab at the end of the line. "For every three Cossacks, there are five Hetman," he said in Ukrainian, shaking his head with disgust. "Welcome to Ukraine."

Nadia checked out his cab. Rust dangled from the body of a filthy white Fiat with Soviet stories to tell. Nadia couldn't see through the indigo tint on the windows, but the phone number stenciled on the side of the door and the license on his dashboard confirmed he was a legitimate operator.

"Hotel Rus. How much?" Nadia said in English. She rubbed her fingers together in the international sign for money.

He put up four fingers and answered in Ukrainian. "Four hundred hryvnia," he said. Fifty dollars. *Should be closer to thirty*, Nadia thought.

Nadia switched to Ukrainian. "I need an honest Hetman. One who'll take this Cossack's daughter to her hotel for two hundred hryvnia."

His lips formed the trace of a smile. "I'm cutting the line. Big violation if they notice. But for a Cossack's daughter returning to her homeland from America, three hundred hryvnia."

Nadia stepped back. "How did you know I'm from America?"

He pointed at the KLM baggage tag on her suitcase. "Newark, New Jersey," he said in broken English, smiling.

Nadia agreed to his rate. He took her bags, opened the door for her, and drove her out of the airport.

"First time here?" he said.

"Yes."

"Are you a language professor? An academic?"

"No. I was born in America, but I was raised in a Ukrainian community. Ukrainian was the first language I learned. I went to night school for twelve years."

"You speak it well. Where was your father from?"

"Bila Tserkva."

The driver nodded. "Sure. My cousins live there. I visit all the time. What do you do for a living in America?"

Nadia hesitated. "Finance," she said. "I work in finance."

He moaned with approval. "So you are beautiful, and you make a good salary. You are half of paradise."

Nadia blushed. She spied his handsome grin in the rearview mirror. "I beg your pardon?"

"In Ukraine, men say that paradise is an American salary, a Ukrainian wife, Chinese food, and an English house. You have the first two covered, so you're half of paradise."

"Oh."

He glanced at her through the mirror. "You know what hell is?"

Nadia shook her head.

"Hell is a Ukrainian salary, an American wife, a Chinese house, and English food."

Nadia chuckled. "Yes. Stay away from those American women. They're selfish and spoiled."

"Really? Ha. What do you know? Just like the men in Ukraine. That makes us two of a kind."

An eight-lane highway cut through a countryside filled with birch groves and white brick farmhouses. A yellow neon sign proclaimed WELCOME TO KYIV in English. The forest yielded to a sequence of billboards and neat rows of apartment buildings topped with satellite dishes. At first, the landscape was reminiscent of the approach to a regional American airport. Once they crossed the Dnipro River and the hills of Kyiv rolled into view, everything changed. A panorama of gilded church domes decorated the horizon. They blended with modern architecture to create a unique urban skyline.

As traffic picked up, the driver accelerated his pace. He used breakdown lanes to pass on the right and darted between cars in lanes that didn't exist. Nadia clung to her armrest.

"There are no atheists in Kyivan taxicabs," he said with a grin. "In fact, you give me an atheist, I'll convert him to the religion of your choice in fifteen minutes."

"That's terrific," Nadia said. "But I'm already a believer. And if I wasn't clear at the airport, I was hoping to arrive at the hotel alive."

The driver laughed and drove more cautiously the rest of the way. When he pulled into the driveway, Nadia tipped him 20 percent.

"Here is my card," he said earnestly. "My name is Anton. If you need reliable transport, call me. Anytime."

Nadia looked at the card. *Anton Medved, Assistant Professor of Sociology, Kyiv Slavonic University.* Why was a professor driving a cab?

"Ukrainian salary," Anton said, as though reading her mind. "It really is hell."

Nadia thanked him and checked into the Hotel Rus. The drab concrete exterior of the former Soviet property conjured images of a soulless country. Her room was small but clean.

After a quick shower, Nadia dialed Clementine Seelick's number in Kyiv and got the same beauty salon she and her mother had reached before. She gathered her valuables in her bag and asked the concierge for directions to Clementine's address.

Just in case the taxi driver tried to take her for a ride or she ended up on foot for whatever reason.

In the taxi, she asked the driver if Start Stadium was on the way. He said it was a slight detour. Nadia asked him to drive by so she could see it. He obliged and stopped at a monument at the front. It was a bronze of a muscular athlete kicking a soccer ball into the beak of a wounded eagle. Nadia felt a lump in her throat. She could hear her father tell the story for the umpteenth time.

On August 9, 1942, Kyiv was under Nazi occupation. A group of German officers believed to be members of artillery and Luftwaffe units challenged a local soccer team consisting primarily of bakery employees. Some of those employees, however, had been members of Kyiv's elite Dynamo team. The local team was warned about the risks of defeating a team consisting of Nazi soldiers, but as one Ukrainian player put it, "Sport is sport." The game that followed would become known as the Death Match.

Before the match started, a Gestapo officer visited the Ukrainians in their locker room and instructed them to give the Nazi salute in a pregame ceremony. The players agreed, but then refused to follow through on the field. The match was tied 3–3 until the Ukrainians rallied for two more goals. They won 5–3.

Within six months, four of the Ukrainian players died. Among them, their three stars.

Yes, exaggerations followed. The Germans probably didn't incapacitate the Ukrainian goalie by kicking him in the head. There was no evidence a Gestapo officer warned them to lose at halftime or face execution. It was unclear if the players' deaths were a function of retribution. And director John Huston's *Victory*, with Michael Caine and Sylvester Stallone, where the players earned a victory and escaped to freedom, was pure Hollywood.

But they were legitimate Ukrainian heroes from World War II. A war during which eight million Ukrainians died, more than in any other European country, and one during which Ukrainians were often collectively labeled Nazi sympathizers.

After the detour, the driver turned back and dropped her off on Yaroslaviv Val. It was a narrow, cozy street. Elaborate balustrades and balconies adorned the facades of architectural masterpieces. Nadia walked for five minutes until she found the five-story neoclassical apartment building. She buzzed the door to Seelick, 8B, took a deep breath, and waited.

No one answered.

A minute later, she buzzed again. No one was home. After two more tries, she buzzed the button for deliveries and asked to speak with the super.

A stout man with a handlebar mustache opened the door. Nadia told him she was looking for Clementine Seelick.

The super soured as soon as he heard the name. "She's gone," he said.

"Gone?"

"This is a monthly rental. She left at the end of March."

"Did she leave a forwarding address?"

The super looked Nadia over from head to toe and turned away as though he was insulted. "No. I don't think she lived here."

"I don't understand."

"She had visitors. Male visitors, if you know what I mean. And now she's gone. Are you interested in renting an apartment?"

"Who, me?" Nadia said. "No, thank you."

The super grunted and slammed the door in her face.

CHAPTER 21

Kirilo Andre hoisted himself to his feet, circled his Louis XIV desk, and faced his daughter. He'd been waiting for this moment since the British kid had asked Isabella to marry him. Kirilo clutched the antique music jewelry box.

"For you," he said in Ukrainian, his voice cracking. "To wear on your wedding day."

"What? For me? For real, Papa?" Isabella said.

"Yes, sunshine. For you."

Tears welled in her eyes. She didn't rush to open it. Instead, she caressed the mother-of-pearl inlay with her elegant fingers, taking pleasure in it.

Kirilo caught his breath. With each passing year, she looked more like her mother. Her black hair fell in silken strands to her shoulders. Her innocent oval face appeared sculpted by God himself from Venetian white marble.

After her mother died when she was sixteen, she told him she wasn't going to be like all the other girls her age. She was saving herself for the man she loved. How proud he had been. Now she was twenty-one, and the time had come. Why did it have to happen so fast?

Isabella opened the box. It sprang to life with the melody of "Lara's Theme."

"*Doctor Zhivago*," Kirilo said. "It was your mother's favorite—"

"Oh, Papa. They're beautiful." Isabella pulled the strand of white pearls out of the box and gasped.

"They were your mother's greatest treasure. She asked me to give them to you for your wedding day. They're natural pearls. Made by oysters. By accident. Just like you. Here, let's try them on."

Isabella stood up. Kirilo's hands trembled as he fit the pearls around his daughter's neck.

"Well..." he said, forgetting his other words as quickly as they came to mind.

She ran to the mirror in his office bathroom, shrieked, and flew back into his arms.

"Thank you. Thank you, Papa."

They discussed the wedding arrangements for a few minutes.

"It doesn't have to be the Hotel Oreanda," Isabella said. "We can have a simple wedding. At a smaller place."

"Nonsense. I've booked all one hundred thirty-three rooms and suites for our guests. I've booked the entire hotel for the weekend."

She beamed and kissed him hard on the cheek.

"Papa," she said when she pulled away, "we want to live in London when we're married."

"London?" he said, alarmed. "Really? I thought your young man was going to open a restaurant in Kyiv. You know. Close by."

"We were thinking about that, but given my experience in the music business—"

"Selling CDs at Virgin Records?"

"And Evan's experience in the nightclub business—"

"Tending bar at Club Revolution?"

"What we really want to do is open a disco in London." She tugged on his cardigan sweater. Her eyes moistened and twinkled.

Kirilo sighed. "If it's a disco you want..."

She hugged and kissed him again. They discussed the wedding invitation list before she said good-bye.

Kirilo sailed to the sitting room next door to his office so he could watch her leave. The opportunity to look out the window and see his baby in a candid moment would be gone in six months.

Beyond his crushed-shell driveway, the turquoise water of Yalta Bay shimmered against the soaring backdrop of the Crimean Mountains. Resorts and spas sprang from the dense forest that surrounded the sandy beach.

Two equally skinny girlfriends waited for Isabella beside her Mercedes. Kirilo rotated a lever to open the window.

"Look what I got," Isabella whispered. "Somewhere My Love" started up again as she pulled the old-fashioned white pearls out of the case. "He wants me to wear them at the wedding."

One of the girls exploded with laughter. The other one looked at the jewelry as though it were a dead rat.

"Oh my God. You'll look like…one hundred years old. You're not going to, are you?" the second one said.

"Hell no," Isabella said. "These crappy strands. They're so old and unreliable. They can snap for no reason. What can you do? Accidents happen."

They climbed into the car. A chorus of giggles erupted. The engine roared to life and drowned them out as the car sped away.

Kirilo's vision went black. He collapsed against a wall and slid down to the floor. He wrapped his arms around his knees and focused on breathing.

He stayed in that position for an indeterminate amount of time. Two different men came by and asked him if he was okay. He didn't bother to look at them. He just told them to fuck off.

Eventually, the stench of a thousand rotten eggs threatened to suffocate him. He wobbled to his feet and closed the window. After marching back to his office, he screamed his adviser's name.

Ten seconds later, Pavel burst inside, breathless. His most trusted adviser had a doctorate in chemical engineering and was a member of the Institute for High Temperatures.

"What's wrong, Boss?" Pavel said.

"The fucking Black Sea. Seventeen waterways shitting all over us. Some Riviera. They don't have this in France, you know. They do not have this in France. Remind me why I should be happy about this stench?"

"It's hydrogen sulfide. Energy of the future. Once the commission decides it's usable, the distribution concession should come our way. Assuming you and the commissioner are still business partners."

"He'll be seated at my table at Isabella's wedding." The mere mention of her made him wince. "Have you heard from Puma?"

"No. It's been twenty-four hours."

"Then she's dead. And the bitch is still alive. Victor Bodnar is still alive. That's not acceptable. Not acceptable at all."

Pavel lowered his head.

A hurricane wind shook the villa.

Kirilo frowned. "The helicopter?" He checked his watch. It was 5:30 p.m.

Pavel cleared his throat. "You have dinner with Steen. Andrew Steen. The money manager in Kyiv."

"That shifty-eyed prick."

"He's meeting a man from America on a delicate matter, and he needs protection."

Kirilo reached into a drawer for his battery-powered cattle prod. "Don't we all?"

CHAPTER 22

CHESTNUT TREES LINED BASEINA STREET. WHITE-AND-PINK blossoms burst from thickets of fernlike leaves. The air smelled of spice and jasmine. Nadia couldn't imagine living anywhere other than in America. Her father had pounded it into her head that she was the luckiest girl in the world to be born in the USA, and Nadia firmly believed it, as much now as she had then. But if there were a short list of alternatives, much to her shock, Kyiv might actually be on it.

The brief thought faded as Nadia wandered back toward her hotel. Her only lead was dead. Why would the woman who had promised to help Damian give him the wrong phone number? Why would she vanish without leaving a forwarding address? Clementine Seelick was acting as though she had lied to Damian, as though she didn't really mean to help him.

A crowd bustled at the *Palats Sportu*, a metro station built in the shape of a stadium. A babushka sold dried meat, cheese, fruit, and nuts from a pushcart at the corner.

"Sunflower seeds?" she said, waving a bag at Nadia.

"No, thank you," Nadia said.

She put her head down and hustled past the old woman. Guilt and shame washed over Nadia. Should she have bought a bag? The poor woman probably relied on the extra income to survive.

Nadia kept walking. The crowd thinned.

A man emerged grinning from behind a chestnut tree. He looked twentysomething, with a day's growth over suspiciously gaunt cheeks. He wore a neat blue sports jacket with gray slacks and shiny cowboy boots.

"Hey," he said to Nadia in heavily accented English, as though they were friends. "How are you?"

Nadia ignored him, but he caught up to her.

"You British or American?" he said.

"How can you tell I'm a foreigner?" she said in English.

"You answer babushka. A local not so polite. Local just walk by."

He tripped over something on the sidewalk and brushed against Nadia's side. She recoiled.

"I practice English. Is okay?" He pulled a lighter out of his right pocket.

Nadia kept walking.

He pulled something out of his left pocket and lit it. Took a drag.

The smell of weed invaded Nadia's nostrils. She glanced at him with shock. Picked up her pace and turned.

A man and a woman blocked her path. They wore jeans and black Windbreakers over athletic physiques.

"Police," the man said in Ukrainian. "Stop. Both of you."

They flashed IDs and badges. His was gold, and hers was silver.

The policeman grabbed Nadia's pursuer by his shirt collar. "Still dealing drugs to tourists, Kolya?"

"It was her marijuana," he said, pointing to the extinguished joint by Nadia's shoe.

"That's a lie," Nadia said in Ukrainian.

The two cops glanced at her sharply when they heard she spoke the language. The policewoman blocked her path. She stayed on her toes as though she expected Nadia to run.

"Passport," the policeman said.

Nadia opened her purse and gave him her passport. He studied and returned it.

"Let me see your bag," he said.

Nadia handed him the bag.

"My partner is going to search you," he said. "Just take it easy and do what she says. You got nothing to worry about if it's like you said."

The policewoman told Nadia to raise her arms. She patted Nadia's pockets. Reached into the left one and pulled out a small bag filled with white powder.

"That's not mine," Nadia said, outraged. She looked at the dealer. "This guy brushed up against me a minute ago. He must have slipped it into my pocket."

The policeman studied the bag of powder. "We all know Kolya deals in cocaine, don't we, Kolya?" He smacked the drug dealer in the head. Turned back to Nadia. Her purse was still in his left hand. "This is very serious. We are going to arrest you and take you to the station. Unless you'd like to pay the fine right here."

"Fine?" Nadia said. She realized they could be thugs scamming her. She didn't live in New York for nothing. "I'm not paying any fine. Go ahead. Arrest me. I want to call the American embassy."

"Look," the policeman said, pulling her purse out of the bag, "we're getting cash out of this one way or another. Why do you have to be such a bitch? You want to get hurt? Is that the thing? Are you the kind of woman that likes to get a beating?"

An SUV screeched to a halt beside them on the street. All eyes went to the road.

It was a black Porsche Cayenne. A man stepped out of the vehicle. He wore a thin cashmere mock turtleneck, pleated slacks, and fine Italian loafers. He moved with the confidence of a bullfighter.

"What's going on here?" Brad Specter said in fluent Russian.

The policeman frowned. "Who the hell are you?" he said, switching from Ukrainian to Russian. "Passport."

"You're the police?" Specter said.

"That's right."

Specter looked them over. "Really. You two…You two don't look like police. Show me your badges."

No one moved or said a thing. The man and the woman looked at his Porsche and each other.

Specter stepped closer. "I understand," he said, nodding sympathetically. "We all have to make a living. Leave now and I'll spare your lives. I won't have all three of you shot tonight." He reached out with an open hand for Nadia's bag.

Kolya, the supposed drug dealer, stepped back. He tapped the man on the arm and motioned for the woman to retreat with him, as though he were in charge.

The man defiantly stood his ground. "Spare our lives? Fuck you, asshole. You don't even know our names."

"I don't need your names," Specter said. "I know your faces."

The man swallowed deeply. He handed Specter the bag. Backpedaled slowly and joined Kolya and the woman. They turned and hustled toward the metro station.

"What are you doing here? When did you get here?" Nadia said.

Specter walked calmly to Nadia and returned her bag to her. "Please get in the car, Nadia. Your life is in danger."

"I'm not going anywhere with you. How did you know they weren't cops?"

"Cops don't hassle Caucasian tourists anymore. And if they did, they'd be wearing uniforms."

"How did you get here so fast? I had a head start."

"I was on the KLM flight with you."

"What? But I…I searched the entire cabin. Even business. How could I have missed you?"

"I was in the backseat by the bathroom and the galley. I could duck into either when I saw you move. And you didn't have a head start. I was tailing you the entire time. I saw you and your friend in Central Park. The guy with the ponytail."

"Why did you stop to help me?" Nadia said.

Specter hesitated. "Just doing my job. Protecting Misha's investment. Who lives at Yaroslaviv Val?"

"Ask the super."

"I did."

"Then you should know who lives there."

"He wouldn't tell me. I'm a foreigner, and I don't speak Ukrainian. He said if I want to speak Russian to go to St. Petersburg and slammed the door in my face."

"Yeah, he does that."

"The man who got shot on Seventh Street," Specter said. "He said something else to you, didn't he? I could tell at Victor's. I could tell you were holding back."

Fate of the free world.

"No. I said it like it was."

"Why did you run? Why did you piss Misha off? Don't you understand that the way you're playing it now, you're dead no matter what?"

"Until he finds Damian, Andrew Steen, and the money, he needs me. I have the only lead. Which means you need me."

"What did the man who got shot really whisper in your ear?" he persisted. "Who told you Damian is alive? Who lives at Yaroslaviv Val? If you tell me, I'll help you get out of the country and get lost for a while. Eventually, Misha will move on to something else and forget about you. We're like that. Sicilians, they remember and hunt. Ukes, we let go and move on. Tribal difference. Our ancestors suffered ten centuries of oppression. Letting go and moving on is in our genes."

"Why would you do that for me? Why would you help me?"

Specter paused and looked away. "So I don't have to do what I'm supposed to do once we find the money."

"What are you supposed to do if you find the money?"

He turned back to Nadia with a blank expression on his face, the same one he'd shown her in Victor's courtroom when he first walked in.

"Kill you."

CHAPTER 23

Andrew Steen, the gray-haired elder statesman who wore tailored British suits, didn't rattle easily, in Kirilo's experience, but he was fidgeting in his seat tonight.

"For the third time," Steen said, "I don't have any clients named Tesla. I have a very profitable business. Why would I possibly lie?"

The evening had begun well but was deteriorating quickly. After a pleasant dinner at a steak house, Kirilo invited Steen and Misha to an old section of Kyiv called Podil. Curved streets wound around churches, cathedrals, and antique merchant homes. The River Palace was a private casino in a fancy old mansion constructed with marble columns. Sculptures of crocodiles, frogs, and nymphs surrounded the house as though they'd crept out of the nearby Dnipro.

Steen, Misha, and Kirilo reclined in crushed-velvet chairs in the soundproof VIP room, overlooking the seven gaming tables through a one-way window. The bodyguards, lubricated with bottles of vodka, busied themselves at the blackjack tables below.

Kirilo had the VIP room prepared for a business meeting beforehand. The temperature was cold enough to store fur, just in case tempers boiled over. A Eurasian minx in a conservative black suit served drinks. Kirilo chose *horilka*, Ukrainian whiskey. Misha drank vodka. Steen chose Coca-Cola Light and turned the color of a beet.

"I apologize, gentlemen," he said. "I can't consume any alcoholic beverages because of certain medication I'm taking."

It was a lame excuse and a sign of weakness, Kirilo thought. The man couldn't hold a single drink.

When they first arrived, Kirilo decided to sit back and enjoy the sparring for a while. Now, however, he sensed it was escalating toward physical violence. Just as well. Misha Markov reminded him of a handsome British television presenter he'd always wanted to pummel.

"Let's see your client roster," Misha said.

"That's out of the question," Steen said. "It's confidential. Look, you're obviously an important man. I respect you. The last thing I need is for you to make life difficult for me."

Misha said, "You're a Jew in Ukraine. You don't need me to make life more difficult for you."

"Hey." Kirilo wagged a finger at Misha. "You're a guest here. Watch your language."

Misha's grin widened, giving him the look of someone who needed psychiatric care. "Don't wave your finger at me, *doob*."

Kirilo's ears rang. *Doob* was the word for "oak," and Russian slang for "dumb Ukrainian." Arrogant Muscovite pig. "Hey, *moscal*," Kirilo said. "Did you just call me a *doob*?"

"What?" Misha exaggerated a look of horror. "No. You must have heard me wrong. I would never call you a *doob*. You're the son of my father's slaves. My father would never hire dumb slaves."

Kirilo burst out laughing, trying his hardest to sound genuinely entertained.

"*Andreyu*," he said to Steen, using the familiar version of his first name. "Would you step outside for a moment and give us some privacy?"

Kirilo escorted Steen to the door and closed it behind him.

Misha grinned as Kirilo circled around him, pretending to be going to the bar for a refill of *horilka*. Instead, Kirilo wrapped his arm around Misha's neck. Secured it in a choke hold.

"Fight me and I'll snap your neck in half," Kirilo said.

Misha froze, the grin finally off his face. Kirilo applied pressure to the carotid arteries. Misha gripped the crook of his arm with both hands but didn't fight him.

"You're going to pass out in twenty seconds," Kirilo said. "And then I'm going to teach you a lesson in manners, *moscal*."

"Thank you," Misha stammered.

Kirilo eased up on the pressure and laughed. "What did you say? Did you say 'thank you'?"

Misha struggled to form words. "Thank you…for the privacy. I knew you'd come through for me."

Kirilo reapplied the pressure. "Come through for you? What are you talking about?" Kirilo burst with laughter. "Listen to this *moscal*."

Misha tapped Kirilo's arm with his fingertips. The tapping was so gentle, born of such confidence, that Kirilo eased up out of sheer curiosity.

"Your cousin," Misha managed to say.

Kirilo eased up some more. "What?"

"I know your cousin in America. He goes by the name of Victor Bodnar."

Kirilo released his grip.

Misha took a deep breath and rubbed his neck. "The courier you sent with a gift didn't do so well."

"You know my cousin?"

Misha sat up. All traces of the shit-eating grin were gone. "He trusts me. I'm sure I could arrange an unexpected reunion between the two of you."

Kirilo stepped aside. Let his pulse slow and digested Misha's revelation. "Interesting," he said, circling to Misha's front. "You know, you are a resourceful young man."

"So who is this Tesla you're looking for?" Kirilo said. "What's his first name?"

"Damian."

"Damian Tesla? Huh," Kirilo said. "I knew a man by that name once, but he died."

"He's alive," Misha said.

"Impossible."

"It's true."

"Are you sure we're talking about the same man?"

"This Damian was well-known in certain circles. His business associates died in an accident involving a truckload of hot asphalt."

Kirilo was struck dumb. "I'll be damned. The ten million dollars."

"Exactly. I know his niece. She was recently told Damian is dying and has ten million dollars for her. I can offer you ten percent to help me find it. And a reunion with cousin Victor."

"Twenty percent."

"Done. We just need to be certain that Steen is telling the truth."

"He is. If he knew something, he would have told me."

"There's believing, and then there's knowing."

Kirilo sighed. He'd known Steen for close to ten years, but $2 million would pay for Isabella's wedding and the disco in London.

He walked to his overcoat, removed the cattle prod from its pocket, and started toward the door.

"What can you do?" he said as he fired it up. "Accidents happen."

CHAPTER 24

VARVARA, THE DECORATIVE BLACK PIG WITH GOLDEN EARrings, welcomed guests to *Varenichnaya* No. 1 from atop its podium near the entrance. In the dining hall, old wall clocks hung beside lace curtains. They mixed with porcelain knickknacks to give the restaurant the feel of a pristine rural kitchen within a Ukrainian antique shop.

Nadia sank her teeth into a *varenik* sautéed in butter and bacon and filled with farmer's cheese. As the oversized ravioli melted in her mouth, her eyes watered.

Anton Medved, the taxi driver, grinned from across the table. "They have twenty-one flavors. When you told me you were a fiend for *vareniky*—hey, why are you crying?"

"It's so good," Nadia said after swallowing. She glanced around the restaurant, still amazed she was here, in her parents' homeland. "My best memories from childhood are the food my mother used to make. No one screamed or yelled or…Everyone was happy when they had a *varenik* in their mouth."

A little after 9:00, the casual restaurant was filled with an eclectic mix of people. Regardless of age or demographic, they were all well dressed.

"The average annual salary in Kyiv is three thousand US," Anton said, "but a Ukrainian will still put on his best clothes when he goes out for any reason."

"I noticed," Nadia said. "Even the criminals dress well."

Anton stopped dipping his blueberry *varenik* in sour cream and raised an eyebrow. "Huh?"

Nadia told him about her incident with the supposed drug dealer and police. She pretended Specter was a Good Samaritan who had helped her escape.

"I'm so sorry you went through that," Anton said. "You're from the States. You have police that protect people."

"And what, you don't?"

Anton sighed. "You know what the slang word for 'police' is in Ukraine?"

Nadia shook her head

"*Musor.* You know what *musor* is?"

Nadia shook her head again.

"*Musor* is 'rubbish.' That is the reputation of law enforcement in Ukraine. But hey, this is Kyiv, and in Kyiv, we have a saying: things will get better. In the meantime, you have to take care of yourself while you are here. Remember, Ukrainians are the greatest con artists in the world."

Nadia had a flash of her uncle Damian. "What? Why do you say that?"

"Because it's true. Ukraine itself has been conned for the last one thousand years. In 1240, Genghis Khan's grandson, Batu, broke a treaty and decimated Kyiv. In the next five centuries, the Liths and the Poles took turns exploiting the countryside. The Russian Black Hundreds killed anyone who wasn't Tsarist, and the Soviets brokered a truce and then tried to wipe all trace of our culture off the face of the earth. That is why Ukrainians are the world heavyweight champions of the long con. They've had more than ten centuries of training."

Nadia and Anton continued chatting about all things Ukrainian. For Nadia, it was another surreal moment: a casual meal and conversation in her parents' native language with an actual native. When they finished their *vareniky* and beer, they split the bill.

"How is your jet lag?" Anton said as they walked to his car at ten fifteen. "Would you like to go to a club? An underground music club? My friend Radek is playing tonight. He has a great thrashabilly-psychobilly band. It's called F in Mathematics."

Nadia's brain was floating in a fog. "No, thank you. I think I've had enough psychobilly for one day. Maybe another night."

"How about dessert? You must have some Kyivan dessert. You like chocolate, Nadia?"

The magic word stifled her protestations.

Fifteen minutes later, they were seated at the mahogany bar in Café Éclair. Light jazz music played in the background. The air smelled of rich cocoa.

"I love this place. Look, the candles are made from chocolate," Anton said. "Imported from Belgium."

The menu featured sixty-five different desserts, including enough mousses and meringues to satisfy all the monarchs of France. Nadia ordered a decaf cappuccino and a petite slice of tiramisu cheesecake. Anton asked for a double espresso.

"Besides your cousins in Bila Tserkva," Nadia said, "you have family?"

"My parents died when I was young. I was married for two years, but my wife died in '05. She was an intellectual from Lviv. She helped run the *Pora* youth group that built the grassroots support for Revolution Orange, when we overturned the fraudulent presidential election." He paused until Nadia nodded, showing she knew about it. "How about you?"

"I have a mother and a brother. My father's dead. And I was married, too, but my husband died in a car crash a while back. He was a professor like you. Religion was his field."

They talked about their spouses until a waiter delivered their coffees.

"So why did you call me, Nadia?" Anton said. "Not that it matters. We love Americans in Ukraine, and it's my privilege to meet you. I enjoy our conversation very much."

Nadia studied his earnest expression. The concierge at Hotel Rus had helped her find the website for Kyiv Slavonic University. Anton Medved really was an assistant professor of sociology, and his picture confirmed his identity. She decided she could trust him.

"I'm looking for someone," Nadia said.

"Who is this person you're looking for? I know people who know people who know a lot of people."

"I'm looking for an uncle I never knew. But first, I have to find a woman who knows his whereabouts. To find her, I need a friend who knows Kyiv."

Anton spread his arms out and pointed at himself. "Who is this woman? What is her name? You have an address?"

"I have a name, an address, and a phone number. Problem is, I went to the address today, and the super told me she doesn't live there anymore. And the phone number belongs to a beauty salon. Which really doesn't make sense, because supposedly she was waiting for me to call her."

"Huh," Anton said, nodding. "You have the number?"

"Yeah, hold on." Nadia pulled her borrowed cell phone out of her purse and read from the memory. "Two-four-four, three-six-eight-three."

Anton stared at her and blinked. "What about the city code?"

"She lives in Kyiv. It's forty-four, right?"

"That depends."

"What do you mean, it depends?"

"If it's a Kyivstar mobile phone, it's sixty-seven."

"What?"

"Everyone thinks there's only one city code for Kyiv. That's not true. If that number is a cell phone and it's Kyivstar, the city code is sixty-seven. Not forty-four."

Nadia realized that she and her mother had been dialing the wrong number. "Is it rude to make a call in here? Should I go outside?"

Anton waved his hand. "Please. Make your call. It's too dangerous to step outside. The temptation for you to smoke pot or buy cocaine will be overwhelming."

Nadia was busy dialing, so she didn't realize what he had said until after the phone started ringing. She chuckled belatedly and held her breath.

One ring, two rings, three rings, four. Five rings, six rings—pause. A commercial female voice greeted Nadia in Ukrainian: "The party you have called is unavailable. Please leave a message at the tone."

Nadia left an urgent message in Ukrainian. Afterward, she called back and left the same information in English.

When she hung up, Anton beamed at her. "Good?" he said.

Nadia shrugged. "I'm not sure. I hope it was her and not someone else's phone."

"I was just thinking that if that wasn't the right phone number, we can go to her apartment and I can talk to that super for you. A local might have more luck, you know?"

"Thanks. Let's hope it doesn't come to that."

"I think it's her. Everyone uses cell phones these days. Relax. It's like I told you. This is Kyiv. Things will get better."

Nadia smiled and thanked him. She took a bite of her cheesecake. The coffee-flavored mascarpone melted in her mouth. She hadn't found Clementine yet, but she was closer to the money today than yesterday, and she'd made a friend. She was in a foreign land, but she felt as though she was visiting her second home. There was ample reason to be optimistic.

An engine wailed. Nadia glanced out the window, but the vehicle disappeared before she could see it. The sound was a sobering reminder, however, that a man in a black Porsche was tailing her. His ultimate job was to kill her. Nadia refused to succumb to fear. Emotions could only interfere with her agenda. If she found the treasure, she'd have something they wanted. She'd have resources to find a way home. Still, the echo of those words was a promise that, regardless of what they said in Kyiv, things were going to get worse before they got better.

CHAPTER 25

NADIA SLEPT FITFULLY FOR SEVEN HOURS, BOLTING UPRIGHT every time she heard a noise in the hallway or next door. Her subconscious feared any one of them might be the phone call she was waiting for. They weren't. By 11:00 the next morning, she couldn't sit still anymore. She put on a light coat and hiked down Khreschatyk, Kyiv's primary north–south boulevard.

During World War II, she remembered from her classes, the Soviet Army had mined Khreschatyk with explosives as it retreated from Kyiv. When the Nazis arrived on September 19, 1941, Red Army commanders detonated the explosives using radio signals from over four hundred kilometers away. More than three hundred buildings were demolished and one thousand troops killed. The Nazis responded by executing twenty thousand Kyivans. It was the first use of long-distance radio signals to trigger explosives in history.

Clouds hung low on a bitter, overcast morning. The air smelled of flowers and gasoline fumes. Bumpy cobblestone promenades for pedestrians and small-vehicle parking flanked cafés, stores, and restaurants. Ornate Stalinist facades adorned an eclectic assortment of government buildings.

Upon entering Independence Square, Nadia paused at a bronze sculpture of the four Slavic tribesmen who founded Kyiv in the fifth century, including the namesake, Kyi.

The phone pulsated in her purse.

Nadia jumped. Looked around to make sure no one else was within earshot. Yanked the phone out of her purse and cleared her throat.

"This is Nadia."

No one answered.

"Hello?"

"What was the boy wearing in the picture?"

"Excuse me?"

"What was the boy wearing in the picture?"

"Is this Clementine?"

"Answer the question. I'm hanging up—"

"No, wait." Nadia remembered the photo her mother had shown her. "Skates. The boy was wearing skates."

"Are you claustrophobic?"

"No. Well…maybe a little—"

"Too bad. One o'clock at the Caves Monastery. Don't buy a ticket. Tickets are for tourists. Use the lower entry where the locals go."

"Okay—"

"Meet me at the entrance to the Far Caves. Not the Near Caves. The Far Caves. Look for the green-roofed walkway. Come alone. I see anyone else, I disappear, eh?"

The phone clicked dead.

Clementine sounded American except for the "eh," which suggested a Canadian influence. Her voice varied in tone and sounded unreliable, as though she were emotionally unstable or an addict suffering from withdrawals.

After Nadia hung up, she looked around Independence Square. Logic dictated that Specter was watching her at this very moment. Perhaps a local was watching her for him. It was 12:05 p.m. She had fifty-five minutes to lose her tail and get to the Caves Monastery on time.

Nadia sat down on a bench beside a lamppost and an elevated grassy promenade in front of the Central Post Office. She removed a pen, notepad, guidebook, and map from her purse. She'd studied the latter two in detail during her flight from New York.

She planned her course of action with the mathematical precision of an experienced cartographer. The entire exercise took her fifteen minutes.

The Caves Monastery was four miles southeast of her present location at Independence Square. Nadia ambled like a tourist south on Khreschatyk, back toward Hotel Rus. After twenty steps, she turned and took a mental snapshot of the scene behind her. Pedestrians crowded the promenades. She didn't try to memorize faces, just shapes and colors. Three beats later, she resumed walking south.

At the corner of Arkhitectora, she took a left to head east. The crowd thinned on the side street. Nadia accelerated her pace. Counted twenty paces. Stopped. Turned. A young couple, a businessman, and a babushka rounded the corner toward her.

Nadia took another left onto a promenade beside the Cinema Ukraina. Jogged twenty paces. Turned. Waited.

The couple walked by. The businessman and the babushka turned left and followed her.

Nadia took her third fast left onto Institutska. Twenty paces later, she was back on Khreshchatyk, right where she'd started. She turned right and headed north, in the opposite direction of the Caves Monastery. Twenty paces later, she stopped and turned.

The babushka rounded the corner alone. She wore an old gray sweater and a floral scarf around her head that obscured her face. She might have been seventy-two or twenty-seven. Twenty meters away, their eyes met. The babushka quickly pulled away to peruse a Benetton store window.

Nadia checked her watch: 12:28. She power walked a kilometer farther north. When she got to the Golden Domes of the Cathedral of St. Mikhail, she asked a young man in a warm-up suit for the entrance to the funicular train. He pointed a block ahead toward the far side of the domes.

Nadia looked around. No sign of the babushka. She glanced at her wrist: 12:38. She pulled out her guidebook and strolled onward, pretending to be sightseeing.

The back of the cathedral hung on a cliff. An ancient-looking tram with a sky-blue roof and immaculate white body sat on steep rails, locked in place by heavy cables. People jammed the interior so tightly their faces seemed plastered against the window.

Nadia started toward the cathedral's rear entrance. She took deep, even breaths.

A bell sounded.

Nadia raced for the funicular.

Snack vendors beneath green-and-white umbrellas gaped as she blew by them. She burst into the domed entrance. The funicular door started to close.

"Wait," she shouted in English, the language of opportunity. The guidebook said conductors loved to fine foreigners for any and all violations.

The door slid to a close.

Nadia leaped onto the edge of the tram. She wedged an arm and a shoulder inside. The door pressed against her.

A heavyset woman reached out with one hand and pulled it open a few inches. A fat man with garlic breath in her way, however, would not move. Nadia pleaded with her eyes.

"Push him," the woman said, aiming her disgust at Nadia for not being more assertive.

"Push," they all shouted, as though her stupidity far outweighed his rudeness.

Nadia spun, stuck her butt into the man's upper thighs, put her head down, and pushed with her rear.

The man swore under his breath. Nadia slid inside. The woman released her grip. The door slammed shut. Nadia looked up.

A fist smashed against the glass door. A fierce young man in a blue warm-up suit pointed a finger at her. He hurled a single word at her. It sounded like Russian slang. Nadia didn't understand the word but was certain it wasn't a compliment.

In the distance, the babushka sprinted toward the empty station like the world's fastest granny. She was closer to twenty-seven than seventy-two after all. Two people were tailing her, and neither was Specter. As the funicular rolled down the cliff toward Podil, the man in the warm-up suit touched the headphone wrapped around his left ear and jabbered into it.

It was too late. The funicular was the fastest way from Upper to Lower Kiev. She'd be in Podil in ten minutes. In daytime rush hour, it would take a car half an hour to catch up.

The tram was packed so tight it was impossible for Nadia to get to the front. She bought a ticket by passing one hryvnia to the conductor through the hands of her fellow passengers. A stamped ticket and fifty kopek were returned to her the same way. No one grumbled. This was the norm.

The tram descended along a wooded cliffside and a white steel fence. Halfway down the mountain, the vista opened up to reveal the waterfront scene of the Dnipro River. Ships lay moored beside venerable warehouses at the harbor's edge. Cranes and derricks elevated the skyline.

At the bottom station, the funicular deposited Nadia in Podil, at the opposite end of Kiev from the Caves Monastery. She raced to the subway across the street. Trains ran every two and a half minutes. She boarded a train within sixty seconds of her arrival, repeating the last-second process she had used to board the funicular.

Nadia got off at Arsenalna and hailed a *Marshrutka*, one of the thousands of Mercedes vans that ran along bus routes. She arrived at her destination at 12:58, certain she wasn't being followed.

Green-and-gold rooftops covered a campus full of white churches and cathedrals. The headquarters of the Orthodox Church in Ukraine, the Caves Monastery was a labyrinth of catacombs and tunnels covering seventy acres.

Clementine Seelick, the only clue to Damian's location, was waiting at one of the entrances to the caves.

Nadia had two minutes to find her.

CHAPTER 26

At 12:45, Kirilo was waiting for Misha at Felix's Lounge on the third floor of the River Palace. After interrogating Steen, they'd stayed up all night gambling before packing it in for four hours' sleep in private suites upstairs.

Twelve cozy seating areas of various sizes offered rich upholstered chairs and sofas. Wide-screen monitors hung along every wall, all tuned to the same program. Four boisterous men in tuxedo shirts and pants dug into steaks and blintzes at one table. Three slinky girls cackled over mixed drinks with a man in safari gear at another.

Misha arrived with puffy eyes and cherry cheeks, hair sopping wet as though he hadn't even bothered with a towel. When he thrust his hand out, Kirilo cringed. A young man never offered his hand to his elder in Ukraine. Did this *moscal* have any manners at all?

"Good morning," Misha said.

Kirilo smiled and shook his hand firmly. He had two million reasons to forgive Misha's lack of etiquette.

Kirilo and Misha sat at the bar. A pyramid of liquor bottles rose against a mirror in front of them. The bartender, a hunk of steel who'd been a Russian Black Beret in a former life, leaned in to them.

"What can I get you, boss?"

Kirilo turned to Misha and raised his eyebrows.

"What kind of beer do you have?" Misha said.

"Bass and Guinness," the bartender said.

"That's all?"

"That's all."

Misha frowned at Kirilo.

Kirilo shrugged. "This country's obsessed with everything British. The majority owner here is the worst. A royal watcher. Ever since Independence Day. I don't really understand it."

After Misha ordered a black and tan, the bartender looked at Kirilo.

"English breakfast tea," Kirilo said.

Misha nodded at the television monitor, where an auburn-haired beauty pulled up in her skates and sprayed ice in a handsome man's face.

"What is this?" Misha said.

The bartender glanced at the screen. "*On Her Majesty's Secret Service.*" He turned back to Misha. "It's Bond twenty-four/seven in here. But only Craig and Connery. No Moore or Brosnan. Dalton and Lazenby, but only in the morning."

Misha frowned. "Lazenby?"

The bartender nodded gravely. "Only in the morning." He moved down the bar to prepare the beverages.

"How did you sleep?" Kirilo said.

"Fine. But I would have slept even better if you'd used the cattle prod a few more times."

"No. Once was enough. Steen was telling the truth. He knows nothing about Damian or the ten million dollars."

"Okay. If you say so. Is there any risk Steen will tell someone about last night? Do we need to worry about him?"

"Not if he values his business and his life, and he values both. It was an accident. We were drinking, I got carried away. Lost my balance. He got some accidental voltage. End of story."

"All right. Well, I appreciate all your help."

"Don't mention it." Kirilo decided to switch the subject. "Tell me more about my cousin."

"What's there to tell? He's not like you. He never graduated to bigger things. He was small time and still is." Misha shrugged. "We did some business together. He taught me how to think ahead."

Kirilo rolled up his right sleeve. A tattoo of a cat sprang from his forearm as he flexed it. "You know what this means?"

"Of course. *Voroskoi Mir.* You were a thief in your prior life."

Kirilo showed Misha his hands. "The tattoos on my fingers and palms, I had to get removed. Laser. So I can mingle in polite society. But the stars on my shoulders and knees are still there. I kneel for no one."

"What did your cousin do to make you so upset?"

"He was born. His father was a bitch for Stalin, and that makes him a bitch. It's a matter of honor. All the bitches who helped Stalin must die. All their offspring must die. I took an oath as a child to see this through. How are you going to help me with this?"

"It's already in the works. I expect him in Kiev any day."

"Why? Are you sure of this?"

"He taught me how to think like my enemy. He's bankrupt. He's got nothing. He'll come to protect his share of the money."

"The ten million dollars. Are you sure it exists?"

"I hired one of Victor's men recently. A man by the name of Stefan. He's playing poker down below with my other bodyguards. Victor is certain about the money. If it's not ten million dollars, it's a treasure of some kind."

"And you believe him?"

Misha nodded.

"Where is she? The Tesla woman. New York?"

"No. She's here. In Kyiv."

"You're having her followed?"

“As we speak.”

The bartender delivered tea and beer. Two sips later, Misha’s cell phone rang.

“We have to go,” he said to Kirilo after hanging up. “It’s the Tesla woman. She lost my men on purpose, as though she’s about to meet someone.”

“Where did they last see her?”

“On the funicular headed to Podil. But that was misdirection. She just arrived at the Caves Monastery.”

CHAPTER 27

NADIA LOOKED AROUND FOR SOMEONE WHO COULD GUIDE her toward the proper entrance. She'd studied the Pecherska Lavra, the Caves Monastery, as a student in Ukrainian School growing up. It was a mythical place, one she read about but wasn't sure really existed. Now, as she stood beneath the peach-and-ivory Lavra Belltower, despite the urgency of the moment, excerpts from lectures came flooding back to mind.

In 1051, St. Anthony Pechersk left Mount Athos in Greece to live in a man-made cave in Kyiv. As his disciples followed him, he expanded his home into an underground city of tunnels, rooms, and chapels. Monks spent lifetimes praying, meditating, and writing in what became known as the Pecherska Lavra. Memoirs suggest the underground network may have once stretched for hundreds of kilometers, from Kyiv to Moscow. By the twentieth century, more than 120 saints were buried in the Caves Monastery.

In 1959, Nikita Khrushchev began a fresh campaign to destroy all remaining traces of Christianity in the Soviet Union. He confiscated religious icons, burned churches, and either executed priests or tortured them into recanting their religious convictions. He also ordered the removal of the bodies of the saints as a prelude to the destruction of the Pecherska Lavra.

No one is certain exactly what happened next, but the accepted story is something like this: A platoon of soldiers arrived in a truck to remove the bodies. They loaded them onto their vehicle, but when they tried to leave, the engine wouldn't start. Mechanics were summoned to examine the truck. They found nothing wrong. Still, it wouldn't start.

A priest told the soldiers that it was impossible for the bodies of the saints to be removed from the caves. At his suggestion, the soldiers unloaded the bodies from the truck. The engine started. When they put the bodies back on the truck, it wouldn't start. After lying outside for three weeks while Soviet officials debated what to do, the bodies were returned to the caves, and Khrushchev gave strict orders: nothing belowground was to be touched again.

Later, Soviet scientists conducted tests to understand why the bodies remained preserved despite no embalming. They determined that lack of moisture prevented decay. An experiment with wheat plants proved that the bodies also emitted an organic matter that influenced the nuclear content of living matter and may have helped preserve the monks' remains.

Nadia got directions to the lower entry to the Far Caves from a tour guide with a badge hanging around her neck. As Nadia hurried down a sidewalk, a flock of monks swooped by her, their long black cloaks billowing in their wake. They appeared to float slightly aboveground like spirits who alternated living among the earthly and the celestial. Nadia followed them down the steep drop along the fifteen-foot-high fortification wall toward the southeast corner of the Lavra, in her black weather-resistant jacket and leggings.

The exit from the Far Caves was in the Church of the Birth of the Blessed Virgin. Its towering gold dome was the landmark for the entrance on the near side of the street in the unassuming and tiny Annozachatiyevskaya Church. Nadia spotted the green-roof walkway Clementine had mentioned on the phone.

The monks disappeared inside the entrance. Nadia stopped beside the wooden door to the church and checked her watch.

It was 1:13. She was thirteen minutes late. She'd underestimated the Lavra's sprawl. The street along the edge of the Lavra teemed with tourists, visitors, and vendors selling food and souvenirs.

At 1:26, three boys ran up to her. They barely came up to her waist, with gaunt, dirt-smeared cheeks and tousled hair. Their eyes were lively, appraising her and her purse.

Homeless children. Nadia had read about them. Abandoned or orphaned, with nowhere to go, no socialist state to take care of them. The shortest of the three stepped forward. "Are you Nadia Tesla?"

"Yes."

He pulled a piece of paper out of his pocket. "A lady told us to give this to you."

"She did?" Nadia looked around. "Where? What lady?"

The boy's tongue flicked out of the corner of his lips, as though he were contemplating mischief. "She told us you'd give us ten hryvnia."

Ten hryvnia was a little more than a dollar. Nadia twisted her body away from them, cracked her purse open, and pulled out two hundred hryvnia. The boy's eyes lit up as though he'd found the biggest sucker in Kyiv. He extended the paper with his left hand and reached out for the money with his right. Nadia did the opposite. Each of them held on to both for two beats and stared at each other. The boy snatched the money and released the paper. He took off with his friends toward the river beyond the lavra.

Nadia unfolded the paper. An unsteady hand had scribbled a note:

Go into the Far Caves. Head for the Church of the Annunciation. Bear left for the Church of the Nativity. Meet me past Saint Sisoi but before Prince Feodor. Beside the body of Saint Damian.

Nadia considered the implications of Clementine's instructions. Perhaps her uncle had buried the money in the tomb of a saint that bore his name, and Clementine was empowered to show her the exact location. Maybe hiding the money in plain sight was the best solution, especially for a man who was surrounded by scavengers and thieves. The tombs were there for any tourist to see, but they would never be moved, not after Khrushchev's experience. How hard was it to hide $10 million in a tomb? Not too hard if the money was in bearer bonds.

Nadia started toward the entrance to the Far Caves.

"Wait," a rawboned babushka said, beside her souvenir stand. "Don't go in there." She patted her head, which was wrapped in a floral scarf. "Women must cover themselves before going in the caves."

A tour group of thirty to forty people was making its way down the fortification wall toward the same entrance. All the women wore shawls on their heads.

Nadia bought a scarf with a bright floral pattern on one side and a plain black one on the other. The babushka said the dark side would come in handy in the unfortunate event of a funeral. She wrapped it around Nadia's head with the floral side on the exterior so that other people could see her better. Nadia also bought a cheap lighter at the babushka's suggestion, to use with the beeswax candle she bought as a donation to the monastery. She stored both in her purse and went into the church.

The plunge down the initial stairway to the caves reminded Nadia of an entry to a medieval wine cellar. Light from the doorway faded as she descended narrow steps. Her shoulders brushed the whitewashed walls on either side.

The staircase turned right at the bottom and deposited her into a twisting, equally narrow tunnel. Candles illuminated the path from bronze sconces along the white walls. The stone tiles beneath her feet pitched downward. Looking forward, she could see that the concave ceiling resembled the top of a keyhole. It created the illusion that she had entered a portal that was leading her to the center of the earth.

Muffled voices echoed around her. The street curved into an elongated S. The voices ahead grew louder until they were audible whispers. A sharp turn, and the street came to a fork. Nadia glanced at her crude black-and-white map. She veered left toward the voices, sniffing incense in the air. An opening in the wall revealed itself on the left.

Nadia looked in. An Asian couple stood with candles beside the body of a saint named Joseph. A maroon shroud covered his remains in an old wooden coffin. The man leaned forward and kissed the shroud atop the body.

Nadia moved on past three more cells containing bodies of the saints and found the Church of the Annunciation. Shimmering gold icons of Saint Mary and Saint Joseph hung against a turquoise wall painted with a gold cross. An African family of three admired an altar covered in green velvet, the little girl clinging to her mother's knees.

As Nadia continued past the church, she idly scratched an itch on her brow. Her fingers left a wet spot on her forehead.

The monastery's floor fell to a depth of 775 feet. That was one-sixth of a mile. The floor seemed to pitch downward forever. Nadia cursed herself for thinking in terms of miles while underground. It was not conducive to sanity. Another interminable S-shaped hike revealed the Church of the Nativity. More gilded iconostasis. The church was empty. Nadia checked her diagram. Another city block and she would be there.

As she marched onward, the air thinned out. Her lungs stretched for oxygen. Sconces and candles grew scarce. Light faded.

Nadia stopped, removed the beeswax candle from her purse, and lit it. Continued forward. Heard whispers up ahead.

There. A coffin.

Nadia raised her candle to the placard on the wall.

A bare skull greeted her with gleaming ivory teeth.

Nadia jumped back. Someone had placed it in a recessed opening in the wall. She took a deep breath and shone her light again to read the name on the wall.

Saint Sisoi.

She checked her diagram. Prince Feodor was the next saint listed. Only prominent saints were listed. Clementine said Saint Damian was after Sisoi and before Prince Feodor.

He was next.

The street became a straightaway. The whispers grew louder. They came from a hole in the wall up ahead. Was that Saint Damian's crypt? Had Clementine brought her uncle with her? Was it she who was whispering to him?

Nadia heard loud, muffled voices behind her. A commotion of some kind.

She crept forward. The hole in the wall was a room. She slid to the edge of the room and peered around the corner inside.

Six figures in black cloaks stood chanting quietly in a refectory, a small room with beds carved in the walls. They were the monks she'd followed down the fortification wall to the monastery.

Nadia forged ahead. A candlestick shone in the distance. She took a deep breath and marched toward it.

A tall, angular figure bent over a coffin in the wall. He straightened and turned to Nadia.

The light of their candles became one. Nadia gazed at the person.

He was an old man with a gigantic crooked nose, dressed in green overalls. An ID hung around his neck. He held a clipboard in his hands. The word *Official* was emblazoned above *Pecherska Lavra* on the ID. He was a curator of some sort.

Nadia looked at the coffin. "Is this Saint Damian?" she whispered.

The man frowned. "Saint Damian?" He nodded at the sign on the wall. "This is the body of Prince Feodor."

Nadia read the sign. "Where is the body of Saint Damian? Is it up ahead?"

The man's frown deepened. "There is no Saint Damian."

Nadia lost her breath. "There is no Saint Damian?"

"No, there isn't. And there is no 'up ahead.'"

The curator picked up the candle and extended his arm beyond the coffin. The tunnel ended. There was a wall dead ahead.

"Some of the caves collapsed through the years," he said. "This is the farthest point west. This…is the end."

Light flashed behind Nadia. Human voices. Women chattering, thinking they were whispering when everyone could hear them.

The curator sighed. "Tour group."

Nadia remembered the group of thirty to forty people.

"We're totally screwed," he said. "We're behind them now. There's no way for anyone to pass. They have to stop and turn in line. It's going to take hours for us to get out of here."

By the glow of lantern flashlights, Nadia saw people round the corner.

Clementine Seelick was not waiting for her. Instead, she'd sent Nadia to the bowels of Kyiv. Now she was eight hundred feet beneath the face of the earth, trapped behind a tour group—being led by Misha Markov and Brad Specter.

CHAPTER 28

KIRILO STOOPED AND SQUINTED OVER MISHA'S SHOULDER AS they squeezed through the tunnel. This was ridiculous. All three of them would be hunchbacks by the time they got out.

He had known it would be like this when he insisted on going along with the two Americans, but what choice did he have? The other American, Specter, had done his college dissertation on the caves and said he knew them well. The Upper Lavra connected with the Lower Lavra. A knowledgeable man knew half a dozen exits. Hell, some thought the tunnels went all the way to Moscow.

He'd be damned if the *moscal* and his man were going to get away with the clue to the money or whatever it was they were certain was so valuable before he got paid.

They approached a doorway. Misha raised his fist in the air for Kirilo and Specter to slow down. The tour group they'd passed at the Church of Nativity dawdled behind them. Kirilo could smell the perfume of the woman who'd screamed when he'd shoved her aside so they could get past her, some sort of rose-infused rat piss.

"You're sure she's here," Kirilo whispered to Specter.

"I'm sure," Specter said. "She lost two of my people and thinks she's alone. Whoever she was trying to meet at Yaroslaviv Val used kids to deliver a note. That person must be here."

"He's the one we want," Misha said.

"What will you do with the Tesla woman?" Kirilo said.

"The Varangian Caves," Specter said. "In the eastern end of the Lower Lavra. Where the Vikings used to bury their loot in the tenth century. There are no bodies there. No one will ever find her."

Specter turned the corner and burst through the doorway. Misha and Kirilo followed him inside the small room.

Seven monks in black cloaks stood chanting with their heads bowed. They didn't look up, as though used to idiot tourists interrupting them. Specter shined the light around the room. Nothing. He looked at Misha, who nodded toward the door.

Kirilo backpedaled, and the other two men came out with them. This was not good. Ukrainians knew better than to mess around with the bodies of the saints or the monks who protected them. They were asking for trouble. He began to wonder if the money was worth tempting God himself.

A single candlelight illuminated a coffin in the distance. Specter shined the light farther down the tunnel. A tall, angular man shielded his eyes. Misha pulled a garrote out of his pocket. The three of them advanced quickly. They were upon him in thirty seconds.

"Who are you?" Kirilo said.

The man raised the badge around his neck while still shielding his eyes. "Lavra official."

"Where are the others?" Misha said in Russian.

"What others?"

Kirilo measured him. "Do you think your body would fit in this tomb if I folded it in three?"

The man hesitated for a second. "One woman. Alone. She went back that way."

"What way?" Specter said.

The man pointed over their shoulder. "This is the end of the caves. She went back in the direction you were coming from."

Kirilo turned and shuffled back toward the refectory as quickly as the tight confines allowed him. When they got there, the tour group was five paces away. The monks were still chanting.

Misha shined the light from floor to ceiling on all the walls. There was no sign of the woman.

"Wait," Kirilo said. "Shine the light again."

Misha aimed the beam at the men cloaked in black.

"There were seven monks a minute ago," Kirilo said. "Now there are only six."

CHAPTER 29

A blast of rose perfume hit Nadia as she came upon a woman with a permanent scowl etched on her face. Behind her, a seemingly endless line of tourists shuffled down the tunnel.

"I'm sorry," Nadia said. "I'm not well. I have to get out. Now."

Feeling like a thief herself, she dropped to her knees and began to crawl through the tour group's legs. As women yelped and protested and the occasional man asked if she was okay, Nadia gave thanks to the babushka outside the Lower Lavra entrance. She'd told Nadia that the black side of the shawl might come in handy in the event of a funeral. In fact, it might have helped postpone hers, for at least a few hours.

After she crawled through her thirty-third pair of legs, Nadia tried to stand up but couldn't straighten her back. She had to lean against the wall and let her vertebrae recover. She would bet her uncle never had to do this.

She heard men shouting from the direction she'd come from. Misha, Specter, and a third man had figured out what she'd done. They were trying to pass the tour group themselves. Impossible. There was no way they were going to crawl on their hands and knees, and even if they tried, they were too big to maneuver through and around people's legs.

Nadia took off toward the churches, looking for signs for the exit. As she wound her way through the underground city, the voices and footsteps behind her faded. She found the exit and emerged near the Church of the Birth of the Blessed Virgin.

Hiding behind a nook in the far wall of the church, she pulled out her cell phone and hit the redial button.

An energetic masculine voice answered above the din of traffic. “Yeah?”

“It’s Nadia.”

“Hey,” Anton Medved said, with a burst of enthusiasm.

“I’m being followed by at least three atheists. I need a taxi driver who can make them believers.”

A bellow of laughter cut short. “Are you all right?”

Nadia started to answer honestly but caught herself. “Yes.”

Anton paused, as though translating the rhythm and tone of her reply into words. “Where are you?” he said.

“Caves Monastery. Far Caves exit. Near the Church of the Blessed—”

“Walk two blocks north to the access road to Dniprovsky Uzviz. Wait on the southeast side.”

“Okay.”

Nine minutes later, Nadia climbed inside the car. The taxi smelled of sautéed mushrooms and musk. Motown blared from the speakers. Anton lowered the volume.

“What happened?” he said. “Are you okay?”

“I’m okay, I’m okay. Thank you, Anton. Thank you so much.”

He whipped the car into a U-turn before Nadia could fasten her seat belt. Slammed the brakes at a red light.

He wore a rumpled white button-down shirt with blue pinstripes. A stylish day’s growth covered his face. His bloodshot eyes reminded Nadia that he worked two jobs to survive.

“Who’s following you? Where are these three men? What kind of car are they driving?” Anton searched in the rearview mirror.

"They're not in a car. They were behind me in the Far Caves."

"*In* the caves?"

"Trapped behind a tour group of thirty-three people. It should be at least a half hour more before they get out."

The light turned green. Anton swerved right onto Naberezhne Expressway, headed south along the Dnipro. He merged into the far right lane and drove calmly with traffic.

"Why were you in the caves?" he said.

"The woman told me to meet her there."

"The woman you're looking for?"

"Yes. She sent a boy with a note. It said to meet her in the Far Caves near the body of Saint Damian. But there is no Saint Damian. And she wasn't there. I tried calling her on her cell while I was waiting for you but got voice mail. Why would she lie to me? Why would she send me down there?"

"Maybe she saw you were being followed and assumed you were setting her up."

Nadia shook her head. "I lost my tail. On the funicular to Podil. I'm a hundred percent sure of it. How could these men know where I was?"

"What men? Who are these men?"

"Some men I'm in trouble with in America. I busted up an art-theft ring of theirs last year. They think I owe them for that, and that this woman can lead them to money."

"And can she?"

"No. She can lead us to my uncle. He may have money…or something of value…or not. I don't know for sure."

Anton murmured something about Jesus under his breath. "Do these men do any business in Ukraine or Russia or the other former Soviet states?"

"One of them was suspected of selling a Soviet submarine to the Colombians. There was a third man with them in the caves. I assume he's their local connection. Why?"

"Because that explains why you were and still are being followed."

Anton gritted his teeth, floored the gas pedal, and exploded into the left lane. He pulled the wheel sharply to the left and hammered the brakes. The car spun 180 degrees and slid into opposing traffic.

Nadia closed her eyes, unable to bear watching what would happen next.

Cars screeched. Horns blared.

The engine wailed again. The car lurched forward.

Nadia opened her eyes. They were going north on Naberezhne now.

Anton pointed at a black sedan stuck behind two cars on the south side. The driver eyeballed the taxi as they sailed by.

"There are more Mercedes in Kyiv than in Stuttgart, but I knew he was following us. I picked him up after you got in the cab."

Nadia watched the driver get out of the car and take two steps toward them as they drove out of sight. "How the hell—"

"Technology," Anton said. "GPS. A satellite tracking device. It's either in your purse or on your clothes."

A crude laugh escaped Nadia's lips. "Oh, come on. You can't be serious. This is the mafia shaking me down for money. Not the government in pursuit of state secrets."

Anton mumbled under his breath. "So naive..."

"What?"

"Nadia, the mafia in Ukraine is not like the mafia in the United States. In the States, the mafia protects criminals from the government so they can steal. In Ukraine, they're one and the same thing."

"What do you mean?"

"You know who's the only person a Ukrainian trusts less than a foreigner?" Anton glanced at her. "A fellow Ukrainian. You know which countrymen he trusts the least?"

"The government."

"Precisely. When Gorbachev was in power in the eighties, the KGB siphoned off six hundred billion dollars into shell accounts—in places as far away as Ireland and Las Vegas—so the party bosses could control Soviet resources no matter what happened with *perestroika*. By the early nineties, the job got too big for them, so they went in with ex-military, ex-KGB, ex-government officials to help them manage all these businesses. The *mafiya* as it exists in Russia and Ukraine—the *avtoritet*—was born. You want a license to import goods into Ukraine? You pay. You want electricity turned on for your barbershop? You pay. Nothing gets done without the mafia, because in Ukraine, the mafia *is* the government. That gives the men who are following you access to any and all resources."

"But there's nothing in my pockets. I've been wearing this jacket, these shoes, the entire time. There's nowhere to hide anything in my leggings. And my purse hasn't been out of my sight."

Anton weaved in and out of traffic. "There had to be a moment. Think."

"I'm trying, dammit," Nadia said, eyes closed.

Her purse was in the seat back in front of her the entire flight. It never left her eyes during the customs inspection. She carried it to 8 Yaroslaviv Val—

"Oh my God," Nadia said, ripping it open. "That incident with the drug dealer and the phony cops." Specter returned her purse to her. It was in his hands. "It was all planned to put something in my purse."

Anton murmured his agreement.

Nadia removed her passport, wallet, hairbrush—

Her phone rang.

She answered. "This is Nadia."

"Who are those men?" Clementine Seelick said.

"Why did you send me to the bowels of the Lavra? Why did you pretend there was a Saint Damian?"

"Because you lied. I saw them following you from the top of the Lavra Belltower. I saw them. I saw them. Three guys. Who are they? You were setting me up, weren't you? You were setting me up."

"No, I was not. I'm…I'm sorry. I thought I'd lost them."

"Who are they?"

Nadia exhaled. "They know about Damian. How doesn't matter. But they think he has something valuable. It's dangerous for you. You should know that."

"Oh, shit." Clementine paused for a beat. Her lungs rasped. "I saw them go in the Far Caves after you. How did you get away from them?"

She wanted to say, "I've discovered I'm sneaky like my uncle," but instead, she said simply, "I'm resilient."

"Did you lose them?"

Nadia's eyes fell on a narrow inside pocket she never used. The zipper was open, and there was a slight bulge to it. She slid her fingers inside and removed a rectangular device the size of a domino.

"Yes," Nadia said, holding the tracking device up so Anton could see it. His eyes widened. "I've lost them."

"All right," she said, her voice twitching. "Are you in a car?"

"Yes."

"In Kyiv?"

"Yes."

"Okay. I have an idea where we can meet."

CHAPTER 30

KIRILO STUDIED THE JALOPY IN THE PARKING LOT. THE Soviet-era Zhiguli sagged in the middle, as though both axles were gradually succumbing to gravity. The taxi's number was painted on the side door. The window tint had turned the color of eggplant.

"That's it," Specter said. "That's the car my man was following on the expressway before it got away."

Kirilo's driver pulled up behind it.

"Don't park near that piece of garbage," Kirilo said. "It looks like the wheels might come off any minute. I don't want its rust anywhere near my Audi."

While the driver rolled forward across the lot toward BMWs and Mercedeses, Kirilo glanced over Specter's shoulder. The light on his handheld GPS device blinked furiously.

"She's here," Specter said. He turned the receiver off and looked at the two-story bar attached to the car wash.

"What, no voice on that thing like navigation?" Misha said. "The bitch-whore you are looking for is…up ahead…on the left."

A black 4Runner with Stefan and Misha's other bodyguards pulled up beside them. A Pathfinder with Kirilo's quartet of men followed in their wake. The men followed Specter, Misha, and Kirilo toward the front door.

"A bar at the car wash?" Misha said.

"It's the safest place in Kyiv," Kirilo said. "No one wants his car scratched. There's an understanding. All grudges and beefs are left at the door."

The first floor featured a long counter and a dozen booths and tables. Small groups of men drank, chatted, and laughed with one another. All were dressed similarly to the others in their group: black leather jackets and designer warm-up suits prevailed among most of them.

Specter asked the slinky bartender if she'd seen an American woman. The bartender reminded Kirilo of Isabella. He wondered what she was doing with her friends at this very moment. Wished he could go back in time and keep his pearls to himself so he could pretend she was good and sweet. But he couldn't, and she wasn't, was she?

"There's an American woman upstairs," the bartender said. "With a man and another woman."

Misha and his crew charged upstairs. Kirilo rowed and lifted weights to stay in good shape and fight off aging, but the infernal caves had almost killed him. He had to pause halfway up. When he heard screams above, however, he hurried to the top.

Four broad-shouldered men with grizzled faces stood around a pool table, watching a scene in the far corner. Kirilo pushed past them.

Two pieces of a broken pool cue lay at an odd angle on the floor. A college-age girl consoled a grungy young man, with chains dangling from his jeans, on the floor. He looked like a poser, with carefully cultivated facial hair and a T-shirt with a picture of hippies holding guitars. Blood trickled down his cheeks. Another young girl, with purple streaks in her hair, stood by them, shouting in English. Specter stood between her and Misha as though keeping her from harm's way. Stefan was rifling through both women's purses.

"It's not her," Specter said, nodding at the girl with the ridiculous hair. "She's a college exchange student."

Kirilo gave Misha a stern look. "Didn't you hear me? No violence in the car wash."

Misha dismissed him with a quick glance and continued rummaging through the purses.

Kirilo glanced at the poser. He looked familiar. "Who are you?"

The poser sneered.

"I asked you a question." Kirilo tried to place the face but couldn't. "Who are you?"

"I'm the bastard who gave birth to Baba Yaga," the poser said, referring to an evil witch from Ukrainian folklore. "What business is it of yours?"

Kirilo took a step toward the poser, and it hit him. He reminded Kirilo of Evan. The spoiled little turd of a fiancé of his bitch daughter. Both carefully cultivated their rat whiskers. Both wore the same shit-eating grins on their patronizing faces. Wouldn't the world be a better place without both of them? A disco in London? It was Evan's fault his daughter was a no-good, conniving little whore-thief who wanted to move far away from her father. It was all the poser's fault—

Kirilo stumbled backward against his will. Someone was pulling him. Men were shouting. Stop! Stop what? His lungs heaved. Blood pounded against the skin of his face. His fists trembled. His knuckles were red.

"Hey, man," Misha said, grinning, as the bodyguards released their grip on Kirilo's shoulders. "No violence in the car wash."

Kirilo righted himself.

Blood streamed from the poser's nose. His right eye swelled. The American girl screamed in English while the Ukrainian girl cradled his head in her hands.

"One more time," Kirilo said. "What is your name?"

When the poser opened his mouth, his teeth appeared stained with beet juice. “Radek,” he said with a nasal twang. “I’m just a singer. A singer in a band.”

“Band?” Kirilo said. “What band?”

“It’s called F in Mathematics.”

Stefan threw both purses to the ground. “Nothing.”

Misha glared at Specter. “How can this be?”

Specter turned on the GPS receiver and showed Kirilo. The light blinked at a slower pace. “The signal’s weaker here. It was stronger outside. The tracking device is outside somewhere.”

They followed Specter outside to the car wash itself. Two vehicles were being hand-washed in separate bays while another six waited behind each. Specter homed in on the tracking device until the light turned solid red. He ended up beside a beer delivery truck parked on a strip of grass on the far side of the car wash. The truck’s hood was open.

The driver chomped nervously on a cigar as Kirilo, Misha, and their entourage approached.

“Engine?” Kirilo said with a sympathetic tone.

“Timing belt,” the driver said.

Kirilo grimaced. “Sorry to hear that. We need to take a look in the back. We think you have something of ours.”

The driver didn’t waste time. He unlocked the rear and swung the doors open. Stefan jumped inside and found the tracking device behind a stack of cases of Obolon beer. They questioned the driver if he had seen anyone hovering around his truck.

“Nope. I made my delivery and broke down on the way out. Some boys helped push my truck out of the way.”

Kirilo, Misha, and Specter stepped away from the van.

“She figured out we were tracking her and threw the device in his truck,” Specter said, “figuring the beer guy would go on to his next delivery and it would take us time to stop and ask questions.”

“Smarter than throwing it out the window,” Misha said.

"More clever," Specter said. "But in this case, too clever. Seventy-two percent of all Soviet-era cars break down every year."

"You were right about this woman," Kirilo said with a savage edge to Misha. "I like her. I haven't killed anyone in eleven years, but in her case, I may have to break that streak. Just to see the look in her eyes at the last second, when she gives up hope, you know?"

Misha and Specter looked at him as though he were insane. Good. That meant they had some morals, which meant there were limits to what they would do, which meant they were vulnerable.

Misha said, "The driver left his taxi here. Why?"

"Your man on the expressway made him," Specter said. "They know we know the car. And this is a safe place where the taxi company can come get it."

"Which means the driver is helping her," Kirilo said. "What do we know about him?"

They paused and looked at each other.

"Phone number," Specter said. "Of the taxi company. On the side of the car." Specter and Stefan ran toward the parking lot on the opposite side of the building.

"If they left the taxi here, how did they get away?" Misha said.

"They got a ride or borrowed someone's car," Kirilo said.

"Someone who got an F in mathematics?" Misha said.

Kirilo and Misha hurried back to the bar. When they got to the second floor, Radek and the two women were gone.

Specter burst inside as they descended back to the first floor. Stefan lagged behind, out of breath.

"Anything?" Kirilo said, lungs heaving.

Specter shook his head. "The taxi's gone. You?"

Misha shook his head. "They're gone."

"It's possible your man got the phone number off the car on the expressway when they lost him," Specter said.

"Find him," Kirilo said. "The taxi driver. He'll lead us to the girl."

CHAPTER 31

NADIA WATCHED THE BLACK-AND-WHITE IMAGES ON THE projection screen. They popped and crackled with distortion at the Chernobyl National Museum in Kyiv. Firemen piled up a stairwell toward the blaze in the reactor. They were never to return. Divers waded into the cooling ponds to seal the pipes. No one told them the water was contaminated.

On April 26, 1986, the world's worst nuclear disaster took place at the Chernobyl Nuclear Power Plant in the Ukrainian SSR, an administrative region of the Soviet Union. It was the only Level 7 event on the International Nuclear Event Scale before Fukushima. A systems test caused a catastrophic power surge. An emergency shutdown caused a rupture in Reactor 4 and exposed it to air.

The ensuing fire sent a cloud of radioactive smoke over the western Soviet Union and Europe. At least 350,000 people were evacuated after the central authorities realized what had really happened. At first, they thought it was a routine fire. Operator error was initially blamed for the disaster. A subsequent investigation concluded that human factors contributed to the explosion but design deficiencies caused it.

The soldiers, coal miners, and construction workers who were assigned the task of ultimately containing the nuclear disaster were called liquidators. In English, the word conjures images of people facilitating a sale at bargain prices. For these liquidators, it was a bad bargain.

The United Nations Atomic Energy Commission estimated that fifty deaths could be directly attributed to the explosion at the power plant, and the final death toll from radiation exposure would be less than four thousand. European parliaments, Greenpeace, and medical institutions in Britain, Germany, and Scandinavia disagreed. Of the two million people who were officially classified as victims of Chernobyl, five hundred thousand were already dead. The UN attributed the death toll to rising poverty and unhealthy lifestyles. Meanwhile, the Ukrainian Scientific Center for Radiation Medicine was overwhelmed with cases of cancer and genetic mutation.

The names of five thousand liquidators hung on a wall at the museum. Pictures of children born after the disaster hung on another. It was a bad bargain for them, too. The incidence of thyroid cancer among children in the area rose twenty-two-fold over the next ten years. According to the World Health Organization, however, no increase in overall cancer mortality could be associated with radiation exposure.

Nadia moved past the display of children's pictures and checked her watch: it was 3:20. Anton was waiting in Radek's Volkswagen van around the block. She heard a clatter of footsteps and turned.

A woman nodded at her. It had to be Clementine. She'd seen Nadia at the Caves Monastery. Clementine's heart-shaped face was the color of muddy water. Her unkempt hair fell to her shoulders in greasy black strands and contrasted sharply with narrow hazel eyes. A pink Juicy Couture warm-up suit hung loosely on her wire-tight frame. She had dark semicircles under her eyes but seemed more composed in person than she'd sounded on the phone, as though she'd had a fix. She bore a distant resemblance to the boy in the photo whom Damian had claimed to be his son.

"You're sure you weren't tailed?" Clementine said.

Nadia said, "I'm sure."

"Follow me."

They passed a pair of ancient computers salvaged from the plant. A sign said DO NOT TOUCH.

"I knew this place would be empty," Clementine said. "No one ever comes here. The tourists would rather go to church, and the locals don't want to know it exists."

A banner across the top of an archway read, *There is a limit to grief, but no limit to fear.*

The exhibit room contained a replica of Reactor 4. A red-and-white chimney enclosed in scaffolding towered over the plant. Nadia did a double take at the smokestack. It looked like the chimney in the background of the photo of the boy.

Clementine put her hand on her hip. "Okay, show me the money."

Nadia frowned. "What? What money?"

"The money you're going to pay me for telling you how to find Damian. Your uncle, right?"

"No one ever said anything about money."

"Well, I'm saying it now. One thousand dollars."

"Show me your driver's license first," Nadia said. "I want to make sure I'm dealing with the right person."

Clementine hesitated before pulling a wallet out of her bag.

Nadia checked the state of issuance. "Alaska?" she said.

"The Last Frontier."

Nadia removed traveler's checks from her wallet. "I can only give you three hundred. If your information's good, I'll send you the rest when I get back home. What's your connection to my uncle?"

"My sister had his child."

"So there really is a boy."

She was puzzled by the statement. "Of course there's a boy."

"Your sister had his child? Where's your sister now?"

"She died. About eleven years ago."

"What was she doing here?"

"She dropped out of school in Kotzebue and moved to LA to make it in Hollywood."

"School?"

"Yeah, school. Community college," Clementine said with a dollop of exasperation. "Her career in Hollywood took a different turn. She got in with the wrong people and couldn't handle it. She ended up in Moscow, then Kyiv. It's none of your business."

"And you? What are you doing here?"

"Succeeding where she failed. What do you care? Five hundred."

"What does my uncle have that might be worth so much money?"

"I don't know, but I get five percent of whatever he gets when he sells it. That's why I'm here."

"Sells what? What does he have to sell?"

"I don't know. He didn't tell me. Just said it was something *countries* would pay money for. That sounded rich to me."

"He didn't say anything about cash?"

"Cash?"

"Yeah, cash. Like ten million dollars."

Clementine cackled. "Uh, no. I think I would have remembered that. No, no cash. He's got something to sell. Or at least he says he does."

"Why couldn't he meet me himself? Why did he have to get you involved?"

"Because he doesn't officially exist."

"What do you mean, he doesn't officially exist?"

"He lives here," Clementine said, pointing to the wall of the exhibit room. "And you're not allowed to live in the Zone, so he doesn't officially exist. He has no address."

Nadia looked around and frowned. "He lives here? In the museum?"

"No." She shook her head as though Nadia were an imbecile. "Not here. *Here*. In the Zone. Near Pripyat."

"Pripyat?"

"Chernobyl is an old village. It's also the name of the power station. Pripyat is the name of the town built right next to the reactors to house the workers. The Zone is the Exclusion Zone. It's a thirty-kilometer radius around the power plant. They set it up right after the disaster. The Zone is radioactive."

The lure of the money and meeting her uncle helped push the thought of radioactivity out of her mind. "Where and when do I meet him?"

"Give me the money first."

Nadia considered her options and handed her the checks.

"Tomorrow. Thursday," Clementine said, backpedaling toward the exit. "Nine p.m. Hotel Polissya. Go to the check-in desk for instructions."

"Sounds very civil."

"Remember you said that when you see it."

They left in opposite directions. Nadia jumped into the passenger seat of Radek's van, a block away from the museum.

"Radek called," Anton said. "The truck broke down."

"What truck?" Nadia said.

"The beer truck where you threw the tracking device. It broke down at the car wash. And Radek stayed to have a drink with the girls instead of leaving right away. They found him. They punched him."

"Oh, no. I'm so sorry, Anton. Is he okay?"

"He has a broken nose. He'll live. They found the tracking device. Radek and his girls got away in the taxi while they were looking for it."

Anton powered onto the expressway.

Nadia summarized the meeting with Clementine. Anton remained mute when she told him she was supposed to meet Damian in Pripyat.

"You're not saying anything," Nadia said.

"There is nothing to say," Anton said quietly. "That is not a place we talk about."

"Is it even safe to go there at all? Do I risk contamination?"

Anton lowered his voice. He did not turn to look at Nadia. "If you talk about it, if you ask questions about radioactivity, no. It will not be safe for you. You may get sick. But if you don't talk about it, if you don't ask questions and you follow the rules there, you will be fine."

"I...I don't understand. Why won't it be safe if I ask questions about it?"

"That's how it is. You talk about it, things go bad. You keep quiet, everything is fine. Trust me, it works."

"Is there a train or bus that goes there?"

"No. You have to go with a licensed tour, and you have to have a guide with you at all times. Technically, you can apply for a pass from the government, but it would take several weeks and good luck getting one. When is your meeting?"

"Tomorrow. Nine p.m."

Anton laughed. "There is no way. Even if you broke away from the tour—which is impossible—everyone is back on the bus by midafternoon."

"That means I have to sneak in somehow."

"That is not a good idea. There are checkpoints with armed militia. No one gets in and out without permission. No one stays overnight except licensed workers. Children under the age of sixteen aren't even allowed to visit more often than once a year. You don't want to stay overnight."

"Great. Surefire proof the risk of contamination is low. Do you know anyone who can help me get in there tomorrow night?"

Anton didn't answer.

"Do you?"

"I might know someone."

"Can you introduce me to him? Please?"

Still he didn't answer.

Nadia squeezed his arm. "Please?"

Anton sighed with exasperation. "Have I ever refused you anything, Half of Paradise?"

CHAPTER 32

Victor Bodnar sat in the back of the old Land Cruiser, studying the diamonds in the display window of the jewelry store across the street through Russian battlefield binoculars. The airplane's engines droned in his clogged ears as though he were still in flight. He'd been in constant motion since landing at Boryspil twelve hours ago; he was afraid to lean his head on the window for fear of nodding off.

The Timkiv twins sat up front, eyeing the shiny gold and silver watches in an adjacent display window. They'd told him their first names when he met them, but they were identical, so he'd forgotten them as soon as he heard them. They looked like volleyball players who liked the lens of a camera, with short blond hair that brushed against the truck's ceiling and easygoing blue eyes.

When Victor first shook their hands, however, their sleeves were rolled up. The tattoos on their forearms told him they were not into fun and games. The brother in the driver's seat wore the markings of a gun beside the ace of spades, a bottle of vodka, a ten-ruble note, and the profile of a girl with serpents for hair. He was the gun. His twin boasted the same backdrop, but instead of the gun, his tattoo featured three bullets. He was the ammunition. The pictures meant the brothers had spent time at Corrective Labor Colony 4.

The tattoos also meant that separated, the brothers were vulnerable, but together, they were invincible. A powerful *vor* must have made this assessment in prison and labeled them as such forever.

A beefy security guard in a black suit opened the door to the jewelry store from the inside and allowed a woman to exit. She carried a small white bag, purse, and matching poodle. She disappeared down the boulevard.

"So how exactly are we going to get the merch?" the Gun said.

"We should do it strong," the Ammunition said before Victor could answer. "We have the weapons, the manpower, and the element of surprise."

Victor said, "A thief who uses a gun is not a thief."

The twins exchanged glances and smiled. "What is he, then?" the Gun said.

"Incompetent," Victor said.

They laughed good-naturedly. "Okay," the Gun said. "If we don't do it strong, we could create a diversion instead. A violent one."

"No one wants to be in a car wreck," the Ammunition said. "But everyone slows down to watch one."

"Exactly," the Gun said. He turned around to face Victor and pointed at the convertible parked a few car lengths away from the jewelry store. "I could ram that Jaguar with the truck. Everyone comes out. All eyes on my brother and me, you and the guys in the van take down the merch."

Victor sighed. "A diversion like that is no diversion at all."

"It's not?" the Gun said, visibly disappointed.

"No."

"Then what is it?" the Ammunition said.

"A summons for the police."

The cabin remained silent for a moment.

The Ammunition turned to face Victor also. "Okay. What do you suggest we do?"

"We use the greatest advantage we have at our disposal."

"Which is?" the Ammunition said.

Victor smiled. "You and your brother's natural good looks."

Victor outlined their strategy. When he was done, the Gun called the driver of the van behind them and shared the plan.

Twenty minutes later, three girls burst from the jewelry store, dancing and shrieking down the steps toward the Mercedes. A lithe, dark-haired beauty waved a jewelry box with her right hand.

"I knew it," she shouted. "They're worth a fortune."

Before the girls could climb into their car, the Timkiv brothers strutted down the opposite side of the street. One of them held a map of Yalta in his hand. They waved to the girls.

"Excuse me, gorgeous," the Ammunition said. "This is Malisleva Street, right?"

The girl with the jewelry box seemed reluctant, as though she didn't like the attention being diverted from her and her newfound wealth. But her two friends swung their hips eagerly across the street and offered to help with directions.

The girl with the jewelry box started to cross the street to join them. A white van pulled up alongside her Mercedes. Its body shielded the girl and her car from her friends and the Timkiv brothers.

The passenger window was rolled down. A colleague of the Timkiv brothers nodded at the keys in her hand. "Are you leaving? We could sure use your parking spot. We have a delivery to make."

The girl frowned. "Oh. Okay. Let me pull out." She turned and lifted the door handle. There was a loud clicking noise as the doors came unlocked.

Two large men came up behind her. One slid a strip of duct tape over her head and covered her mouth. The second corralled her legs and taped them together. They lifted her and tossed her gently into the back of the open van. A third man slammed the door shut from inside.

She shimmied to the wall of the van and twisted to a semi-seated position. Her eyes stretched their sockets as though she were a wounded animal.

"Hello, Isabella. Don't be alarmed. You will not be harmed. It is so nice to meet you. My name is Victor. I am your uncle."

CHAPTER 33

STEAM BILLOWED FROM THE BOILED DUMPLINGS IN ANTON'S kitchen. The cover to the simmering pot of borscht rattled in place as though the slightest increase in heat would make it blow. They'd already shared half a bottle of an Alsace wine, during which time Nadia's desires had become inexplicably carnal. Anton began to grin with increasing frequency during their conversation, as though he could tell where her mind was drifting based simply on her body language. When he finally put his glass down and approached her, Nadia didn't run.

Anton bent at the knees, reached down, thrust his arms between her legs, and cupped her buttocks. She grabbed his shoulders to keep from falling backward.

"Anton, what are you—"

As he straightened, she teetered. Her hands went around his neck. He lifted her off the ground. She urged him on. He stepped forward, slid her butt onto the granite kitchen countertop, and released his grip. Her legs were splayed, and his hips pressed against her.

He kissed her, letting his lips sink into hers barely enough to make an impression before sealing them and kneading her gently. He tasted of apples and lemon. When he parted, Nadia lost her breath. What was she going to ask him? What was her problem now?

His left hand pressed against her lower back. His right hand massaged her shoulder, her spine, the back of her neck. The lips—those big, juicy fucking lips—caressed and nuzzled the rest of her neck, seemingly forever, slowly sucking on every pore between her head and shoulders, sending blood rushing to her face and turning her brain to mush. He finally, mercifully, slid his lips to hers and kissed her again, this time more urgently.

"Bedroom," he said.

Even though her hip bone ached, Nadia slid her hands through his hair and clumped it in her fists. "No," she said. "Right here. Right now."

They tore at their clothing and unleashed themselves on each other. Ten minutes later, Anton carried her into the bedroom. They rolled for over an hour in the cool gray sheets. When they finished the second time, Anton held Nadia in his arms and sang a tragic Ukrainian folk song about the maiden, the Cossack, and their unrequited love.

The popular song reminded Nadia of her childhood, when her father would play it on the stereo in the living room and light his pipe, and she knew that they were safe from his tirades for at least a few hours. She curled away from Anton and dabbed at the moisture in the corners of her eyes, lest he ask her why she was crying.

Anton lived in an old Soviet high-rise, a bland cement structure that explained a nation's unquenchable thirst for vodka on first sight. His penthouse loft, however, was an entirely different matter. Stainless steel appliances gleamed in the gourmet kitchen, and sterling silver antiques complemented a huge bureau full of first-edition books in the living room. The quality of his possessions didn't jibe with a man holding down two jobs in Kyiv, Nadia thought.

"What's this?" she said, holding up a silver box.

Anton stirred the pot of borscht in the kitchen. "An English tea caddy. My entire collection is English. That one's Victorian regency."

Nadia replaced it on the antique mahogany sideboard. "You have impeccable taste, Anton. This is quite a collection."

"I know what you're thinking. No, I didn't steal anything. Most of it belonged to my parents. My father was a renowned professor back in the day when the communists rewarded their academics. My mother was a translator in the diplomatic corps. I inherited the apartment from them. As for the kitchen, I had everything updated because I'm a fiend for gourmet cooking. Thus the second job."

Two candles lit the kitchen table while they wolfed down dinner: borscht, mushroom dumplings, cheese, and black bread.

"I want to tell you why I'm really here," Nadia said. "I want you to know everything."

"Don't. Please. I don't need to know anything more."

"But I trust you."

"No. No, you don't. And you shouldn't trust anyone in this country. Why should you? If you need something and I can help, I will. No questions asked."

"But—"

He raised his hand for her to stop. "Please. There's been no one for me since my wife died. These moments…You can rely on me unconditionally while you're in Kyiv."

Behind the circle of candlelight, his eyes seemed enormous, even moist. Nadia was already recovering, though, from her moment of naive passion. He was right. She didn't know him at all, so why was she being such a sap?

"That's incredibly sweet, Anton. I don't know what I would do without you. Really."

He smiled and stabbed a dumpling in his borscht.

"So tell me about this friend you have who knows Chernobyl," she said.

Anton tore the slice of bread in half. "His name is Hayder. I'm going to call him tonight. He owes me a favor and he's an honorable man, so I think he'll help. But there's something you should know."

"What's that?"

"He's a Crimean Tatar. From Crimea. It's an autonomous republic in the south of Ukraine."

Nadia shrugged. "Great. Why is that something I should know?"

"Because he's a Sunni Muslim. And he hates Americans."

CHAPTER 34

On Thursday morning, Kirilo drove forty kilometers south of Kiev to the small village of Trypillia, population 2,700. He'd made inquiries with business associates at the SBU, the Ukrainian State Security Service, into the whereabouts of Damian Tesla's old crew of thieves. Besides Damian, there were six of them. Three had disappeared, presumably to Western Europe or America, and the other three were dead. Buried in asphalt. One of the latter three, however, had remained close to his sister while still alive, in direct violation of the *Vorskoi Mir*, the Thieves' Code. He might have confided in her about the $10 million Damian allegedly stole.

Kirilo's driver guided the Audi along an unpaved road to a small house with a thatch roof. A sculpture, carved from the trunk of a massive oak tree, confirmed it was the right home. It featured a woman in helmet and full body armor, leaning on a staff with a serpent coiled at her feet.

In April, wheat looks like grass. It undulated like an ocean wave beneath the cool morning breeze throughout the prairie that surrounded the house. A hearty babushka chopped wood beside an apiary of bees.

Another woman greeted Kirilo at the front door. This one was middle-aged, with lustrous brown hair, deep-set oval eyes, and a shockingly thin waist. She wore a golden leather vest over a billowy white shirt and painted-on auburn pants.

The woman raised her eyebrows. "Kirilo Andre?"

Kirilo had to pull his eyes away from her torso. "Pardon? Oh, yes."

"May I see some identification?"

It was a common request in Ukraine. He showed her his domestic passport.

She nodded. "My name is Zirka." It was the Ukrainian word for "star." "The *militsiya* called and told me you'd be around. Come in."

A stifling heat greeted him in the small living room. Kirilo looked around. The windows were nailed shut. He knew the reason: every breeze was a potential source of colds and influenza. Sweat trickled inside his shirt down his armpit. Damn the peasants. Damn their superstitions.

Zirka served them tea in cups that matched a collection of wall plates, a vase, and a serving bowl filled with apples and chestnuts. They were all variations of the same wild geometric patterns, each with swirls of red, black, and white. It was similar to a traditional Ukrainian pattern, yet entirely different, more extreme.

The sound of manual labor echoed through the walls: wood splintered, an ax thumped, the babushka paused. Splinter, thump, pause. Splinter, thump, pause.

"What is that statue in front?" he said. "The woman in armor."

"That is Athena," she said. "The goddess of wisdom and weaving."

Kirilo frowned. "Who?"

"Athena. The Greek goddess. The goddess of wisdom and weaving. Also the goddess of heroic behavior."

"Well, you don't see that every day," he said.

"It's not every day you're in Trypillia."

"Excuse me?"

"You don't know about Trypillia?"

"Should I?"

"Trypillia is an ancient culture dating back to 5000 BC. It originated right here, in Trypillia. In Ukraine. At one time, it spread through Moldova and the Black Sea, halfway into Romania. It was a matriarchal society. Women took care of the agriculture, made the pottery, and ran the household. Men hunted, kept domestic animals, and made tools. Do you know how to make tools, Kirilo?"

Wood splintered, an ax thumped.

Kirilo spit tea out of his mouth. "I…I know how to use one or two, but I've never made one."

She wasn't smiling or laughing. Instead, she measured him up and down. "It's never too late to learn."

Unsure if she was serious, he fidgeted in his seat. "As the police may have told you, I'm conducting an investigation into a swindle your brother was involved in before he died. I'm sorry to bring up bad memories."

"It's all right. That was a long time ago. You know the communists killed my brother by burying him alive in asphalt?" She said it in a detached manner, as though she were describing an innovative way of road building.

Kirilo wiped his brow with the back of his shirtsleeve and took a deep breath. "Yes. Again, I'm sorry to bring this up." He described Damian's alleged theft of $10 million. "Did your brother ever tell you about this?"

"It was the reason he was killed. He did more than tell me about it. He and Damian hid the money here." She eyed his Patek Philippe watch. "Are you married, Kirilo?"

"Married?" Kirilo said. He was vaguely aware that the rhythmic sounds of the babushka's work had ceased. "No. I'm not the marrying kind." Had he heard her correctly? He leaned forward. "They hid the money here? My God. *Here*?"

"Yes. They buried it in a box in our vegetable garden."

"Where is the money now?" Kirilo took a deep breath.

A shuffling noise directly behind him.

He turned.

The babushka stood a foot away, left hand curled beneath the head of the ax, right hand gripping the bottom of the handle, ready to rear back and swing.

Kirilo ducked. His instincts told him to run, but he couldn't move. Who had put the lead in his shoes? It was so damned hot.

"Is your guest staying for lunch?" she said to Zirka. "You want me to prepare a fresh chicken?"

"No, no. No lunch, thank you, Babushka," he said. His kingdom for his cattle prod and an air conditioner.

Zirka tried to change his mind, but he told her he had appointments. Many, many appointments.

She shrugged. "No, thank you, Mama," she said, and the babushka left the room.

"Where were we?" Kirilo said. "The money. What happened to the money?"

"The KGB came and took it," Zirka said.

"KGB? You're certain of this?"

"Of course. I was here." Zirka thrust her shoulders back slightly and shifted her hips on the edge of the sofa. "Did you grow up in the city or the countryside?"

"Countryside," he said. "But then I ran away from home, so no, city." He gritted his teeth and shook the cobwebs from his brain. "You saw KGB agents take the ten million dollars? You actually *saw* them?"

"Better than that. My brother bought me a camera because I wanted to be a photographer." She chuckled. "I say bought, but he probably stole it. I hid in the cellar and took pictures through the window with a telephoto lens."

Zirka went to her bedroom and came back with black-and-white photos. One showed two men in shirts and ties digging a hole beside the house. A second showed two others, counting hundred-dollar bills. A third showed them leading her brother away in handcuffs.

"There really is no ten million dollars," Kirilo said under his breath.

Zirka poured him a second cup of tea. "Are you a hunter, Kirilo?" She parted her lips slightly. "There is good hunting here, in the land of Athena."

He started to answer her with tall tales of elk and bear hunts, her remarkable body exercising some sort of magnetic pull on him yet again, when a crack and a thud broke his spell. Wood splintered, an ax thumped.

Kirilo offered excuses, made apologies, and dashed out the front door, pictures in hand.

"Get me the hell out of here," he said to his driver after jumping into the backseat. "Fast."

They tore down the dirt driveway away from Athena, Zirka waving good-bye in the rearview mirror, the thud of the babushka's ax echoing in the background.

"This isn't about Damian's ten million dollars," Kirilo said to Misha when he got him on his cell phone. "The KGB confiscated the money. I saw pictures."

"So it's about a different pot of money. Or something else. Something that's worth millions."

"Has she gone back to her hotel?"

"No."

Kirilo grunted. "She's too smart for that."

"Where will you be?"

"Kyiv today, Yalta tonight. I have a breakfast in less than twenty-four hours with a wedding planner. And my daughter. She's getting married. My daughter, Isabella."

CHAPTER 35

At 7:00 on Thursday night, Anton sped north from Kyiv up the expressway along the Dnipro River in Radek's van. Nadia sat upright in the backseat while Hayder slouched in front beside Anton. He had ebony skin with rich Turkish features. He wore a dark turtleneck, blue jeans, and a mid-length black coat, with a thin black scarf wrapped around his neck.

Hayder spoke Crimean, Russian, and English, but not Ukrainian. He spoke Russian with Anton but insisted on speaking English with Nadia.

"What is your business in the Exclusion Zone?" Nadia said.

"What?" Hayder twisted and glowered at her. "Why do you inquisition me about my business?"

He turned to Anton and asked him a question under his breath. Nadia couldn't hear a word except for *kurva*, the Russian and Ukrainian word for "whore."

"You want to know about my business?" Hayder said. "I tell you about my business. One, I'm in the import business. Two, I'm in the export business. And three, I'm in the 'none of your fucking business.' That's my business."

Nadia looked away and let a few seconds pass. "I'm sorry. I wasn't trying to pry," she lied. "I was just trying to get acquainted."

"Okay, okay," Anton said. He murmured some soothing words in Hayder's direction. "We're all friends here, right?"

"Tell *him* that," she said.

"Sure, we are all friends," Hayder said. "My father can't get the job in Crimea because he is Muslim. My brother, who was the best chef in Sevastopol, is kidnapped by American government and locked up in Gitmo for no reason when he go to Chicago to open restaurant. And here I am, the black man, in the car with the Ukrainian and the American. Oh, yeah. We are the *best* friends."

Nadia studied Anton's reflection in the rearview mirror. "Anton, are you sure about this?"

Anton cracked a reassuring smile. "Don't worry. Hayder likes to rant. But Hayder is good people. He went to the London School of Economics."

The most dangerous people in the world weren't the extremists, Nadia thought; they were the highly educated and super-intelligent extremists. Hayder's presence made her trip—in the dead of the night, to a radioactive wasteland, in search of a notorious uncle she'd never known existed—all the more surreal. Less than a week ago, she thought she was meeting a nice old man who'd known her father. And now, here she was.

While Anton exited the expressway and turned right, Hayder handed her a small device the size of an old-fashioned transistor radio.

"Dosimeter," he said. "It measures your exposure to radiation per hour. After the explosion, the reading in the control room was three hundred sieverts. You died in one minute. Today the reading in the control room is thirty-four sieverts. You die in fifteen minutes. In States or in Moscow, normal reading is ten microsieverts. In Kyiv, the normal reading is twelve to sixteen micros. In the Zone, the reading is up to one thousand micros, depending how close to the reactor."

Nadia held the device gingerly. "That sounds like a problem."

Hayder shook his head. “No. That is not the problem. Exposure is not the problem. Accumulation is the problem. If you spend five hours in the Zone, you radiate as much as if you spend two hours in the airplane or on the beach in Rio de Janeiro.”

“Then why bother with the dosimeter?”

“To avoid getting particles on the clothes or body. Reactor Four explosion released twenty nuclear substances. Most are not harmful anymore. Three are harmful: plutonium, strontium, and cesium-137. Cesium-137 is in the dust. If cesium-137 gets on body, accumulation is problem. You must scrub quickly or die. The particles are the very big problem.”

The road curved through the night. A pine forest hovered over both sides. The truck’s headlights provided the only illumination. Hayder pointed at something up ahead and whispered to Anton.

Anton swerved left onto a dirt road. Nadia bounced in her seat as the van rolled over uneven terrain. Ten minutes later, Anton killed the lights. They drove five miles per hour until they came upon a barbed-wire fence and stopped. Anton flashed his lights twice. A pair of headlights flashed three times from the other side of the fence.

“Bingo,” Hayder said. “My man. Let’s go.”

The barbed wire meant they were at the border of the Zone of Exclusion, thirty kilometers from the reactors, and thirty-three kilometers from the Hotel Polissya in Pripyat.

“I would go with you,” Anton said, “but we can’t leave the car here unattended. It might not be here when we got back. And we can’t take the car inside the Zone. It would be too hot by the time we were done. Cars that go in the Zone stay in the Zone.”

“Don’t worry about it,” Nadia said. “I can take care of myself.”

“I know you can,” Anton said. “I’ll be here. Waiting for you.”

“You better be.”

A steel pole stabilized the hole in the fence so that it opened and closed like a door. A covered military-supply truck was parked on the other side. Hayder opened the passenger door and told Nadia to get in. She slid next to a sullen driver in camouflage gear. The cabin smelled like diesel, cigarettes, and hair tonic.

"This is Volodya," Hayder said, after climbing inside and sitting beside her. "Volodya will be the driver tonight." He switched to Russian. "Volodya, this is Nadia."

Volodya barked a hello in Russian, turned the truck around, and took off down a path with the lights on. A dosimeter on the front dashboard chattered lightly.

The forest gave way to the steppe, which yielded to pockets of woodlands. They passed eleven abandoned homes, all made of square logs with thatch roofs. With fifteen kilometers to go, they sneaked through another barbed-wire fence. The roof of the next house they saw protruded from the ground at an odd angle. The home had been bulldozed and buried. "After the reactor explodes," Hayder said, "they water and bury everything."

"Why the water?" Nadia said.

"To keep radioactivity dust from blowing to the other cities. Government tells people: bury vegetable gardens, bury topsoil, too. But people do not believe anything is really wrong. They think it is just the fire. They say, 'We won't get propagandized again.' So they bury topsoil but eat the vegetables. And keep the manure from the top. They think, 'Why waste good shit over government scam?'

"While he tells people in Chernobyl to destroy the farms, Gorbachev goes on television and tells the world there is no radioactive leak. They put dosimeters in the food in Pripyat and show all is good. But government dosimeters are only good to measure the air. You need different dosimeter for the food. The truth is that Gorbachev does not want to mess up the May Day parade in Kyiv. So he does the Soviet thing."

"He lies," Nadia said.

"He denies," Hayder said. "The explosion is on April twenty-sixth, but the government does not tell about radioactivity leak until May fifth. That was the end of the Soviet Union and the birth of the free Ukraine. Chernobyl is the single-biggest reason this is the free country. Chernobyl containment cost eighteen billion rubles. Destroyed the economy. Proved the communists could not take care of their peoples. Destroyed the Soviet Union."

They sat quietly for a moment as Volodya guided the truck through a patch of brush.

"You know a lot about the history here," Nadia said, "don't you?"

Hayder let a quiet moment pass between them. "I am from here," he said.

"I don't understand. I thought you were from Crimea."

"Born in Crimea, yes. But I am the child of the Zone. My father was the bio-robot. My father was...Robot Hayder. The Soviet government gives order: biological resource are dispensable. The liquidators who work on the reactor call themselves bio-robots. Like dispensable machines. Robot Ivan, Robot Volodya, Robot Hayder...No one tells them radioactivity leak. No one tells them they will die. Some are militia, some are volunteer. My father came for the money. By the time they know the true gig is up, it is too late. My father moves blocks of radioactive graphite in reactor with bare hands. He dies two weeks after explosion. My mother lives in Pripyat. I am born eight months later."

Lights shone a hundred yards away over the top of a grove of pine trees. Volodya stopped at the edge of the woods.

"We get out here," Hayder said. "Bicycles on the other side of trees. Dosimeter on. Follow me."

He bent low to the ground and scampered along a well-worn path to the edge of the clearing. Nadia followed his footsteps carefully, wondering how many particles of cesium were dangling within a foot of her clothing. She burst out of the forest behind Hayder and knelt down beside him on a block of cracked asphalt.

Two rusty bicycles with headlights bolted to the handlebars lay beneath a tree. In the foreground, spotlights illuminated a giant chimney encased in scaffolding. It rose from a dome a few hundred yards away. The silhouettes of two other smokestacks and a dozen cranes surrounded it.

"Welcome to the village of Chernobyl," Hayder said.

He scanned the reactors and the buildings around them, his eyes blazing with anticipation.

"The thing people don't know about the Zone," he said, wetting his lips, "is once you are here, you want to come back. You need to come back. The Zone…It pulls you in."

Hayder loosened his scarf. He turned to Nadia and revealed a V-shaped scar on his neck.

"Last chance to turn back," he said.

Nadia recognized the scar from photographs of children at the Chernobyl Museum. Cancer of the thyroid.

Her dosimeter chattered steadily. Meeting her uncle suddenly seemed far less compelling than it had in Kiev. But then again, she needed the money, and there was also the boy, her cousin. How dangerous could Pripyat be if they offered daily tours of the place?

Nadia swallowed but shook her head.

"You go on?" he said.

Nadia imagined having a little cousin who looked up to her, and logging onto her brokerage account and seeing a seven- or eight-figure cash balance. "I go on."

"Okay. You go on." The tips of his silver-and-gold teeth shined in the dark. It was the first time she'd seen him grin. "You go on. I have some respectability for you."

Hayder disappeared into the forest to tell Volodya he could leave and returned thirty seconds later. The truck rumbled away in the darkness.

Nadia checked her watch. It was 8:34 p.m. "I have twenty-six minutes. Will I make it to Pripyat in time?"

"Sure, sure. Three kilometers. I put you on the main road to Pripyat before I go. We meet back here ten thirty p.m."

Nadia recoiled. "You go? Go where? You told us you'd take me to Pripyat yourself. To the Hotel Polissya. That I would wait for you afterward in the Chernobyl café. Where there are people."

He pursed his lips sympathetically. "Small change in the plan. Very small. Before we go in the truck, Volodya relay message from the business contact. Schedule change. I meet him at nine o'clock now, so cannot go with you. You must go alone."

"But isn't Pripyat a ghost town? Are there any lights there at all?"

"Sure, sure. Good light on the bicycle, and I give flashlight, too," he said. "Check cell phone. The coverage good. Is very good."

Nadia pulled out her phone. Five bars lit up in green. Hayder did the same and nodded reassuringly. She punched his number into her phone and hung up as soon as it rang.

"See?" Hayder said. "No worries. Hayder is the stand-up guy. You get lost, any problem, you call me, we work out together. Just like New York."

"Yeah," Nadia said. She eyed the wreckage on the horizon and imagined a team of human robots cleaning it all up. "Just like New York."

At the outskirts of the power station, the edge of a cooling pond shimmered in the night. Nadia remembered the skates the boy was wearing in the photo and wondered if he played hockey on it during the winter. Perhaps that was as good as it got for her cousin out here, a topless Madison Square Garden manufactured out of radioactive water, as frozen during the winter as Chernobyl was in time.

CHAPTER 36

ADAM FELL TO HIS KNEES IN THE FIELD, GASPING. HIS NECKlace popped out of his shirt. The locket bobbed before him. He reached out to tuck it back in.

"No strength," his hockey coach said.

The snap of the homemade whip cracked the air. The braided rope lashed Adam's shoulders and back. It dug through his sweatshirt and T-shirt and burned his skin. Adam's hands fell to the ground for support before he could grasp the locket. He gritted his teeth, determined not to make a sound no matter how much it hurt.

"No stamina," the coach said.

He snapped the whip again.

Moisture blurred Adam's vision. The whip thrashed his spine.

"No heart," the coach said.

He whipped Adam again.

Tears streamed down Adam's cheeks.

The locket. Where was the locket? He focused, grabbed it, and tucked it under his shirt.

The coach towered over him, his huge potbelly hanging over his waist like a sack of potatoes, rope coiled in his right hand, slapping his left as though counting the seconds until the next beating.

"I've been training you to play hockey since you were seven. Seven years old! And you are what—fifteen now? That's eight years. And you still can't climb that hill? You really are a useless bastard. The son of a scumbag Ukrainian thief and an ugly American whore. How many times have I told you? If you can't climb that hill, there's no hope for you. There's no future for you. And guess what? You'll never climb that hill."

The hill was one hundred meters long and as steep as a snow mountain. The problem with the sprint was that it was a rigged game. The coach made him run with a fifty-meter rubber band around his waist. It was as thick as a man's wrist. The coach tied the other end of the rubber band around his own belly. When he decided it was time for Adam to fall, he yanked on the band and pulled him back.

The coach was right. He would never climb that hill. He would never be strong enough to pull the coach with him.

Rusty hinges creaked behind them. Three huge men in overalls shuffled out the back door of the Korosten Porcelain Factory. They carried pails as wide as tractor tires to the field and placed them in front of three wooden blocks. The first block went up to Adam's knees, the second to his hips, and the third to his chest.

Adam knew the routine. He did it three to five times a week. He quickly ripped off his tattered sneakers and pulled off his torn socks.

The coach removed a stopwatch from his pants pocket. "Five…four…"

Damian scampered to his bare feet and faced the column of pails and boxes.

"Three…two…one…Begin!" The coach squeezed the stopwatch with his left hand.

Adam jumped. As soon as he landed on the first box, he bent his knees and leaped onto the second. He did the same to land on the third. Once on the highest box, he spun in the air 180 degrees and reversed course. When he landed on the ground, he spun again and repeated the process.

"Five minutes on," the coach screamed. "One minute off. Total exercise time: *thirty-five minutes*!"

Thirty-five minutes? The coach was trying to kill him. He'd always been brutal, but now he was insane. It had started after he got back from visiting his father in Chernobyl on Sunday. It was as though the coach knew he would be leaving soon forever. The coach had taken him in years ago as a favor to his father. He'd promised to turn Adam into a professional-caliber hockey player. But now it was as though he didn't want Adam to go away. If he did leave, the coach wanted to make sure he did so in a casket.

If the coach was planning to kill him, he might have to kill the coach first.

"You won't last thirty-five minutes," the coach said. "Makarov would have lasted thirty-five minutes. Tretiak would have surely lasted thirty-five minutes. You? You won't last thirty-five minutes."

After twenty-five minutes of jumping, Adam shook off a dizzy spell. His lungs were ready to burst. His legs were spaghetti.

He was moving at a snail's pace. Each leap required maximum concentration and effort now. But he wouldn't quit. He wouldn't give the fat bastard the satisfaction. He'd rather die than quit.

He leaped for the second block. Landed flat on the edge of the square. Bobbled. Wavered. Held his position.

"You want to know why you won't last?" the coach said. "Because you have no heart. Because you have no soul. You're the product of a radioactive cesspool. If I were a betting man, I would never bet on you."

Adam took aim for the third block. He bent his knees. Swung his arms back and jumped.

His toes kissed the block. His heels came up short. He teetered, reached out for an imaginary handle—

There wasn't one. He tumbled down into the pail of sizzling charcoal rock below him.

The coal burned his feet. He rolled to one side. The rocks singed his arm. He rolled to the other side. The rocks scalded the other arm. He kept rolling until he fell out of the bucket and collapsed on the grass.

The coach convulsed with laughter. "You look like the village idiot taking a bath. Better than television. Much better. Thank you, boy. I knew there was a reason I was training you all these years. Put your shoes back on. Puck-handling drill in two minutes. Two minutes. Prepare yourself!"

Adam caught his breath during the first minute. With sixty seconds left, he staggered to his feet and walked around the field, trying to shake the blood out of his arms and legs.

That evening, Adam slept beside the chicken coop of the coach's house, not in the barn, where he usually did. He stole three apples from the neighbor's cart and ate them instead of his usual dinner of buckwheat bread and cheese.

It didn't matter. It didn't matter what the coach tried to do to him. Adam had the necklace.

The necklace held the locket, the locket held the future, and the future was his.

CHAPTER 37

LIGHT SPILLED FROM NADIA'S BICYCLE ONTO THE NARROW road to Pripyat.

A pothole.

She pulled on the handlebars to the right to avoid it. Her dosimeter screeched. Nadia yanked the handlebars farther to the right. The bicycle swerved. She teetered and tottered. Pedaled to stay upright. The dosimeter hushed.

The bicycle turned in a circle. Nadia regained her balance. Ended up right back where she had started. The dosimeter screeched again. She cursed and pedaled through it. The dosimeter quieted down.

Her headlight was aimed ten feet in front of her, a compromise that let her see the road and some of what lay ahead. She weaved around the ubiquitous potholes, sticking to the right side of the road, avoiding the column of grass and weeds growing down the middle.

Hayder told her to avoid all vegetation, especially the moss. Water infuses moss, and cesium hides in water. She'd probably driven over a small patch and sent the dosimeter into a frenzy. So what? Her tires were already hot. Bicycles that entered the Zone stayed in the Zone. It was the rider you had to worry about. Hopefully, this rider was destined to leave the Zone.

Chernobyl's red forest pressed in on the narrow road from both sides. A quarter moon illuminated their dense canopies and irradiated coral trunks. Power lines crisscrossed above her head. In a clearing along the forest's edge, cars, trucks, and ambulances protruded from the ground where they'd been buried.

Nadia passed the first block of apartment buildings. The thought occurred to her that her uncle might live there. Logic dictated she keep her eyes on the road, but she couldn't resist. She aimed her headlight at the apartment complex and stole a glance. Dark windows against a white-and-orange facade, terraces with wooden banisters. It might have been a glimpse of urban slumber, as opposed to a nuclear apocalypse, until she looked again.

The windows were black holes: all the glass had been removed. The banisters dripped with mildew. Trees sprouted around the perimeter of the building and rendered the first two floors invisible. A branch from a taller specimen disappeared into a window on the fifth floor. Her uncle didn't live there. Only ghosts were sleeping inside.

Nadia fixed the light back on the street and exhaled. There was no trace of life in Pripyat. What did she expect? The population was zero. The atmosphere reminded her of a black-and-white movie from her childhood where the last man on the planet searched for another survivor.

She arrived at the city center at 8:54. Three sets of buildings framed the main square. Trees, shrubs, and grass protruded randomly from cracks in the asphalt. A sign above the building on the left said RESTAURANT. Beside it was the CINEMA. The building in the middle was the CULTURAL CENTER. Beyond the building stood a Ferris wheel. It was frozen in time, its yellow chairs reaching hopelessly for the moon. Nadia headed toward the building on the right, as Hayder had instructed.

Halfway there, a light flashed on the hotel's first floor. It flamed like a cigarette lighter and went off just as quickly.

It was Damian. It had to be. He was signaling that he was waiting for her.

When she arrived at the hotel, Nadia laid her bicycle on a clean stretch of asphalt. The front doors were chained shut. The glass, however, had been removed from all the windows. There was no light inside. Why didn't he keep the light on inside?

Nadia climbed through a window. Her feet found a perch on top of a radiator. As she jumped to the floor, a cloud of dust gagged her. She suppressed a wave of panic. Took three steps into the lobby and turned on her flashlight.

Strips of wood and Sheetrock on the floor. Debris everywhere. An elevator shaft, door removed. Two light switches turned up in the on position. A high-powered rifle was aimed at her head.

"Don't make a sound," the man with the rifle said quietly in coarse Ukrainian. He was hiding behind a desk. "Turn off your flashlight and get down on your knees, real, real slow. Do it now."

Nadia clicked off her flashlight. She looked down. An infrared beam blazed a path from the rifle to her chest. She fell to her knees. Was this her Uncle Damian? Why would he be pointing a rifle at her?

The room was silent. The man with the rifle didn't say anything. He didn't lower his rifle's aim. The infrared beam streamed over Nadia's head.

An animal growled. It sounded like the raspy exhalation of a wild cat. The growl came from behind her. The animal sounded poised to pounce.

Footsteps. Two high-pitched roars in rapid succession.

A muted shot rang out. The animal whimpered. Hit the floor with a thud.

A powerful lantern battery shone at Nadia from the hunter's perch. She shielded her eyes with her forearm and turned away.

A giant lynx lay behind her, gorgeous silver-and-gold fur with spectacular black ears. It looked like a sleeping baby. Its lungs filled and contracted. A dart protruded from its skin. There was no sign of blood.

"You haven't seen my face," the hunter said. "Go. Now."

Not Uncle Damian. Nadia climbed back out the window and ran to her bicycle. She pedaled furiously, paying no heed to the dosimeter. Halfway to Chernobyl village, she stopped and called Hayder. She got his voice mail. She left him a message that her meeting was over and she would be at the Chernobyl village café at 9:30. She was supposed to meet him across the street from the café at 10:30. She would be an hour early.

Afterward, she pedaled through the darkness toward the bright lights of Reactor 4.

CHAPTER 38

NADIA STRADDLED THE BICYCLE AT THE JUNCTION TO THE village center. A sign warned all unauthorized personnel to leave.

A barbed-wire fence surrounded the Chernobyl Power Station. Floodlights burst with light. The sarcophagus and chimneys loomed in the background. A guard smoked beside his booth at the entrance.

Nadia checked her watch: 9:25.

A monument beside the power station displayed six firefighters lugging a hose to put out the reactor fire. They were not wearing respirators or hazard suits. In the monument, a globe was fixed to the side of the reactor smokestack. It looked like a miniature replica of the New York City Unisphere from the World's Fair.

A door crashed open. Raucous laughter. A hip-hop beat.

Nadia followed the sound. A hundred yards away was a small square building that resembled an emergency military barracks.

The café. Built for workers who still labored in the village and the power plants in the center of the Zone.

She waited until the guard turned to walk back to his booth and pedaled to the side of the café. Leaned her bicycle against the wall, set her cell phone to vibrate, and stepped inside.

She gagged. Cigarette smoke hung in the air as though fire were leaking from beyond its walls. Rap music pounded from small suspended speakers. The beat was American, but the words were Ukrainian. Laughter and conversation spilled from one clique to another and filled the room. She looked around for an older man, but there were a half dozen possible candidates.

Slicing her way into the far corner, she counted thirty to forty people, split evenly between the sexes. Most wore camouflage uniforms or warm-ups. One couple danced dirty in the center of the room, lips and hips mashed together.

Nadia ordered a beer from an agreeable bartender. As she sipped it, a series of men stood up at a long table and raised toasts to a pair of newlyweds. Champagne flowed from multiple bottles.

One of the men saw her and did a double take. Nadia cringed. She looked away and stepped to her left to try to hide behind a burly Cossack downing shots of *horilka*.

"Hey, you can't drink alone," he said, rushing up to her. He had Einstein hair, a spindly body, and a lovable nerd's face fully equipped with black-rimmed Superman glasses. "Haven't seen you here before, *kotiku*." The literal translation of the popular Ukrainian endearment was "kitty." "What's your name? Where are you from? Where have you been all my life?"

Nadia smiled and nodded toward the table. "I think the party's over there, not here."

He grinned. "You won't get rid of me that easy, *kotiku*. My name is Karel. What is yours?"

"My name is Nadia."

"Nadia, Panya. My beauty. First time in the Zone?"

"How can you tell?"

He laughed and tapped his nose. "The Zone knows its own. Where are you from? Who are you with?"

Nadia followed the script she'd written with Hayder and Anton. "I'm a newspaper reporter from New York City." The media had helped the Green Revolution succeed. They would respect and admire an American newspaper reporter.

His eyes lit up even more. "A reporter? From New York City? Your Ukrainian is excellent." He grabbed Nadia by the crook of her elbow and dragged her to the table.

"Look, everyone," he said, as though she were a major celebrity, "a friend from New York City."

The table exploded with cheers. She searched the faces, looking for a welcoming smile on the face of an older man. An amiable fellow raised a toast to America, the bastion of freedom and free enterprise. Someone shoved a glass of champagne into Nadia's hands. She sipped some, knowing it would be an insult to do otherwise.

Everyone drank to the bottom, set their glasses down, and looked expectantly at her.

Nadia felt herself blush. Glanced at Karel. "Should I raise a toast?" she whispered.

"Better you tell us a joke," he said loudly, so that everyone could hear.

The table roared with approval. "A joke. A joke. Give us an American joke," they said.

Nadia scoured her mind for something funny to say. Only one idea came to mind. "How many actors does it take to change a lightbulb?"

She waited a beat.

"Three," she said. "One to change the bulb, and two to say, 'That could be me up there.'"

For reasons beyond her comprehension, the translation from English didn't work. She got a few chuckles, but no guffaws.

"That joke doesn't work in the Zone," Karel said with mock seriousness. "Because there is no electricity. So the lightbulb *never* goes on."

The table exploded. Karel buckled with laughter.

Nadia waved good luck to the newlyweds as Karel pulled her back to a spot in the corner. He nestled her beer glass back in her hands and ordered a brandy from the bar.

"So what did you learn about the Zone today?" he said.

Nadia considered her answer. "I'm not sure. I saw a lynx in a condemned hotel today. A big, beautiful wild cat. You tell me what that means."

Karel stuck out his chest. "It's one of the world's best-kept secrets. The Zone is the greatest wildlife preserve in Europe, and the second best in the entire former Soviet Union."

"You're kidding me. How is that possible?" Nadia said.

"The common theory is that the absence of man has triumphed over the presence of radioactivity. We have formerly extinct species of wild boar and lynx. Wild horses roam the steppe. Storks nest low, unafraid of human predators. Insects, birds, wolves, rodents. We have species we never had before. Like the lynx. We have species the world hasn't seen for a century."

"That is amazing," Nadia said. "Has word gotten out about this? Do you have poachers hunting for these animals?"

Karel's right eye twitched. "Poachers? Here? No," he said, swatting the idea away. "Sometimes a drunken idiot may go after a wild boar for sport, but that is all. There is no crime in the Zone."

His brandy arrived. He knocked back a third right away and ended up pressed against the side of Nadia's hip. She tried to retreat, but her back was already up against the wall.

"So what do you do, Karel? And who are all these people?"

"I am a zoologist," he said. He gestured toward the newlyweds with drunken inaccuracy. "The others at our table are botanists and scientists who conduct ecological experiments for the government." He motioned toward the men and women in camos. "Then there are the scientists who work in the Shelter."

"The Shelter?"

"The sarcophagus that covers Unit Four. Here, we call it the Shelter."

"Ah."

"No one knows what those people really do in the Shelter. All we know about one another is that we are all volunteers. None of us have to be here. But there is no other place that we would rather be."

Nadia looked around the café. The party was devoid of pretension. People were just plain having fun.

Nadia raised her beer. "To the Zone," she said, and clinked her glass against Karel's snifter.

"To the Zone."

They finished their drinks. Nadia glanced at her watch. It was 10:17. Hayder was due in thirteen minutes.

Karel leaned into her unsteadily, his breath reeking. "I will share a secret with you, if you share one with me." He pulled back and did a little jig in place with eager anticipation.

Nadia laughed. "Okay."

He leaned forward. "There may be a little crime in the Zone." He raised his right hand and left an inch gap between thumb and forefinger. "Just a little," he whispered.

Nadia laughed again. "If there is more than one human being in a place, there will be crime. Now, let me think. What kind of secret can I tell you?"

Karel raised a drunken finger. "I have a suggestion." He leaned into her ear one more time. "True or false. You are not really a reporter, are you?"

"What? Of course I am. Why do you say that?"

His voice shed its alcoholic tinge. "Because your name is Nadia Tesla and you have come to see a man named Damian about the fate of the free world."

CHAPTER 39

KIRILO MARCHED DOWN THE PIER AT THE YALTA YACHT Club flanked by the two bodyguards who had accompanied him on the helicopter from Kyiv. Splashes of moonlight shimmered on the Black Sea.

A pair of identical twins chatted up a trio of girls beside his neighbor's yacht. They were tall, with golden hair and sparkling smiles, young posers who would benefit from a conversation with his cattle prod, like his scumbag future son-in-law.

He boarded his eighty-two-foot yacht and took a deep breath. "Isabella?" he called.

Pavel appeared on the main deck. "Still no sign of her, Boss."

"Something's wrong. Something's happened to her."

"How can you be sure, Boss? She might be out with friends or at a movie."

"We have a pact. She never turns her cell phone off. And if she's late, she always calls." He glanced at his diamond-studded watch. "She was supposed to be here at nine o'clock for a late supper. To discuss the meeting with the wedding planner tomorrow. She's an hour late. Did you call her best friends? Ivanka and Marta?"

Pavel shook his head.

"Why not? Call them. Call them now, dammit." He started toward his office and stopped. "Anything on the taxi driver?"

"Not yet," Pavel said. "We're working on it."

Kirilo looked out at the water. A green dinghy floated freely ten meters from his yacht.

"Look," Kirilo said, pointing at the rowboat. "Those idiots at the club let one get away again. It's going to hit us." When Pavel didn't react, he said, "It's going to hit us, I tell you. Is anyone on this boat awake, or should I just have all of you shot and thrown overboard?"

Pavel and a crewman rushed starboard. Kirilo stomped to his office port side and locked the door behind him. The stereo dispensed a soothing dose of Mozart. The television monitor, linked to his computer, projected a portrait of Isabella at age sixteen. Reluctant eyes and unblemished cheeks, hands demurely folded in her lap.

Pictures lied. Isabella wasn't all that. Daughters lied. She hated the pearls, thought they were a joke. Mozart lied. Life was no symphony.

Kirilo removed his coat with the cattle prod tucked in its lining and hung it on the rack in the corner. Released the latch to his bathroom.

The stench hit him. It couldn't be. He sniffed again. Did one of the crewmen have the gall to use his private bathroom? If he found out which one, he'd kill him tonight.

Kirilo opened the door. A withered old man sat fully dressed on the toilet bowl, arms folded across his chest. He looked like a cigarette butt that needed to be stomped out.

Kirilo froze. Victor? Victor Bodnar? On his yacht? In his bathroom?

"Greetings, cousin," Victor said. "My men have your daughter. Isabella will die if I don't walk off this boat unharmed within thirty minutes. Do we understand each other?"

Kirilo burst inside and wrapped his hands around Victor's neck. Lifted him up and off the toilet bowl. Victor's feet dangled six centimeters in the air. Kirilo squeezed with all his might.

"Your father was a bitch, and so you are you," Kirilo said through clenched teeth. Victor grabbed Kirilo's wrists, but it was no match. His cousin had the grip of a daisy. The bitch was as good as dead.

Victor's cheeks inflated. His face turned purple.

Kirilo eased his grip a bit. Victor gulped air.

"Breathe, bitch. Breathe," Kirilo said, struggling to catch his own breath. "Don't die just yet. No, no. I'm going to enjoy this over a span of an hour, or two, or seven. Only then will you die."

Victor opened his mouth. "Isabella," he said.

Kirilo's eyes fell on the television monitor outside the bedroom: Isabella. Victor had her.

Kirilo released his grip.

A knock on the office door.

"Everything okay in there, Boss?"

Kirilo hustled to the door and unlocked it. Pavel stepped inside.

"Help me get this man to the sofa," Kirilo said.

They rushed to the bathroom, where Victor lay on the tile, panting.

"Who is he, Boss? Where did he come from? How did he get on board?"

Pavel and Kirilo lifted Victor by his shoulders and carried him to the couch.

"He snuck on board when you were or weren't watching," Kirilo said. "You wouldn't have seen him either way. He's a pickpocket. He's a thief. He's the shadow on the street."

While Victor recovered, Pavel brought them tumblers of single-malt scotch and tall glasses of ice water. He closed the door behind him as Kirilo instructed.

"Here, cousin," Kirilo said, handing him the water and the scotch. "Drink. Drink."

Victor drank the water and sipped the scotch. He coughed and repeated. Reclined on the cushions and sighed.

"Where is Isabella?" Kirilo said.

"She is safe," Victor said.

"Safe? What does that mean, safe? Where are you hiding her? Has someone touched her? Is she hurt? Has anyone looked at her the wrong way?"

"She hasn't been touched. I've been gone a long time, but even an old man has friends in his homeland. The men who are helping me are professional."

"Why have you done this?"

"Why did you send an assassin to kill me?"

"You know why."

"Why now? After all these years?"

"Think of it as a gift to myself on my daughter's wedding. I don't want you to die a natural death."

"Well, I do want to die a natural death. That is one of the reasons I've taken your daughter."

"What's the other reason?"

"You've met my business partner, Misha Markov. He intends to cut me out of this money we're chasing. I want us to put our animosities aside—for now. I want you to keep me involved in this Tesla thing."

"That's all?"

Victor sipped his scotch and then cracked a smile. "Almost. I want you to also consider a simple mathematical fact."

"What?"

"Ten million divided by two is greater than ten million divided by three."

"You want me to kill your business partner?" Kirilo knocked back some scotch, put his tumbler down, and scratched his chin. "No, that I cannot do. I have no love for him. After all, he's a *moscal*. But it would not be good for business. He's an important man with important contacts. Someone could be out revenue because of his death, and I don't need the aggravation. No, there has to be a good reason to kill him, and there isn't one. And besides, I'm not a barbarian."

"Of course not," Victor said dryly. "When you die, they're going to bury you with the saints in the Caves Monastery."

A spasm ripped through Kirilo's back. "Don't even mention that place to me. Back to my daughter."

"Isabella will be returned to you unharmed."

"How do I know you won't kill her after you get your money?"

"You have my word. A thief doesn't lie to another thief."

"I need proof that she is well."

"You have my word."

"I need proof."

"My word is good. You know that."

Kirilo grunted. It was true. Victor was a thief. Under the certain circumstances, he could become a killer. But he would never lie to another *vor.*

"Where is the Tesla woman?" Victor said. "Where do we stand?"

The impulse to strangle the bitch seized Kirilo again. He took a deep breath to calm himself before briefing Victor. He had no choice. Isabella's rant about her mother's pearls faded to a distant memory. He longed only to hold her in his arms again.

CHAPTER 40

KAREL'S WORDS RANG IN NADIA'S EARS. HE KNEW WHO SHE was. He knew her agenda.

Back against the wall, Nadia smiled. She wrapped her arms around Karel's waist and moved in for a kiss. His eyes widened with shock and confusion. When her lips came within an inch of his, she swung him around.

Nadia spun out of the corner. Karel fell into it. His back pressed against the wall. Hers pointed toward the exit. The dominant American woman was asserting herself in barroom foreplay. Nothing unusual. Wasn't the American woman always on top?

"Who are you?" Nadia said, hands around his neck.

"What?" Karel glanced around furtively to make sure no one was listening. He whispered. "I told you. I am Karel. I'm just a zoologist—"

Nadia gripped his Adam's apple with the first three fingers of her right hand, her body obscuring the act from everyone's view.

Karel tensed.

"I'm not asking you who you are," Nadia said. "I'm asking you, *who are you*? Who sent you? How do you know me?"

"Your uncle sent me. Damian sent me."

Nadia squeezed. "Why?"

Karel rose to his tiptoes. “Because he’s ill. He couldn’t come to the meet himself.”

“What meet? The meet here, at the bar?”

“No. The meet in Pripyat. At the Hotel Polissya. I got there early and saw the poacher. I knew the meeting was a bust. So I came here. For the party. I was planning to tell Damian later, and he would set up another meeting through the woman.”

“Woman? What woman?”

“The boy’s aunt. She speaks English. Seelick. Clementine Seelick.”

Nadia released her grip. Karel swallowed and massaged his throat. Nadia checked her watch. It was 10:33. She was three minutes late for her rendezvous with Hayder.

She studied Karel. Sweat beaded on his forehead.

“What is your relationship with my uncle?” she said.

He looked her in the eye and spat the words out with conviction. “He’s my friend.”

Nadia considered her options. “Where is Damian?”

“Damian is a squatter.”

“A squatter? What does that mean?”

“He lives illegally in an abandoned home.”

“Where?”

“Here. In the Zone. In Chernobyl village.”

“Can you take me to him?”

“Take you to him?” Karel’s jaw dropped. “Tonight?”

“Now,” Nadia said. She checked her watch. 10:36. She prayed Hayder was still waiting for her.

Karel shrank. “No…I don’t think that would be a good idea.”

“Why not?”

“Well…Damian is very ill. And…And he is not prepared for your arrival. It would be better to plan for another time.”

Nadia tapped him on the cheek three times. “I’m doing the planning. Once I leave, I’m not coming back to the Zone. It has to be tonight. How do we get there? On foot? Bicycle?”

He hesitated. "Motorbike."

"You have one?"

"Outside."

"Let's go."

They stopped at the table with the newlyweds to say good night.

"*Na dobranich*," Karel said. "The lightbulb went out in my dormitory room. Nadia Panya here insists there is an American way of screwing one in that will make it burn brighter and last longer."

The men moaned. The women shrieked.

Nadia threaded her arm through Karel's and smiled lasciviously.

"There will be electricity tonight," one of the men shouted as they left the café.

They found Hayder at the rendezvous point, crouching on the swath of asphalt farthest from the power station, near the edge of the forest through which they'd arrived. A rectangular container shaped like a dog carrier was strapped to the back of his bicycle. It was wrapped in black fabric. A handle protruded through the top.

Hayder stood up. "Who the fuck is he?"

"This is Karel. He's a zoologist. I'm staying the night with him."

Karel smiled good-naturedly at Hayder.

Hayder measured him and tilted his head at Nadia. "You cocksure about this?"

"Yes," Nadia said. "I'm sure about this."

Hayder grinned. "See? What did I tell to you? The Zone. It pulls you in, right?"

"Tell Anton I'm sorry. I'll call him as soon as I can. I'll need help getting out of here. But I'll understand if he can't help me. My staying here tonight—it wasn't part of the plan."

"To stay night in the Zone, you must have the balls like the Crimean Tatar warrior. Like the descendant of Genghis Khan himself. I have more respectability for you. But I borrowed the two bicycles. I must return the two bicycles. Someone will come looking for them at eleven o'clock sharp. If they're not there, someone will come looking for me. You know what I am meaning?"

Nadia retrieved her bicycle and followed Hayder to the point where they'd picked them up. Karel kept pace on a toy motorbike that looked like a Soviet-era Vespa. After dropping off the bike, Nadia climbed up behind Karel.

"I've seen that man before," Karel said as Hayder disappeared into the woods. "He is a scavenger. He steals from the Zone and sells to the world. A scavenger cannot be trusted."

"A friend of mine vouched for him."

"Then your friend cannot be trusted, either."

"What about my uncle?"

Karel paused. "There is no lying in a man who is dying."

"There's no time to waste. Take me to him."

Karel took a deep breath as though fortifying himself. "So be it. He lives in a black village, six miles away. There will be ditches, potholes, and graveyards. Hang on."

CHAPTER 41

"My name is Oksana Hauk. I am a Chernobyl survivor. My grandmother died fighting the Nazis in World War II, and my mother was cannibalized in the famine of 1933. Welcome to my home."

Nadia struggled to digest the enormity of the babushka's revelations while simultaneously crafting a similar greeting, in case doing otherwise was rude.

"My name is Nadia Tesla. I am an American. My father was an officer in the Ukrainian Partisan Army. He died in America. Thank you for having me."

Karel and Nadia crossed the threshold into the kitchen. Two lanterns lit the room.

Oksana Hauk was less than five feet tall, with the face of a pitted prune. She measured Nadia before she said, "You are from New York City. From downtown, yes?" Oksana pronounced the word in broken English, as though it were a city in and of itself, or a special destination whose meaning could not be translated.

Nadia looked at Karel, who smiled and shrugged as though he, too, was amused. Nadia laughed. "Yes, I am from New York City. But actually, I live uptown."

Oksana frowned and glanced at Karel. "I don't understand," she said softly.

Karel turned to Nadia. "She thinks downtown *is* New York City. You confused her."

"Ah," Nadia said, touching the babushka on the shoulder with her hand. "I'm so sorry. Yes, yes. You're right. Downtown. I come from downtown."

Oksana nodded and smiled with relief, as though her sense of geography had been restored.

"My mother received letters from a man claiming to be my uncle. My uncle Damian. Is he here?"

Oksana glanced down the narrow corridor past the kitchen. "Yes."

"May I see him?"

She made a sour face. "No, no. He is very sick. He is resting now. He is usually much better in the morning."

Nadia didn't hide her disappointment. "May I just take a peek? To see that he exists? I've come so far…It would mean so much to me just to see him."

"No," she said before brightening. "Sometimes he wakes up in the middle of the night. If that happens…Otherwise, in the morning."

"So close," Nadia said under her breath. She forced herself to smile. "I understand, I understand. In the morning."

The house was a crooked wooden shack with a thatch roof. A wood-burning brick oven heated the kitchen, which opened to a small dining area. An Orthodox crucifix hung on one wall, and a picture of a boy skating among men hung on another. Nadia looked closer. The boy looked younger, but Nadia recognized the dark skin, pinched eyes, and broad face. It was the boy in the picture her mother had received. The boy Damian wanted her to take home to America. Where was the boy?

Karel and Nadia sat at a beaten, bruised wooden table. Oksana lit a fire under a teakettle and prepared plates of food.

Nadia eyed her preparations with dread. "Where do they get their food?" she whispered.

"They grow it themselves," Karel said. "They have all the land they want, and it's very fertile."

"How can it be safe?"

"Radiation doesn't spread evenly. One lot may be cool, the one beside it hot. Avoid the mushrooms, the fruit, and the fish, and you'll be fine. Don't talk about it, and you'll be fine. But if you keep asking questions..."

"That's what people keep telling me. So, how did you come to be in Chernobyl, Karel? Were you born nearby?"

"More questions." Karel said, but he didn't seem to mind. "I was a college student conducting field studies here when the reactor exploded. I stayed to study animal behavior in the event of a nuclear catastrophe. Who can refuse the cutting edge?"

"Indeed," Nadia said.

"My head hurt, my mouth was dry, and I walked around like a drunk for a month. But I stayed—for science, for my country, and to get my research published. Now I live on one lung with a pulmonary disorder. I can't walk half a kilometer without fainting."

Nadia wondered what her life would be like if her father had never escaped to America and had ended up in Chernobyl. She cringed and thought of the boy. How could he have survived eating the local food? Hell, how could he have survived, period? What kept him going?

Karel pulled a small booklet out of his pocket. "Dosimetric passport. The Division of Nervous Pathologies in Kyiv keeps track of the radiation in my body. Another fifty rem on my passport and I will go from Level One Disabled to Level Three Sufferer. You must prove you are a sufferer or a prospective invalid of Chernobyl to get help from the State. And it is very difficult to do. Otherwise, we are like American capitalists now. You are on your own."

"Some people say the worst is to be healthy here," Oksana said, placing a ceramic pitcher of liquid beside the three plates of food on the table. She sat down. "They are used to the state taking care of them. Me, I just want to live in my home. I lived through World War II as a child. I'll take my chances against the silent enemy. Now, please eat, you two."

Nadia knew it was a Ukrainian custom for the host to offer her guest the best food in the house. The bread, cheese, hard-boiled eggs, and pickled vegetables on the plates were veritable delicacies in a black village of Chernobyl. To not sample them—let alone not gorge herself on them—would be a great insult. Yet the same food could kill her. What was she supposed to do?

"This is *kvass*," Oksana said, touching the pitcher. "You know *kvass*?"

"Yes, I've had *kvass*," Nadia said. It was a nonalcoholic cider made from fermented rye and herbs. Sweet, tasty, and in this case, quite possibly lethal. "But I'm more hungry than thirsty. I would love some of this bread. May I?"

"Take, take," Oksana said.

The center consisted of fresh rye, and the crust offered a tangy caraway kicker. It was as dense as five loaves of American bread condensed into one. It tasted, she recalled her father saying long ago, "like food one could happily live on."

"This is the best bread I've ever had," Nadia said.

Oksana beamed.

Karel stuffed his mouth with egg, bread, and pickled mushrooms. "Mmm," he said, winking at Nadia. "Delicious. You should try everything."

Nadia ignored him and asked Oksana, "Did you live in this house before the explosion?"

"I was born here. This was my mother's home, and my grandmother's before her. My husband was an electrician at the power station. When Unit Four exploded, he became a dosimetric scout. He walked along the rooftop of the reactor with a dosimeter to measure the radiation levels for the bio-robots who were cleaning up. To help guide them to the cooler spots as the wind changed. He died five years later. In 1991."

"Babushka is a famous figure in Chernobyl history," Karel said while chewing. "There is no record of her courage, but those who know her will never forget. Tell her, Babushka."

She dismissed him with a wave of her hand. "Eh. Who wants to hear about old people?"

"Tell her, Babushka."

"Please," Nadia said.

Oksana pursed her lips, sighed, and looked out a window. "They came from Kyiv on the fifth day. The government hired them. They were experienced hunters, the best the government could find. They came with orders to kill on sight. To exterminate. And when they got here, the shooting began right away."

Nadia sat up. "What? They shot people? I've never heard of this. They shot their own people?"

"No," Oksana said. "To many of us, it would have been better if they had shot people. Government people. No, the hunters didn't come for the people. They came for the pets."

Nadia processed the words. "The pets."

"The wind carried nuclear dust," Oksana said. "It was white like snow, but it wouldn't melt. The snow would not melt. It came in through the windows, the chimneys, under the doors, through tiny holes in the walls. It landed everywhere."

"Including fur," Nadia said.

"I would hear gunshots and then a woman wailing. Once, I saw a man with a bottle of vodka throw himself under a tank to try to kill himself because his dog was the only friend he had. Trucks overflowed with dead dogs and cats...They bulldozed them with the cows."

Karel placed his fork on his plate. "It had to be done. They were radioactive."

"One pair of hunters," Oksana said, "they were not well. They went into a home with a machete. They butchered the animals. It happened once. It happened twice." Her eyes smoldered. "When I finally heard about it, I invited them here for some vodka. While they were drinking, I stole their guns. I put a Kalashnikov to one of their heads and told them to leave Chernobyl or they would be buried with the animals. It did not happen a third time."

While the images flashed before Nadia, the table turned silent. Karel and Oksana bowed their heads. Nadia did the same.

"The best way to deal with people you want to get rid of is to invite them into your home first," Oksana said. "That way, if you need to, you can kill them and bury them in your root cellar, where the militia won't find them. Where no one will ever find them."

Nadia looked up at Oksana in shock. Lines sprang from the babushka's weathered face. Karel kept his head bowed. No one said anything.

A moan from beyond the kitchen. Karel and Oksana looked up.

A faded voice followed.

"Syanya."

Syanya. The nickname for Oksana.

"He's up," Oksana said. "He's calling for me. He heard us. He is probably hoping you are here. Let me see to him."

Karel resumed feasting.

Oksana returned a moment later. "Come. He wants to see you. He comes in and out quickly these days. So you won't have long to talk. The morning will still be better."

Nadia followed Oksana down the short hall and almost stepped on her heels from behind. The air smelled of liniment. Oksana stopped at the doorway and motioned with her arm for Nadia to go inside. The shadow of a lit candle flickered on the door. Nadia hesitated.

"Please. There is no reason to be scared. You are with your uncle now. He is your family."

Nadia stepped inside. A man lay wrapped in blankets on a narrow bed. Judging by the length of the bed, he was just a little over five feet tall. His cheeks were sunken and his skin discolored yellow. Red burn marks covered his face. This was the notorious Damian? This was the legendary thief? She felt a pang of disappointment. He looked more like a friendly farmer who'd fallen ill.

A portable Walkman cassette player from a prior century rested on a nightstand. A scratched and smeared cassette box lay beside it: the greatest hits of Petula Clark.

Damian's parched lips spread into a smile. He curled his right index finger for her to come forward.

Without warning, a fit of coughing seized him. He wheezed and convulsed violently on the bed. Nadia wondered if she should call for Oksana but doubted there was anything the babushka could do.

The spasms slowly subsided. He inhaled through his nose and exhaled through his mouth three times to normalize his breathing. Motioned for Nadia to come closer. Nadia wished she felt a connection of some kind, but she didn't. She was just a stranger in the house of an old man who happened to be her uncle.

She pressed her ear closer to his lips.

"Did a man give you a message in New York City?"

Nadia pulled back. How could he know about that?

"Did you send him?" she said.

He nodded. "What was the message?"

She pressed her lips close to his ears. "He said, in English, 'Find Damian. Find Andrew Steen. They all…Millions of dollars. Fate of the free world.'"

She pulled back again and waited for a reaction. His lips parted slowly. He said something, but Nadia couldn't decipher the words.

"I'm sorry," she said. "I can't understand you."

He took three more deep breaths. She leaned in to his ear again.

"Five-androstenediol," he said.

"Excuse me?"

"Five-androstenediol."

His eyes closed, and his head rolled to its side on the pillow. He passed out.

Nadia staggered to the door. Glanced back at Damian. His chest filled and contracted slowly.

She'd heard the man wrong on Seventh Street. He hadn't said, "Find." There was no Andrew Steen. And he hadn't said, "They all."

Find Damian.

Five-androstenediol.

Millions of dollars.

Fate of the free world.

CHAPTER 42

"It's one forty, and I don't want to arouse suspicion," Karel said after they snuck into his laboratory at the Chernobyl Power Station through a rear entrance. "So I'm not going to turn the overhead lights on."

He grabbed a bottle of spring water from a portable refrigerator and handed it to Nadia. "Eat a bag of these mixed nuts, too," he said, offering her a sealed plastic bag. "They're from Kyiv. Grown in eastern Ukraine. I know you're a bit paranoid about food at this moment. It's to be expected. Eat, drink, while I prepare these slides for you."

The lab smelled of formaldehyde. Nadia moved a stack of journals and books off a folding metal chair, sat down, and inhaled the nuts. Her eyes had grown accustomed to the dark during the ride back to the power station from Oksana's home. A green lamp cast a faint circle of light around Karel's desk.

Images appeared in charcoal gray beyond the desk. A dozen mice squeaked in individual cages arranged on portable shelves. A chart of the anatomy of a wolf hung on one wall. A poster illustrating the effects of radiation on a wild boar hung on another. In the center of the room, a rectangular table held an array of tools, dishes, and vials.

An hour ago, when Nadia had emerged from Damian's bedroom, she pulled Karel away from Oksana and asked him if he'd heard of a substance called 5-androstenediol. He stared at her for a moment with a blank expression and burst into action. He told her they were taking a trip on his motorbike. It would be easier to explain at his laboratory. In the event of unforeseen circumstances, he urged her to forget Damian had ever uttered that term to her. If interrogated as to what she was doing in the Zone without proper papers, she would tell the police she was visiting the dying uncle she'd never known.

The only thing Nadia knew for certain was that she was going back to see Damian in the morning. Regardless of what Karel explained to her, she still had questions about her father, the boy, and Damian himself. And she had the distinct impression her uncle might not live long enough to answer them if she didn't hurry.

"Come take a look at these slides," Karel said, lifting his head from a high-powered microscope on the large table.

Nadia pressed her right eye to the lens. The picture resembled a scatter plot of pink circles on a white background. Some of the circles were darker, while others were lighter. More than a third of the picture, however, was white.

"That is the bone marrow of a primate that has been exposed to ionizing radiation," he said. "Ionizing radiation is radiation with energy high enough to change an atom or molecule. Like X-rays or a nuclear reaction. As opposed to non-ionizing radiation, which is low energy. It excites the atom or molecule but doesn't change its shape. Like radio or microwave. For our purposes, we are talking about ionizing radiation."

Nadia kept her eye pressed to the lens. "What do the pink circles represent?"

"Red blood cells," Karel said. "When a human being is exposed to radiation, the bone marrow is the most susceptible tissue, especially the stem cells that give rise to new blood cells."

"There's a lot of white here. Does that mean blood cells are not reproducing properly?"

"Correct. When stem cells die, blood counts drop. Two types of blood cells are especially crucial. The neutrophils, which fight infection and stimulate the immune system. And the platelets, which stimulate blood clots. When neutrophils and platelets drop, the risk of infection and hemorrhaging rises. At very high doses of radiation, the gastrointestinal and central nervous systems are also affected."

Nadia pulled away from the microscope and batted her eyelid to straighten her lash. "If the body is already infected and hemorrhaging..."

"Treatments like blood transfusions and fluid management are basically comfort measures. Death is certain. Now, take a look at this one."

Karel changed the slide in the microscope and stooped to adjust the focus. When he stepped aside, Nadia took his place and lowered her head.

A crash outside.

Nadia straightened herself. Glanced at Karel. He raised an index finger to his lips. They both looked at the front door, where the sound originated.

"Probably just a wild dog," Karel said, motioning for her to take a look.

Nadia peered into the microscope. "I see clusters of pink horseshoes filling most of the white background."

"Progenitors of neutrophils. New blood cells are being created despite exposure to radiation because the mouse was given an oral dose of five-androstenediol."

Nadia stood up from the microscope. "What?"

"Five-androstenediol is a steroid that occurs naturally in the human body. Its benefits as a radioprotectant were first discovered by your Armed Forces Radiobiology Research Institute in 1996. It's known as five-AED. Five-AED stimulates blood cell growth and improves survival rates. But it's not a true countermeasure. A true radiation countermeasure would have to do one of three things: prevent initial injury, repair all molecular damage, or stimulate surviving stem cells so aggressively that they counter the original injury."

Karel picked up a third slide. When he was done loading it, he stepped back. His eyes gleamed.

"Take a look at this," he said, swallowing the last word.

Nadia peered in. "The entire slide is pink," she said.

"Surviving cells have proliferated at an exponential pace. The five-AED has been modified. New enzymes have been introduced. Proteins have been added that result in the synergistic benefits of a true radiation countermeasure."

Nadia looked at Karel. "You?"

"No, no. I'm just a zoologist."

"Then who?"

"A biologist by the name of Arkady Shatan. He conducted the original experiments with wheat in the Caves Monastery to discover why the bodies of the saints did not decompose. It was he who discovered that they produced a protective field of radiation. After the explosion at Unit Four, he was sent to Clinic Number Six in Moscow, where the most serious work was done on radiation effects on humans."

"Is he here? Is his laboratory in Chernobyl?"

"He retired in 1997. He came back here to do his own research, though. Which is how we met in the café one day. Just as you and I met today—"

Fists pounded on the front door.

"Station Security," a man said. "I am armed. Open the door. Now."

"Quick, you must hide," Karel said. "You have no papers. They cannot find you here."

Nadia looked around. "Hide where?" Then a new idea came to her. "Open the door. I'll handle this."

Karel blanched. "What?"

"Trust me. Let him in."

Fists pounded on the door again.

In a panic, Karel gathered himself and opened the door.

A wiry young man in a camouflage uniform pointed his rifle at Karel and sneered. "Oh. It's you. What are you doing here so late?"

"Working. Why are you bothering me?"

The guard looked over Karel's shoulder toward Nadia and squinted in the darkness. "Who's that over there? Is someone else here?"

Nadia had yanked her shirt out of her pants. Unbuttoned it quickly and unzipped her pants. Swept the papers off Karel's desk with the outside of her arm and straddled the corner of the table.

"Who else is here?" the guard said. He pushed Karel aside with his rifle and marched into the light.

Nadia grasped the desk with both hands and thrust her shoulders back. She thought of Anton and channeled his memory into her facial expression.

The guard froze when he saw Nadia. His eyes drew a line from her head to her waist and back up again. His mouth fell open. He glanced at Karel, face twisted with jealousy and disbelief.

Karel managed a grin and shrugged.

The guard looked at Nadia again and shook his head. "Fucking scientists," he muttered as he headed back to the door. "No guests in the facilities after six o'clock. You know the rules. Make sure she's out of here within ten minutes. Ten minutes. That should be plenty for you, eh, old man?"

"I wouldn't be so sure about that," Karel said. "We scientists know the benefits of being deliberate and patient with our research."

After he left, Nadia dressed quickly. Karel looked interested, but her face told him it was for show only. They left via the rear path along the cooling ponds, circled back to the main road, and took off back toward the village. When he got to Oksana's house, Karel continued along a dirt road for another mile. He stopped beside a tree with a purple ribbon tied around it near a thick patch of evergreens.

Nadia crouched behind a large boulder. Her dosimeter chattered lightly. Karel put on a pair of long rubber gloves and walked thirty yards away from Nadia toward a stream. He tossed some brush to the side and revealed a circular container buried underground. Its top protruded four inches and had the circumference of a manhole cover. He pulled a chain of keys out of his pocket, found the right one, and unlocked the cover. Lifted it off the container and placed it to the side.

When he joined Nadia behind the boulder, he was out of breath. "Now we wait," he said.

"For what?"

"You'll see."

A minute passed. Nothing happened. Four more minutes passed. Nothing happened.

Nadia's knees ached. She stood up to stretch them.

A rustle among the evergreens. Karel grabbed her hand and yanked her back down.

A wolf emerged from the brush. Muscles flowed beneath its gray-and-black coat as it stalked around the container. It stuck its mouth inside the bin for a moment. Walked around the periphery of the container again and stopped. Turned toward Nadia and Karel. Its eyes glowed yellow-green in the dark.

The wolf's eyes met Nadia's. It pulled its pointed ears back in an aggressive posture but relaxed them just as quickly. It howled.

Five more wolves appeared. They looked inside the container also. When they found nothing, they followed the leader of the pack upstream.

"The wolf saw us," Nadia said. "But it didn't run."

"Only in the Zone," Karel said. "Let's go back to the house."

When they arrived at Oksana's home, she let them in and went to bed. Nadia and Karel sat in the small dining area.

Karel said, "The common explanation for the wolf not running is that humans are no longer present in the Zone. If you remove the hunter, you remove the fear. That is certainly true, but it's not the only reason."

"What was in that container?"

"It once contained a sample of modified five-AED. Notice there was a stream nearby. I wanted to see if animals would gravitate to the medicated water on sheer instinct. They did. Within two weeks of when I put it out, every local species was drinking out of that container."

"It looked empty."

"It is. But the wolves were waiting for more. They want to protect themselves from the next nuclear catastrophe."

"Animals sense things."

"Ever see a cat an hour before a storm? Maybe Reactor Four will blow again. Maybe it will be one of the other reactors. Or a terrorist. Or nuclear war. But it will happen. The wolves are telling us it will happen. But now there is a countermeasure."

"Are you telling me that modified five-AED cures existing radiation damage in a living organism?"

"The longer you wait after exposure, the more blood cells break down and the less effective it becomes. It's most effective when administered immediately after exposure. It has all the necessary attributes. Arkady said it is cheap and easy to make, has a long shelf life, and is easy to administer."

"Chemotherapy and radiation treatment will be changed forever. This formula will save lives."

"Or cost them," Karel said. "In 2004, the United States commissioned a test to determine what would happen to a city like Washington, DC, if a ten-kiloton nuclear device were detonated. The conclusion was that sixty thousand people would die from the explosion, but two hundred and fifty-five thousand would die from radiation poisoning. More than eighty percent of the deaths would be caused by radiation. In the hands of a single country, possession of this formula would be a tactical advantage."

"It could turn their enemies' nuclear weapons into conventional bombs."

"We cannot let the wrong man get his hands on this."

"Still," Nadia said. "You have to get this formula out there. There are people dying every day from treatments their bodies could handle if they had this drug. Why haven't you and Arkady published this yet?"

"We were waiting for you."

Nadia pulled back in surprise. "Me? Why me? Surely a scientist and a zoologist—"

"No," Karel said. "We cannot trust our government. We cannot trust our colleagues because they work for the government. But we can trust you. That is why your uncle sent your mother letters asking for your help. Your uncle told us you are a person of integrity."

"Oh, I don't know about that."

"You broke up a criminal enterprise in America."

"I had a lot of help."

"You are a mathematician skilled at problem solving. You are resourceful. You know people in America."

Nadia's vision went green. "Millions of dollars" was a gross understatement. "You have the formula? On you right now?"

Karel shook his head. "No. Arkady was an eccentric man. He shared his results with me but never the formula."

"He *was* an eccentric man? Past tense?"

"He died ten days ago from natural causes."

Nadia felt the air go out of her. "That's terrible. I'm so sorry. And the formula?"

Karel shook his head sadly. "He kept everything in his head. He put nothing on paper. He was notorious for it."

"What about his laboratory? Didn't he have a laboratory?"

"Yes. In Kyiv. I must confess, I searched it before I destroyed it. But there was nothing."

"You destroyed it? Why?"

"Because that was his wish. He wanted all trace of his work to die with him."

"But you must know the chemical compounds."

Karel shook his head firmly. "No. I only saw the product of his labor. Never the formula. I swear to you on my wife and child's graves that I am telling you the truth."

"The formula's lost?"

"Gone. You asked me what five-androstenediol is. You deserved an explanation. I have given it to you. But I'm afraid you are too late. The formula is gone forever."

CHAPTER 43

DAMIAN AWOKE AT 7:45 A.M. NADIA WAITED PATIENTLY AS Oksana made him tea and fed him stewed prunes. After she was done, Nadia went into his bedroom.

Damian didn't waste any time. "Karel says I have Chernobyl syndrome," he said, propped up and lucid. "That the structure of my brain is changing. I have fevers, rashes, and paralysis of the legs. The fevers come and go. I faint during the day for no reason. My brain is like a computer going bad."

"Why aren't you in a hospital?" Nadia said.

He smiled. "Hospitals are for citizens, not for ghosts. I don't exist. There's no record of me. No hospital in Ukraine would admit me. Besides, Karel brought a doctor from the power station who looks in on squatters from time to time. He told me I have two to three weeks to live. That was two weeks ago."

Saddened by this news, Nadia started to reach for his hand.

"No, no," he said, pulling it back. "It's not safe for you to touch me at this point. I'm too hot."

Nadia fidgeted, uncertain what to do. She had wanted this connection to her father, to the family she had never known, and now her nearest relative over here was at death's door. "It's okay," he said. "I'm at peace now that I know you'll take my son with you to America."

"What?" She had forgotten about that part. "Oh, no. That's not—"

But Damian was already off down memory lane. "I met his mother in the café eighteen years ago. She was for hire. They earn extra here in the Zone, where a woman never knows if a man is infected with a lot more than a venereal disease. I paid. We danced. She fell in love. I did not pay again."

"I'm sure you charmed her."

His eyes bored into Nadia. "A true thief can make anyone his willing accomplice."

"What happened to her?"

"She was addicted to painkilling medication. And other drugs. She died of an overdose."

"Oh. I'm very sorry." Nadia returned to what they'd been talking about before. Ever since she had come to Ukraine, she had been followed by men who were trying to kill her. How could she bring a boy into that situation? "What is your son's name?"

"Adam."

"Where is he now? I ask, but please understand, there's no way—"

"He lives with a man who used to work in the shelter with me. He played on the Soviet Olympic Hockey Team in the 1970s. When he killed a man in a barroom brawl, he was given the choice of life in prison or fifteen years' labor in the shelter because of his status as a national hero of the old Soviet Republic. He chose the latter, and this is how we met."

She was relieved to hear that the boy lived somewhere else. She couldn't imagine a child growing up here. "That explains the hockey uniform."

"Eh?"

"The hockey uniform. In the picture you sent."

"Ah, yes. You saw the picture. Good, good. How is your mother?"

"She is well."

"And your father, he died."

"Yes. Did you know my father?" she asked hopefully.

"Of course."

"He told me about his time with the Partisans. It sounded so exciting, so noble."

Damian studied her for a moment, as though debating something internally, and shook his head. "I'm not going to lie to you."

"Lie to me? Lie to me about what?"

"Yes, your father joined the Ukrainian Partisan Army. After he moved to Lviv with your mother. But he was with me first."

"With you?"

"Yes."

"What does that mean, he was with you?"

"What do you think it means?"

Nadia felt like a building block of her past had been yanked loose. "I don't know." But of course, that was a lie. She knew exactly what he meant.

"Your father was one of my crew. One of the three that got away."

"What are you saying?"

"Your father was a thief, Nadia. You are a thief's daughter."

The walls closed in on Nadia. Her father wasn't who she'd thought he was. Whatever her issues with his parenting, however demanding, strict, and unrelenting he'd been, she had always respected him. He was a man of integrity. Maybe she didn't always like him, but she looked up to him. Now it turned out he'd been a thief, a criminal, and, by definition, a liar.

"Surely you've noticed that you have a certain resourcefulness. Who do you think you inherited that from?"

She was a thief's daughter, Nadia thought. It was in her genes. And all this time she had thought she was just clever.

Damian saw how shocked she was. "What does it matter? Let go of the past. Look to your future. Your father would want it that way. You are his legacy. My boy is my legacy. He is a good boy. You must take care of him."

They were returning to the big problem. "Uncle Damian, that's just not realistic."

"He has never been hugged," Damian said, ignoring her comment.

"What?"

"He has never been hugged. His mother never touched him after she gave birth. She had problems, and she wasn't the mothering type. Oksana takes care of me for the money. As for the coach and me…Men don't hug their sons." Damian nodded confidently. "You will hug him."

Nadia shook her head as she searched for the right words to tell him that just wasn't realistic.

"There are the hockey games, of course," Damian said. "But they don't count."

"Excuse me?"

"The hockey games. Hockey is the main sport in Pripyat. There is a winter league for all the workers in the Zone. Coach brings my son to the games. He is the best player in the league. He is a defensemen. Defensemen usually don't score many goals. But when he scored his first goal, at age thirteen, he got hugs from his teammates. They do that in hockey. So he started scoring more goals. Lots and lots of goals. But now that won't matter so much. Because you are a woman. And you will give him proper hugs."

Nadia needed to stop this fantasy before it went any further. "Uncle, I'm sorry. It's just not possible." Rather than discuss the dangers with a dying father, she tried to point out, "He doesn't even speak English…How would he manage in America?"

"Once you sell the formula, you can use the money to help him build a life."

"Excuse me?"

"The formula. Karel told me he took you to his laboratory."

"And he told me Arkady never gave him the formula."

"He didn't. He gave it to me instead."

"He what? He gave *you* the formula?"

"Yes."

"Why you?"

"Because he trusted me."

"Why?"

"Because I made him my willing accomplice."

The gears in her head started to whirl. "Where is it? Is it here? Is it written down or stored on an electronic device? You must have several copies."

"Arkady was an old Soviet scientist—he wrote it on a piece of paper and reduced it to a strip of microfilm. Then he burned the paper."

"You mean there's only one copy?"

"Yes. There is one, and only one, copy."

Nadia nodded and let a few seconds pass. "Where is the microfilm?"

"In a locket. On a necklace. Around my son's neck."

Nadia straightened to her full height. The calculations weren't hard to make. Hell, for the money this kind of trade secret would bring, she could buy her way out of trouble. She could hire an English language instructor and tutors and send him to private schools.

"Don't share any of this with Oksana," Damian said. "She takes care of me because she thinks there are ten million American dollars buried in the house somewhere."

"The money you stole fifty years ago from the Soviet *apparatchik*?"

"How did you hear about that?"

"From a thief named Victor Bodnar."

He cracked a wistful smile. "Victor Bodnar. The pickpocket lives."

"Whatever happened to that money?"

"The KGB found it. After they tortured and killed three of my men."

"I heard about that, too."

"I have no money. What little I had I gave to Oksana for her to take care of me." The creases in his face deepened. "Wait a minute. Are you in debt to Victor Bodnar?"

"He thinks so," she said. "So does one of his associates. A young *avtoritet* originally from Moscow. And now there is another man from Kyiv with them. Older, distinguished."

"These men are following you?"

"Yes."

He paused and stared at Nadia. "This is not good. This was not part of my plan. If one of the men is from Kyiv, he must be both thief and government. They are one and the same. They have all the country's resources to find you. You should assume they are close."

"Oh, I don't think so—"

"You will never get through customs if you try to leave Ukraine the way you came in. The man from Kyiv must have people waiting for you at the airport." He seemed to make a decision. "I will get a message to my son that the time has come. He will meet you in Kyiv tonight."

"You can't be serious. Then what?"

"The formula must get to America. You will figure out how to sell it once you are there. You will sell it to men of science. Not to your government. Promise me that."

"Uncle, the American government and the Ukrainian government are not the same—"

"Promise."

"Okay, I promise not to give the formula to the government."

"Good." A cunning look came into his eyes. "The only way you will escape the men who are following you is by going where they will be least expecting you to go."

"And where's that?"

"Along the route I arranged for my son once I gave up hope you would come. Before, I didn't know how he would sell the formula once he got to America, but now that won't be a problem. Now there will be two of you, and you will help each other."

Nadia didn't want them to get ahead of themselves. "Tell me more about this route you've planned."

"My son knows everything you need to know."

"Look, if I'm going to be taking care of him, I think I deserve to know details."

The old thief shrugged. "My son has all the details."

"Can you at least give me a general outline?"

He stared at her with a blank expression.

Nadia sighed. "Okay. I get it. Where and when do I meet him?"

"He is coming from the north. There is a metro stop at Dorohozhychi. He will meet you across the street. At the new bronze statue at Babi Yar."

"When?"

"Six o'clock. And now I have a question for you. The stranger who delivered my message to you in New York City. What happened to him?"

Nadia told him the story.

"Was he a friend of yours?" she said.

"Yuri Banya. He was one of my men. One of the three who escaped to the West before the KGB caught the rest of us. He pretended to be this Max Milan, an upstanding member of the community, to make sure you met with him. He was supposed to send me a message after he met you, but I never heard from him. You say he was shot, but later, when the police went to look, there was no body?"

"And he still had a pulse when I left him. Did you tell him about the formula?"

"No. He only knew words. But if someone interrogated him—"

"Find Damian. Five-androstenediol. Fate of the free world."

"Or had heard them already and didn't want you to hear them," Damian said.

"What if Yuri shared the message with someone else? Someone who realized what 'five-androstenediol' and 'fate of the free world' implied?"

Damian's expression tightened. "Three things are certain. Someone shot him, and someone lifted him off the street. And someone has yet to reveal himself to you."

Nadia let his words sink in. *Someone has yet to reveal himself.*

"I'm fading," Damian said abruptly, his eyes drooping. "I can feel it. You should go. Karel will help get you out of the Zone."

Nadia looked at his emaciated frame. They'd had so little time to spend together. "How do I say good-bye to an uncle I just met and will never see again?"

"You don't. Just take care of my boy."

It was a surreal moment. She'd solved the mystery of Damian, discovered he was her uncle, and traveled across the globe to find him. Now here he was, on his deathbed.

She would never see him again. She should have felt an overwhelming sadness, but she didn't. How could she? She'd just met him. Still, she had to do something. She couldn't just walk away.

Nadia stepped sideways to the foot of his bed. His legs were covered in blankets. She gently grasped the meat of his left foot over the blanket, squeezed with both hands, and held it for a count of ten. A sigh of relief escaped his lips. Nadia slid her hands up to his toes and did the same. His eyes closed. After the second ten-count, she lowered the left leg to the bed and performed the same routine on his right one. The pain in his expression evaporated. When she was done, she stepped away from the bed and let her hands fall to her sides.

"So you can dance with the angels," she said. The words sounded ridiculous as soon as they left her lips. He was a thief, a notorious criminal. If there was an afterlife, odds were low he'd be waltzing with celestials.

He laughed so hard he winced. Although he didn't say anything, the pain in his face melted into an expression of gratitude.

She lowered her head and started for the door.

"Nadia?" he said, gravel in his voice.

She turned.

"One more thing."

"Yes?"

His eyes opened to weary slits. "Remember what the hare said to the hen when he opened the barn door."

She raised her eyebrows. "What's that?"

"With foxes, we must play the fox."

CHAPTER 44

KIRILO, MISHA, AND VICTOR SAT AT A TRIANGULAR TABLE IN the middle of Kozak Egoiste. The air smelled of spices and flesh. A young waiter served their entrées. Blood oozed from Kirilo's steak as he set it before him. The tall, golden-haired waiter looked vaguely familiar to Kirilo, but he couldn't place him.

Kirilo tore a bite out of his *kovbanos*, a thin kielbasa served as a cold appetizer. It was tough, narrow, and veined, like Victor the Bitch's neck across the table from him. Soon he would have his hands around it, and this time he would not let go. He could feel his fingers crushing his cousin's airway, see Victor's final breath—

He cursed himself. Isabella was close. She had to be near. He had to get her back first. Nothing else mattered. He'd scoured Kyiv through all his contacts, but no one knew where Victor was keeping her.

After an hour of prodding with no further revelations, Lalo the Cook proved to be speaking the truth. He didn't know why Victor had chosen his restaurant. But there was a reason, Kirilo was sure. Before lunch was over, he was certain, he'd find out one way or another. As a result, he'd brought maximum security.

Two of Kirilo's men guarded the front door, two secured the rear. Four other men watched Lalo and the other cooks in the kitchen. Four more sat at the bar, watching the dining room. Misha had also brought four men with him. Two sat at the bar, including the impressive American, Specter, while the others guarded the front and rear entrances with Kirilo's men. How was Victor planning to kill Misha with sixteen men watching?

The waiter served Victor a bowl of borscht with mushroom dumplings, and Misha a plate of stuffed cabbage with pickles on the side. Victor looked inscrutable and the *moscal* aloof as always.

They dug into their food. Kirilo sliced a tiny piece of steak and stuck it in his mouth. He checked his watch for the fifth time in the last ten minutes. It was 1:47. How long would it take these bastards to finish? Would they insist on coffee and dessert? Where was Isabella? Where was she right now?

Victor slurped his stew. Misha crunched away. Kirilo nibbled on his steak to stay busy and keep his knife occupied, lest he stab Victor in the left eye out of frustration. Victor and Misha ate their entire entrées without saying a word.

"So," Misha said to Victor when he was done. "You came to Kyiv and you called this lunch. What's your agenda?"

Victor shrugged as though it were obvious. "Nadia Tesla." He looked from Misha to Kirilo and back to Misha. "So where do we stand?"

Misha gave him a summary of how they had lost Nadia in the Pecherska Lavra and her subsequent discovery of the GPS device.

"Outsmarted by a woman?" Victor said, with a twinkle in his eye.

Misha laughed the way a man did to hide his fury. "Hey, it's not *my* country." He turned to Kirilo.

"There's been a development," Kirilo said. "We found the owner of the taxi company. The one the driver works for. The driver that helped her."

Misha stopped noshing on another pickle and blinked at Kirilo. "You didn't tell me that."

Kirilo glared at him. "I'm telling you now. Two of my men just had a conversation with the owner before I got here. The driver's name is Anton Medved. He's a professor of sociology at Kyiv-Slavonic. Lives in Chorna Hora. He wasn't home, but two of my men are waiting for him at his apartment as we speak."

"And the ten million dollars?" Victor said.

Kirilo shook his head. "There is no ten million dollars. The KGB caught them and took it back. I have pictures to prove it."

"Pictures?" Victor said.

"A woman took them from her hiding place. The day the KGB came. It's a long story."

"No matter," Misha said, reaching for another pickle. "A guy gets shot on the street in New York after whispering something in the Tesla woman's ear. She comes to Kyiv and gives us the slip. Whatever she's after is valuable. I can smell it."

Kirilo grunted his agreement. Were they done? Could he ask for the check? He waved to a waiter.

"About that man who was shot on the street in New York," Victor said. "Someone shot him. Someone took him away. So presumably, someone else knows she's pursuing something valuable."

"Yeah. And?" Misha said, between bites.

"I was just wondering if you'd run into anyone else looking for the same thing you are. If anyone else is following Nadia Tesla."

Misha shook his head. He looked at Kirilo, who did the same.

The waiter arrived with a vase filled with tulips in his left hand. "Coffee? Tea? Dessert?" he said.

"No," Kirilo said, before anyone else could answer. "Check, please."

The waiter pulled a black folio out of his apron pocket with his right hand and slid it beside Kirilo. He placed the vase in the middle of the table and left.

Kirilo glanced at the bill. He tried to check every line to make sure they weren't padding it, but he couldn't concentrate.

Instead, he threw his Visa card in the folio and shut it, vaguely aware that Misha was raising his voice to Victor.

"You made us come to this shithole because you wanted an update on the Tesla woman? That's it? That's all you wanted?"

Kirilo noticed the tulips the waiter had left. They were yellow. In Ukraine, yellow flowers mean separation.

"No," Victor said. "I admit it. That's not all I wanted. I had another agenda."

Misha glared at him. "Yeah, well, what is it?"

Kirilo counted the flowers. There were ten of them. Ten. An even number. An even number of flowers was given only at funerals.

Someone was about to die.

"I came to say good-bye to you," Victor said.

"Oh yeah?" Misha said. "You leaving the country?"

Kirilo pushed his seat away from the table. Stuck his right foot out in case he needed to run.

"No, Misha," Victor said. "You're leaving this world."

Misha darkened before his shit-eating grin reasserted itself. His laugh echoed with uncertainty. "Oh yeah? Where am I going, Old School?"

"To the afterlife." Victor put his elbows on the table and folded his hands under his chin. "How were the pickles, Misha?"

Misha stopped chewing.

"A friend of mine knows a woman who grows them in a black village outside Chernobyl. Was the finish a bit salty? Did you detect the aftertaste of cesium-137?"

Misha's lips parted in shock. A few seconds later, they slowly spread into a smile. He shook his index finger at Victor. "You had me for a second, there, Old School. You had me real good. It would be just like you to pretend to poison me to get me thinking about it. To get me to die from the stress. Well, I hate to disappoint you, but it's not gonna work on Misha."

Victor pursed his lips and nodded, like a doctor who was used to his patients' disbelief. "The sugar she adds to the pickles acts as a delivery device. It propels the cesium into your bloodstream quickly." He picked up a saltshaker. "If you dilute this with water and force yourself to throw up before you've digested all of them, you might live ten days instead of five, like the last two people who ate them."

Misha grinned and stared at Victor, head bobbing up and down in mock agreement. Victor stared back. Five seconds passed, and then five more—

Misha grabbed the saltshaker. Unscrewed the cap. Dumped half its contents into his water. Stirred with his finger and drank.

Five seconds later, he vomited on the floor.

While Misha hacked and spit, the waiter returned with Kirilo's credit card bill. In the background, another waiter wheeled out a dessert tray toward the bar where the bodyguards sat.

Kirilo signed the bill, threw the pen on the table, and leaned over.

"Are we done here?" he whispered to Victor.

"Yes," Victor said.

"I want my daughter now. Where is she?"

"In a better place than Misha."

CHAPTER 45

NADIA HELD ON TO KAREL'S HIPS AS HE GUIDED HIS MOTORbike toward the center of Chernobyl. Despite the urgency of the situation, she couldn't stop thinking about Damian's revelation that her father had lied about his past. He was a thief, not a war hero. The freedom-fighter image she'd romanticized was just a figment of her imagination.

Much to Nadia's surprise, however, it didn't bother her. Her mother was right. Her father had moved to America. He gave her citizenship and set an example by working tirelessly collecting garbage for the City of Hartford. He took his family to church almost every Sunday and did his best to be a family man, even if it was clear it gave him no joy. So what if he had a past? So what if he wasn't a doting father? He hadn't been part of the stolen-art and antiquities ring she'd uncovered in Hartford. Wasn't that evidence he'd changed?

Not only did Damian's revelation about her father not disturb her, his proclamation that she was a thief's daughter felt strangely empowering. Perhaps if her father hadn't changed and become a better man, her new identity would have bothered her. Instead, much to her own surprise, Nadia hung on to Karel loosely, comfortable in the moment, more confident she could outwit any adversary who tried to prevent her from getting to New York with the formula.

It was only 2:15, but the sky looked like dusk. Purple clouds swirled overhead. A squall had given way to a steady rain. Karel skidded and slid along the path from Oksana's house, kicking mud onto their pant legs, his headlight barely illuminating the way. When they emerged on the main road, Nadia pulled a hand away from his waist to wipe rain from her eyes.

A clap of thunder erupted. The gate to the power station lifted. A truck passed through. Seven others waited in a queue to enter. A guard studied a driver's papers beneath the hood of a poncho pulled down low. Derricks and cranes working on the shelter grumbled and groaned above the din of the bike's engine and the relentless patter of rain.

Karel circled to the edge of forest at the far side of the station. He sliced through another muddy path toward the thicket of trees from which Nadia had emerged last night. Halfway down, one of the trees seemed to step forward into their path. Nadia shook the rain out of her eyes and looked again.

It was Hayder. He held the same covered carrier in his right hand.

Karel pulled up twenty feet away from him, as though he wanted privacy. Nadia climbed off the bike. Her hiking shoes sank in the mud.

"We will probably see each other again someday, yes?" he said.

Nadia hesitated. "Yes," she said, smiling once she realized what he needed to hear. "I'm sure we will."

"You are a poor liar, but thank you for trying." He squinted. "Is there something you can share with a humble zoologist before you leave?"

"Such as?"

"You had a glint in your eye when you came out of Damian's bedroom this morning."

"I did?"

"Yes. You did. What did he tell you?"

"It was a family matter."

Karel arched an eyebrow. "A family matter?" He revved the engine. "Come, now. You can tell me. He has the formula, doesn't he? Did he give it to you? Are you taking it with you to the West?"

Nadia smiled. "Karel, I can tell you with one hundred percent honesty that I have only one formula in my possession. It's the one I was born with, for getting into constant trouble."

He studied her. "You have this talent for lying yet telling the truth at the same time. Somehow, it makes all your lies even more beguiling."

"I have to go. I couldn't have made it through the night without you. Thank you, Karel. Thank you so much."

Nadia kissed him three times on the cheeks.

Karel nodded. "It was animal attraction from the beginning for you, too, wasn't it?"

"Oh, yes." She puckered her lips and blew him a kiss without her hands.

"Good-bye, Nadia Panya."

Karel took off. Nadia sloshed down the path toward Hayder. She hadn't given Anton much lead time. She'd called two hours ago asking for help. Hayder wasn't pleased to have dropped everything to come get her out of the Zone. He looked like a king cobra ready to strike.

"This is what's wrong with your fucking country," he said, shaking his index finger when she was within earshot. "You think the whole world revolutions around you."

Nadia stopped in her tracks, rainwater trickling down her nose. The bicycles rested on a clearing beside him.

"Excuse me?" she said.

"You couldn't call Anton earlier to make the arrangements? You couldn't call earlier this morning?"

"I know. I'm sorry. I was indisposed."

"In what?"

"Indisposed. Busy—"

"You couldn't wait for the storm to pass? You couldn't get laid low for a while?"

"No. I'm sorry. I need to leave now. It's important—"

"What's so important? What? It's urgent, Anton. Come get me. It is the matter of life and the death, Anton. Whose life and death? Yours? What makes you so special?"

"I know. It was inconsiderate. I apologize, Hayder. I'm in your debt."

"Yurdet? What is this place? I am not familiar with it."

"Your debt. I owe you."

"Damn right you owe me." He nodded at the carrier in his right hand. "Lucky for you, I transplant my business to an earlier time. Lucky for you, my business people are stand-up. Like your Martin Luther King and Chuck Norris. Not many stand-up Americans, but there's two of them. Okay, we go now."

Hayder strapped his carrier to the back of a bicycle and climbed aboard. Nadia followed him. The dense canopy of trees provided some relief from the rain. Traction was better than during the trip from Oksana's house. When they arrived at the fifteen-kilometer fence, a truck was waiting for them on the opposite side. The driver, however, was not Volodya.

Hayder stepped off his bike. Nadia followed his lead.

"Stay here," he said with a cautious edge. "I don't know this guy. It is not the same truck. Volodya drove me here. Volodya should be here. I go, check it out, be right back. You watch my box for me, okay?"

"Okay," Nadia said.

Hayder pulled the wire fence open and slipped through it. The driver rolled down the window, but Hayder motioned for him to step outside. At first, the driver refused, but Hayder insisted. A hairy brute donned a baseball cap that matched his camouflage uniform and stepped out of the vehicle. They began to speak in earnest, the woolly mammoth and the cobra.

Nadia's eyes fell to Hayder's crate. What was inside? Last night she had assumed it was the tranquilized lynx, headed to a private zoo or, heaven forbid, a taxidermist. Was it another exotic animal? A different species of wild cat? Growing up, Nadia loved wild cats. The cougar and the cheetah were her favorites. Whatever was inside wasn't moving. What was the harm in taking a peek?

Nadia glanced at Hayder. He was still in the middle of an animated conversation. She looked down at the crate. Saw the hinges on one side and the small clasp below it. Flicked the clasp and lifted the top before she could change her mind.

The three sides of the crate were reinforced with steel, as was the cover. A large metal object lay inside. It had a six-inch diameter. It looked like a motor of some kind. Beside it were two metal rods. Rigid steel dividers kept all three items from touching each other.

Nadia closed the box and secured the clasp. She looked up.

Hayder was running toward her through the rain, left arm extended, gun pointed at her face.

"What the fuck are you doing?" he said, bug-eyed with disbelief.

"I heard a noise inside the cage. I thought it was an animal. I thought it was hurt."

A maniacal laugh escaped his lips. "An animal? What kind of crock are you shitting here?"

"You took a lynx out yesterday, didn't you? When I went to Pripyat last night, a poacher tranquilized a lynx in the Hotel Polissya. I just assumed that's what you took out...and when I saw you with the same carrier...I thought I heard a noise. I swear."

"Lynx? What lynx?" Hayder blinked hard twice, as though processing her words. His eyes widened with supposed recognition. "Mother of God. You are not here on the personal family business, like you tell Anton. You are here to hurt my business. You hunt scavengers, don't you?"

"What? Hayder, no—"

Twin bolts of lightning cracked the sky. A clap of thunder erupted.

Hayder pressed the gun to her forehead. "Who sent you, bitch? Did the American government send you? Did the CIA? What is your real business here?"

"Hayder, please. You're being paranoid. I'm sorry I opened your case. I didn't mean any harm. I am not here to mess with your business. I'm exactly who I say I am."

"No. No, you're not. You're the American. You're the liar. And now you're dead."

"Hayder, stop."

The voice came from the direction of the fence. The voice was familiar. Nadia strained to peer over Hayder's shoulder.

It was Anton. He slipped through the fence and bounded up to Hayder. Radek's van was parked behind the truck.

"Hayder," he said. "Put the gun down. What are you doing?"

"She opens my box, man. She opens my box. Why did she do that?"

"Calm down."

"She's the government, man. She's the CIA. She's here to shut me down."

"Hayder. She's not government. She's an American tourist. I picked her up at the airport in my cab. America couldn't care less about the Zone. They don't even know what the Zone is. To them, it's a type of defense played by basketball teams."

"What?"

Anton made soothing noises as though quieting an infant. He reached out and gently lowered Hayder's arm. The gun fell to his side.

Anton glanced at Nadia. The bags beneath his eyes looked inflated with air, the stubble on his beard no longer stylish but in desperate need of a shave.

"Anton," Nadia said, bouncing on her tiptoes.

He stepped past Hayder, smiled, and hugged her. Nadia buried her head in a nook between his chest and his shoulder. He smelled of mango, nicotine, and musk. It was the most pleasant place to spend a moment, a month, a year, or longer.

"You okay?" he said, holding her face in both hands.

"Yeah. Sorry for all this. And for calling on the spur of the moment. It's been crazy—"

He put his index finger on her lip and shushed her. "Let's talk about it in the van." Anton twisted his body so he could see Hayder, too. "I'll pay the man. You get in the van."

Hayder shook his head. "I am not sure about her."

"We have to get out of here. We can talk about it in the van. Agreed?"

Hayder glanced at Nadia, bit his lower lip, and nodded reluctantly. He thrust his gun beneath his forest-green rain jacket and under his belt.

He sat in the back of the van with his crate beside him. Nadia had no choice but to sit directly in front of him. She imagined his gun pressed to her back from the moment her butt kissed the tattered and torn vinyl. Anton paid the woolly mammoth for his troubles. After the truck disappeared, he turned the van around and started toward the thirty-kilometer fence.

"When we get out of the Zone," Anton said, "I'm going to drop Hayder off first. Then you can tell me what's next for you."

"That sounds good," Nadia said. "Thank you for coming to get me. I think the reality is…I think the reality is, I'll be going back to America shortly."

Her words must have been comprehensible in Russian, because Hayder cackled in the backseat. "Yeah, go back to America," he said. "Go back where you belong. The American dream is dead. You think you are better than the Russians and Chinese. You used to be. But you aren't anymore. You used to care about others. Now you care only about your oil. The world used to love you. Now the world hates you. Yeah, you go back to

America and have the good time. The American dream is over. You hear me? It is over."

They slipped through the hole in the second fence and drove to Kyiv without talking.

At 3:45, Anton stopped at the first metro station on the outskirts of Kyiv, called Petrivka. He stepped out of the van with Hayder and had a brief conversation with him before climbing back in.

"We go for a quick bite?" Anton said. "You must be hungry. You have time?"

"Hungry and thirsty," Nadia said, "and yes, I have time."

Anton drove back on the highway.

"So, what was that all about?" Nadia said.

"What, the talk with Hayder? I was smoothing things over with him."

"No. Not the talk. The crate and what's in it. What's he stealing from the Zone, Anton?"

Anton shook his head. "I have a policy. It's best not to ask questions about other people's business."

"That's not true. When you picked me up at the airport, you started asking me questions about my business as soon as I sat down. Remember?"

Anton didn't answer her.

"What's in the case, Anton?"

He licked his lips and remained mute.

"What's in the case?"

He sighed. "Spare parts."

"Spare parts?"

"Spare parts from automobiles, ambulances, and bulldozers. In this case, a starter."

"A starter?"

"Yes, yes, a starter. From an ambulance. A starter is a motor. A battery supplies electricity to the starter. The starter gives power to the engine."

Nadia remembered the vehicular burial ground on the way to Pripyat. "You mean from a radioactive ambulance? That starter is hot?"

"Yes, from an ambulance from the Zone. It may or may not be hot. Who knows?"

"Anton…"

"Okay, yes. It's probably hot. And it will find its way into an ambulance in Kyiv someday. All the vehicles in the Zone have been stripped. Anything of value can be sold."

"What about the two rods?"

"What rods?" Anton said.

"There were two rods, about six inches long and an inch in diameter—sorry, about fifteen centimeters long by three centimeters in diameter."

Anton mumbled something under his breath in Russian.

"What's wrong?" Nadia said. "Your partner holding out on you?"

"Partner? What partner? Who, me?"

"You have a nice apartment. With a beautifully equipped kitchen. Even if you supplement your income by driving a cab…Oh. Wait. What was it you said to me when we first met? Ukrainian salary. It's hell."

A moment of silence passed between them.

"Okay," Anton said. "Hayder is a scavenger. And I am his driver. I help with logistics. A good starter on the open market, it's worth three hundred US dollars. Three hundred US. You have to live here to understand how much money that is and how hard it is to make it."

"But you're helping put radioactive parts in vehicles in Kyiv. Some mechanic is going to touch that with his bare hands."

"Well, then that's his bad luck. Water overflows from the cooling ponds, seeps into the streams, and empties into the Dnipro. I drink that water every day. This isn't America. This is Ukraine. You have no idea how good you have it. Here, life is hard, then you die."

They drove for a while without saying anything more. The rain subsided. White clouds chased each other across the sky. The sun peeked between them.

"After we eat, I'll be leaving," Nadia said. "Tonight."

He nodded. "I understand."

He took an exit and merged onto a main thoroughfare. Nadia didn't recognize the street, but a sign said NOVOKOSTANTINIVSKA STREET.

"I meant to ask you," Nadia said. "Why did you drive the van through the fence in Chernobyl? I thought all cars that are in the Zone stay in the Zone."

"They do."

"But now the van is hot, isn't it? I mean, at least its tires are."

"Yup. I have to have them stripped, burned, and replaced tonight before I give it back to Radek." Anton took a sharp left. "But it was worth it."

"That's sweet. Thank you. Thank you for caring."

"That's not what I meant."

He smiled, turned right, and mashed the gas pedal. The Volkswagen hesitated before surging forward. Nadia's head snapped back against her headrest. In front of them rose a dilapidated gray warehouse on an abandoned lot. A pair of doors swung open sideways, as they would on a barn.

The van hurtled into the building. The brakes screeched.

Nadia lurched forward until the seat belt strangled her. She fell back. The belt loosened and slid back down around her chest.

A black Audi and two black SUVs were parked in front of them. One of the SUVs was a Porsche Cayenne. Nadia didn't recognize the six men lollygagging in front of the SUVs, but she'd seen the other three before. Victor, Misha, and the distinguished-looking man she'd evaded in the Caves Monastery were waiting for her.

"What I meant," Anton said, "is that you're worth more alive than you are dead."

CHAPTER 46

THE HOCKEY COACH MIGHT KILL HIM.

He might have to kill the coach first.

Adam's folding knife bounced around his warm-up pants pocket as he ripped through a set of burpees:

Squat down, thrust the legs back, fall nose to the ground, and do a push-up; squat up, leap as high as possible, bringing knees to chin, and land, prepared to squat down immediately into the next rep.

"You look anxious today, loser," the coach said. "Like something is weighing on your mind. Like you're planning a trip somewhere."

He stuck his face a few centimeters from Adam's head as he landed on the top block.

A whiff of raw garlic breath. Adam gagged.

"You planning a trip somewhere, loser? You think you're going somewhere without my knowing about it? Without my approval?"

Adam jumped down the blocks on his right foot and switched back to his left. The coach knew. The coach knew he was leaving. Either his father had told him or the fat bastard had figured it out himself.

The coach might kill him.

He might have to kill the coach first.

Adam resumed box jumps off his weighted left foot.

"Your report card came today," Coach said. "All 'outstandings,' except for one 'very good.' That is impressive for the son of a scumbag thief and an ugly whore from Alaska. For the product of a radioactive cesspool. When I was your age, my coach was Anatoly Tarasov. The father of Soviet hockey. He always said, 'Education is important. An educated hockey player is easier to coach.'"

Adam landed on the top block and turned. Sweat streamed down his cheeks. He hopped down to the middle and lower blocks and turned.

"Of course, in your case, education makes no difference. You'll still be the village idiot forever. Let me tell you where you're going. You're going nowhere. That's where you're going."

The coach cracked the whip in the air.

"Stop! Rest for ninety seconds. Lateral box jumps next!"

Ninety seconds later, Adam began jumping sideways from the ground to one box, back to the ground, and up to the next. Each jump was successively higher.

"In 1979, I played in the Challenge Cup in Madison Square Garden," Coach said. "NHL All-Stars versus Soviet National Team. We split the first two games, but we won the last game six to nothing. Yes. Of course we won."

Adam tried to focus on the height of his knees and ignore the story. He'd heard it only five hundred million times before. Hard as he tried to ignore the coach, though, he couldn't.

"New. York. City," Coach said, emphasizing each word as though it were the name of a woman he once loved. "New. York. City. The restaurants. Oak Room in the Plaza. Steak fit for a czar. The theater. Angela Lansbury. *Sweeney Todd.* The people. Black, white, yellow, millions of them walking up and down Broadway. I will never forget it. That is a place where I've been, loser, and you will never see. Pick up your feet!"

Adam jumped.

Coach cracked the whip on the ground below him. Missed his feet by a centimeter.

Adam's knees shot up and touched his chest.

"Chin music, loser. That is what I call chin music. Twenty seconds more!"

When time was up, Adam collapsed to the ground. The coach gave him two minutes' rest before moving into clapping push-ups. Adam clapped his hands twice during each exercise, performing three sets of fifty repetitions for a total of 150 clappers in four minutes.

He lay faint on the ground when he was done, lungs heaving, legs bent to keep the blood flowing to his face.

"Want to see another place you'll never go, loser?"

Adam glanced at the coach from an upside-down position.

The coach pointed to the top of the hill with his whip. "There will be sunbathing in Siberia before you ever see the summit of that hill, loser. No strength. No heart. No soul. Wrap the rubber band around your waist. Sprints in one minute. Prepare to fail the way you always do. Prepare yourself!"

Ten seconds later, Adam staggered to his feet and collected the rubber band. It was ten centimeters thick and fifty meters long. He wrapped one end around his waist and tied it into a knot.

He'd tied it loosely on purpose two years ago, when he'd decided he'd had enough of the fat bastard. When the coach gave it a yank, the band came loose and Adam kept running until he heard the gunshot. The coach always kept a handgun in his waistband. Adam didn't make it to the top of the hill that day, either, and had always tied the band properly from then on.

After tying the band around his waist, Adam stood at the starting line at the bottom of the hill. The coach tied the other end of the band around his own waist. Adam noticed the bulge on the coach's lower back where he always kept his gun.

The coach brought the whistle to his lips. Adam looked up at the hill. Something moved in his peripheral vision. A man stepped out from behind a Dumpster by the far side of the porcelain factory so that Adam could see him. Adam recognized the chaotic hair and scarecrow body of his father's friend Karel, the zoologist from the Zone.

Karel raised the second and third fingers of his right hand to form a V.

That was the signal. The signal they'd agreed on.

It was time.

Adam considered the coach's warning, that he was going nowhere, and the gun behind his back. He stuck his hand in his pocket and gripped his folding knife.

The coach blew the whistle.

Adam pulled his right hand out of his pocket, knife in fist, thrust it up in the air, and took off up the hill. After three swings with both arms to catapult himself forward, he unsheathed the knife. He tightened his fist around the handle and pumped his legs furiously. The horizon blurred.

Twenty meters. Thirty meters. Forty meters.

Adam hit the wall. The rubber band tightened. His steps shortened. Resistance increased. He stopped moving forward.

As soon as he felt the familiar tug, Adam turned and sprinted ten meters back down the hill. The hand with his knife swung by his side. He locked eyes with the man who'd fed and trained him for most of his life. The coach's eyes went to the blade and back to Adam. His lips parted with surprise as Adam raced toward him.

The ten-meter sprint downhill had created slack in the band. The coach couldn't pull him in if he tried. At least not for a few seconds. And that was all he would need.

Adam slid to a halt. Sliced the rubber band with his knife. It fell to the grass. He turned again, put his head down, and raced back up the hill. His legs moved in slow motion. He had nothing left. He expected bullets to whiz by him any second. They didn't.

When he got to the top of the hill, he looked down. Karel was in his car, looping around to pick him up on the road half a kilometer away. The coach stood in the same place where he'd been, arms folded across his chest, whip at his feet, rubber band still tied around his bulging waist. He thrust his head back with pride. It was the same pose the parents in Korosten struck when they bragged about their sons after games over beer.

Adam squinted to see if he was just imagining it, when he remembered there was no time. His father had given him explicit instructions to follow when Karel gave him the signal.

Run.

CHAPTER 47

THE BODYGUARDS SURROUNDED THE VOLKSWAGEN. NADIA looked daggers at Anton, wishing there were a pocket chain saw handy in the glove box. His eyes dropped to the steering wheel.

"You slimy prick," she said. "Since when? Since the airport?"

He glanced at her with a pained expression. "No, no. That was all genuine. My love for you was real. They were waiting for me at my apartment this afternoon."

"Really?"

"Really. They gave me two choices. Which is to say, they gave me one choice. I'm sorry, Nadia. Really, I am. This is Ukraine. The politics change all the time. It's a constant power struggle. The winners know how to go with the flow."

"Yeah. You're a real winner, Anton. You're a walking testament to why Ukraine's leading export is its women. Do the men in this country realize how pathetic that is?"

He snarled. "Hey. You wanted to get in the Zone. I got you in the Zone. You wanted to get out of the Zone. I got you out of the Zone. At my own risk. I asked for nothing in return. Nothing. And let's remember how it was two nights ago. You were the one begging for it, *from me*."

"You bastard."

He shrugged. "Hey. You can't say I didn't warn you."

"What?"

"I told you when I drove you from the airport. Ukrainian salary. It really is hell."

Nadia shifted in her seat and squared her hips toward him. "So is an American woman."

She pummeled his nose.

Bone crunched. Blood spurted. Anton screamed.

Nadia stepped out of the car.

"We missed you at the Veselka Restaurant," Victor said. "Your ponytailed lawyer friend didn't cut quite the same figure across the table from me."

Nadia didn't answer him. There was no benefit to saying a word.

"Let me have her, Kirilo," Misha said.

The distinguished man from Kyiv sliced through the circle of bodyguards. He looked fat yet fit, like a former heavyweight prizefighter who carefully balanced his love of food and fitness. His clothes and carriage spoke of confidence and power. He gave Nadia a quick once-over that ended with a dismissive smirk.

She'd seen that smirk on Wall Street: how could a woman have given him this much trouble?

"You remind me of what my daughter might look like in fifteen years," Kirilo said. "You have the same coloring. She's the joy of my life, my daughter."

Without warning, the back of his hand crushed Nadia's face. As she toppled to the cement, pain shot through her jaw. Her eyes watered. Her nose stung. A bitter taste flooded her mouth.

"Let me have her," Misha said. "I can make a woman do anything in fifteen minutes flat."

Kirilo motioned to a man who looked more like a malnourished librarian than a bodyguard. "Pavel, take her to the office. Search her and make her comfortable."

Pavel and two burly men grasped Nadia by her elbows and guided her toward an office in the far corner of the warehouse. They passed a harness attached to an elaborate pulley, one that could be used to hoist engines from a truck—or crucify uncooperative American women. A pair of stylish black shoes and slacks appeared beneath the pulley as a man circled around it. Brad Specter cast an indifferent look at her as she walked by. His footsteps stopped short as the bodyguards pushed her into the office.

The office contained portable orange shelving, a bare metal desk, and three chairs. A row of well-worn manuals lined one shelf. Nadia deciphered the Russian words for "truck repair." The bodyguards tied her feet to the chair and her hands behind her back with duct tape. One of the men tore a final piece of tape with his mouth and sealed her lips.

They searched her body without inhibitions and did the same with her purse.

Kirilo entered the office. He removed his coat. As he placed it on the table, it didn't bend, as though he were performing a sartorial levitation. He ripped the duct tape off Nadia's mouth.

Her lips stung, but she didn't scream.

"I hear you speak the language well for an American," he said.

"I can get by," Nadia said.

His eyes widened. "Refined. Like a college professor. You know about Ukrainian Hetman? Military commanders during the Cossack era?"

"I studied history. I know some things about them."

He sat down on the corner of the desk and tapped his coat with his left hand. It made a solid noise, as though it were reinforced with steel.

"Then you know more than I do," he said. "I never studied anything. I got my education on the street. I had to fight for everything I have. A smart man on the docks of Podil once told me—before I drowned him for his fishing boat—that the Cossacks believed that when you killed an enemy, the power of that enemy became yours. It literally seeped out of his soul into yours. The stronger the enemy you defeated, the more powerful you became."

"I'm not your enemy."

"I'm glad you said that. It's true. Not only are you not an enemy, but it's possible we can be business associates. Look at your friend Anton. He helped us, he got paid, and he's going back to his life. A bit bloody, thanks to you, but back to his life. There's no reason we can't strike the same bargain. Tell me what it is you found in the Zone, and we can come up with a fair price."

"I didn't find anything in the Zone. I went to meet my long-lost uncle. He's on his deathbed, and my mother told me of his existence just recently."

"Oh, really? What is your uncle's name?"

Nadia kept her lips sealed.

Kirilo smiled and tapped a muted tune along the coat, from shoulder to hip.

"What did the man say to you on Seventh Street? We both know there's no ten million dollars. Damian Tesla is your uncle. Where did you meet him? What did he give you?"

Nadia focused on her breathing and reminded herself: once she told him, she was dead.

He grasped the lapel to his coat and started to pull it back.

A knock on the door behind her.

Nadia tried to turn but couldn't.

Kirilo glared at whoever was standing in the doorway. "What?"

"Pavel needs you." It was Specter's voice.

"Not now," Kirilo said.

"I thought I heard him say your daughter is on the phone."

Kirilo tore out of the office.

Once he was out of sight, Specter rushed in and cut the binds around her ankles with a switchblade.

"What are you doing?" Nadia said, astonished.

Sirens blared outside the warehouse. "The police are here," he said.

Nadia wriggled her legs free. "They are? How do you know that?"

"I called them. I gave them an anonymous tip that a big drug deal was going down." He freed her wrists.

An emphatic metallic clang in the warehouse. Feet stomped, men shouted.

Nadia shook her hands loose. "Why are you doing this?"

Specter folded the knife and stored it in his pocket. "I'll tell Misha and Kirilo I did this to make sure the cops didn't find you all tied up and they didn't arrest us for kidnapping. When we walk out there, tell the cops we're together."

"Why are you—"

"Listen," he said, exasperated. "The story is, Misha and I do business with Kirilo, and we're here to look at a warehouse for storing auto parts from the States. You and I just had a lovers' quarrel. Tell them I'm a cheat. Ask them to drive you to the police station. Tip them a hundred hryvnia. They'll do it in a heartbeat. Kirilo will get us out of this, but you'll have a lead on us again."

Nadia stood up, still mystified. "Why are you helping me?"

Specter gathered the duct tape and threw it over the top of the shelving. "What were you doing in Chernobyl? You need to get to the embassy and get out of this country."

"No. I have to meet someone first."

"Who are you meeting?"

"Who are you?"

Footsteps clattered through the warehouse toward them.

"I can help you," Specter said.

Two men with the word *Militsiya* stenciled on their light-blue warm-up jackets burst into the room. They drew their guns.

"Police," one of them said. "Hands in the air. Don't move."

Nadia and Specter raised their hands.

"I'm an American tourist," Nadia said in perfect Ukrainian. "Thank God you're here. You've prevented a murder."

"Murder?" the other cop said.

"Yes," Nadia said. "This is my cheating shit of an American boyfriend. I was about to kill him."

CHAPTER 48

POLICE SWARMED THE WAREHOUSE.

Nadia watched Kirilo's eyes widen with disbelief when he saw her marching toward him with Specter. Then he gave Specter a nod of approval, as though he realized it was not in his interest for the police to find her tied up.

Fifteen to twenty policemen lined up the bodyguards against the wall, searched them, and checked their domestic passports. Nadia, Specter, and Misha stood beside Kirilo.

A police cruiser pulled into the warehouse. A cop emerged from the passenger side. Veins pulsated on his bald cinder block head as he chewed gum slowly. Ropes of muscle flexed under the ribbed white T-shirt beneath his powder-blue tracksuit. The index and middle fingers were missing from his right hand. He appraised each of them with a poker player's expression before turning to speak with a uniformed cop.

"He looks familiar," Kirilo said, just loud enough for Nadia, Misha, and Specter to hear. He squinted. "Have I seen him before? Wait…Is he an Eagle? By God, I think that's it. I think he's an Eagle." He nudged Misha. "We may have gotten lucky here."

Nadia had no idea what Kirilo was talking about.

The man with the missing fingers finished giving instructions and ambled over. "I am Detective Novak," he said.

"You've made a mistake," Kirilo said.

"Passport, please."

"There are no drugs here."

"Passport."

Kirilo handed him a blue booklet similar to the US passport.

"There's been no crime committed here," Kirilo said. "This warehouse belongs to me. These two men are from America. We're negotiating a business deal."

Detective Novak compared the photo in the book to the man before him. "What kind of business deal?"

"Auto parts," Kirilo said. "American-made auto parts for the do-it-yourself repair market. It's big in America, and it's going to take off here."

The detective returned Kirilo's passport and turned to Nadia. "Who are you?"

Nadia glanced at Kirilo and Misha. They stared at her, radiating a ferocity that belied their inscrutable expressions. Victor, meanwhile, stood calmly behind them.

"Until an hour ago, I was this man's girlfriend," Nadia said, shaking her thumb at Specter. "Now I'm his *ex*-girlfriend. I'm an American."

"Passport," Detective Novak said.

Nadia handed it to him. Kirilo, Misha, and Victor exchanged blank stares with one another, as though processing her story.

Detective Novak studied and returned her passport, and did the same with Victor and Misha.

"We got an anonymous tip," Detective Novak said, arms folded. "It was made by a man with a lot of urgency. He was very specific about the location." The detective glanced at Kirilo. "Why would someone send us here for no reason?"

"Do I look like I give a damn?" Kirilo took a step forward. "Do you know who I am?"

Detective Novak kept chewing slowly. "No. Should I?"

"The deputy minister of internal affairs is a personal friend of mine. He is an investor in my Black Sea energy project and a frequent guest at my villa in Yalta. Your police chief is also a friend. Didn't I see an eagle fly over your shoulder when you stepped out of the car?"

Detective Novak stopped chewing. He blinked. "What did you say?"

"I said, we both know the same people. We're both businessmen. Surely we can come to some sort of arrangement."

Detective Novak frowned. "It's you who's made a mistake. There was no eagle flying over my shoulder. There are no Eagles of Kravchenko here. Procedure will be followed. Any more discussion, and I will take you all to the station and we will sit there all night getting to the bottom of this. Procedure *will* be followed."

He turned, snapped his fingers, and shouted a pair of names. Two uniformed young cops with clipboards came running.

Misha looked at Kirilo. "Eagles of Kravchenko?"

Kirilo grunted. "In 2000, the president, Kuchma, complained about a journalist by the name of Georgiy Gongadze. Kravchenko, the minister of the interior, told him he'd 'take care of him.' Kravchenko said he had a team of elite detectives 'without any morals, prepared to do anything.' His words were recorded on cassette tape by a major who was in the meeting. They found Gongadze later, decapitated in a forest. They called the detectives the Eagles of Kravchenko. This fellow looks just like one of them, but apparently he's someone altogether different."

Detective Novak returned with the two cops. "Look at their papers again. I want names, addresses, and phone numbers. Hotel names from the Americans." He turned back to Nadia, Misha, and Kirilo. "Now we will search the warehouse and the cars."

The searches and interviews proceeded at a glacial pace. Nadia checked her watch every five minutes and fidgeted in place. Half an hour later, at 5:15 p.m., the cops finished collecting information and stepped away.

"I'm looking forward to finishing our conversation," Kirilo said to Nadia. "I think we were close to coming to a business arrangement."

Nadia ignored him.

Detective Novak returned with Kirilo's coat. He removed a long, cylindrical object from a special pouch in the lining. It was made of stainless steel and had a green handle and trigger at one end. It reminded Nadia of a spear gun.

"You are carrying a concealed weapon," Detective Novak said.

"It's not a weapon. It is a cattle prod."

"Do you herd cattle?"

"Do you value your career?"

Detective Novak smiled, walked up to Kirilo, and handed him the coat and the cattle prod.

"We've completed our search," he said. "You're free to go, as are your men."

Kirilo stepped between Specter and Nadia and put his arm around her shoulder. "Come with me, dear. Let me give you a ride to your hotel in my Audi."

Nadia wrangled out of his grasp and stepped forward. "Detective, may I get a lift to the station, please? I'm not with these men anymore."

Detective Novak glanced from Nadia to the men and back to her again. He stopped chewing.

"I was going to offer to pay for the gasoline or any inconvenience," she said, "but that would be an insult. So I can only say please."

Detective Novak paused, resumed chewing, and smiled. He marched over to a police cruiser and opened the door to the backseat without saying a word. Motioned for Nadia to get in with a sweep of his right hand. After closing the door behind her, he stood before Kirilo, Misha, and Specter.

"I don't want to see any of these vehicles following us to the station. The lady is no longer interested in your company. Is that understood?"

They didn't answer.

"In fact," Detective Novak said, glancing at one of his men with a clipboard, "check registrations for all these cars before these men leave." He turned back to Kirilo. "For my report. To make it perfect. Because I value my career." He winked.

He climbed into the passenger seat while another cop got in the driver's seat. As he pulled away, Nadia snuck a peek out the window. Kirilo followed the car on foot for a few steps, as though letting her know they would be coming soon.

Specter stood tapping his cell phone. The motion suggested he wanted Nadia to call him later.

"May we take you to the Hotel Rus?" Detective Novak said.

"No, thank you," Nadia said. "That's very kind of you. If you wouldn't mind...There is a destination...I'm leaving tomorrow, and I haven't had a chance to see the new statue. The new statue at Babi Yar."

CHAPTER 49

THE COPS KEPT KIRILO, VICTOR, MISHA, AND THE BODY-guards in the warehouse for another hour. Kirilo fumed at the irritation until the cops finally left at 7:25.

"We have to stop her from leaving the country," Kirilo said. "If she's still here. Pavel, call the deputy minister of the interior. Get him on the line for me."

Pavel pulled out his cell phone and stepped away.

"Who has a picture of her?" Kirilo said.

Misha pointed to Specter, who nodded.

"Good," Kirilo said. "Get it to Pavel right away. I'll see that the deputy minister gets it to Passport Control and that she's held for suspicion of illegally entering the Zone of Exclusion. We don't even have to make up a phony charge. It's legitimate. The taxi driver confessed to it."

"She has a head start," Misha said. "She could be on a plane before they have her picture."

"She won't go to the airport," Victor said.

Kirilo forced himself to look at his cousin. "Why do you say that?"

"She'll be expecting us to be expecting her there. It's how she came in. It's the easy way out. It's too big a risk, and she's too smart to take it."

"Then she'll go by boat or by rail," Misha said.

"It doesn't matter how she travels," Kirilo said. "She has to clear Passport Control somewhere, and we will either have that picture in time for her to be stopped or we won't. Which is why we will pursue our other leads while we wait."

"What other leads?" Misha said.

"We know from the taxi driver that she met with a zoologist. A man named Karel who conducts experiments in Chernobyl village. The deputy minister will get Pavel his home address, and we'll go pay him a visit immediately. Meanwhile, the deputy minister will get us emergency clearance to enter the Zone of Exclusion tonight."

"Chernobyl?" Misha said. "You're going to Chernobyl? When? Tonight?"

"That's where she went to see her uncle," Kirilo said. "Damian Tesla is there, somewhere. He can tell us what we're chasing after. And he might be able to tell us how she's leaving the country."

Misha fidgeted in place. "For real? You would go there? I mean, like, is it safe?"

"Of course it's not safe," Kirilo said, amused by the *moscal*'s obvious fear.

Victor slapped his young protégé on the shoulder. "You don't have to go, Misha," he said. "I'll go with Kirilo, and we'll fill you in with whatever we find out. You can trust us. You know that."

Misha blinked several times in rapid succession. He straightened his posture and balled his fists. "Fuck you, old man."

As soon as he got the words out, Misha whitened. He raised his hand to cover his mouth, turned, and vomited on the warehouse floor.

Kirilo stepped back. Victor hadn't been kidding, he realized. The Bitch really had poisoned the *moscal*.

"You okay?" Kirilo said.

"I'm fine," Misha barked, face flushed. "Don't you worry about me."

As Kirilo passed him, Victor whispered under his breath, "Ten million divided by two is greater than ten million divided by three."

The mere sound of the Bitch's voice made Kirilo want to bite his ear off and spit it out in his face.

"I'm on hold," Pavel said, cupping the phone with one hand.

Kirilo edged closer to Pavel, glancing over his shoulder to make sure Victor couldn't hear him.

"Anything on Isabella's whereabouts?" Kirilo said.

"No," Pavel said. "I have calls in to all our contacts. The only thing I've learned so far is that the Timkiv twins may be helping him. They run a small crew in Odessa and were seen in Yalta by one of our men. They match the description of the two young men you saw outside your boat when Victor came aboard."

"Good," Kirilo said. "How can we squeeze them where it hurts? Are their parents alive? Are they married with children?"

"I don't know about their family. I know they're single. And they worship only money."

"That is a church I'm familiar with. Let's find their bishop. I'm sure I can threaten to disrobe him to reveal their location."

CHAPTER 50

NADIA ASKED DETECTIVE NOVAK TO GIVE HER A QUICK TOUR of the park at Babi Yar so she could orient herself. He dropped her off two kilometers away from the ravine itself. She'd learned her lesson at the Caves Monastery: she wasn't going to expose herself at the rendezvous point. She would approach the boy only after she saw him.

Nadia hoped the picture of him was recent and that she would recognize him. Of greater concern was her responsibility to help get him out of Ukraine. She could take care of herself under any circumstances. Of that she was certain. A teenage boy she'd never even met, however, was an entirely different matter.

She stepped out of the police cruiser at 5:43. After the car disappeared, she hid behind a tree and waited for a few minutes to make sure Kirilo or Misha hadn't somehow followed her. When no one appeared, she slipped out of hiding.

Tall lampposts illuminated the tree-lined path that wove its way around the perimeter of the park. The air smelled of dew and worms. A young couple, their fancy backpacks identifying them as tourists, walked solemnly around the Menorah Monument. A family of seven stood at the ravine's edge.

Nadia was certain she and the family were thinking about the same thing. On September 29, 1941, all Jews in Kyiv were ordered to report for relocation. The Nazis spread the word by nailing bulletins to telephone poles and taping signs to windows. At the time, the Jewish population in Kyiv numbered fifty thousand, with another hundred thousand having fled deeper into the Soviet Union and Central Asia. Non-Jews were told that their Jewish countrymen were going to be deported to Israel. In fact, 33,771 of them were lined up at a ravine called Babi Yar, stripped naked, and slaughtered over a two-day span.

A total of one hundred thousand people were executed at Babi Yar during the Nazi occupation of Kyiv, including Ukrainian priests, nationalists, and gypsies. Yet, after the war, the Soviet Union refused to acknowledge the murders. The first Jewish memorial was built only when Ukraine proclaimed independence from the Soviet Union in 1991. A bronze statue dedicated to all the Ukrainians who perished was added in 2009.

The ravine was not what Nadia had expected. Its shockingly small size stood in sharp contrast with the number of bodies the Nazis had buried within it. Nadia snaked along a fence of decorative trees to a rolling meadow. A sports complex loomed in the foreground. She clung to the shadows as she marched two kilometers through the park, eyes swiveling around to the back of her head. The sound of traffic grew louder. A metro station came into view. Cars crisscrossed at a major intersection ahead. When the outline of the new statue appeared, Nadia circled around a maintenance building and hid behind a corner. From her perch, she couldn't make out the details of the monument.

As if on cue, a boy emerged from behind the statue. He wore an old blue warm-up suit, muddy track shoes from the seventies, and an army knapsack that looked as if it had survived a world war. He carried a duffel bag in his right hand. He was close to six feet tall and lanky, with a knit cap pulled low over his forehead.

Nadia decided to approach. A light shone over the monument. On the granite wall to the left, a series of human silhouettes toppled into a ravine. A mother clung to her baby below.

On the right, a bronze child read the announcement on the wall, ordering him to report to Babi Yar.

Nadia came within ten feet of Adam and stopped. He was the boy from her mother's photo, although he looked taller and more mature. He looked ready to run on a second's notice.

"Hi. My name is Nadia. Your father told me to meet you here."

"Passport," he said, like a young customs officer in training.

"What?"

"Passport."

Surprised by his officious manner, Nadia pulled the booklet out of her bag. Adam studied her photo, her personal information, and the entrance stamp, and returned it. She stowed it back in her bag and put her left hand on her hip.

"Passport," she said.

His sullen expression didn't change.

She put her hand out. "Passport."

He removed a sealed plastic bag from the front of his pants. The bag contained his two passports, as though there were a risk they would get wet during his journey. One of the passports was a domestic ID, the other international. Nadia read the inside page of the international one.

"It says you were born in Korosten," she said. "Your father told me you were born in Chernobyl village."

"No one lives in Chernobyl, so no one can be born in Chernobyl, even if he was really born in Chernobyl."

He reached out with an open palm. She leafed through the domestic one quickly and slapped the passports into his hand. He stuffed them back in the plastic bag, sealed it tight, and stowed it in his knapsack.

The boy was very stiff, and she could understand that. She tried to put him at ease. "So you're the man with the plan," she said. "What next?"

"We go see the forger."

"Who?"

"The forger. My father, he knows some people. It's all arranged."

"What do we need to see a forger for?"

"You need a visa."

"I do? Where am I going?"

"Moscow." He checked a battered watch with a red hammer and sickle on a discolored white dial. "It's ten after six. The forger's expecting us at six thirty. The express to Moscow leaves Central Station at eight-oh-nine tonight."

"Moscow? Why are we going to Moscow?"

He remained very cautious. "I can tell you once we're on the train but not before."

"Why not?"

"Because those are the instructions my father gave me. If you get captured by the men chasing you, you won't know anything more."

Nadia studied his neck. A sliver of gold protruded along the left collar of his T-shirt.

"Your father told me about a locket. A locket that has some very special information in it. Where is that locket?"

He slid his hand under his shirt and lifted the necklace high enough to reveal a pendant. It was a golden square with a black trident carved on the front.

"I'd like to see inside—"

"No." Adam took a step back. "I don't open the locket for anyone."

"I'm not anyone. I'm your cousin."

"I don't care who you are. My father told me. Keep it simple. If you don't open the locket, you can't lose the formula inside. So I won't open the locket. Not for you, not for him if he showed up here right now. Not for anyone."

"Okay," Nadia said. "So be it. There are men following me. We should hurry."

Adam suddenly loped toward the train station across the street. Nadia raced after him. As a teen, she'd run the mile in 5:37. At home, she still worked out religiously. It didn't matter. The kid had the propulsion of a locomotive and the stride of a deer. The faster Nadia ran, the more ground Adam gained. He disappeared across the street into the Dorohozhychi metro station fifty yards ahead of Nadia.

When she got there, she was out of breath. The station teemed with commuters. Informal queues lined food kiosks. Nadia found Adam waiting for her at one of the yellow vending machines.

"I'll get this," she said.

He slipped two hryvnia into the machine and bought his own token before she could open her purse. Nadia did the same. Their tokens rattled to the metallic cup at the bottom, one after the other. As they walked toward the platform, a babushka stepped in their way. Nadia put her hand on Adam's shoulder to guide him around the old woman.

Adam stopped sharply and pulled back. "Don't touch me. Don't ever touch me again."

This wasn't exactly a family reunion. The boy was scared, and he obviously didn't trust her. That was okay, Nadia thought. She was scared, too.

Seven minutes later, a train arrived. They climbed aboard and headed south toward the center of Kyiv without saying another word to each other.

CHAPTER 51

"THE POLICE MAY BE ONTO ME," THE FORGER SAID AFTER opening the door. She glanced over Nadia's shoulder. "One of my clients was arrested this morning. Come in. We must hurry."

The forger lived in the basement of a small coffee shop with a Wi-Fi sign in its window, three blocks away from a hospital near the Pecherska metro station.

At first glance, she appeared to be the prototype for the churchgoing spinster: a middle-aged woman with alabaster skin, meticulously combed short hair, and a smile that could charm a priest into eating anything she baked. On second glance, the tattoo on her forearm that peeked out from beneath the sleeve of her dress suggested she was less devout. It was a picture of the queen of diamonds, an inkwell, and a feathered pen in the shape of a gun.

Her office was a bookkeeper's dream, with stacks of accounting ledgers and textbooks lining the shelves. A high-powered lamp illuminated a sturdy wooden desk. A computer, a printer, and an array of well-organized office supplies rested on top.

Adam removed his backpack. The forger pointed to a plate of poppy seed rolls and a pitcher of milk. He grabbed a massive hunk of pastry and dug into it like a Cro-Magnon man.

"Let me see your passport," the forger said. "Do you have two blank pages facing each other? Do you? You must have two blank pages facing each other, or I cannot help you."

Nadia opened her passport to a pair of blank pages.

"Good. Stand in the corner against the white wall. We need to take a passport photo."

Nadia backpedaled toward the corner. "Why? Since when do visas have pictures?"

"When you cross the border, a customs agent will check your visa against the computer. If your information isn't there, you'll be arrested. My son will download your application into the Russian Federation database. He will also enter your picture."

A man in his thirties with wire-rimmed glasses and an air of ambivalence shuffled into the room. He held an instant camera and a blue knit sweater the size of a pup tent in his hands.

The forger gave the sweater to Nadia. "Put this on. Quickly."

"Why?" Nadia said.

"It will look suspicious if you are wearing the same clothes as you are in your photo, no? Put it on."

Nadia took her coat off and put the sweater on. She stifled her horror at how she must have looked. Yet the photo would be shoulders up, she reminded herself. Who cared?

She stood against the wall and cracked a sympathetic smile. The son snapped three photos in rapid succession and disappeared into a back room with the pictures.

"Now fill out this visa application," the forger said. "In English, as though you walked into the Russian embassy in New York. Date it February nineteenth. I will fill in the name of your hotel in Moscow. It will also be the entity that's inviting you."

"Inviting me?"

"To get a Russian visa, you must be invited by an authorized party. Usually it's a travel agency or a hotel. You are going to be invited by the Hotel Ekaterina."

"Does it even exist?"

"Yes. It exists. My son will book a reservation for you in their system as well."

When she was done with the application, the forger made a copy on the printer and took it to the adjacent room to her son. She returned and began typing as quickly as her fingers allowed.

"What is your connection to my uncle?"

She looked up. "Your uncle?"

"Damian. The young man's father."

"My brother spent six years with him at the *gulag* in Sevvostlag. When he got so weak he couldn't produce his daily quota in the gold mine, your uncle got him an easy job picking needles off dwarf cedar trees. They used to grind them into soup as a cure for scurvy. That saved his life."

"That was decent of him."

"Decent had nothing to do with it. It was about money. He knew I sent my brother sweaters, cigarettes, and food every three months. That all went to your uncle, or whatever the guards didn't take."

Nadia glanced at Adam, who was on his second hunk of poppy seed roll. "How did you learn this trade?"

"I worked in the Ministry. Department of Tourism. First in Moscow, then Kyiv. When independence came, capitalism came with it. I lost my job and had to find another one."

The forger printed a single sheet of paper, moved to a side table, and inserted it into a paper cutter. As she lined it up, Nadia walked over to the doorway where the forger's son had disappeared. He sat in a small room, surrounded by six computer screens. The passport photo of a pale woman with a prematurely aging face and a forced smile appeared on one of the monitors. Nadia gasped. The son turned to see who'd made the noise, then returned to work.

Nadia paced the main room for five more minutes while the forger worked. Adam burped and leaned against a wall.

"Come look at your visa," the forger said.

A yellow, intricately manufactured discoloration marred its complexion. The faint stencil of a blue coat of arms decorated the center. Russian words and numbers ran along the top in distinct shades of red. A multicolored stamp featuring churches, a ship, and a coat of arms was pressed on the left. Nadia's name and date of birth appeared in dull blue toward the middle.

The forger took the visa and placed it in an envelope. "This is good for ten days, and ten days only. They are very strict about this. You must be out of Russia within ten days from today."

"That will not be a problem," Nadia said.

The forger held the envelope by her side. "Payment, please."

"Excuse me?" Nadia said.

"Your uncle didn't tell you?"

Shuffling noises behind them. Nadia turned. The son stood behind them with a rifle in his hand.

"No," Nadia said. She glanced at Adam. He wiped crumbs off his lips, oblivious to the conversation. "My uncle didn't tell me."

"The bargain he struck with me was that I would give you a visa and you would give me all the jewelry on either one of your hands."

"I never heard anything like that."

The forger shrugged. "Surprise."

Nadia looked down. Her stainless steel Bedat watch was wrapped around her left wrist. She'd paid $4,000 for it back when she'd had a job, earned a bonus, and could afford it. Her favorite ruby ring shimmered on her right hand. It was probably worth a fraction of the watch, but it had sentimental value. Her mother had given it to her when she graduated college.

Nadia glanced at Adam. His eyes were glued to the gun in the son's hand. She turned back to the forger.

"Well," Nadia said, "which hand is it going to be?"

"Let me see the ring."

Nadia raised her right hand. The forger removed a loupe from her desk drawer and studied it.

"I'll take your left hand," the forger said. Sirens sounded in the distance. "Quickly."

Nadia took the watch off and exchanged it for the visa. Nadia and Adam flew up the exterior stairs to street level and took off for the subway.

The sirens grew louder as they speed-walked out of sight.

CHAPTER 52

THE ZOOLOGIST RAISED HIS HAND FROM HIS PLUSH VELVET seat. It trembled from residual electrical current.

"No more," he said.

Kirilo sighed and replaced the cattle prod in his coat's lining. After bringing Karel a glass of water, he sat down on the sofa directly across from him, beside Victor. The River Casino's gaming floor bustled with activity beyond the soundproof glass wall.

Misha returned from the restroom. Sweat dotted his forehead even though it was cool in the room.

"Diarrhea," he said as he sat down on the couch.

Kirilo slid a few centimeters farther away from him. "You're from America. Some of our fine water probably got into your system. Happens to tourists all the time. Victor didn't really poison you, did you, Victor?"

Victor didn't react; instead, he kept his head tilted at an angle at Misha.

"You old prick," Misha said, wiping his brow. "If this is a joke, I'm going to more than even the score back in New York."

This time, Victor grinned. "And if it's not?"

Kirilo had gotten the zoologist's name and address in Kyiv from the deputy minister of the interior. Pavel's men had identified themselves as *militsiya* and dragged Karel out of his apartment. By 8:00, he was in his current seat. Twenty minutes later, after substantial prodding, he motioned for Kirilo to stop.

"I didn't think a zoologist could be so tough," Kirilo said.

"He watches animals all day," Victor said. "He should have learned something by now."

"Good point," Kirilo said.

Karel tipped the glass to his lips. Water trickled around his lips, down his chin, and onto the velvet around him.

Kirilo winced. "The furniture, dammit. Watch the furniture."

Karel drank some more. Kirilo took the glass away from him, put it on a coaster where he couldn't knock it over, and sat back down.

"Why did the Tesla woman go to the Zone?" Kirilo said.

"To see her uncle."

"What uncle?"

"Damian. Damian Tesla."

"He's alive?"

"As far as I know. I haven't seen him since he asked me to do a favor."

"What favor?"

"To go to Korosten and bring his son to Kyiv."

"Does this have anything to do with the Tesla woman?"

"Yes. He's meeting her tonight."

"Why?"

"They will travel together."

"Where are they going?"

"I don't know."

Kirilo squinted.

Karel sighed. "Honestly. I don't know. My instructions were to leave him at Babi Yar."

"Babi Yar?" Misha said. "What's at Babi Yar?"

"Nothing," Kirilo said. "Monuments and a park. Nothing that would give their ultimate destination away. That's why he picked Babi Yar. What do they have in their possession? Why did the Tesla woman come here?"

Karel shook his head. "I don't know."

Kirilo chuckled. "What's that, you say? You haven't really had enough? You want some more?"

Karel raised his hand in self-defense. "No. Honestly. I don't know. There was a formula. The scientist died. I thought the formula died with him. But maybe that's just what I was led to believe. Maybe the truth is that Damian and the scientist didn't trust me."

Kirilo moved to the edge of his seat. "And you suffer for them? For these so-called friends? You owe them nothing. Nothing, I say to you. You are a prospective Chernobyl invalid?"

Karel nodded.

"Then you have suffered enough. My sources tell me you have published books of great importance regarding animal behavior in a nuclear environment."

Karel lowered his head.

"No. Now is not the time to be humble. This country owes you a great debt. A great debt that is long overdue. I can guarantee you invalid status by the end of the month. The deputy minister of health is a close friend of mine. We've hunted caribou together on the Taimyr Peninsula. Your full pension will begin the first of June, and you will be free to continue with your important research."

"Full pension?"

"Full pension." Kirilo leaned over and tapped Karel on the thigh. "Now, my good friend, tell us, what formula?"

CHAPTER 53

A THREE-TIERED GOLDEN CHANDELIER HUNG FROM THE soaring ceiling above the steps to the concourse at the Central Railway Station. Ornate murals of baroque castles with vivid blue stained-glass windows and churches with gleaming golden domes decorated the walls. The brass hands of a giant clock suspended above an electronic message board announced the time: 7:23.

As Nadia and Adam cut across the tiled floor toward a ticket booth, Nadia scanned the concourse for familiar faces. Tourists in khakis and jeans mixed with businesspeople in suits, sports jackets, and light coats. She didn't recognize any of them. Still, Kirilo's men could be watching her at this very moment, and Victor and Misha could be waiting for her around the corner. Anton's words echoed in her ears: in Ukraine, the criminals and the government were one and the same. If she stayed in this country, it was just a matter of time until they caught up with her.

With Kirilo's local influence, their first step would be to seal all borders. Nadia figured she had two tactical advantages. First, they didn't know she was traveling with a boy. Border guards would be looking for a woman traveling alone. Second, and more important, she had a head start. If the police delayed her pursuers long enough, she and Adam might be able to sneak through

Passport Control before Kirilo notified anyone. If not, they were at risk of being arrested imminently.

"Are you buying a ticket, too?" Nadia said.

"No," Adam said. "I have mine. You want the eight-oh-nine express to Moscow. Coupe."

"Coupe?"

"Second-class cabin."

"What does that mean?"

"Four people per cabin."

"We're going to have strangers in our cabin?"

"No. No one else is going to stay in our cabin."

"How can you be sure?"

"Trust me." He looked down at the floor, face flushed. "You don't have to worry about that."

The ticket agent asked Nadia for her destination, time of departure, and passport. Nadia paid the equivalent of $170 in hryvnia, waited an interminable few minutes, and received her ticket.

Passport Control was the same disorganized madhouse as when she had arrived at the airport.

Nadia jostled her way forward, glancing back every thirty seconds to make sure Adam was following. He kept his knit hat pulled low over his ears. Knapsack and duffel bag in each hand, he shuffled forward with his eyes planted firmly at his feet. Removed from the countryside, he seemed out of his element.

When the mass of bodies finally converged into a line, Nadia counted twenty-one people ahead of them. She tried to prepare herself to look nonchalant, which inevitably had the opposite effect. She focused on the formula and wondered how much a radiation countermeasure was worth on the open market. The thought of riches beyond her dreams was a pleasant way to calm her nerves.

The agent returned the passports to a family in front, and they moved along. After glancing at his computer, the agent scanned the line awaiting him. Nadia dropped her gaze to the floor so that their eyes didn't meet, lest she appear anxious.

When she looked up again, she saw, to her alarm, a supervisor had joined the agent at his booth. Both of them peered in Nadia's direction. Nadia swiveled her head, glanced over her shoulder, and realized they were staring at Adam.

"You!" the agent said. He pointed an index finger at the boy and then directed it toward Nadia. He must have seen her tense when he shouted at Adam. "Are you together? Is that your boy?"

Nadia's gut instinct was to protect him, rude and insolent though he was. "Yes," she said. "We're together."

"Step forward, please," the agent said.

As Nadia and Adam cut to the front of the line, two beefy policemen with bulging sidearms joined the supervisor and the agent at his booth. Their expressions conveyed suspicion and fear.

The couple in front moved aside, pushing the line back to leave as much space between them and Nadia and Adam as possible, as though they knew she was about to be arrested for some sort of crime against the State.

At least she was an American citizen, Nadia thought. Whatever else happened, that still had to count for something.

Didn't it?

The Passport Control agent opened Adam's passport and studied his picture. The supervisor peered over his shoulder as the two cops stood by with their hands on their weapons.

"Take your hat off," the agent said.

Blushing deeply, Adam grasped the edges of his knit hat with both hands. As he slowly peeled it off his head, his ears popped out. They rose from the side of his head and stopped halfway, just above the canal. They looked as though they'd been sawed in half with a hacksaw. Jagged grooves ran along the square tops like the edge of an unfinished cardboard puzzle. Nadia recalled a picture of similar ears on a child at the Chernobyl museum.

She absorbed the visual shock without flinching, realized she was staring, and tore her eyes away.

People in line gasped. The agent, the supervisor, and the cops averted their eyes. Their collective gaze was one of acute discomfort. The cops folded their arms across their chests in a defensive posture. The supervisor nodded at the agent as though he'd known all along what was hidden beneath Adam's hat. The agent himself pursed his lips in deep disapproval.

Nadia held her breath when he turned to her visa, but he didn't bother checking it. He stamped their passports quickly and firmly. The cops pointed in the direction of their track as though they wanted to make sure Nadia and Adam got out of the country as quickly as possible.

The entire process had taken sixty seconds.

As they marched toward the train, Nadia's initial feelings of horror swiftly transmuted to compassion. She had seen that stricken look on Adam's face. He must be embarrassed by his ears every day of his life, and he was not to blame. Not at all. He was a teenager, at the point in his life when looks were so important. Now she understood why he distrusted people so much.

When they boarded the train, static cracked through the speakers.

"This is the eight-oh-nine Stolichny Express to Moscow. Train number one. Eight-oh-nine Stolichny Express to Moscow. Welcome aboard."

They found an empty cabin. Nadia sat opposite Adam. Fresh white linen and burgundy blankets covered their beds. Above them, another pair of bunks remained folded against the wall.

Light poured in from the platform through the window. Outside, passengers rushed on board.

"Kyivans," Adam said as he took off his hat again and sighed. "They know when someone is from the Zone. They can smell it off you. You see? Even before I took my hat off, they knew. The supervisor knew. Some of the people in line, they knew, too."

Nadia was outraged for him. "And? So what? Why do they care?"

"No one wants to be near anyone who is from the Zone. Years ago, no one wanted to be near anyone who might be radioactive. Even though twenty-four years have passed, nothing's changed. They couldn't wait to get me out of the country."

"Well, that's just wrong."

He scowled at her. "Would you be here if I didn't have the locket?"

Nadia's gaze fell to the gold shimmering around his neck. She looked up at his face. "That's different. I wouldn't even be in Kyiv if your father hadn't written."

"Good, at least you admit it. You wouldn't be here if it wasn't for the locket. Just so we both know where we stand." Adam turned, fluffed up his pillows, and kicked his legs up onto the bed, filthy shoes and all.

Nadia had to hold in a burst of temper. "You told me you'd tell me why we're going to Moscow when we got on the train," she said. "We're on the train."

He folded his hands behind his head and stared at the ceiling.

"Are *you* a man of *your word*?" she said.

He bolted upright. Tossed his legs back over the side and faced Nadia.

"We are going by train because they expect you to go by plane. We are going to Moscow because they do not expect you to go there. But mostly, we are going to Moscow because that is the route that was arranged for me by my father and his friends when they thought I would be alone. It is the route where there are people my father knows. Where there are people who will help me."

"What route, Adam?"

He told her. There were five waypoints. Five people would meet them along the way and guide them forward. Once they got to the last waypoint, they were on their own.

She bought chips, candy bars, and bottled water in the restaurant car and consumed them in the cabin. She tried to share them, but Adam wouldn't accept anything from her. He drank the hot tea provided by the carriage attendant and ate nothing. Nadia slept fitfully during the last four hours of the nine-hour trip, falling into a deep slumber just as the conductor announced their arrival at 6:39 a.m.

Language was not a concern. Nadia had studied Russian from seventh grade through college. Her mother had tried to dissuade her, for fear it would pollute her Ukrainian, but Nadia thought it might help her business career someday. It never did. But now it just might help keep her alive, she thought.

After a three-hour wait to clear customs, they emerged at Kievskaia Station in Moscow at 11:00. Exchanged her remaining hryvnia and dollars for rubles. Adam set his watch forward one hour. Nadia made a beeline for a McDonald's and ate two hamburgers, a large fries, and a chocolate milkshake. She offered to buy Adam lunch, but he refused, eating a grotesque piece of sausage wrapped in onionskin paper and buying his own bottled water instead.

After lunch, they went shopping. Nadia had never had the opportunity to return to her hotel room. All her luggage was still in Kyiv. She bought a cell phone charger, blue jeans, a denim shirt, a fleece pullover, a ski jacket, ski gloves, and hat, hiking socks and boots, a compass, toiletries, and a roll of toilet paper. She changed into the shirt, jeans, socks, and boots, and stored everything else in the knapsack she'd also bought.

At 4:00, she ate an early dinner of bread and borscht at a cheap joint called the *Elki-Pelki*. The waiter seated them near the kitchen in the far corner of the restaurant. Nadia ordered Adam steak and boiled potatoes without asking him. When the food arrived, he played with the potatoes as though they were hockey pucks but didn't eat anything. They hadn't spoken the entire day except to discuss where they were going next.

After dinner, Nadia called Johnny Tanner in New Jersey and left him a voice mail that she would be calling him again for help within six to ten days. She also called her brother's club and confirmed that he was still out of harm's way in Thailand.

They still had time to burn, so they walked the ten kilometers to Yaroslavsky Station. The entire way, Nadia kept her head on a swivel out of sheer paranoia that Kirilo and Misha had somehow tracked her down. She and Adam covered the distance in two hours and arrived at 7:45.

Adam already had his ticket. He said a man who owed his father a debt had sent it to them. Nadia showed the vendor her passport and bought a one-way ticket for the Trans-Siberian Express. The train departed Moscow with Nadia and Adam on board at 9:25 on Saturday, April 24.

It was the No. 2 train, headed from Moscow to Vladivostok, on the Sea of Japan.

CHAPTER 54

At 11:00 p.m. on Saturday, Kirilo sat in the front seat of a car bumping down a spooky abandoned road in the Zone. The deputy minister had finally secured emergency entrance passes for the Zone of Exclusion after a two-hour delay. Kirilo had to promise the deputy minister more shares in his alternative-energy fund in exchange for the discretion of two superintendents. No doubt the deputy minister was compensating the superintendents somehow. Now that he understood the value of the formula they were chasing, Kirilo considered it a bargain.

Kirilo slept during the drive to Chernobyl until they passed the thirty-kilometer radius to the power plant. The red forest and vehicle graveyards kept him awake and wondering if it really was safe to be in the region, no matter how brief his stay. Chernobyl was not a place people discussed, let alone visited.

Kirilo had gotten good news from Pavel at the River Casino earlier in the evening.

"Nadia Tesla left Ukraine on the night train to Moscow," he said. "The deputy minister made inquiries for us. She entered Russia at ten fifty a.m."

"And?" Kirilo said.

"She's still in Russia," Pavel said.

Kirilo rubbed his hands together.

Misha said, "Why didn't anyone tell us earlier she left the country?"

Pavel shrugged. "This is Ukraine, man. That's how things work."

Misha turned to Kirilo. "Why didn't you have her detained?"

"I don't want to arouse suspicions, end up sharing the bounty from the formula, or worse. If she'd gone to an airport, she would have been detained. There would have been no choice," he explained. "If she's on a train, we can catch her. There's no need to get the government involved." He looked at Pavel. "Where is she now?"

"Her visa says she's staying at the Hotel Ekaterina, but that's a lie. She bought a ticket for the Trans-Sib. She had to show her passport and visa to buy a ticket. They've been flagged."

"The Trans-Sib?"

Pavel nodded. "Nine twenty-five to Vladivostok."

Kirilo checked his watch. "It's midnight in Moscow. See if the jet is available. If not, charter another immediately. Three hours to Moscow, plus one to get through Customs and Passport Control. They have a six-and-a-half-hour lead."

"We won't get out tonight," Pavel said.

Kirilo opened his mouth to shout but realized Pavel was right.

"Airport's closing, pilot's out on a Saturday night, we have to file flight plans with Moscow. Even if you make phone calls and pull strings, it will take you all night to find people. Get you nowhere."

"Set it up for the morning, then. As early as you can make it happen. It's seven days to Vladivostok. Four to Irkutsk if they wanted to throw a curve and go south from there. She's not going anywhere fast. Check the train schedule. Find the airports along the way. Plot two courses to intercept. Best case and worst case. You never know with Passport Control in Russia."

"Trans-Sib? Where the hell is she going?" Misha said. "Ferry from Vladivostok to Japan? Plane to Hawaii and on to San Francisco?"

"That sounds like the longest route possible for her to get home," Pavel said.

"And the last place anyone would look for her, my friend," Victor added. "The last place anyone would look."

His bitch cousin was right, Kirilo thought as the car cratered in and out of a pothole. Everybody lurched inside the car. Victor and Karel remained quiet, but Misha groaned.

"I didn't think it was possible for a head to hurt this much," he said.

"How do you feel otherwise?" Kirilo said. "The nausea? The diarrhea?"

Misha shrugged. "Dunno. Not that bad, I guess."

"Good, good," Kirilo said, hiding his disappointment.

"But then again, I haven't been eating."

"You sure you don't want something? Some pickles, perhaps?"

Misha glared at him.

Kirilo cackled and slapped him again. "Forgive me, my friend. I couldn't resist."

At last, the car pulled to a stop outside a farmhouse. "This is it, Boss," the driver said.

"Okay," Kirilo told the others, "we go in fast and we go in hard."

Kirilo burst inside Damian's house, pushing the babushka aside. A single lantern flickered in the kitchen.

"Where is he?" Kirilo said.

"Who do you think you are?" the babushka said. "This is my home. Get out. Get out now."

Kirilo raised his hand to strike her. "Don't make me ask you twice, old woman."

The babushka didn't flinch. "The bedroom," she said.

Kirilo motioned for his driver to go first. Kirilo followed, his bodyguard's flashlight illuminating the path.

Kirilo marched into Damian's room, confident he could get the old man to talk. He had a son. That meant he had a weakness

Kirilo could exploit, just as Victor had done with him. Kirilo's driver found a lantern and lit it.

They found a shambles. Thieves had ransacked the room. The mattress was pulled off its box spring. It was sliced in four places, the lining ripped out and strewn all over the room. A bureau sat empty, its drawers pulled out and overturned. Clothes lay scattered. Among them lay the corpse of a small old man. His lips were curled into a slight smile. Blisters festered on his face.

Karel ran in to take his pulse, even though it was clear he was dead.

"Is that him?" Kirilo said.

Karel nodded.

"Huh. I never met the man, but I certainly heard of him," Kirilo said. "And so I have to ask: How could he end up dead in squalor in a nuclear ghost town? Couldn't a thief steal a better ending for himself?"

"Maybe he was more concerned about someone else," Victor said.

Kirilo glanced at the doorway. Misha and Victor had slipped inside.

"You mean he has a son," Kirilo said.

"Just as you have a daughter," Victor said.

Whom I am going to find within the hour, you bitch, Kirilo thought.

As Kirilo scanned the wreckage in the room, Victor walked around examining its contents.

"What's this all about, though?" Kirilo said. "It's as though someone else is looking for the same thing we are. Where is that babushka?"

A bolt slammed shut. Kirilo recognized the sound of a bullet entering a chamber.

The babushka stood in the doorway with her rifle pointed at Kirilo.

"You're a rude city bastard," the babushka said. "I have a place reserved for you beneath my root cellar next to a couple of pet hunters from Kyiv. Come. Let me show it to you."

She pressed the stock into her armpit and tightened her lips. Kirilo realized she really was going to shoot him. The crazy old woman was going to shoot him, and there was nothing he could do about it.

A pair of massive hands reached over the babushka's shoulders and ripped the weapon out of her hands. Misha's bodyguard towered over her, his massive frame spilling outside the doorway.

Kirilo exhaled and nodded his thanks. The man nodded back.

Kirilo glared at the babushka. "That wasn't very hospitable. Fortunately for you, you have some information I require. So let's all go to the kitchen and talk like civilized people, shall we?"

When Kirilo turned to look at Damian one last time, he saw Victor's hand on a side table on the opposite side of the bed.

"What's there?" Kirilo said. "Did you find something?"

Victor picked up a cassette tape. "Petula Clark," he said in English.

"Who?"

"Petula Clark. English singer. Very popular in America when I first arrived in '65. You know the song 'Downtown'?"

"No, but I'll make sure it's played at your funeral. Get in the kitchen. Now."

The babushka turned on a lantern and lit four candles in the kitchen. Kirilo, Victor, and Misha joined her at a wooden dining table.

"What is your name, Babushka?" Kirilo said.

"Oksana Houk."

"Oksana. Good. I'm sorry to barge into your home in the middle of the night. I understand if you think I'm your adversary. How can you not? But it's not true. In fact, not only am I not your adversary, I can be your friend."

Kirilo pulled his billfold out of his inside jacket pocket and placed it on the table. Oksana's eyes widened when she saw it was stuffed three inches thick with bills.

"Why did you turn the bedroom upside down?" Kirilo said. "What were you looking for?"

Oksana glanced at the billfold.

"Money," Kirilo said. "You were looking for money. Were you looking for the ten million dollars Damian stole many years ago?"

"Aren't you?"

"No. That money was confiscated by the KGB when they killed three of his men. There is no ten million dollars."

"Then what *are* you looking for?"

"A piece of microfilm," Kirilo said. "With some very valuable information on it."

Oksana considered his statement and shook her head. "I don't know anything about any microfilm."

"Damian didn't tell her anything," Karel said. He stood between the two bodyguards. "He only told people what was necessary to get their help. Never enough for them to fully understand what he was planning."

Kirilo turned his attention back to Oksana. "Did Damian request your help with anything before he died?"

"No. Nothing out of the ordinary. He asked me to clean and polish a locket and necklace that he gave to his son as a keepsake. Other than that—"

"A locket, you say?" Kirilo said. "Interesting. Did he put anything in the locket when you gave it to him?"

"I wouldn't know."

Kirilo glanced at Victor. They communicated without speaking. They both knew the locket held the microfilm and it was hanging around Damian's son's neck.

"What is Damian's son's name?" Kirilo said.

"Adam," Oksana said. "He is from the Zone, so he doesn't have many friends. But he's a good boy."

"I'm sure he is," Kirilo said. "Where has he gone? Where have he and Nadia Tesla gone?"

"I don't know." Oksana's eyes fell to the billfold again. "I wish I knew, but I don't."

Kirilo tapped her palm with an open hand. "I understand, Babushka. I understand." He counted ten thousand hryvnia and handed it to her.

Oksana wet her lips and snatched it from him. "Thank you, kind sir. Thank you."

"We're going to search your home before we leave just in case there might be an item of interest. Do you mind?"

Kirilo insisted that they attack one room at a time so that he could keep an eye on Misha and Victor the entire time. When they returned to the bedroom, Kirilo cornered Misha's bodyguard, blocking the others' view with his back so Misha couldn't see their hands or hear their discussion.

"Thank you for your help with the rifle, my friend," Kirilo said. "What is your name?"

"Stefan," the man said. "My name is Stefan."

"Stefan," Kirilo said. "I'll have to remember that." Kirilo offered him a wad of bills. "I'd like to discuss some business with you later."

Stefan glanced over Kirilo's shoulder to make sure Misha wasn't watching and shoved the money in his pocket.

"Now, let's finish this search so we can get out of this godforsaken place," Kirilo said.

CHAPTER 55

THE CABIN ATTENDANT, A SURLY CHAIN-SMOKER WITH HIPS the width of the corridor, instructed Nadia and Adam on how to use the *blokirator*, a Club-like plastic device that secured the door handle in the locked position from the inside. This prevented even the attendant from opening the door with her key.

"When you leave your room," she said, "let me know. I will lock it behind you. There are thieves on these trains, you know."

Nadia slept fitfully, gradually drifting to the border of consciousness before bolting upright at each of the three stops they made through the night. Each time, she glanced at Adam's cot to make sure he was still there; he was lost in the depths of sleep that only teenagers can find.

In the morning, she paid the attendant the US equivalent of three dollars to prepare hot water. Half an hour later, with Adam awake to secure the *blokirator*, she took her first shower in three days in a special carriage located beside the restaurant car. Unlike the dreaded bathroom she shared with other passengers, the shower room was surprisingly clean.

Returning to the cabin with a bounce in her step, she offered to pay for a shower for Adam, but he refused. When she asked him to do it for her as a favor, however, he got the message.

"Wait," Nadia said. "I'll get the attendant to lock the door behind us," she said.

"Why?"

"I have to go with you. It's too dangerous."

"What? For who? For me? And what, it wasn't dangerous for you?"

Nadia sighed.

"Oh. I get it. You mean it's too dangerous for the locket."

"You know what I mean."

"Yeah, yeah. I know what you mean."

The attendant locked the door behind them.

Adam emerged from the shower with his wet hair carefully combed to hide his ears. On the way back, they stopped at the restaurant car. Light poured in past teal curtains pulled to the side. A dozen booths with steel-blue upholstery lined both sides of the car, half of them occupied. Four men jammed in front of a semicircular bar made of cheap marble, smoke curling upward from the cigarettes in their hands. A television above the bar was tuned to a hockey game. The announcers chattered and buzzed.

Upon their entrance, everyone in the car turned to appraise them. Nadia ignored them and pointed to an empty booth. Adam rushed ahead and took the side that let him watch television. A sullen waiter dumped two menus in front of them. They were fifty pages long and weighed five pounds. Most of the items had a line drawn through them and were unavailable. The latest offerings were handwritten on the front page, as though the kitchen was picking up whatever it could along the way.

Nadia saw that other people at the booths had brought their own food in baskets and shopping bags.

"We can get good food on the platform," Adam said. "When the train stops. Next stop, Balyezino."

"When is that?"

He checked his watch. "Around one thirty. In about three hours. It's a good stop. Twenty-three minutes long."

"How do you know all this? You been here before?"

"I've never been anywhere except Korosten and the Zone," he said. When she sat there waiting for the explanation, he relented. "My father used to work the railway. He gave me a train schedule. Told me some things."

Nadia looked around and saw that everyone was watching them. "Then we should go back to the cabin. There's no advantage in being here."

"I'm sick of being all cooped up. You go back," he said. He nodded at the television. "I'm going to watch the game."

That was not an option. The *samovar* provided boiled water, so Nadia ordered two cups of tea and two bottled waters. Adam didn't touch his. Instead, he stared like a zombie over Nadia's shoulder at the screen.

As soon as Nadia began to sip her tea, an elderly woman with an overbite leaned over from a booth diagonally across the way and smiled.

"Your skin is incredible. Where are you from, dear? Italy? Greece?"

"No, America," Nadia said, her hand touching her face.

The woman's eyes widened with curiosity. "America. When I was a child, we used to fear this place, America." She opened a plastic container filled with raspberries, strawberries, blueberries, and whipped cream. "Please," she said. "To share. I wish I had meat to offer you, but my pension hasn't arrived in four months. This is all I have. Please."

Nadia thanked her profusely, but when the woman persisted, she slid over to her booth. Adam was ten feet away. He wasn't going anywhere. Nadia passed on the berries and cream, and stuck to her tea and water.

"I was a stenographer for Brezhnev in the Kremlin," she said, "until they accused me of helping circulate rumors that he was in bad mental health to help Andropov unseat him. For this I spent two years in a *gulag*."

As the woman spoke of her struggle to survive a labor camp, people leaned in from adjacent booths. A small crowd gathered and began to participate.

"Tell me," she said, "what do Americans think of Russians?"

Nadia foraged for an honest and congenial answer. "That you are soulful. That you're rich in family and tradition and, above all else, soulful."

A murmur of approval surrounded Nadia. The woman glowed.

"A soul must work to survive," a voice said.

The crowd murmured more approval. Those who were standing parted. A man sprawled at a booth in front of Adam with a bottle of vodka and a shot glass in front of him.

"Since they closed the collective farms in 1991, it's all gone to shit," he says.

"Papers," a woman shouted.

Conversations ceased. Lips formed straight lines. A pair of heels clicked together at the back of the car.

People scurried about. Some escaped into the car ahead. Others returned to their booths or the bar.

A petite woman in a gray military uniform bustled up to Adam with a fierce look on her face, as though he'd trampled her garden. From the neck up, she resembled an aging porcupine, with spiked black hair that sprang from gray roots. A younger man accompanied her. He was tall, with a square face, gaunt cheeks, and a sidearm attached to his belt.

"Papers," she screamed at Adam. "Where is your guardian?"

Adam lowered his head. He stuttered, "I…I…"

For the first time since Nadia had met Adam, he looked like a child and not a man, one reared to respect and fear authority, like Soviet citizens of the past. An unfamiliar sense of maternal protectiveness sent Nadia springing to her feet.

"Hey," she said to the cop. "I'm the boy's guardian. Who are you?"

The woman flashed a legitimate-looking police ID. "You are in Kirov Oblast. We are the police. Passport Control. Papers. Both of you. Do not make me ask you again."

Nadia turned over her passport and told Adam to do the same.

"Your papers are out of order," she said after studying Nadia's passport.

"Why?"

"Because you must register with the local prefecture upon entering Russia. You are in Kirov Oblast. There is no stamp of registration."

"I'm on a train, just passing through. How am I supposed to register?"

Instead of returning the passports, she clutched them by her side. "You will get off with us at the next stop. You will register at the local prefecture. And you will have to pay a fine."

Adam shrank in his booth.

"A fine?" Nadia said. The lies of a thief sprang to her mind. "I see. Well, we cannot and will not get off this train. I'm on important business."

The policewoman smirked. "Oh, really? What kind of business?"

Nadia whipped out her New York City library card. "You see this? It says *New York Chronicle*. That is the biggest newspaper in America. I went to Moscow to interview Aline Kabaeva. You know Aline Kabaeva? She's the Olympic gold medalist who's now a member of parliament and a very close friend of Prime Minister Putin. After writing a story on women in politics in Russia, I'm enjoying your beautiful countryside with my nephew. But you...You don't want me to enjoy it, do you? You want me to write another story instead?"

The policewoman's lips quivered as though she didn't know if she should be angry or afraid. The soldier put his hand on his sidearm uncertainly. He looked from his partner to Nadia and back to her again.

After a momentary pause, she returned the passports. "But you must register," she grumbled. Her partner followed her to the next car, the badge sewn on his right shoulder barely hanging on by a few threads.

When Nadia turned back, she found Adam staring at her with wonder. She led the way back to their compartment. Worn and weathered passengers loitered in front of their cabins. Smoking was prohibited, but a white cloud hung in the air and the corridor reeked of nicotine. Nadia savored the thrill of outwitting the cop. She was a thief's daughter. She could wrangle her way out of any situation, couldn't she? Equally thrilling was the thought that she'd impressed Adam and earned a modicum of respect.

"Was that…Was that all true?" Adam said, close on her heels.

"Was what true?"

"What you said back there. To that *musor*. Was that all true?"

"Of course it was true. Are you calling your aunt a liar?"

"You're my cousin, not my aunt."

"I prefer aunt. It gives me a sense of power with no real responsibility."

"You're not my aunt."

"I disagree."

"Are you really a reporter? Do you really know Aline Kabaeva?"

"No. But I read an article about her in a New York paper once."

"Huh?"

When they got to their cabin, Nadia locked the door behind them.

"From now on," she said, "we don't leave the room unless we need to use the bathroom. And we watch each other's back at all times. Agreed?"

Adam hesitated and then nodded. "Agreed."

CHAPTER 56

KIRILO SLIPPED A FIVE HUNDRED–RUBLE NOTE TO THE BARtender in the restaurant car.

"Car Three, Cabin Two," the bartender said, snatching the bill from the counter and burying it in his pocket. "She and the boy."

"The boy? What boy?" Misha said.

"Ugly boy. Not Russian. Face like a reindeer's ass after Christmas Eve. Looks like he's from the North. Not Yakut or Evenk. More like Chukchi. Smells like he's from the Zone, though."

"The Zone?" Victor said. "Why do you say that?"

"I worked in Kyiv for twelve years. You get a feeling." The bartender shrugged. "I can't explain it."

Misha's neck buckled. Warned, Kirilo stepped away. Misha vomited. The bartender recoiled. Misha hurled again. Blood mixed with chunks of partially digested chips and nuts. The bartender groaned. A putrid smell filled the air. Kirilo gagged.

Misha straightened. Blood dripped from his nose onto the counter. He raised his sleeve to his ashen face. A red droplet seeped into the white cotton and spread.

His lips parted and his eyes widened. He glanced at Victor with a mixture of disbelief and disdain. "Did you really poison me, old man?"

Victor laughed. "Of course not. You really must have caught a bug or a parasite."

Kirilo now knew Victor was lying. Misha looked worse every hour. But there was no sense in telling Misha. They couldn't afford any delays to see a doctor, and even if they could, there was no hope for the *moscal.*

"You should really see a doctor," Specter said.

Misha babbled incoherently for a few seconds before glancing at Specter. "What? Doctor? And let you guys make out with the formula? You'd like that, wouldn't you, Specter? No, no doctor."

"Misha," Specter said, "you're not well."

"The formula," Misha said. A maniacal glint shone in his eyes. "All I need is the formula. Let's go."

They bounded down the corridor toward the third car. Kirilo let Misha, Specter, and the four bodyguards go ahead of him to put distance between the radioactive *moscal* and himself.

Kirilo checked his watch. It was 4:00 p.m. on Tuesday. It had taken them two and a half days to catch up to Nadia. When they had finally arrived in Moscow at 2:00 p.m. on Sunday, some pipsqueak in Passport Control had flagged Misha as an undesirable based on his criminal record as a youth in Moscow. It didn't help that Misha was sweating profusely, like someone who had something to hide. Kirilo explained that the deputy minister of the interior of Russia was an investor in his Black Sea energy project and would vouch for the American. The deputy was away at a conference in Prague, however, and couldn't be reached until midnight.

On Tuesday morning, they flew to Yemelyanovo Airport and tried to catch the Trans-Siberian thirty-seven kilometers away at Krasnoyarsk, but the taxi arrived seven minutes late. They drove an additional four hundred kilometers and finally boarded it at Tayshet, halfway to Vladivostok.

When they arrived at Cabin 2, Misha tried to open the door. It wouldn't budge. He cursed and kicked at it. Loitering passengers disappeared.

Something clanged inside the cabin. It was metal on metal, like a lead pipe accidentally banging into the steel frame of a bed.

"Who are you? What are you doing?" A very large female attendant barreled down the corridor. No wonder the restaurant car had no food to offer, Kirilo thought.

Kirilo had the *pyatichatka* out of his wallet before she arrived. He offered her the fifty-hryvnia bill.

"Please open this door," he said.

She licked her lips at the money and frowned as though she wished she could accept it but couldn't.

"It's okay, dear," he said. "The American woman is my granddaughter. The boy is a troubled child. She is adopting him. I am here to help them."

"That's no business of mine," she said. "But I can't open the door for you because it's locked from the inside."

"How do you get in if it's an emergency?"

"They have to open it themselves."

"What if they can't?"

"Well, that's never happened. But if we had to, we could break it down. Though, in this case, it would be a waste of time."

Kirilo sighed with exasperation. "Why do you say that?"

"Because the woman and the boy aren't in there. They got off the train at Tayshet."

"What?" Misha said.

"As soon as we arrived at Tayshet, they got off the train and disappeared."

The lock was unbolted from the inside. The door slid open. An ancient couple jabbered in Chinese. The man held a metal cane.

"Where could they possibly be going that they would get off at Tayshet?" Victor said.

"The Baikal-Amur Mainline begins in Tayshet," the attendant said. "It goes north and then runs parallel to the Trans-Siberian. It is a slower train."

"Then why on God's earth would anyone use it besides a local?" Kirilo said.

"It used to be a transit stop for *gulag* prisoners. Now it is the gateway to Yakutsk and the North," she said.

Kirilo howled. "Yakutsk? The North? There's nothing in the North but *gulags* and mines. No roads, no civilization, nothing." Kirilo's voice faded as he listened to his own words.

"Which makes it the last place anyone would look for her," Victor said.

Kirilo swore under his breath. "What is the fastest way for us to get on the Baikal-Amur headed north?"

The attendant eyed the *pyatichatka* again. "Once you pass Irkutsk, the train turns back north. You can get off at Bamovskaya, take the Amur Yakutsk line, and cut them off."

Kirilo handed her the five hundred–ruble note. "Where can we cut them off, dear?"

She snapped the bill out of his hands and buried it in her pocket in one motion. "At Tynda," she said. "You can cut them off at Tynda."

CHAPTER 57

THE TRAIN RUMBLED NORTH BY NORTHEAST, PITCHING AND tossing Nadia in her ramshackle seat every half hour. She spent the hours sleeping and gazing out the grimy bolted-down window of their second-class cabin. Whenever she checked to see how Adam was faring, she found him slumped in torpor. He didn't mind the endless travel. It must be some Eastern European thing that living in America expunged, Nadia thought.

Mile after mile of conifers stretched across the taiga amidst patches of red-and-gold birch trees. Signs of industry and life rolled into view occasionally. Factories sprawled along the Bratsk High Dam, while coots and geese buzzed the marshes. The vista gave way to the untamed forest and served as a reminder that Siberia was larger than the United States and Western Europe combined.

Twenty-four hours after Nadia and Adam had boarded, they passed Severobaikalsk. The train plunged along its tracks past groves of stunted pines into a valley surrounded by jagged mountains with snowcapped peaks. The afternoon sun shimmered on the northern tip of icy Lake Baikal. It was the Pearl of Siberia, the attendant said when she brought hot tea, and the world's largest freshwater lake. They passed through four tunnels along the lake and emerged surrounded by glazed tundra. From there, the permafrost extended forever.

Adam kept busy by reading the same torn and tattered hockey magazine over and over again. The cover featured an action shot of a huge player with a penguin on his jersey driving toward the net. Wavy black locks flowed from his black helmet, fierce determination etched on a surprisingly cherubic face. From her viewing angle, Nadia could see the name *Jagr* in bold letters beneath the picture.

"You have a favorite team?" Nadia said.

He lifted the magazine and flashed the page he was reading. The top of the page said, *New York Rangers*. The page was a mess. The left side had a hole the size of an adult's fist punched through it.

They bought food and bottled water on the platforms during stops along the way. Forty-eight hours after they'd boarded, the Baikal-Amur train headed to Sovetskaya Gavan, the Sea of Okhotsk, and the Pacific Ocean, and Nadia and Adam made a scheduled stop. The local time was 7:31 p.m., five hours later than Moscow. It was now Thursday, April 29.

The name on the train station read *TYNDA*.

Nadia and Adam climbed off the train onto the platform at Track 2. Their matronly attendant did the same.

"Where can we catch the northbound Amur-Yakutsk to Tommot?" Adam said.

"Track Six," the attendant said. "It arrives at seven forty. In nine minutes."

CHAPTER 58

KIRILO AND HIS TWO BODYGUARDS STEPPED OFF THE NORTH-bound Amur-Yakutsk at Tynda on Track 6 at 7:42. Misha followed, propped up by Specter, looking like a corpse who'd escaped from the morgue. His pair of bodyguards brought up the rear.

Kirilo marched up to a transit employee on the platform.

"Which track for the Baikal-Amur? The one that's just arrived, from Tayshet?"

"Track Two," the employee said.

Kirilo had expected a small railway station. What the hell did they have out here that required twelve or more tracks? Timber? What else could it be?

They bolted up the stairs to Track 2, where the Baikal-Amur had arrived twelve minutes earlier. The train sat on the track, waiting to depart. Kirilo and Specter hurried to the far end. A woman wearing a blue vest and a matching cap puffed on a cigarette.

"I'm looking for my niece," Kirilo said. "She's American. Traveling with her adopted son. An unfortunate sort. Have you seen them?"

The attendant's eyes flickered for a second before registering confusion. She looked Kirilo up and down. "An American, you say? Gee, I don't know if I've seen any Americans."

Kirilo whipped out his wallet and held out a *pyatichatka*. "Is your memory getting any better, dear?"

The attendant snatched the dough. "Oh, that American. Sure. They were in Car Two, Cabin Four."

"*Were*?" Kirilo said.

"Yes. *Were*. They got off when we arrived."

"Do you know where they went?"

She scratched her chin. "Gee. They may have asked me how to connect to a train, but I'm not sure I remember which one."

Kirilo gave her another *pyatichatka*.

"Oh, that train. Sure," she said. "Now I remember. It was the Amur-Yakutsk."

"What?" Kirilo said.

"The Amur-Yakutsk. They're headed north to Tommot." She glanced at her watch. "It leaves at seven fifty-five. In two minutes."

CHAPTER 59

NADIA SAW THEM JUST AS THEY GOT OFF THE TRAIN. SHE grabbed Adam by the collar and yanked him behind a massive iron pillar on the platform of Track 6.

"Oh my God. That's them," she said.

"Who?"

"*Them*. Don't look, don't look."

Adam slipped the knapsack off his back and stood sideways beside Nadia to make himself smaller.

They approached. Nadia rotated her body around the pillar to hide. Adam followed her lead. She heard footsteps, recognized a familiar voice.

Specter.

Another rotation and they passed. Nadia glanced at their backs. Specter was twenty feet away from her. He was so close.

Specter disappeared down the stairwell toward the central concourse with the others.

Nadia nudged Adam. They hurried onto the Amur-Yakutsk headed north, the same train the others had just gotten off.

The doors closed. The engine hissed. The train rolled away from the station. Nadia peered through a narrow gap between the curtains on the window in her cabin.

Specter and Kirilo exploded out of the stairwell, three bodyguards close on their heels.

"Let me look," Adam said beside her.

She held him back with a straight-arm.

Kirilo and Specter raced for the edge of the platform. Nadia's viewing angle narrowed until she lost sight of them.

"What if they jump on the back of the train?" Adam said.

"Lock the door," Nadia said.

She bolted out of the cabin, sprinted down the corridor, passed through a doorway, and entered the rear car. Weary faces looked up at her from benches. She didn't recognize any of them.

She slowed as she approached the window of the rear door, fearful that Kirilo or one of his bodyguards could be climbing aboard. The bottom of the window was filthy, covered with grime. The top, however, was still translucent.

From a distance, she could see five men turning back on the platform toward the stairs.

CHAPTER 60

FOUR TAXIS WAITED OUTSIDE THE TRAIN STATION AT TYNDA.

"Who knows the road to Tommot?" Kirilo said.

All of them raised their hands.

"Who's driven it recently?" Kirilo said.

All of them raised their hands again.

"Who knows my brother Theodore's hotel, the Tommot Vista Inn?"

Three of the men raised their hands. Kirilo approached the fourth, the youngest of the bunch. He looked as though he didn't shave yet. He stood beside a beaten-up Volvo station wagon with his arms folded across his chest.

"How long a drive to Tommot?" Kirilo said.

"About six hundred kilometers. But there is no Vista Inn in Tommot. And I don't know any Theodore."

"Neither do I. I'd like to hire you."

"It's going to be expensive."

"How much?"

The kid hesitated. "Eight thousand rubles. Plus gasoline. Half up front."

Kirilo laughed. "Half up front. Good for you. Done. There are six of us."

The kid looked them over, pausing when he got to Misha. "What's wrong with him?"

Misha brandished his gun, pointed it at him, and grinned. "This is what's wrong with me." Spit flew from his lips and connected with the kid's shirt.

The kid looked at his shirt with disgust and backed away. "You'd be better off with two cars," he said to Kirilo. "More space. More comfortable."

Kirilo could see the kid's mind working. He was using comfort as an excuse to put Misha in someone else's car. Smart boy.

"Fine." Kirilo looked at the other drivers. "You decide who else goes."

"All right. The road is bad. There are many holes. It's a brutal drive. You sure you don't want to wait for the train?"

"We're sure."

"In the dark, it's going to be slow going."

"The train arrives at Tommot in fifteen hours. We must be there before the train."

"I've done it twice. It took me sixteen to eighteen hours. And that was daylight."

Kirilo pulled out his wallet. "I will give you three thousand rubles up front. And another nine thousand if you make it before the train."

The kid's eyes lit up. "I think I can make it in fifteen, though."

"I thought you might."

CHAPTER 61

THE GLACIAL PEAKS OF THE STANOVOY RANGE GLISTENED IN the dark. The train hurtled through a tunnel beneath them. A hundred miles past Tynda, they entered the Sakha Republic of Russia, also known as Yakutia.

The train crossed three rivers and rumbled past the coal mines at Berkakit and Neryungri. Smog hung over the stations at the mining towns. They passed abandoned collectives and empty wooden cottages with fenced-in gardens overgrown with weeds. When the train pulled in to Tommot at 11:00 a.m. on Friday, the Aldan River shimmered beneath the morning sun.

Adam followed Nadia as she skulked her way through the train station. She was fearful that Kirilo, Victor, and Misha had somehow caught up with her, but they were nowhere in sight. "Where do we wait?" Nadia said.

"Outside, in front of the station," Adam said. "My father said the man will find us."

"And he didn't tell you what he'd look like?"

"Just that he is a Yakut, and he will look a little more like me, and a little less like you."

"What is a Yakut?" Nadia said.

"They're one of the indigenous people of Siberia. Close to five hundred thousand live in northern Russia. Great hunters. Really intense."

The Tommot station was a plain cement building but boasted three yellow domes like a church. Nadia put on her hat, gloves, and winter coat. Adam did the same. A wind blasted them when they stepped outside. According to the oversized thermometer by the entrance, the temperature was negative five degrees Celsius. That was about twenty degrees Fahrenheit.

A man got out of a vintage SUV parked a few steps away. He looked like the offspring of a Slav and an Asian. A fur hat covered his bald head. Although the creases in his weathered face suggested he was in his late sixties or older, the bounce in his step said otherwise.

After glancing at Nadia, he looked at Adam cautiously. "There is much talk about you. Can it be true?"

"Yes," Adam said. "She betrayed me for a Yakut."

The Yakut smiled. "Old Cossack song. Your father loved it. Yeah, good. We go."

The SUV was a square-shaped model Nadia had never heard of, called a Nissan Patrol. The exterior was dented and dinged, but the interior was spotless, the cloth upholstery impeccably maintained. They stored their bags in the cavernous cargo area, which contained three spare tires and four cans of gasoline. Nadia sat behind the Yakut so she could watch him. Adam sat beside him.

"My name is Fyodor," he said as he guided the car away from the station.

Nadia introduced herself and Adam. Fyodor spoke in a strange dialect. Nadia had to focus on the words to understand him.

"How did you know my father?" Adam said. "Did you work together on the railroad?"

"No. I knew father from *gulag* in Kolyma. Many years ago. We did business together."

"Business?" Nadia said. "At the *gulag*?"

"Were you a prisoner, too?" Adam said.

Fyodor shook his head and glared at Adam. "No Yakuts in *gulag*. Bounty hunter."

"Bounty hunter?" Nadia said.

"Yakut is hunter. Government hire Yakut to hunt prisoners who escape from *gulag*."

"So how did you do business with my father?" Adam said.

"Your father arrange for prisoner to escape. Bounty hunter catch prisoner and bring him back. Bounty hunter get paid. I get paid. Father get paid. Prisoner get paid—if live."

Nadia envisioned prisoners escaping and returning, and money changing hands.

"Didn't the guards catch on after a while?" she said.

"Guard, no problem," Fyodor said. "Other gang leader, problem. He set trap. Prisoner caught. Bounty hunter caught."

A horn blared. Nadia craned her neck to the right. A massive cargo truck headed straight toward them.

Fyodor swerved into a pothole to avoid it. Nadia's head hit the ceiling. She yelped.

"Sorry," Fyodor said. "They work on railroad, extend all way to Yakutsk. Supply come to Tommot. Many trucks. Many holes in road." He turned to Adam. "When I caught in *gulag*, your father pay money to guards. Bounty hunter escapes. Owes father debt. Yakut always pay debt."

They drove farther north for a hundred kilometers until they reached a small village beside a river surrounded by rolling hilltops.

"This is Anga," Fyodor said. "Oldest Russian settlement in Siberia. We are headed to one hundred kilometers from Yakutsk, near Sharlam's lodge. Evenk meet you there, yes?"

"Outside Yakutsk," Adam said. "Yes. An Evenk. Another friend of my father's."

"Evenk," Fyodor said with a derisive sneer. "Yeah, good."

Nadia whispered to Adam. "What's an Evenk?"

"Another indigenous people of Siberia. About eighty thousand of them. Great herdsmen. Laid-back. Total opposite of Yakut."

They drove on for another three hours along an increasingly awful road. Nadia was starting to think that it might just be possible to jar a person's brains out of his skull, when Fyodor pulled to a stop.

Everyone climbed out of the vehicle. The sun burst into an orange ball of fire as it set over the horizon. Beneath the ridge, water rushed packs of rocks and ice along a river. After three hours in the van's cloying heat, the Arctic chill was a welcome relief.

"You okay?" Nadia said.

Adam shivered and nodded.

"You see the trapper's lodge where we're supposed to meet this guy? I don't see any lodge."

Fyodor pointed at a cluster of pine trees a hundred yards away. "There."

The corner of a roofline formed by three intersecting logs protruded through the trees.

"Five fifteen," Adam said. "He's supposed to be there at five. From five to nine."

Thanking Fyodor for the ride, they ran to the lodge.

When they got there, a man was waiting. Like the Yakut, the Evenk was of medium height and lean build. His chin and cheekbones, however, were less pronounced, and his nose was sharper. He had a darker complexion, like an Australian aborigine.

The Evenk raised a shotgun and aimed it between them. "Who goes there?" he said in coarse Russian. He was even harder to understand than the Yakut.

Nadia and Adam froze.

"*Umukon*," Adam said. "*Umukon Khalganchuluk*."

"Then let's run from here," the Evenk said, "because it's a place where evil spirits live."

The Evenk laughed heartily and lowered his gun. He bounded forward and hugged them as though they were long-lost friends.

"Sorry late. Stopped by to see friends on way. In, in," he said. "Leave quick."

They climbed into a vehicle similar to the white van they had just left.

"Who is *Umukon Khalganchuluk*?" Nadia said.

"I don't know," Adam said. "It's just something my father made me memorize."

"*Umukon Khalganchuluk*. One-arm, one-leg, one-eye evil spirit," the Evenk said.

"Why is he evil?" Nadia said.

"Because," the Evenk said as he turned the van around, "he steal children from their sleep."

CHAPTER 62

A SHOTGUN EXPLODED BEHIND HIM.

Kirilo ducked. The kid behind the wheel swore. The Volvo screeched and swerved to a halt on the bridge.

Kirilo waited, turned, and looked back through the rear window.

The second taxi, an old Peugeot, wobbled to a halt. The rubber on the front driver's side wheel lay flat in a pothole. It wasn't a shotgun. The tire had exploded.

"How far are we from Tommot?" Kirilo said.

"Ten kilometers."

Kirilo glanced at his watch. It was 11:05 a.m. The train had probably arrived on time five minutes ago.

"You almost made it," Kirilo said. "Excellent job."

The kid frowned into the rearview mirror. "But I didn't make it. I failed."

Kirilo pushed his door open. Water rushed and chattered below the bridge. Victor opened the other rear door beside him.

"Failure creates opportunity, my friend," Kirilo said. "You will be paid your bonus in full. Stay in the car and keep the engine running. We will be moving in a few minutes." Kirilo turned to Pavel and the other bodyguard. "Step outside and keep our friends company. Especially the American." He glanced at Victor. "You. Follow me."

Kirilo put on his fur hat and a pair of finger-hugging Italian driving gloves. He stepped out of the car, leaving his warm cashmere gloves behind.

The other driver opened the trunk and removed the spare tire.

Misha had already gotten out of the other car. He pointed a gun at the driver's head. Pus oozed from a sore festering on his sunken left cheek. Misha waved the gun as though it were a pointer. "You've got thirty seconds to change that tire," he said. "Thirty seconds. We would have been on time. We were almost there. But no. You had to screw it all up."

The driver's hands shook so badly he couldn't get his fingers under the spare tire to lift it out of storage. Specter and Misha's other bodyguard helped him.

Kirilo made soothing noises and motioned for Misha to lower his gun. "There, there, my friend," Kirilo said. "Sometimes bad news brings good news with it. Siberian waters are known for their antioxidants. The Lena River is known for its healing powers. People travel from all over Europe to bathe in it. Come down to the river with me. Fortunately for us, it's late April, so the river melts during the day before freezing at night. Come splash some water on your face, and you will be instantly rejuvenated."

Misha appeared baffled. "Where?"

"To the river. Down below," Kirilo said.

"No," Misha said. "Where are we?"

Specter started toward him.

Kirilo put his hand out for him to stop. "No, no. We're fine. He's just a little feverish from all the travel. You all help the man with the tires." He turned to Misha. "You are in Russia. Past Tommot on the way to Yakutsk. The formula, my friend, the formula."

"The formula." Misha's eyes lit up. "The formula."

Specter stepped aside tentatively. He took the jack and lug wrench while Misha's bodyguard grabbed the spare tire. As they began to work, Specter kept glancing over his shoulder.

Kirilo motioned for Victor to follow. He guided Misha around the bridge to an embankment that fell gently to the river's edge, out of sight. When he got to the water, Misha placed his gun on a rock and bent over. He reached into the water with both hands.

Kirilo thrust the cattle prod against his neck. Misha convulsed and made gurgling noises. He collapsed into the water. Kirilo put the prod beside the gun. He hoisted Misha out of the river and rolled him on his back. Misha coughed and wheezed.

Kirilo wrapped his hands around his neck and squeezed.

Misha brought his hands around Kirilo's. They felt weak, weaker than Victor's had when he'd almost strangled him on his boat. Misha tried to speak. Kirilo eased his grip.

"American citizen," Misha said.

"That doesn't mean anything anymore."

Kirilo resumed squeezing until Misha's body went limp and his pants moistened. Kirilo relaxed for a minute to catch his breath. After taking Misha's wallet, passport, and diamond-crusted watch, he pushed the body into the water. The current swept it down the river around patches of ice.

Kirilo walked up to Victor beside the bridge, cattle prod in hand. "You were wrong," he said, still wheezing.

"About what?" Victor said.

"Ten million divided by two is not much more than ten million divided by three. But this formula…That's a different matter."

Kirilo replaced the cattle prod in the lining of his coat and put Misha's gun in his pocket. When Victor and he climbed to the road, Misha's bodyguard was changing the tire with his back to him. Pavel and Kirilo's other bodyguard immediately drew weapons.

The bodyguard turned, dropped the lug wrench, and raised his hands.

"Your boss had an accident," Kirilo said. "You were local hired help anyways. You want a job?"

"Yes, please," the bodyguard said.

"Where is Specter?" Kirilo said.

"He went to take a piss," Pavel said. "That way." Pavel nodded at the wooded knoll on the near side of the bridge headed back toward Tommot.

Pavel stayed with one of the bodyguards while the other went with Kirilo to find Specter. They searched for five minutes but didn't find him. When they got back to the car, the tire was changed.

"Nothing?" Pavel said.

"No," Kirilo said. "He's gone. He lied in the warehouse when we had the Tesla woman. He told me Isabella was on the phone to get me away until the police came. But Isabella never called."

"Why would he do that?" Pavel said.

"Because he's not who he seems to be."

"Then who is he?"

"Looks like a bitch to me."

"A government agent? Who infiltrated Misha's operation? In America?"

Kirilo glanced at Victor.

Victor shrugged. "He was Misha's man. I didn't know him until a week ago. I don't know where he came from."

"Bitches die," Kirilo said. "Who cares where they're from."

Kirilo turned to the two taxi drivers. "You guys have two choices. You can be paid handsomely for your work and forget that you had two more passengers. Or you and your families can cease to exist. Which will it be?"

Pavel joined Kirilo and Victor in the Volvo. The other two bodyguards remained in the other car. Kirilo told the kid to pass the other car. The kid gunned the engine, and the Volvo took the lead.

"Slow down, slow down," Kirilo said. "There's no need to hurry anymore."

The kid eased up on the gas. "There isn't?"

"No," Kirilo said.

Pavel turned from the front seat and frowned. "Why not?"

"We know where she's going. We've known where she's been going all along." Kirilo glanced at Victor. "Haven't we, cousin?"

Victor didn't answer him. Instead, he just looked out the window.

"It's best to dispose of garbage in remote areas where no one will find it," Kirilo said. "So we chase. But now that we're rid of the garbage, we can stop chasing. She is going to Yakutsk. What is Yakutsk known for?"

"Diamonds," Pavel said. "Twenty percent of the world's diamond production."

"What else?"

"*Gulag*," Victor said.

"Yes. *Gulag.* Where did they bury the bodies in the *gulags*?"

"Ah," Pavel said. "Of course. The Road of Bones."

Kirilo looked at his hands. He tried to uncurl his fingers and straighten them completely, but he hadn't been able to do so since wielding a pickax at the *gulag* for eight years straight.

"Yes. The Kolyma Highway. And where does the Kolyma Highway lead?"

"Magadan," Pavel said. He turned forward, sighed with contentment, and relaxed in his seat. "It leads to Magadan."

"Exactly," Kirilo said. "Gateway to the Kolyma Region. Former transit center for prisoners being shipped to the *gulag*. The only major port in the area. Now services the lumber trade. We are five hundred kilometers from the Arctic Circle. The ice is melting. The rivers and lakes are flooding. There is one, and only one, road in the taiga, which may or may not be passable in late April. It is the Road of Bones."

"They could fly from Yakutsk," Victor said.

"No. They are not flying for a reason. It may have something to do with the boy, or it may be to stay off the radar. They will take the Road of Bones from Yakutsk to Magadan. Once in Magadan, they *must* take an airplane or a boat to leave Russia."

"How will we get from Tommot to Yakutsk?"

Kirilo leaned forward and tapped the kid on the shoulder. "This young man will drive us for ten thousand rubles more. Won't you, my friend?"

CHAPTER 63

"NO ONE IN RUSSIA CALL ROAD OF BONES. IN RUSSIA, KOLYMA *Trakt*." The Evenk peppered his phrases with affirmative grunting noises and Evenki words Nadia didn't understand.

"Why is that?" Nadia said.

"Many people die in old Russia. Now new Russia. No more Road of Bones. Kolyma *Trakt* now. We take new Kolyma *Trakt*. Old Kolyma *Trakt* no good. Too late."

"Excuse me? What new Kolyma *Trakt*?"

She glanced at Adam, who was sitting beside her behind the driver. He shrugged.

"Two roads," the Evenk said. "Old and new. Old, twelve hundred kilometers. New, two thousand kilometers. Too late April for old. River melting, bridges and road risky. We take new road via Ust-Nera."

Nadia leaned toward Adam. "Did your father say anything about a new road?"

"No," Adam said. "Road of Bones."

"New *Trakt* finish 2009," the Evenk said. "Good, good, all year. My name Sharlam. Sharlam take care of you."

Sharlam turned right onto a cracked asphalt road.

Nadia bounced lightly on her seat as the van's suspension squeaked and groaned. Ivory figurines of dancing bears and children riding wolves were glued to the dashboard. There were two additional rows of seats behind them. A mattress and sleeping bag were rolled out on each of them. Eight spare tires, two windshields, and a cardboard box full of windshield wipers and headlights lay in the back beside a huge toolbox.

"What is this vehicle?" Nadia said.

"*Buhanka*," Sharlam said with pride. "Also call *wazzik*, *hiebobulka*. You know *buhanka* in America?"

"No," Nadia said. "But I know some neighborhoods in New York City where a *buhanka* might work."

"*Buhanka* best. It break, Sharlam fix. Anyone can fix. Easy as Evenk. You see."

"I can't wait," Nadia said.

"How do you know my father?" Adam said.

"Know father from *gulag*. From Sevvostlag. Father save Sharlam's life. Sharlam remember. Sharlam help boy."

"Did you do business with my father?" Adam said.

"Yes, business. Government hire Evenki to manage horses at *gulag*. Sharlam in charge of oat supply for horses at Sevvostlag. Father buy oats from Sharlam. Yes, business."

"Oats," Nadia said. "For food. I understand the rations were horrible."

"One bowl soup, two pieces bread for dinner. When bring soup, if thin, prisoner cry. If thick, prisoner so happy, cry more. Many tears in *gulag*. But father no buy oat for food."

Nadia frowned. "No?"

"Then why?" Adam said.

"To burn so other prison gang leader no get. Estonian, Lithuanian prisoner much bigger. Bigger prisoner die first in Sevvostlag. Portions same no matter what size. Father burn oats so other gang leader no get, die first."

A moment of silence passed.

"How did my father save you?" Adam said.

"Guard find out. Sharlam sentenced to death. Father paid guard to let Sharlam escape. Sharlam remember. Sharlam always remember."

In Kolyma, the taiga is infinite, signs of life rare. Time is measured in distance. Nadia alternated shifts with Sharlam. She drove four hours for each of his twelve. She tried to persuade him to let her do more, but he refused. His concern for her and Adam's safety and their need for speed were the only reasons he agreed to allow her to drive.

Sharlam knew precisely which outposts had food and bottled water and, more important, 92 octane fuel. Their first stop was Khandyga, 380 kilometers past Yakutsk. Subsequent stops included Ust-Nera, Susuman, Ust-Omchug, and Palatka.

They suffered five flat tires and one broken windshield when a windstorm felled a branch onto the *buhanka.* Adam stayed quiet through the trip, returning to his hockey magazine time and time again.

The two thousand–kilometer trip took two and a half days. Sharlam dropped them off with a tearful hug a quarter mile from their destination at 8:45 a.m. on Sunday, May 2. Nadia and Adam were sore, hungry, and exhausted.

They were near an airport on the outskirts of the administrative headquarters of the Russian Far East, four hours ahead of schedule. It was a port town on the Sea of Okhotsk and the gateway to Kolyma, where most *gulag* prisoners had been processed.

The town was called Magadan.

CHAPTER 64

"It seems you have some influence in Russia," Deputy Director Krylov said. "The director told me to give you full cooperation."

"We're old friends," Kirilo said. "We went to university together. We're always on the lookout for the best interests of our countries, the way neighbors and brothers should be."

In addition to Deputy Director Krylov, Kirilo, Victor, and five other men sat at a large rectangular table at the Magadan headquarters of the FSB, the Russian Federal Security Service and successor to the KGB.

After quick introductions, it was clear from their titles that the first four were the deputy director's lackeys. The fifth one, however, wore an everyday olive military uniform with a single gold star on the insignia on his shoulder.

"This is Major General Yashko of the Russian Ground Forces from the Far Eastern Military District," Krylov said. "Your exact command, General? Forgive me; in all this excitement, I've forgotten."

"The Fourteenth Independent Spetsnaz Bridage in Ussuriysk."

"Special Forces," Kirilo said.

"Yes," Major General Yashko said with a dismissive smile. "To catch a woman and a child." He enunciated slowly and precisely to convey his disgust with his assignment.

"You'd be surprised how elusive American women can be," Victor said. "Especially if they're from New York. I see them outside my apartment on the sidewalk chasing their dreams every day. They move so quickly. One second they're there. Then you blink. And they're gone."

Major General Yashko measured Victor and smirked. He turned to the deputy director. "Who is this little man?"

"He is with me," Kirilo said. "Do I need to get the director and the general on the phone and ask them for reassignments?"

"No, you most certainly do not," Krylov said.

He turned to a wall with twenty television monitors featuring live video feeds. Some showed passengers wheeling suitcases and checking in, while others offered wide-angle views of piers and ships.

"We have security monitors at Sokol Airport," Krylov said. "Arrival, check-in gate, security, luggage, departure. There are five international flights departing this evening from Magadan. We also have security monitors along the pier. There are three ships leaving this evening. We have agents all over the airport and the pier."

"But you're not certain she's even in Magadan," Major General Yashko said, "are you?"

"We're certain she's either in Magadan or is on her way," Kirilo said. "She's getting local help, so she could be coming in slightly off the grid. On a parallel road of some kind."

"Passport Control is on full alert throughout Russia," Krylov said. "It is impossible for her to get out of Russia legally."

"Then she will get out of Russia illegally," Victor said.

Shortly thereafter, two shapely assistants came in with lunch and coffee.

It was 12:00 p.m. on Friday.

CHAPTER 65

"THE PLAN FROM HERE ON OUT..." NADIA SAID. "ADAM. IT'S dangerous."

"No," Adam said. "The plan is good."

"It's really dangerous and unnecessary."

"No, it's necessary."

"The man who's chasing us is Ukrainian. He's powerful in Ukraine. Not in Russia. If he were, he would have caught us by now. Let me buy tickets for the flight to New York tonight."

"No."

"Actually, it's New Jersey. United Airlines. It connects through Los Angeles."

"No. You don't understand how it is here. Russia, Ukraine, the other Soviet countries—they're all independent, but they're still linked. They're linked by bad governments. We follow my father's plan. He may be dying, but he's still smart. He's never told me a lie."

"I'm not saying he's not smart, Adam, but he's not here now—"

"My father's plan. We stick to my father's plan."

"Adam—"

"No."

Nadia looked across the street at the airport and sighed. She checked her wrist, forgetting it was bare. "What time is it?" she said.

"Twelve thirty."

"Okay. We stick with the plan. God help us."

Four trees stood in front of the modest peach-yellow cement terminal. The grass along the front hadn't been cut for a year. They entered through a pair of rusty steel-framed glass doors. Two weathered men in plaid shirts and jeans were buying Fanta sodas from a babushka at a small convenience shop. A fourth old man, with his back to Nadia, was chatting up a woman in a uniform at the check-in counter. When the woman glanced at Nadia and Adam, he turned.

He looked like a tunnel rat made of sinew and bone, with a fair Russian complexion. Gray stubble covered his sunken face. A cigarette hung on the edge of his lips. After glancing at Nadia and Adam, he pulled a small white envelope out of his coat pocket and handed it to the woman. After peeking inside the envelope, she turned away. He approached with the swagger of a younger, albeit equally short, man.

"Why do policemen work in pairs?" he said to Adam in guttural Russian.

"Specialization," Adam said. "One can read, the other can write."

"Ruchkin," he said, tapping his chest. *Ruchka* is also the word for "hand." "Quick. This way." He pointed toward a side door with a sign that said AUTHORIZED PERSONNEL ONLY.

They rushed down a short corridor and exited through a sheet-metal door. Power lines ran along a grassy field on one side of the single runway. Two white planes with red propellers sat along the other side. One of the wheels on one of the planes rested at an angle, as though it were ready to break. A red-and-white smokestack dominated the horizon. There was no control tower in sight, though there was a small shack beside the terminal.

A black delivery truck was backed up to the plane with better wheels. A pair of burly young men in army fatigues finished loading it with wooden crates. They nodded at Ruchkin and took off in the truck.

Nadia and Adam boarded the plane. Ruchkin started the engine and guided the plane to the far end of the runway. Pointing the nose toward the other end, he exchanged words with someone on the other end of the radio.

The plane teetered and tottered down the short runway with the speed of a broken-down Yugo. The engine groaned. Nadia bounced on her seat as though it were a trampoline. As the runway ended, the nose slowly lifted in the air and, against all odds, the plane took off.

Ruchkin said something over his shoulder, but Nadia and Adam couldn't hear him over the engine's wail. Nadia unbuckled her seat belt and leaned forward.

"Vodka and water in the cooler on the floor," he said. "Help yourself."

"Thank you," Nadia said.

"How did you know my father?" Adam said. "Were you in business with him?"

"No. I was in *gulag* with him. Nine years." He turned and flashed a smile filled with gold and decayed teeth. "For bootlegging."

"Oh," Adam said. "Were you friends?"

"We ran the Red Cross together."

"Red Cross?" Nadia said. "I didn't know there was Red Cross assistance in the *gulags*. I thought the West was clueless about what went on there."

"It was. In *gulag*, control of the infirmary was everything. Who got sent, who got treated, who survived. To control the infirmary, you had to control the doctors. In *gulag*, Red Cross meant control of the doctors."

"How did you do that?" Adam said.

Nadia shot him a glance to stop asking questions, but it was too late.

"We bought them vodka, candy, and cigarettes. And made friends with them."

"Really?" Adam said.

Ruchkin shrugged. "Sure. That didn't always work. Some didn't want to listen. That's where the Red Cross came in." Ruchkin twisted his face toward Adam. He wore an earnest expression. "But we never killed anyone who wasn't an asshole. Except this woman doctor. And even that was an accident..."

Adam looked down and sank back in his seat. Nadia raised her hand to touch him and remembered he had told her never to do so. She pulled it away and looked out the window instead.

Adam didn't ask any more questions.

The plane never reached a high elevation, as though Ruchkin were purposefully avoiding detection. Half an hour into the flight, a snippet of coastline came into view on the right side.

"It's going to get bumpy here along the coast," he said. "But don't worry. I've done this trip many, many times. You know what they call this route, don't you? Magadan to Chukotka? They call it 'Gateway to Hell.' "

Four hours later, they landed on a runway at Ugolny Airport, serving Anadyr, the capital of the Chukotka Autonomous Okrug. Anadyr is the largest town in the extreme northeastern part of Russia and the last before land yields to water.

At Ugolny, they never left the runway. Two men hauled two dozen crates from the plane into a large helicopter with camouflage paint. Ruchkin then flew Nadia and Adam an additional three hundred kilometers to a secluded landing spot in Provideniya, the largest settlement at the tip of Chukotka.

They flew for six hours cumulatively and crossed one time zone during the trip. It was 8:35 p.m. on Saturday when they arrived in Provideniya.

CHAPTER 66

KIRILO PACED THE FSB OFFICE. HE GLANCED AT THE CLOCK: it was 9:00 p.m. on Saturday.

"So much for the airport tonight," Deputy Director Krylov said. "The last international flight just left Sokol."

"Nothing from the pier or Passport Control?" Victor said.

"Nothing."

Kirilo swore under his breath. Krylov brushed his hand through his thinning hair and reached for his fifth cup of coffee since lunch.

Major General Yashko marched into the room as though he were reporting for duty. His customary indignation was absent from his expression. He clicked his heels together and cleared his throat.

"I have a development to report," he said.

Krylov raised his eyebrows.

"Magadan-Thirteen," Major General Yashko said.

"Magadan-Thirteen?" Krylov said.

"What's Magadan-Thirteen?" Kirilo said.

"Airfield," Krylov said. "Thirteen kilometers northeast of Magadan. Basically abandoned. An occasional prop plane. Domestic. By appointment only."

"Actually, that may not be true. I was discussing our problem with one of my men when he made me aware of certain rumors," Major General Yashko said.

"What rumors?" Krylov said.

"A bootlegging operation," Major General Yashko said, his eyes falling to the floor.

"Bootlegging?" Krylov said. "What does that mean, bootlegging?"

"Government employees in the Chukotka Oblast get paid once a month. When their paychecks arrive, there's a big demand for alcohol. Especially among the locals, the Chukchis. It's a big business. Thousands of people. Big enough to command a monthly run under the radar from Magadan-Thirteen."

"What?" Krylov said. "Under whose protection?"

The major general's face turned a darker shade of red. "I honestly don't know. I'm sure the deputy director can launch an appropriate investigation and find out."

"You can count on that," Krylov said. He reached for his phone. "First we have to find out if there's been a flight today."

"There has," Major General Yashko said. "That's the development. I had my man make inquiries. A woman and teenage boy were seen boarding the plane at one o'clock this afternoon."

"My God," Krylov said. "What was the destination?"

"Provideniya. Via Anadyr."

"The Chukchi Sea," Victor said.

"What resources do you have up there?" Kirilo said.

"The Maritime Border Guard Unit," Krylov said. "When did they land in Provideniya?"

"Hard to say," the major general said. "Sometime in the last hour."

"We have a modified Tupolev TU at our disposal," Krylov said. "We can be in Provideniya in two and a half hours. I'll have the Border Guard set up a perimeter with a radius of one hundred kilometers up and down the coast."

As Deputy Director Krylov barked instructions into the phone, Major General Yashko walked up to Kirilo. "So there's no doubt now. Her plan was to escape by ship after all."

Kirilo didn't argue. He simply nodded and smiled. Then he glanced at Victor. He could tell from the Bitch's expression he was thinking the same thing as Kirilo.

Now that it appeared Nadia Tesla was planning to escape by ship, there was no doubt she was going to leave Russia some other way.

CHAPTER 67

NADIA AND ADAM STOOD SHIVERING BESIDE EACH OTHER. Light poured from the headlights of an idling *buhanka* beside the makeshift helicopter landing pad. A Caucasian man gave Ruchkin an envelope. He and another Slav transferred the crates from the helicopter to the *buhanka*.

A light flashed three times at the base of the knoll.

"Your Chukchis are waiting for you," Ruchkin said. "Go."

Nadia and Adam thanked him. They descended down the snow-covered hilltop to a ridge, walking and sliding in diagonal fashion to keep from falling. The hike warmed them up after they'd been standing so long in the biting cold.

Two men sat in another *buhanka*. One of the men climbed out of the vehicle and walked over to Nadia and Adam. He bore a startling resemblance to Adam, more so than the Yakut or Evenk. His face was the roundest of the three, his features the smallest, and his complexion lightly tanned. His lustrous black hair fell beneath his fur hat to his shoulders, but he had the heavily lined face of a prematurely aged man.

"You Adam?" he said, in coarse, barely comprehensible Russian.

"Yes," Adam said.

"Skinny, though. What, no food in Ukraine?"

"No," Adam said. "I mean, yes. There's food in Ukraine."

"Then why you no eat?" The Chukchi turned to Nadia. "You American, though?"

"Yes," Nadia said. "I'm American."

"America poor, though. Not much money."

Nadia hesitated, unsure of what he meant. "Well, yes, our economy's in trouble. The American government has borrowed a lot of money to keep us out of the recession, but I wouldn't say we're poor."

The Chukchi frowned as though he had no clue what she'd said. "You say America not poor? America has money, though?"

"Well..."

"Then if you buy Alaska, why you no buy Chukotka, too?"

"Oh," Nadia said, feeling her face flush in the darkness. "Now I see what you meant about money. Yeah, you're right. Big mistake. We should have bought Chukotka, too."

"How did you know my father?" Adam said.

"Didn't know father. Don't know father. Not your father, or mine. We go, though."

Adam and Nadia climbed into the back of the *buhanka*. Heat poured from the *buhanka*'s vents, but the other Chukchi pointed at reindeer skins and told them to cover themselves anyway.

They traveled four hours over snow-covered paths and trails until they arrived at the edge of a salt pit.

The Chukchi driver pointed beyond the salt pit. "My cousin waiting at shore," he said.

When Nadia and Adam circled around the salt pit, another pair of Chukchi were waiting for them at the edge of a lagoon.

They were in Uelen, the easternmost settlement in Russia, and the closest to the United States.

CHAPTER 68

VICTOR WATCHED KIRILO PACE AROUND THE MEETING ROOM in Provideniya's *Militsiya* headquarters. It was 6:00 on Sunday morning. Major General Yashko sipped coffee while Deputy Director Krylov was on the phone.

Victor worried about the Timkiv twins and hoped they were moving Isabella every twenty-four hours, as planned. It concerned him that they were incommunicado. In Kyiv, he could sneak away to a pay phone every now and then. Out here, in Siberian hell, there were no pay phones. And he purposely didn't carry a cell phone, for fear Kirilo would steal it and trace the number he'd dialed. The boys were professional and reliable, but they weren't planners.

If they could just hang on for another twenty-four hours, Nadia would cross the international date line and the playing field would tilt in his favor. Victor was certain he knew where she was going. Once she was on American soil, Kirilo would be playing on Victor's turf. The advantage of familiarity would shift in his favor. The probability of victory would shift in his favor as well.

One of Deputy Director Krylov's lackeys burst inside.

"Border Patrol officers just found a *buhanka* with crates of vodka and brandy by the pier where the Yupik whalers take off in the morning. The driver said he took a delivery tonight. A woman and a boy got off the helicopter."

"I'll call you back, sir," Krylov said into the phone, and hung up. "What? What's this?"

"A pair of Chukchis were waiting for them in a *buhanka*. The driver said one of the Chukchis tried to buy a bottle off him. Said they had a long, cold trip ahead of them."

"Did he say where to?" Major General Yashko said.

"Uelen."

"Uelen?" Krylov said. "Why, that's at the tip. Near Dezhnev."

Kirilo stood up. "The Bering Strait," he mumbled.

"Gvozdev Islands," Major General Yashko said. "Forty kilometers from shore. Big island, Russia. Small island, America. Four kilometers between the two islands. Four kilometers from Russia to America."

The major general hustled toward Krylov's desk and reached for the phone. Krylov must have read his mind, because he stood up and made way.

"Have you got anyone on Gvozdev that can help?" Kirilo said. "Or is it all natives?"

Major General Yashko was busy dialing.

"It's all natives on the American side," Yashko said. "One hundred sixty-two at last count. And two sentries and a telescope. We shipped our natives to Chukotka in 1948 and razed our island. Now it's a military base. About twenty square kilometers. Company strength. Helicopters, artillery. It's under military command."

Deputy Director Krylov nodded toward the major general.

"Get me the commander at Gvozdev," the major general said into the phone. "Yes, yes, wake him up. It's an emergency, dammit. Hurry!"

The major general cupped the phone, sighed, and glanced at Kirilo.

"Not by plane or by ship," Kirilo said. "On foot. The strait is still frozen. They're going to walk. They're going to walk from Russia to America."

When the major general started barking instructions, Kirilo glanced at Victor and did a double take.

"You don't seem surprised," Kirilo said.

"Why should I be?" Victor said. "Damian planned a route where people would help his son. The zoologist told us. Plus, the boy's mother was from the American tundra. Don't you get it? The boy's mother is from Alaska."

CHAPTER 69

DAYLIGHT ARRIVED SHROUDED IN FOG. ON THE SHORE OF the rocky beach in Uelen, Nadia couldn't see more than twenty feet in front of her.

Two other Chukchi men met Nadia and Adam. They wore the same sullen, inscrutable expressions and had identical weathered appearances. They were somewhere between twenty and fifty years old. It was impossible to discern more.

Their wooden boat seated four. It had oars in the front and the back where the Chukchi sat. It also had an outboard motor surrounded by a rib cage of pipes. When one of them started the engine, it whirred gently like an electric razor, suggesting the extra pipes were a noise-reduction system. Nadia and Adam didn't speak, and the Chukchi didn't ask them any questions.

The lagoon had melted. The boat chopped and skipped over water toward an invisible target. The cliffs surrounding the inlet tempered the winds. Small waves slapped the boat and rolled by without incident. The Chukchi in the lead checked his compass every five minutes and made minor adjustments in navigation.

Time passed. Nadia didn't know how much, but it had to be pushing two hours. Russia's Big Diomede Island was somewhere up ahead. Two miles beyond it was Little Diomede Island. American soil. Adam wore his anxiety on his face, continually mashing his upper lip into his lower one. He appeared stiff, as he had when the policewoman had accosted him on the train.

The boat came to a stall in a pocket of slush. The Chukchi killed the engine and rowed through the icy sludge to water. They started the engine again, but the boat promptly groaned to a halt again. The Chukchi in the back muttered something to the one in front. That one nodded. From then on, they kept the engine off and rowed. They navigated through an unpredictable maze of water, slush, and ice. When a wave crashed over the edge of the boat and doused the deck, the Chukchi continued rowing as though nothing had happened.

Nadia looked around for something to do, but there was no way for her to help. She was baggage. Feeling impotent, she suppressed an urge to scream.

The current nudged them southward while the Chukchi forged eastward. That was the plan. Uelen was northwest of the Diomedes Islands.

Water gave way to more slush, and the latter yielded to more ice. They stopped rowing. The Chukchi in the lead turned and held his finger to his lips.

"Keep your voice low," he said. "Keep your voices low."

They rowed for another five minutes until they careened in a circle and ended up pressed between two blocks of ice. The Chukchi muttered something incomprehensible to each other and set their oars aside.

The Chukchi in front turned and whispered to Nadia. The wind swallowed his words, however, and Nadia had to ask him to repeat everything he had said.

"Ice from here to Imaqliq," he said. "Four, five kilometer to Ignaluk. Chukchi can do. American? Not sure, though."

By "Imaqliq," he must have meant the Russian Island, Big Diomede. By "Ignaluk," he must have meant Little Diomede. Five kilometers was a little more than two miles. Big Diomede was in the way, but the fog would protect them. The Russians had no reason to know Nadia and Adam were coming anyway. The lookout would never see them.

Nadia pulled out her compass and looked at the Chukchi. "Where is Big Diomede?"

The Chukchi frowned.

"Imaqliq. Where is Imaqliq?"

The Chukchi turned and pointed forward into the fog at a forty-five-degree angle to the right. "That way," he whispered. "Close. Real close, though." He pointed to Nadia's compass. "Fog lift soon. You see Imaqliq and Ignaluk. Beach on Ignaluk on west side. Remember, though. West side."

Nadia and Adam stepped carefully out of the boat onto a massive sheet of ice. The boy was no longer sullen. He was oddly cautious, looking to step where she'd stepped. The Chukchi tossed them their bags and two pairs of webbed rubber spikes. Nadia and Adam stretched the rubbers and slipped them over their boots for traction.

"Russian side—sea is warm. Chukchi warm. Many pieces ice," the Chukchi said. "American side island—sea is cold. America cold. Big ice, though. Travel good, other side. Tell cousin said hello."

"Cousin?" Nadia said.

The Chukchi didn't answer. He and his partner turned their boat around and disappeared into the thick white clouds.

Nadia helped Adam with his backpack and other bag, and he did the same for her. She studied the compass and pointed south with her arm. They took three steps and stopped.

A strange mechanical noise sounded above them. Nadia looked up into the fog. It sounded shrill, like a motor, grew louder as it approached, and became deafening. Adam squatted to the ice out of sheer instinct, as though he feared they were about to be bombed. Nadia stood tall, to appear brave for the boy, but when the noise got even louder, she bent down beside him.

Under her breath, so that Adam couldn't hear, she began a constant rotation of Hail Marys. Halfway through her third round, she realized she was squeezing Adam's arm tightly. She pulled her hand away, repulsed she might have shown weakness. If this was going to be the end for her, so be it.

But she'd be damned if she went out any way other than fighting.

CHAPTER 70

KIRILO RACED DOWN THE STAIRS BEHIND MAJOR GENERAL Yashko and the soldier who'd met them at the heliport toward the observation room at Gvozdev. He could hear Victor and Deputy Director Krylov trying to keep up behind them.

"I have a helicopter, my friend," Kirilo said, "but I've never been on a flight like that before."

"That is the Bering Strait," Major General Yashko said.

Krylov staggered in behind them, looking like a sweaty piece of moldy cheese. Victor looked a bit winded but otherwise unaffected, like the immortal bitch that he was.

Another military officer introduced himself as a colonel and the commander of the island.

"Are your men in position?" Major General Yashko said.

"They are leaving the garrison as we speak," the colonel said.

"And the helicopters? Why are your helicopters not in the air?"

The colonel appeared flustered. "Why...We agreed to wait... to allow you safe landing...prevent a collision."

Major General Yashko slammed his fist on a table. "Well, I've landed, dammit. Why are they not in the air?"

"Yes, sir."

"We prefer them alive rather than dead," Kirilo said, "but above all, Colonel, we must have the bodies and their possessions. Don't let them drown. Do we understand each other, Colonel?"

The colonel appraised Kirilo hesitantly, reluctant to take orders from a man in a suit. Yet he couldn't disobey someone powerful enough to be on Gvozdev right now. He turned to Major General Yashko for guidance.

"Don't even let them get wet," Yashko added.

CHAPTER 71

THE NOISE IN THE AIR STOPPED ABRUPTLY.

The small hard-rubber spikes gripped the ice well and provided excellent traction. Nadia and Adam scampered twenty feet forward before they had to make their first jump. Although the gap was only two feet wide, the leap still unnerved her.

The water deep below was hypnotic. It lapped the edges of both blocks of ice and reminded Nadia of harsh reality. She was standing on the Bering Strait, halfway between Russia and the USA, nothing but the principle of freezing keeping her from the bottom of the sea. No one had told her there would be gaps in the ice. The strait was supposed to be frozen. This was not the plan.

The second jump came thirty feet later. This time the gap was closer to four feet. Adam took off his knapsack, bent low, swung his arms back, and leaped.

He flew through the air like an Olympic athlete, landing four feet in on the other block of ice, covering twice the necessary distance. He slipped, fell, and righted himself. He got up, rubbing his left hand.

"You okay?" Nadia said.

He nodded.

Nadia threw their bags to him. He caught them and motioned for her to jump.

She inched closer to the edge. How close should she be? Six inches? Four inches? Nadia looked down at the water.

"Don't look down," Adam said with authority, as though he'd done this many times before. "Look at me. Look only at me."

Nadia set her feet. Looked at Adam. Took a deep breath. Bent her legs and swung her arms back. She vaulted.

An alarm sounded.

Her foot slipped.

She flailed forward. Her left leg sailed forward. Hit the far block of ice. Her right leg lagged behind. Would she make it?

Adam bounded forward and rammed the heel of his shoe into the ice to create a foothold.

No way she would make it. She was going down. She reached out with her hand.

Nadia's right foot hit the water. She teetered backward.

"Help—"

Adam grabbed her hand. Braced himself against the foothold and pulled.

Nadia slid forward onto the ice beside him. Pulled her right boot out of the water as though it were fire.

Human voices shouted to one another in the distance. Startled, Nadia looked up and around. Visibility was a mere ten feet. She couldn't see anything, but people were approaching.

The whirring noise from before started up again, multiplied by five. Helicopters, Nadia realized. Within ten seconds, they were buzzing overhead, invisible through the fog. The voices belonged to soldiers or border guards. They were searching and hunting.

For them.

"They're here," Nadia whispered. "They knew we were coming. They were waiting for us."

Adam stared at her, eyes wide, looking for guidance as to what they should do next.

CHAPTER 72

THE PERIPHERY OF THE ISLAND WAS CAPTURED BY STRATEGICALLY positioned cameras and displayed on a wall of security monitors in the observation room. Two men manned the equipment. This morning, however, the monitors were all white with fog.

Kirilo kept his eyes glued to the telescope on the southwest side of the island. He scanned from left to right and came upon three of the soldiers who had been sent out to form a human chain, twenty meters apart. There was no woman or child among them.

"Twenty meters is too far apart in this fog," Kirilo said. "You need more men out there."

"This is Gvozdev," Major General Yashko snapped. "There are no more men."

The telescope wouldn't swing farther to the right. Kirilo began scanning backward to the left. "What are the odds someone can cross the Bering this way? Not likely, right? The ice, the water. The wind, the current. How many people have done it? Two? Three?"

"Thirty-three, excluding the Chukchis and the Inupiat," the general said. "I say excluding the Chukchis and the Inupiat because they visit each other all the time. If you count them, thousands."

Kirilo pulled his eye away from the telescope. "Thousands? You must be joking. The world thinks it's two or three."

"That's what we want it to think. Neither we nor the Americans want the publicity, or we'll have every thrill seeker in the world here. So we keep it quiet. But it is not as hard as the world is led to believe. It all depends on the fog and the ice. The natives know the weather and the terrain. They have it down to a science. They communicate with each other all the time. If the natives have guided the woman and the boy, then they can most certainly do this. The only question is if they're getting such help."

"No," Victor said.

"No?" Krylov said. "They're not getting help?"

Victor smiled and shook his head. "I meant no. There's no question about it."

Major General Yashko grabbed a radio transmitter. "Get those helicopters lower. Seventy meters. They're useless up there."

Kirilo resumed scanning. An empty block of ice. A soldier. Another block of ice—wait. Something dark against the white background. He swiveled the telescope back a few centimeters. Someone was emerging from the fog. Was it another soldier?

No. It was the boy.

"The boy, the boy," Kirilo said. "There he is."

A chorus of voices. "What? Where?"

A soldier surprised the boy.

"Wait," Kirilo said. "He's one of ours."

The soldier raised his rifle. The boy dropped his bag and raised his hands.

"We've got him," Kirilo said. "By God, we've got him."

CHAPTER 73

Adam stared at the barrel of the rifle. The soldier was either going to shoot him or take him prisoner to get the locket. The first option was bad. He didn't want to die. But the second was worse. To come this close to executing his father's plan and then be taken without a fight was unacceptable.

The soldier had a face that could have grated potatoes. He looked as happy as the coach the morning after a vodka bender. His rifle was wedged in his armpit as he operated the radio transmitter that was attached with Velcro to his shoulder.

"Yes, sir," he said. "Standing by."

Adam had to make a move, and he had to make it now. He had quickness and the element of surprise in his favor. Lunge, lift, wrestle. Lunge forward, lift the barrel, and wrestle it out of the guy's hands.

"Up. Up," the soldier shouted, stabbing the air with the point of his rifle. "Get your hands up."

He'd let some slack develop near his elbow. It was a big mistake. Now the soldier was even further on edge. He raised the rifle to eye level and pointed it between Adam's eyes.

"The order is shoot if necessary but don't kill," the soldier said. "So wounding is okay." He lowered his aim to Adam's right knee. "You want to live in a wheelchair the rest of your life?"

Adam raised his hands as high as he could and shook his head. No. Not the knees. If he got shot in the knees, he might never skate again. Better the heart or the head than the knees.

"Why are you staring at me, boy? You shouldn't have stared at me, boy." He cocked his head to the side, moved one eye to the sight, and closed the other.

A figure rushed out of the fog from the soldier's blind side and rammed him with a shoulder. The soldier and his gun went flying. He landed hard on the ice. Didn't move.

Adam glanced at the figure. He couldn't believe his eyes. It was Nadia. Of course it was, he thought. Who else could it have been? But it was a woman. An American woman had knocked out a Russian soldier.

"Awesome," Adam said.

A look of pride washed over Nadia's face. Replaced with her usual intensity. "Quick, get your bags," she said.

Adam grabbed his knapsack and satchel.

They disappeared into the fog.

CHAPTER 74

"THEY'RE GETTING AWAY," KIRILO SAID.

"It's the damned fog," the colonel said. "My men can't see anything. The helicopters are useless."

"Tell them to go lower," Major General Yashko ordered.

"They're getting away," Kirilo said. "Lower, dammit."

The colonel said, "Any lower and they will collide. Do you want to be the one who explains to the highest authorities why two helicopters collided in the fog over Gvozdev? Do you want to explain the nature of the mission to your superiors, Major General?"

Major General Yashko glanced alternately at Deputy Director Krylov and the fog in the observation window. The two men shrugged at each other.

"Call the choppers back," Yashko said.

Kirilo pounded his fist on a table. "No, no, no. Are you people out of your minds? Do you know what's at stake? Do you? Get those helicopters lower. Now."

Yashko glared at Kirilo. No doubt he wasn't used to being screamed at by a civilian. But Kirilo had to give him credit. He wasn't fuming. He was thinking. He turned to the colonel.

"Call the choppers back," Yashko said, "but radio the coordinates where we last saw the woman and the boy to the men you have out there. Quick."

"They cannot cross the international date line," the colonel said. "That's less than two kilometers from where we saw them last. That could be interpreted as an act of war. And we cannot have any incidents."

"Do it," Yashko said.

The colonel radioed the coordinates. The soldiers formed a line and marched in the fog toward the American island. But it was an impossible assignment. All the woman and the boy had to do was detour half a kilometer east or west and take a circuitous route to the American island, and they'd never be found. That assumed they had a compass, and Kirilo was certain they did. The woman was too resourceful to be unprepared.

The solders searched in the fog to no avail.

Victor stood quietly in the corner through the entire event. He never said a word. Kirilo kept peering through the telescope even though he knew there was nothing more he could do. His influence had reached its limit. The Tesla woman, the boy, and the formula had been so close he could have touched them, but now they were gone.

They were in America.

CHAPTER 75

NADIA AND ADAM FORGED ONWARD FOR TWO HOURS UNTIL they were stranded on the ice. The wind whipped their faces. They made fists constantly to keep the blood flowing in their hands. Nadia felt as though her nose were frozen. Adam said his feet ached. He knew he had blisters.

As the fog broke up and the clouds rolled over the strait, the cliffs of Little Diomede flashed in and out of sight a quarter mile to the right. Seabirds screamed as they swooped to the water from their bluff-side perches. Excluding the birds, this side of the island was completely deserted.

Ten minutes after they stopped moving, a skiff circled to them from the far side.

"You made it," a man said in perfect English. He wore a hooded parka made of animal skin and resembled the Chukchi. "My name is Sam. Get in quick. The Border Patrol rarely comes out this way and the fog is thick this morning, but we heard helicopter noise coming from Imaqliq."

"Your cousin said to say hello," Nadia said after they got in the boat.

"Which cousin?"

"The grumpy one who's mad the US didn't buy Chukotka, too."

"I have twenty-six cousins on Imaqliq and in Chukotka. You've just described every one of them."

He rowed to a rocky beach. After Adam helped him hide his skiff behind a giant boulder, he guided them along a rocky path for half a mile to a cluster of huts on the other side of the island. Nadia focused on each step. Her breath was labored and her legs were expiring, but she refused to fall behind.

Sam took them into his home, a three-room shack wedged into the bottom of a cliff. He introduced them to his wife and two toddlers. By American standards, it was a small, humble home, but Adam thought it was paradise. He marveled at the quantity of food in the refrigerator and the wide-screen TV.

"Welcome to my home," Sam said. "I'll go out and melt some snow for you to drink."

"You don't have running water?" Nadia said.

"No. We store water from a spring in a tank for the winter. By March we run out and have to melt snow instead. There's some water in the basin in the washroom, and the honey bucket is around the corner if you need it."

"Honey bucket?" Nadia said.

"Only the washateria and the clinic have septic systems. My wife will prepare some food for you. You must be exhausted. After that, you can get some rest."

"Thank you so much, Sam," Nadia said. "This is very generous of you. When will we go on to the mainland?"

He frowned. "The mainland? You mean the Lower Forty-Eight?"

Nadia figured out his reference. "No, no. I mean Alaska proper."

"Oh. Right. Day after tomorrow. On Monday."

Nadia frowned. "You mean tomorrow. Today is Sunday."

"No. Today is Saturday. When you crossed the international date line, the clock went back twenty-one hours. It's one p.m. on Saturday. That's why they call them 'Tomorrow's Island' and 'Yesterday's Island.'"

After Sam left, Adam tugged on Nadia's sleeve and asked her to translate. Nadia repeated what Sam had said.

"You're on Yesterday's Island," she said. "You get to live the day again. As of today, you get to start over."

Nadia and Adam had developed blisters around their eyes from the wind on the strait. Adam had also earned some hard black blisters on the soles of his feet because his boots were so worn. Sam's wife treated them with an antibiotic ointment.

They ate, recuperated, and stayed indoors so as not to attract attention for two days. On Monday, a large helicopter delivered the mail. While his wife feigned illness and distracted the officer of the Border Patrol, Sam escorted Nadia and Adam into the back of the helicopter. The pilot, a longtime friend, took off.

They flew south to the Nome Airport, where they met an old bush pilot with a Cessna. He flew Nadia and Adam back north to Kotzebue, a small town with a population of three thousand. It looked more like an industrial park that had been plunked down on a massive gravel pit at the tip of a peninsula on the edge of the Arctic Circle.

A middle-aged man met them in an old Jeep at the Kotzebue Airport. While the Chukchi and Sam had the same bone structure and skin color as Adam, this man looked like an artist's impression of the boy himself in thirty years. The one exception was the huge smile on his face that was evident from the moment Nadia and Adam stepped off the plane.

He hugged each of them as though he'd known them since birth.

"Hello, Adam," he said in English. "My name is Robert. Robert Seelick. I am your mother's brother. I am your uncle."

CHAPTER 76

KIRILO CHARTERED A PLANE IN MAGADAN. VICTOR FLEW with him to Anchorage. Kirilo kept a select array of temporary business visas up to date in case he needed to travel on the spur of the moment, including the Category B visa for visits to America. Pavel and three of Kirilo's bodyguards, who were waiting in Magadan, had similar documentation and joined him. Kirilo had been to New York City and Los Angeles three times each and enjoyed none of the visits. The excess of wealth and power reminded him that he was relatively poor and powerless on a global scale. After each of his visits, he couldn't wait to get back to Kyiv.

Victor was an American citizen, so they parted ways at US Customs and Border Protection. When Kirilo caught up with Victor at the gate to their connecting flight, Victor handed him a cell phone.

"Where did you get this?" Kirilo said.

Victor nodded at a kiosk for a cell phone vendor. "There's someone on the other end of the line who wants to talk to you."

Kirilo pressed the phone to his ear.

"Papa?" It was Isabella's voice.

"Bella?"

"Papa." Isabella sounded teary, as though she'd been crying.

"Are you all right?"

She sniffed some tears in. "Yes, I'm okay. Oh, but it's horrible, Papa. It's horrible."

"Are you hurt? Have they touched you in any way?"

"Well, no…"

"Are you getting enough to eat? Are they taking care of you?"

"Well, yes…"

"Good. Listen to me, Bella. Be good. Do whatever they tell you to do, and don't show them any of your sass. Do you hear me, Isabella?"

She didn't answer. By the time Kirilo realized the line had gone dead, Victor had already stretched his hand out to retrieve the phone. Kirilo gave it to him.

"You didn't have a phone before," Kirilo said. "You were worried I'd take it from you, triangulate the number you called, and find her. But you're not worried anymore."

"The boys are expecting me to call every hour on the hour from now on," Victor said. "And you're in my country now."

"Yes, we're in your country now. So why don't you just let her go?"

"Soon, cousin. Soon."

An airline employee announced that the flight to New York City would begin boarding in half an hour.

"You have her residence under surveillance right now?" Kirilo said.

"Yes, but she won't go there. That would be too obvious."

"Where will she go?"

"The question isn't where she's going. We can't even be sure she's going to New York. The question is, who does she trust? The question is, who's going to know where she's going?"

"Why do I feel as though you're saving the best for last?"

"He wears his hair in an elastic band like a schoolgirl, is built like a man who worked the docks, and dresses like an Italian fashion designer."

"What is this abomination's name?"

"He calls himself Johnny Tanner, and I'm going to make him my willing accomplice."

CHAPTER 77

As soon as she stepped foot in Robert Seelick's house, Nadia called Johnny Tanner.

"How are you? Where are you?" Johnny said.

"That's not important," Nadia said. "I need you to do something for me and not ask questions."

"Shoot."

"I need you to find a biologist in or around New York City. A radiobiologist would be even better. Private sector or academic. But not a government employee. You hear me? He can't be a government employee."

"I hear you. What am I supposed to tell this guy?"

"That you have a friend in possession of a scientific formula with epic ramifications. And she'll only reveal it to an American man of science. Can you sell that, Johnny?"

"I'll try."

"You have to do more than try. You have to make it happen. I need to go directly from the airport to a meeting with him as soon as I land."

"When will that be?"

"Wednesday morning. I'll call you back with the details when I have them."

After she hung up, Nadia whispered to Adam, "Locket?"

He nodded confidently and pulled it out from under his shirt to show her.

That evening, Robert's wife served a dinner of caribou steak, steamed vegetables, bannock bread, and frozen berries. She was a slight woman, with lithe features and a kind face. After dinner, they sat in the living room and had coffee, tea, milk, and fresh chocolate chip–walnut cookies.

"In Inupiat culture," Robert said, "there is a supreme being called *Silap Inua*, but there is no afterlife. Instead, Inupiat believe that, after spending some time in limbo, the soul of a deceased is reincarnated in the body of a newborn infant."

He paused for Nadia to translate for Adam from English to Ukrainian.

"There was a boy in our village some years ago named Aagayuk," Robert said. "He vanished when he was two. He may have been kidnapped, he may have wandered off and drowned accidentally. No one ever figured it out. He had a lot of energy and showed promise to be a good hunter. He would have been seventeen in September if he were still alive. How old are you, Adam?"

"Sixteen," Nadia said. She translated for Adam.

"Sixteen," Robert said, nodding. "This boy's parents, the Kungenooks, were older when they had their child. They lived in a nearby village and were close friends of ours. They've also died since then. They had no other children."

Robert coughed to clear his throat while Nadia translated. When she was done, he opened the manila envelope.

"This is your new birth certificate," he said, handing Adam a letter with a raised stamp on it. "And this is your Social Security card. A death certificate was never issued. This will allow you to travel to the Lower Forty-Eight with Nadia. You are under eighteen. No photo ID is required."

Adam reached for the papers.

"There is one thing you must do first, though," Robert said. "You must choose an Anglo name. It can be the name of any person that you admire."

Nadia translated.

Adam appeared flustered for a moment. "Can I use your name, Uncle?" he said. "Can I be Robert, too?"

Robert didn't need a translation.

"Robert was my father's name. He chose it because it was the name of a man he admired very much. It was a man he worked for as a member of his campaign for president of the United States. This man's name was Robert Kennedy. He was the brother of the former president John Kennedy. Will you remember that name, Robert Kennedy? Will you promise to learn more about him in America?"

Nadia translated. Adam nodded eagerly.

"Good," Robert said. "If I am Robert, though, then you should be Bobby. Let it be so, then. From this day forward, you will be known as Aagayuk Bobby Kungenook."

They started a small bonfire in the backyard and burned Adam's Ukrainian passports. Robert's wife trimmed and styled his hair so that it covered his ears seamlessly. Later in the afternoon, they bought him some new clothes in town, including a collared shirt, khaki pants, brown moccasins, sunglasses, and a plain blue baseball cap made of wool. Robert gave him an old navy blazer that was a little too loose in the waist but otherwise fit well. When he tried on his entire ensemble, Adam looked like a college student.

Nadia also bought him a cheap wallet and gave him five twenty-dollar bills to put inside, fresh out of an ATM.

"A young man should always have emergency cash in his pocket," she said.

Nadia plotted a route back to New York with Robert's help. After checking flight schedules on his computer, she called Johnny and gave him the details of her arrival. He called her back a few hours later.

"I found your man," Johnny said. "Professor John Horton, Department of Radiobiology, Columbia University. He lives near the United Nations. We can meet there. In a public place. One thing we haven't talked about. You realize you're returning to Victor Bodnar's home turf, right?"

"It's my home turf, too. I'm tired of running, and I have nowhere else to go. Besides, I have you, don't I?"

Johnny remained silent for a moment. "I'm not sure I'm a match for Victor Bodnar, but yes. Yes, you do."

At 10:00 on Tuesday morning, they said their good-byes at the Kotzebue Airport. The bush pilot, a childhood friend of Robert's, flew them to Seattle, stopping in Anchorage to refuel along the way. In Seattle, Nadia bought two one-way tickets for the Delta red-eye, Flight 1642, to JFK Airport.

There were no unoccupied adjacent seats in the economy cabin when Nadia booked the flights. When they got on board, she put Adam in the front so she could keep an eye on him from the other seat fifteen rows back during the flight.

Their cumulative flight time was fourteen hours. With the time change, they arrived at JFK on schedule at 7:13 a.m. on Wednesday. Nadia watched with pride as Adam helped an elderly lady wheel her carry-on off the plane, with his own bags slung over his shoulders. Five minutes later, it was her turn to leave.

She hustled up the ramp to the gate to catch up to Adam. Her quads and hamstrings ached. When she burst into the terminal, six armed Port Authority policemen and four burly men in suits surrounded an unremarkable businessman in a suit and tie. The man's hands were cuffed behind his back, and one of the officers was searching his briefcase. Nadia looked around for Adam but couldn't find him. She walked around the perimeter of the gate, checked the food court, and asked a restroom attendant washing the floor to check the men's room for him. Adam wasn't there.

Nadia finished where she'd started, at the gate where she'd arrived. As the cops escorted the businessman in cuffs out of the area, she realized that Adam must have emerged from the ramp to find cops converging. The men in plainclothes looked like Homeland Security agents—government men, to borrow Adam's phrase. His paranoia was such that he had probably assumed they were there to arrest him and send him back to Ukraine. In a panic, he ran.

Adam didn't speak English. He didn't know anyone in America and didn't understand the city. As Nadia wondered what she would do if she were in his shoes, she realized that she wasn't as concerned about the locket as she was about Adam himself. Nadia remembered when her mother had paced the kitchen, wondering where her brother was and what harm might have come to him, when he disappeared for days as a teen.

Nadia bolted in search of a customer service desk. Halfway down the main aisle, her cell phone rang.

It was Johnny, calling with details of the meeting he'd arranged.

CHAPTER 78

ADAM DIDN'T HAVE TIME TO STOP AND TRY TO FIND SOMEONE who spoke Russian. He had to get out of the airport fast. He'd seen the government people as soon as he climbed up the ramp from the airplane. Fortunately, they didn't recognize him because he was dressed differently and helping the old lady.

He found a perky woman in front of a computer with a first-aid symbol embedded in the sign above her desk. Adam had studied English in school and knew some basic words.

"New York City. Train. For downtown," he said.

She answered so quickly he couldn't understand a word. She also pointed down the corridor—didn't Americans know it was rude to point?—and Adam took off in that direction. He followed others down a long stairwell, past a shiny silver carousel rotating with no luggage on it, and emerged in a giant lobby. Men in suits and ties held big white cards with words written on them. Other men, some of them not so well dressed, bombarded him with questions.

Adam had never seen so much dark skin in his life. He'd seen pictures of black men and Indian men, but he'd never seen them in person. It was incredible. This must be why the United Nations was in New York. Every type of person on the planet had to live in New York.

A beady-eyed woman behind a wall full of pictures of gleaming hotels helped him find the train. She drew a picture of an airplane beside a railroad track and slowly repeated a single word:

AirTrain.

After climbing stairs and finding the AirTrain, Adam gave the ticket man a twenty-dollar bill. The ticket man barked the word "peak" at him and gave him twelve dollars back. Adam didn't understand what "peak" meant and guessed he was charged more for having two bags. It was just like Ukraine. People were looking to make money any way they could.

The AirTrain circled around JFK Airport like a limousine in the sky. Adam noticed a sign on the subway and realized that JFK stood for John F. Kennedy Airport. He felt a little less like a foreigner after he read this. After all, he was named after the former president's brother.

Adam followed the ticket seller's instructions and switched trains at a stop called Howard Beach. He paid $2.25 for a ticket for the underground A train. He made sure he was on the right train before boarding by asking two different people if he was headed downtown. They both nodded.

When the train arrived at Washington Square, Adam got out and climbed the stairs to the street. He gaped at the size of the buildings. Gawked at the number of people on the sidewalks. But mostly, he tried to contain an overwhelming sense of joy.

He pulled a piece of paper out of his pocket that his father had given him in case of emergency.

The first person he approached was a dapper man in a pinstripe suit.

"Excuse me," Adam said, holding out the paper his father had given him. "To help, please?"

The man glared at Adam as though he were a criminal about to rob him and hurried by.

The second person Adam approached was a chic young woman with a miniskirt and legs as long as the skyscrapers around him.

"Excuse me," Adam said, holding out the paper again. "To help, please?"

The woman took one look at him, wrapped her arms around her chest, and circled around him, leaving a berth far and wide, like a Kyivan who feared he might be radioactive.

Before Adam could approach a third person, a glamorous woman with dark skin ambled up to him. She had the shoulders of a Black Beret and a masculine face but wore makeup and high heels. In fact, Adam wasn't sure if the person was a man or a woman, but he decided on the latter because only women wore high heels.

The woman said something and smiled. She had teeth the size of piano keys.

Adam showed her the paper.

She read what was on the paper and asked another question.

Adam pleaded with his eyes. "Downtown," he said.

The woman studied Adam for a moment and then pointed to a bench. They sat down together. The woman removed a notepad from her briefcase and drew a beautiful map. She put a big X next to a square and pointed to the ground.

"Here," she said.

Afterward, she drew a second X next to a street corner far away and pointed to the paper her father had given him.

"There," she said.

Adam thanked her profusely in Ukrainian and took off toward the second X.

CHAPTER 79

After killing Misha, Kirilo had struck a bargain with his excellent bodyguard, Stefan, who'd saved him from being shot by the babushka. He put him and his crew on retainer, paying them the equivalent of US$50,000 to become his American security consultants. In fact, Kirilo was paying to prevent them from seeking retribution and to agree that Misha had left the casino complaining of stomach pains and had simply vanished with his friend Specter. If Specter was a *musor*, as Kirilo suspected, that would convince those who profited from Misha's existence that he had turned snitch for the American police. Hence, no one would regret the *moscal*'s disappearance.

That Stefan had worked for Victor previously was of no consequence. It was not unusual for men to shift allegiances as their bosses faded. Victor was on the decline. His power had eroded to younger men such as Misha. More important, he was broke. Stefan's betrayal of Victor for Misha implied he was a rational economic being. He followed the money. Kirilo had money. Still, since some allegiances died hard, Kirilo instructed Pavel and his team of bodyguards to maintain a safe distance from him.

Two of Stefan's men picked them up at Newark International on Saturday morning. Pavel, the bodyguards, and Stefan drove in one car. Kirilo and Victor rode in the other.

Victor had been on the cell phone when Kirilo finally got through Customs. Strangely, it made Kirilo happy to see him talking to his men in Kyiv because they were taking care of Isabella. Their line of dialogue brought Kirilo closer to his daughter, if only in his imagination.

"How is she?" Kirilo said, once they were on the highway to New York.

"Demure, humble, and compliant. Just like her father."

"You're such a bitch."

"She is fine. Just as she was two hours ago on the plane when I called."

"And this Johnny Tanner?"

"I have two men watching him now. We're going to meet with him straight away."

Kirilo's hand went to his coat pocket, where he usually kept his cattle prod. "Damn," he muttered. It had been confiscated at Customs.

"Don't worry," Victor said, looking out the window at a giant sports stadium. "You're not going to need it. This is America. It's a civilized country."

"Oh yeah. I forgot. You're just going to ask him where the Tesla woman is, and he's going to tell you, right?"

"Exactly," Victor said.

"This I can't wait to see."

Forty-five minutes later, both drivers pulled up next to a deli called Vichkovski's on a long, wide avenue in New York City. Kielbasa necklaces hung in the display window. A middle-aged man with a bloodstained apron stood waiting for them. He lifted a metal door handle and opened a hole in the sidewalk. Kirilo and Pavel followed Victor down a set of steep metal steps in front of the deli to its basement.

Pavel was essential. He'd attended the California Institute of Technology and spoke fluent English. They wound their way through a storage room to a thick stainless steel door where a second man was waiting for them. This one was younger and bigger, dressed in a leather bomber jacket and jeans: a soldier type Kirilo knew well.

He opened the door. Victor, Kirilo, and Pavel stepped inside.

Sides of beef dangled from hooks. Nooses made of blood sausage hung from the ceiling. A muscular man in a ponytail sat strapped to a folding metal chair, wearing a tank top and pinstripe pants. Fear was etched on his face.

Kirilo looked at Victor. "Civilized country? I thought you were going to make him your willing accomplice."

"I am. As soon as I put a gun to his head, I'm certain he'll be willing."

"You really are such a bitch."

Victor walked up to his boys. "Did he cooperate?"

"Not yet," one of them said.

Victor motioned with his hand for one of his boys to give him something, and the man pulled a gun from his waistband. It was a semiautomatic with a noise suppressor. Victor held it by his side as he approached Johnny Tanner.

"We met at the Veselka Restaurant," Victor said. "You came in Nadia's place, which means she told you who I am." Victor racked the slide to load the chamber and put the barrel to Johnny Tanner's head. "One chance, and one chance only. Where is Nadia Tesla?"

Johnny Tanner gnashed his teeth as though preparing to live with the consequences of giving up the girl. Kirilo had respect for the man. He'd refused to tell the boys anything, and even now, with a gun to his head, he was hesitating. That took balls. This Johnny Tanner was unlike any lawyer he'd ever met in Ukraine.

Victor pressed the gun into the skin of his forehead. "And the count from three begins. Three, two—"

"Turtle Bay," Johnny Tanner said.

Victor frowned. "What?"

"Turtle Bay. She's meeting him in Turtle Bay."

"Meeting who?"

"A professor. Radiobiologist from Columbia University."

"What is this Turtle Bay?"

"It's a neighborhood. Around the United Nations."

"United Nations?"

"He lives there. Three United Nations Plaza. They're meeting at the Plaza Deli. Between First and Second. Near the United Nations, where he lives."

"What is this professor's name?" Victor said.

"John Horton."

"When is the meeting?"

Johnny Tanner hesitated.

Victor pressed the gun deeper into his flesh. "When is it?"

"Today. The meeting is today. At noon."

CHAPTER 80

"BOBBY KUNGENOOK. BOBBY KUNGENOOK. PLEASE PICK UP any courtesy phone and dial two-one-one."

Nadia had Adam paged, figuring it was safe to do so since no one knew his new identity. It was a long shot: even if he was still in the airport and heard his new name, would he understand the rest of the message?

She waited half an hour, but no one showed. After leaving her cell phone number with Emergency Services, Nadia hustled down to arrivals at Terminal 4. If he wasn't in the airport, he'd left. Given his limited knowledge of English, he would have needed help to secure transportation.

The arrivals area was a melting pot of people and languages. Two Port Authority cops stood by the entrance, studying everyone, but Nadia didn't want to arouse their suspicions by asking questions. She walked across the street to the taxi dispatcher.

"I'm looking for a teenager," she said. "About six feet tall, athletic but thin. Black hair over his ears. He's wearing a blue blazer. Speaks broken English."

The dispatcher scratched his forehead. "Nope. Haven't seen anyone like that."

She ran back into the terminal. The cops and Homeland Security officers looked like the government. She could understand why Adam had gotten spooked, but why didn't he wait down the corridor or in the arrivals area?

The information desk was no longer empty. An intense-looking woman with slits for eyes was standing behind it now. Nadia sliced her way through a group of tourists jabbering at each other in German.

"Have you seen a boy?" Nadia said. "He doesn't speak English. Five foot ten. Hundred seventy pounds. Looks like an Eskimo. He had a knapsack and a duffel bag. He's wearing a blue—"

"AirTrain."

"I beg your pardon?"

"He wanted to know how to catch the train to Manhattan. I told him how to get to the AirTrain."

"Manhattan?" Nadia said.

"He had an address written on a piece of paper. He showed it to me because he wanted to make sure he got on the right train."

"Do you remember the address?"

"Let's see. Seven…Seven East Thirty-Third. That's right. Seven East Thirty-Third."

Nadia frowned. Murray Hill? Why would Adam visit someone in Murray Hill?

"Are you sure?" Nadia said.

The woman started to nod and stopped. "No. Wait. Other way around. It was thirty-three East Seventh Street. That's it. A place called the Underground. Thirty-three East Seventh Street."

The Underground was a Ukrainian dive bar favored by an older generation of immigrants. Maybe it was an emergency address his father had given him, a place to go to if he got lost. If that were the case, though, why hadn't Adam shared it with her? An eerie feeling washed over Nadia. Was Adam's disappearance related to the formula? It had to be. Had Damian arranged a sale to a less-than-savory party in New York City? Had that been the plan all along?

Nadia called information and got a phone number for the Underground. She called the bar four times on the way to Manhattan, but no one answered. It probably didn't open until the afternoon. Was Adam waiting on the doorstep? When her taxi from the airport merged onto FDR Drive, Nadia checked her watch. It was 11:41. She'd never be on time for her appointment with the radiobiologist if she tried to go to the Underground first. But Adam and the locket were essential to the meeting.

She tried calling Johnny to tell him to call the professor and inform him she'd be late, but it went straight to voice mail. While she left him a message, her driver passed the United Nations.

She was on her way back to the East Village, where it all had started.

CHAPTER 81

AT 11:05 A.M., ADAM WALKED INTO A BAR CALLED THE Underground below a doctor's office at 33 East Seventh Street. The inside of the bar was dark and smelled of dried booze, like the coach's kitchen in Korosten. A babushka was wiping down the bar. Adam was amazed to see a babushka in New York. He'd assumed all women in New York were glamorous, like the Victoria's Secret models. The babushka stopped work when she saw him.

"Is Yuri here?" Adam said in Ukrainian.

"Who's asking?"

"Adam. Adam Tesla."

An old man appeared in front of a curtain in the back of the bar. He looked as though he could slip through closed doors at will. The creases in his face deepened.

"Adam? Is it really you? Praise be to God. You've made it." He smiled, limped forward, and pumped Adam's hand with both of his.

"You're my father's friend?" Adam said.

"I knew your father since we were this tall," Yuri said, holding his hand at his waist. "Welcome. Welcome, my boy. You've done it." Yuri looked over Adam's shoulder. "But why are you alone? Where is your cousin? Where is Nadia? Is she not with you?"

"We got separated. At the airport. Police and government men were there, waiting to send me back."

"The police were waiting for you?"

"Yes."

"They approached you? You ran away from them?"

"No. They didn't recognize me. My clothes. My hair. I slipped away. But now I feel bad I left Nadia behind."

"Don't worry about your cousin. She'll find us. Worst case, we have her number."

"You do?"

"Yes. The important thing is you're here and you're safe. Maria, bring the boy a glass of water. And something to eat."

"Thank you. But I don't want to eat. I promised my father I'd call him as soon as I got here. My father said you would have a cell phone and a calling card for me. I must call Karel. Karel will go to my father, and I will speak with him to let him know I'm here."

Yuri's face fell. "I'm sorry, son. I have bad news. Your father… Your father is dead."

"What?"

"He died five days ago. Karel called to tell me. I'm sorry." Yuri patted his shoulder. "He's at peace now. He was suffering for a long time. It's for the best. You know that."

All the joy seeped out of Adam. He had known his father was going to die soon. There was never any doubt about that. But it had never occurred to him he'd die before Adam would be able to call him from New York City.

"He was supposed to see it through," Adam said.

"He did see it through. That was your father's gift. He knew what people would do before they did it. He knew you would succeed, Adam."

Adam perked up a bit upon hearing someone call him a success. "I have a new name now. An American name. From now on, people will call me Bobby. Like Bobby Kennedy."

"Really? Well, sit down, Senator, and have a glass of water and something to eat, even if you're not hungry, and let's see if we can locate Nadia for you. You know, it wouldn't surprise me if she was on her way here right now."

CHAPTER 82

VICTOR'S PHONE RANG. KIRILO WATCHED THE BITCH STEP into the storage room to take the call. In the meat locker, Victor's two men were removing the binds from Johnny Tanner's hands and feet. Kirilo's two bodyguards looked on beside a slab of ribs. Thirty seconds later, Kirilo's own phone rang.

"Papa, I'm free!" Isabella said.

"Bella. Is it really you?"

"Yes, Papa. It's me!"

"You're free? What do you mean, you're free?"

"They let me go."

"They let you go?"

"Yes. They just let me go. They said they could see people were following us, but they couldn't tell if it was your men or someone else. Since they couldn't guarantee my safety anymore, they drove me to your apartment in Kyiv."

"What? You're home?"

"Yes! I'm home."

"I'm overjoyed. How are you? Are you okay?"

While Isabella answered, Kirilo cupped the phone and whispered to Pavel, "Isabella's free. Go get Stefan and the other man. Tell them to be ready."

"I'm going to take a bath and order something to eat," Isabella said.

"Good, good," Kirilo said, returning his attention to the phone. "Lock all the doors. I'm going to arrange for some men to come guard the house. When they get there, call me before you let them in."

The men who were tracking the Timkiv twins on his behalf must have gotten close, Kirilo thought. Victor, not knowing if it was his men or someone else, didn't want to take the chance that something would happen to her on their watch, so he let her go. This meant Victor had never truly intended to hurt Isabella under any circumstances.

Still, the Bitch had to die.

Pavel, Stefan, and Kirilo's other bodyguard were descending down the stairs to the cellar.

Kirilo rushed out of the meat locker and slammed the freezer door shut. He slid the deadbolt in place, leaving Victor's men, his two other bodyguards, and Johnny Tanner trapped inside.

Victor dropped his phone and reached for his gun.

"Don't," Kirilo said, pointing at Stefan and the other bodyguard, who'd already brandished their weapons and were aiming them at Victor from the bottom of the steps.

Victor raised his arms with a look of resignation.

Fists pounded against the meat locker door. The men inside screamed for someone to open it.

Kirilo walked up to Victor, took his gun, and handed it to Pavel. Kirilo ripped his belt from around his waist. He wrapped it around the Bitch's neck and savored the look of futility in his eyes.

"The key to leverage is to maintain your advantage," Kirilo said. "Because the minute you lose it, you're dead."

Kirilo stared into Victor's eyes and pulled on the ends of the belt.

Two thumps sounded in rapid succession behind Kirilo. The sounds were muted but loud enough for him to recognize them. They were gunshots. Muted by a silencer.

Kirilo swung around, dragging Victor with him like an unwilling dance partner.

Pavel and the bodyguard were lying on the floor with holes in their heads. Stefan aimed his gun at Kirilo, a silencer attached to its barrel.

"Release him," Stefan said.

Kirilo removed his belt from Victor's neck.

"You were right," Victor said. "Ten million divided by two is not much more than ten million divided by three. But this formula…It really is a different matter."

Victor took the gun from Stefan.

It was all happening so quickly, yet in slow motion. Kirilo wanted to bargain, to offer Victor a deal in exchange for his life, but he knew it was hopeless. Victor was going to kill him. The Bitch was going to kill *him*, and there was nothing he could do about it.

"Isabella," Kirilo said, pleading with his eyes, embarrassed at the weakness in his voice.

"I would never harm my niece," Victor said. "You have my word as a thief."

The last thing Kirilo saw was an image of his daughter, innocent and sweet.

The last thing he heard was the suppressed sound of a gun firing a bullet into his brain.

CHAPTER 83

VICTOR HELPED STEFAN MOVE THE BODIES INTO A CLOSET until he could dispose of them the way they disposed of all the bad meat at the deli.

"You're the best chess player the world never knew," Stefan said.

"No. The best chess player the world never knew died in Chernobyl village last week. Did your men have any problem getting into my apartment?"

"No. No problem."

"How is she?"

"The maiden and the dove, the dove and the maiden." Stefan sighed with uncharacteristic delight. "They look at home on my living room wall. I love them so."

"Of course you do. You have one hundred thousand reasons to love them. Have you heard from my—have you heard from Tara? Did she get the money you wired for me?"

"She did. She is good. She's still hiding in upstate New York. You should call her and tell her to come home. Your word was good, Victor. Misha will never harm her again."

"No," Victor said, remembering the moment when Kirilo killed him. "No, he won't. But first, we have to take care of business. You're going to have to dispose of the two inside the meat locker, too."

"What about Johnny Tanner?"

"No, no. A man does not survive in America by killing officers of the court. Send him out to me while you take care of Kirilo's two men in the meat locker. I'll make sure he understands that he was never here, that a dozen people will swear we were playing chess in the park all morning, and that no one in this neighborhood ever saw him, even if they did. He'll listen. He's a survivor. Look at him. He's from the streets. He won't risk his life or Nadia's."

Thirty seconds later, Johnny Tanner emerged from the freezer, shirt and suit jacket in hand, looking surprisingly composed. Stefan remained inside and closed the door behind him. While Johnny Tanner dressed, Victor explained the reality of life to him, in accordance with what he'd told Stefan. A cell phone in one of the lawyer's pockets vibrated twice before Victor finished.

"Do we understand each other?" Victor said.

"I don't know," Johnny Tanner said as he straightened his tie. "If any harm comes to Nadia, I'm going to find you and square it, and if I don't, I got friends who will. So you tell me. Do we understand each other?"

His cell phone vibrated again.

Victor waved his gun at Johnny's pants pocket. "Is someone calling you?"

"No. Voice mail."

"Let's hear it."

"Excuse me?"

"Let's hear your voice mail. Maybe a mutual friend of ours left you a message. Let's hear what she has to say."

CHAPTER 84

As soon as Nadia entered the Underground, she didn't have to wonder anymore if anyone had found the body of the man who was shot before her eyes. There, at a small table, reading a Ukrainian newspaper and looking decidedly alive and healthy, sat Yuri Banya, the man who'd pretended to be Max Milan.

Yuri said to Nadia, "I'm not surprised to see you. We knew you'd figure it all out eventually."

"You're giving me more credit than I deserve," Nadia said. The scene that had started it all flashed in her mind. Banya. A gunshot. A big old American sedan. "I haven't figured anything out. I thought you were dead. But you're alive."

"Yes. Last I checked."

"And looking none the worse for wear."

"Thank the Lord."

"In fact, you don't look like a man who cheated death…How many days ago was it? Seventeen? No, eighteen. You don't look like a man who spent eighteen days in a hospital recovering from a gunshot wound to the chest."

His eyes twinkled. "I've always been a fast healer."

"I'm looking for a boy. My nephew—"

"Adam," Yuri said. "You're looking for Adam. He's here."

"He is? Where? Is he okay?"

"Yes. He's fine. He's using the bathroom in back. Maria is fixing him a sandwich and some borscht. He'll be out in a minute. Have a seat, please." Yuri gestured with his hand toward a chair.

Nadia glanced at the chair and spotted Adam's knapsack and bag against the wall beyond it. A wave of relief washed over her. Instead of sitting, though, she remained standing. Something Yuri had said sounded wrong, but she couldn't figure out what it was. Then it hit her.

"You said, 'We knew you'd figure it out.' Who's 'we'?"

Feet shuffled. A curtain parted. A tall, gangly man with a round face and a shock of red hair came into the room. He stopped beside Yuri, bowed, and smiled.

"Good morning, Nadia," he said, as though they were friends.

Nadia mumbled a greeting in return. She didn't recognize him, but something about him looked disturbingly familiar. She'd seen that shock of hair somewhere before. It was the stuff of nightmares, the kind that caused her to wake up in the middle of the night elated that she'd only been dreaming. Except in this case, he'd been all too real…

"The big old American sedan," Nadia said. "You were the shooter. The supposed shooter, I should say."

"This is my old friend," Yuri said, "Simon Stanislavski."

"Blanks," Simon said. "I was shooting blanks."

"Why?" Nadia said.

"We had to motivate you," Yuri said.

"Excuse me?" Nadia said.

"We had to motivate you to go to Kyiv," Yuri said. "If there wasn't the promise of untold millions, whether in cash or from the sale of a formula, would you have gone to Kyiv?"

"What?" Nadia said.

Yuri said, "If you got letters in November and January, the way your mother did, and learned your long-lost uncle was alive, a long-lost uncle who was the most notorious thief and con man the country ever knew, would you have packed your bags and gone just because he asked you to?"

Nadia tried to process everything they were saying and form a logical conclusion, but her brain didn't seem to want to go there.

"Damian sent letters to your mother in November of last year and in January. He was honest. He said he was dying and he had a boy, a good boy, for whom he wanted a better life. Your mother never answered. It was no surprise. Damian was a thief. People thought he was long dead. And who wants a boy from Chernobyl?"

"No one wants a boy from the Zone," Simon said.

"So he wrote a third letter. This time he talked about having some information that could change the fate of the free world. And he asked us to lure you in. To lure you into the con."

"We were members of his crew in Kyiv back in the day," Simon said.

Yuri said, "We're two of the three who got away."

Nadia collapsed into a chair. She stared at the geometric pattern of the wood grain in the table. The pattern seemed to be moving in a circle for her benefit.

"You're saying that everything that happened on Seventh Street was an act," she said. "A ruse just to pull me in. You said, 'The sale of *a* formula.' Not *the* formula. *A* formula. Which suggests there is no real formula. That it was all just a sick game of some kind. That everything I went through was for nothing. For nothing at all."

The men exchanged gratified looks with each other and turned to Nadia.

"No," Yuri said. "Not for nothing. It was most definitely for something. It was for *someone*."

"No one wants a boy from the Zone," Simon said. He stepped over to the bar and reached up into a storage rack for glasses.

"What?" Nadia said.

"No one wants a boy from the Zone," Simon said.

"That's not entirely true," Yuri said.

Simon raised his eyebrows. "Oh?"

"There is a country."

"Really? Where is this country?"

"North of the equator and just south of heaven."

"What's so special about this country?"

"It takes everyone," Yuri said. "Everyone has a chance to prosper."

"Everyone? You really mean *everyone*? Does an Arab have a chance?"

"Yes."

"Does a Jew have a chance?"

"Yes."

"Does a black man have a chance?" Simon said.

"A black man can become president."

"What about a boy from the Zone?"

"Even he may have a chance," Yuri said. "Especially in one particular city."

"Oh? What kind of city is this?"

"It is a city that was built on the backs of the unwanted."

"And where is this city?"

"At the mouth of the river where the woman stands guard by the harbor."

Simon poured three vodkas. Yuri and Simon raised their glasses. Yuri and Simon glanced at Nadia as though waiting for her to do the same. She did not.

"Three days ago, a thief died," Yuri said. "But still he steals from his grave. Today he steals freedom for his son."

"To the best there ever was."

"To Damian. *Na zdorovye.*"

They downed their shots.

"When I saw Damian," Nadia said to Yuri, "he told me that, given your body had disappeared from Seventh Street, someone had yet to reveal himself to me. That someone…was *him*. He was pulling my string the entire time."

"We had no idea you were in trouble with Victor and Misha because of that antiques business," Yuri said. "We had no idea you would be followed and your life would be in danger."

"That...That was never part of our plan," Simon said. "This should have been much, much easier."

Nadia glanced at Yuri again. "On Seventh Street...When you asked me if I was the Nadia Tesla who worked on Wall Street and I said, 'Not anymore,' you seemed disappointed. Upset, even. Why?"

Yuri shrugged. "It costs money to bring a boy to America. To raise him. To live in New York. Simon and I live on a fixed income. We barely get by. And that's in southern New Jersey."

Nadia laughed. "Well, there's one on you guys. I'm unemployed and rapidly depleting my savings." She tossed the vodka down her throat, coughed up a storm, and cleared her throat. "So if there's no formula, what's in the locket?"

"Locket?" Yuri said. He glanced at Simon, who shook his head. "What locket?"

A toilet flushed in the distant background. Everyone turned toward the curtain leading to the back room.

Adam walked into the bar looking refreshed. His eyes widened with excitement when they met Nadia's. His lips parted, but no words came out, as though he couldn't find the words to express himself.

Nadia bounded up to him and folded her arms across her chest. "Why did you run away from me? Why didn't you wait?"

"I saw the government men. They were there for me. They were there to send me back, weren't they?"

"No. They were there to arrest some other man. It had nothing to do with you or me."

"Really?"

"Really." Nadia lowered her gaze and found a few links of the necklace peeking out from beneath his shirt. "Where's the locket?"

Adam swallowed, like a boy who'd done something wrong and knew he was about to be scolded, and touched his upper chest area.

"It's time we opened it and took a look at exactly what's inside," Nadia said.

A shuffling noise from the direction of the front door broke the silence.

Nadia turned.

Victor Bodnar stood in the foyer. Stefan and another huge bodyguard held guns in their hands behind him.

"Yes," Victor said, smiling. "Exactly what I was thinking. Let's see what's inside that locket."

CHAPTER 85

VICTOR LOOKED TWICE AT THE TWO OLD MEN AS HE WALKED past their table. They looked vaguely familiar and recalled memories from his youth, but he couldn't place them. He quickly turned his attention back to the necklace around the boy's neck. All the riches of the world finally within his grasp. He never could have imagined they'd be in the form of a piece of microfilm in the possession of a boy from the Zone.

Adam's face was burned and his lips chapped from crossing the strait. Nadia's face was similarly damaged, and she looked as though she'd lost ten pounds since he'd seen her last in Ukraine. Victor detected fear in Adam's eyes, but it was noticeably absent in Nadia's. In its place was an element of disbelief. She was probably surprised he'd found them, Victor thought.

Stefan and Victor's other man aimed their guns at Nadia and Adam.

"Be a good boy and remove the necklace from your neck," Victor said. "And open the locket."

Adam lifted the necklace over his head, ruffling his hair and exposing his ears in the process. Victor saw they were half ears and felt a measure of compassion for the boy. As Adam struggled to unlock the tiny clasp, Victor had to take a deep breath to remain patient. When it finally unsnapped, Adam opened the locket.

A piece of paper the size of a stamp fell out into his palm. Adam unfolded the paper into a three-inch-by-three-inch square. He held it up for everyone to see. Victor squinted, but without his glasses, he couldn't read it. He could tell it wasn't microfilm, however, and experienced an immediate sting of disappointment.

"What is that?" Victor said, reaching into his jacket pocket for his glasses.

Nadia regarded him with a wistful smile. "No one wants a boy from the Zone."

Victor found his glasses, slid them out of their case, and wrapped them around his head. "What? What's that you say?"

He studied the paper. It was a torn and tattered picture of the Statue of Liberty. It was the symbol of freedom and all that America offered, and if it was this picture the boy had been carrying around all this time...

Victor spun around toward the two men. Banya. Yuri Banya. And Stanislavski. He couldn't remember the latter's first name, but he realized who they were and why he recognized them. They were part of Damian's crew, long thought dead by everyone—

It was a con, Victor realized. There was no formula. It was all about the boy. It was all about getting him to America.

Victor wheeled back to Nadia. He could tell just by looking at her expression that she knew he'd figured it out.

"A thief made me his willing accomplice," she said.

Victor nodded.

"FBI. Drop your weapons."

The order came from the doorway. Victor turned. Specter and a swarm of other men in blue Windbreakers buzzed into the bar, guns aimed at Victor and his men.

Something crashed to the floor.

Stefan and the other bodyguard fired. Muted thumps rang out from their suppressed weapons. An FBI agent collapsed before everyone dove for cover.

As Victor hit the ground, he saw a woman scurrying back into the kitchen with her hands wrapped around her head, leaving an empty tray, broken china, buckwheat bread, and a puddle of beet soup in her wake.

Specter and the agents fired back. The noise became deafening.

Victor crawled toward the curtain leading to the back, not giving a damn about the formula or Nadia Tesla. After all, he could take over Misha's businesses now. He hadn't prayed to God in decades. Yet here he was, on all fours, begging God for a clean escape so he could see his daughter again. So he could hold his grandson in his arms. His grandson.

Halfway to the curtain, Victor thought of Specter and the possibility of jail, but realized the man had never seen him commit a crime. The authorities had nothing on him. When Victor burst through the curtain, his religious inspiration left him. He became the greedy bastard he'd always been. Once he knew he was safe, and that he'd see Tara and her child again, he thought of what all men thought of when they were conscious. Money.

As he escaped the Underground through the back door onto the street, it occurred to Victor that if Stefan were killed, the dove and the maiden would be his once again.

CHAPTER 86

When the bullets started flying, Nadia tackled Adam. They stayed low. The floor shook before her eyes when bullets felled Stefan and Victor's other bodyguard.

The firefight ended as abruptly as it had started.

Specter rushed over to them. Nadia and Adam were still on the ground.

"Are you all right?" he said.

His words sounded distant. Nadia realized her hearing was impaired from the gunshots.

Nadia glanced at Adam, who was rubbing his ears.

"I think so," she said, collecting herself. She studied Specter. "Who are you, really?"

Specter pulled out a wallet and flipped it open to reveal an ID. "John Dzen. FBI. I work for the joint Hungarian-American task force on organized crime. We started there, ended up here. Where's Victor Bodnar? He was here, wasn't he?"

Nadia stood up. Her body trembled. She looked around. An agent was tending to a wounded colleague near the front door. Yuri and Simon were sitting on the floor, unscathed. Another agent was checking the pulses of Stefan and the other bodyguard. But there was no sign of Victor.

"These two are dead," the agent said.

"He must have slipped away," Nadia said. "You're going to get him, though, right?"

"Did he have a gun? Did you see him shoot anyone?"

Nadia remembered Victor standing beside his bodyguards with his hands by his sides. "I don't think so."

Specter frowned. Raised his eyebrows. "Where's the formula?"

Adam stood up.

"There is no formula," Nadia said.

"Nadia, please," Specter said. "The formula is a matter of national security. You must hand it over to the federal government. Let me put it to you this way. You will hand it over to us one way or another."

"There's no formula, Specter," Nadia said. "Adam, show this man what was in the locket. Show this man what this was all about."

Adam held the picture of the Statue of Liberty in his left hand. He extended his arm so Specter could see it.

Specter frowned. "What's this? Is this a joke? Do you think I'm stupid enough to fall for this? Where's the microfilm—"

Adam was staring with disbelief at a purple stain on his sports jacket. It was near his upper chest on his left side.

"He's been shot," Nadia said. "Specter, you shot an innocent child."

"Stray bullet," Specter said.

"Get an ambulance. Now."

Adam's knees wobbled. Nadia caught him. Specter helped her ease him back to the floor and peeled his jacket back. His white shirt was stained with blood, like Yuri's the night he'd pretended to be Max Milan. Only this time, the blood was real.

Specter barked orders for a second ambulance and a first-aid kit. When it arrived, he opened a sterile bandage and told Nadia to apply direct pressure on the wound.

"It's the upper chest," he said. "Near the deltoid-pectoral tie-in. Nothing vital. Worst case, a muscle got hit. He'll be fine. Ambulance is on the way."

Adam, near the border of consciousness, studied Specter and turned to Nadia. "Government man," he said. "Can't trust a government man."

"No," Nadia said, giving Specter an evil eye. "No, you most certainly cannot."

Nadia followed Adam's gaze to the paper in his hand. The glossy newsprint and its dimensions struck a chord within Nadia. The hockey magazine. Adam had held up a page when she first asked about it on the Trans-Siberian. The page had a hole in it. It was the page for the New York Rangers. He'd torn the picture of the Statue of Liberty out of the magazine and put it in the locket.

Adam nodded at the picture of Lady Liberty. "Downtown?" he said.

Nadia nodded. "Downtown. I'll take you to see her."

For the first time since she'd met him, Adam smiled.

Nadia continued to press her hand to his wound gently. "It's going to be okay. I'll take care of you. But no more lies between us. Okay, Bobby?"

He took a second to absorb the comment. "Okay. No more lies, Auntie."

CHAPTER 87

SHE WAS THE MIGHTY WOMAN WITH THE TORCH.

Back in school in Korosten, Adam had badgered a teacher into translating the poem with which the Mother of Exiles greeted new arrivals:

Give me your tired, your poor,
Your masses that want to breathe free,
The human garbage that washed upon your shore.
Send these, the beaten and homeless to me,
I lift my lamp beside the golden door!

Those were the lines he liked the most. Those were the phrases he recited before he went to sleep.

Now that he was here in person, though, she seemed to have more to say. It was a simple message. The wind carried it across the harbor and onto the bridge. It echoed in his ears over and over again:

Anything can happen in New York City.

Any dream can be fulfilled.

EPILOGUE

Early in the third period, Fordham Prep cut its deficit to 2–1. The pace quickened, play sharpened. The teams traded power plays and numerous quality scoring chances. With five minutes left in the game, Coach Terry Hilliard tapped Bobby Kungenook on the shoulder for the first time since benching him.

With two minutes left to play, Iona broke in on a two-on-one. A third goal would put the game out of reach and end any chance of Fordham continuing its undefeated season. Bobby Kungenook skated backward as the two Iona forwards converged on the goalie. He moved his stick toward the puck carrier and shifted his body as though he were going to lunge for him. The Iona forward assumed he was about to get hit and shuffled the puck across to his teammate. Bobby pushed off with his back skate, righted himself, and intercepted the pass.

He exploded up ice. One stride. Two strides. Bobby blew past the third Iona forward at full speed. He shoveled the puck to his center. An Iona defenseman leaned toward the center, who left a drop pass behind his back. Bobby collected the puck again a second later and streaked by them.

His black hair flowed behind his helmet as he rushed toward the net, gleaming like a bat's wing under the arena lights. He faked right, slid the puck between the second defenseman's legs, collected it, deked the goalie low, and tucked the puck into the upper-right-hand corner of the net.

The crowd erupted. Goose bumps sprouted on Lauren's neck. She realized she was standing and clapping, though she never remembered having risen to her feet.

After the goal, Bobby circled the net but didn't raise his hands in jubilation as most hockey players do. Instead, he rounded the corner of the rink and stopped in his tracks. As his four teammates mobbed him, he kept his hands by his sides and stuck his head out to receive their congratulations, like a cat eager to butt heads with its owner. They hugged him and rubbed their gloves over his helmet, and when he skated to his bench to butt fists with his other teammates, he looked like a long-lost boy who'd finally found his home.

After the game ended in a tie, Lauren waited alone in the visiting coach's office. Ten minutes later, a woman came in and closed the door behind her. She was stylish but not flashy, a classy dresser in a simple black suit. She wore a ruby ring and a Timex sports chronograph—no other jewelry. She had what Lauren called active eyes, the type that shone with a special light because the people behind them were readers and interpreters and not just lookers.

"Nadia Tesla," she said.

"Hi. Lauren Ross."

They exchanged cool smiles and still-cooler handshakes.

Nadia circled her way to the coach's desk and assumed the seat of authority. Lauren sat down in front of her and opened her pad.

"So you're Bobby's guardian."

"That's right."

Lauren scribbled on her pad. "Coach Hilliard told me your relation, but I forget. You're Bobby's…aunt, is it?"

"I'm his guardian."

Lauren smiled. "No. I understand that, but—"

"Bobby's not going to be joining us today."

Lauren shifted in her seat. "Oh? Why? Is he okay? Is he hurt?"

"He's fine. But it's not realistic for him to be interviewed right now. He's adjusting to a new life. New home. New friends. New school. This race in Central Park has caused a bit of a hullabaloo, but it will blow over in time."

"Okay, fine. But you understand that this is a story. My guess is it's a big story. It's my job to dig. And I'm going to do my job."

"You'll fail," Nadia said. "The more you dig, the less you'll find. Say you go to Kotzebue and ask questions. All you'll learn is that there are more questions to ask. And that will be it. You'll hit a dead end. You'll have your wasted time, and you won't have a story."

"You seem very sure of this."

"I am. I'm Bobby's guardian."

"Well, no good journalist is going to resist the challenge just because someone tells her it's a dead end. If anything, you've only piqued my curiosity even more."

"Of course, there's an alternative course of action."

Lauren raised her eyebrows.

"Give Bobby until June of next year. He'll be done with his first year at Fordham. He'll be substantially fluent by then—except for certain humor and inside jokes that take forever. If you leave him alone until June of next year, we'll sit down with you together and give you an exclusive story."

Lauren chuckled. "You're telling me this is something worth waiting for?"

"I think so, but you'll have to be the judge of that."

"This is about…more than hockey?"

"Hockey is about more than hockey. But yes, it's about more than hockey."

"And you won't talk to anyone else in the meantime?"

"As long as you keep your word and leave the story alone until then."

"I like what you propose. But I'd like to think about it overnight. Do you have a business card?"

Nadia handed her a card with her name, a 917 area code cell phone number, no address, and a title.

"What's a forensic investment analyst?"

"Someone who digs until they find the truth. You might say I'm following in my father's footsteps."

Lauren chuckled again and put the card in her purse. "I'll call you tomorrow. Maybe we can have lunch soon, and I can give you my final decision."

"All right."

Lauren stood up to leave. "Just tell me one thing. That necklace that fell off Bobby's neck during the game. What's in the locket?"

Nadia's lip quivered for a split second. "The Statue of Liberty," she said.

"I beg your pardon?"

"A folded-up picture of the Statue of Liberty. Bobby was named after Robert F. Kennedy. He's very patriotic."

Adam sat in the bathroom stall, studying the indent on the back of the locket. He'd accidentally scraped it with the edge of his skate blade, removing some of the gilding. He closed his eyes, took a deep breath, and opened them again to make sure he wasn't imagining things. The indent was still there.

It was the shape of a hexagon, the kind chemists used to write formulas. The scientist Arkady had given his father the locket shortly before his death as a token of appreciation for their friendship. His father, in turn, had passed it on to him so he could keep the mighty woman close to his heart during the trip to America. Were there more symbols beneath the rest of the gilding?

Adam's next thought was to confide in his aunt. She had taken care of him and proven herself beyond any doubt to be someone he could rely on. Still, it was probably best not to rush into any course of action. Adam came to this conclusion by remembering his father's final words to him.

With foxes, we must play the fox.

ACKNOWLEDGMENTS

THE FOLLOWING BOOKS SERVED AS REFERENCE: SVETLANA Alexievich's *Voices from Chernobyl*, C.C. Bailey's *The Aftermath of Chernobyl*, R.F. Mould's *Chernobyl Record*, Adriana Petryna's *Life Exposed*, James Forsyth's *A History of the Peoples of Siberia*, John Ziker's *Peoples of the Tundra*, Ian Halliday's *Native Peoples of Alaska*, and *Russian Criminal Tattoo Encyclopaedia*, Volumes I and III.

I am indebted to the following people for their assistance with this enterprise. Jaromir Jagr unwittingly inspired the plot. The men, women and children of Chernobyl inspired the writer. Lou Paglia, Neil McMahon, Jeff Palmer, Mary Jane Cronin, and Jim Cronin read early drafts. Elaine Thomas offered exhaustive input, infectious enthusiasm, and moral support. Scott and James Palmer of Palmer Group Media provided invaluable web design and social media exposure. Scott also created brilliant alternate cover art. Charlotte Herscher guided me to a superior final draft and made the experience a pleasure. Daphne Durham and Andy Bartlett turned a writer's dream into reality. It's a privilege to work with them and the rest of the Thomas & Mercer team. Erica Spellman-Silverman of Trident Media Group discovered the book and promoted it relentlessly. She is agent, counsel, and friend. My parents, Eudokia and Bohdan Stelmach, provided an education and instilled in their children a love and appreciation for America that remains the same today.

First and last, of course, I thank Robin for her love and unwavering support.

ABOUT THE AUTHOR

Photo by Robin Stelmach, 2011

Orest Stelmach was born in Connecticut, the child of Ukrainian immigrants. He didn't speak English until he began school as a child, going on to earn academic degrees from Dartmouth College and the University of Chicago. Along the way, he earned his living washing dishes and stocking department-store shelves, later teaching English in Japan and managing international investments. In 2012, his short story "In Persona Christi" was published in the Mystery Writers of America anthology *Vengeance.* He speaks Ukrainian, Spanish, and Japanese. *The Boy from Reactor 4* is his first novel.